“Can I bathe Comet with the cast on his back leg?”

Chase nodded. “We’ll just wrap it with a plastic bag and a rubber band. Do you have those two things?”

“I do.” Sophie laughed, which was a good sign. A lot of new and inexperienced pet owners might be having second thoughts right about now as they realized what they’d gotten themselves into. A dog was a nice thought but it was also a lot of work. There would be training, bathing, and losing a few precious items to a puppy’s teething. “I told you this would be an adventure,” he said.

Her smile fell just a notch. “You weren’t kidding.” She handed Comet back to him. “I’ll just go change before we bathe him.”

“We?” Chase asked.

“I assumed you were going to stay. You don’t have to. I’m sure I can figure out the plastic bag over his cast.”

Chase shook his head as she talked. “No, I’ll stay,” he said once she’d taken a breath. “I’m all yours tonight.”

PRAISE FOR ANNIE RAINS AND HER SWEETWATER SPRINGS SERIES

Sunshine on Silver Lake

"Readers will have no trouble falling in love with Rains's realistically flawed hero and heroine as they do their best to overcome their pasts and embrace their futures. A strong cast of supporting characters—especially Emma's stepmother, Angel, and the many returning faces from earlier books—underpin Rains's engaging prose and perfectly paced plot. Lovers of small-town tales won't be able to resist."

—*Publishers Weekly*

"*Sunshine on Silver Lake* was an endearing second-chance romance that pulled at the heartstrings as often as it tickled my funny bone!"

—TheGenreMinx.com

"Annie Rains delivers hope."

—ReallyIntoThis.com

Starting Over at Blueberry Creek

"This gentle love story, complete with cameos from fan-favorite characters, will enchant readers."

—*Publishers Weekly*

"A sweet, fun, and swoony romantic read that was both entertaining and heartfelt."

—TheGenreMinx.com

Snowfall on Cedar Trail

"Rains makes a delightful return to tiny Sweetwater Springs, N.C., in this sweet Christmas-themed contemporary. Rains highlights the happily-ever-afters of past books, making even new readers feel like residents catching up with the town gossip and giving romance fans plenty of sappy happiness."

—*Publishers Weekly*

"Over the past year I've become a huge Annie Rains fangirl with her Sweetwater Springs series. I'm (not so) patiently waiting for Netflix or Hallmark to just pick up this entire series and make all my dreams come true."

—CandiceZablan.com

Springtime at Hope Cottage

"A touching tale brimming with romance, drama, and feels! I really enjoyed what I found between the pages of this newest offering from Ms. Rains...Highly recommend!"

—RedsRomanceReviews.blogspot.com

"A wonderfully written romance that will make you wish you could visit this town."

—RomancingtheReaders.com

"Annie Rains puts her heart in every word!"

—Brenda Novak, *New York Times* bestselling author

"Annie Rains is a gifted storyteller, and I can't wait for my next visit to Sweetwater Springs!"

—RaeAnne Thayne, *New York Times* bestselling author

Christmas on Mistletoe Lane

"Top Pick! Five stars! Romance author Annie Rains was blessed with an empathetic voice that shines through each character she writes. *Christmas on Mistletoe Lane* is the latest example of that gift."

—NightOwlReviews.com

"The premise is entertaining, engaging and endearing; the characters are dynamic and lively...the romance is tender and dramatic...A wonderful holiday read, *Christmas on Mistletoe Lane* is a great start to the holiday season."

—TheReadingCafe.com

"Settle in with a mug of hot chocolate and prepare to find holiday joy in a story you won't forget."

—RaeAnne Thayne, *New York Times* bestselling author

"Don't miss this sparkling debut full of heart and emotion!"

—Lori Wilde, *New York Times* bestselling author

"How does Annie Rains do it? This is a lovely book, perfect for warming your heart on a long winter night."

—Grace Burrowes, *New York Times* bestselling author

REUNITED ON DRAGONFLY LANE

Also by Annie Rains

Christmas on Mistletoe Lane

A Wedding on Lavender Hill (short story)

Springtime at Hope Cottage

Kiss Me in Sweetwater Springs (short story)

Snowfall on Cedar Trail

Starting Over at Blueberry Creek

Sunshine on Silver Lake

Season of Joy

REUNITED ON DRAGONFLY LANE

ANNIE RAINS

FOREVER

NEW YORK BOSTON

Cover design and illustration by Daniela Medina
Cover photographs © Shutterstock
Cover copyright © 2021 by Hachette Book Group, Inc.

Bonus novella *A Wedding on Lavender Hill* by Annie Rains © 2019 by Annie Rains

Forever
Hachette Book Group
1290 Avenue of the Americas, New York, NY 10104
read-forever.com
twitter.com/readforeverpub

First Edition: January 2021

Forever is an imprint of Grand Central Publishing. The Forever name and logo are trademarks of Hachette Book Group, Inc.

The publisher is not responsible for websites (or their content) that are not owned by the publisher.

ISBN: 978-1-5387-0340-3 (mass market), 978-1-5387-0341-0 (ebook)

Printed in the United States of America

CW

10 9 8 7 6 5 4 3 2 1

For Doc, my favorite animal lover

Acknowledgments

There are so many people to thank for helping me with this book. First and foremost, I want to thank my husband, Sonny, for getting me "unstuck" when it came to this story. Thanks as well for your financial planner expertise for helping me develop Pete's character and for guarding my time so that I could work through this book. I couldn't have written *The End* without your help.

Thank you to my amazing editor at Grand Central Publishing, Alex Logan, for always knowing what my stories need to make them the best they can be. And to the rest of the Forever team for the behind-the-scenes work that every book requires to come to life and to the digital and literal shelves. I am so honored to work with so many talented professionals.

I also want to thank my amazing agent, Sarah Younger, who is always in my corner for whatever I need. I do believe this is our eighteenth book together. What a journey! I'm so glad to be on it with you.

Thanks a million to my critique partner, first reader, and friend, Rachel Lacey. And to my #GirlsWriteNight crew—Tif Marcelo,

Rachel Lacey, April Hunt, and Sidney Halston—who keep me motivated and inspire me every day. I love you ladies!

Thank you to Helen Atkin for opening my eyes to local libraries around me. Every author should know their libraries and librarians.

I also want to thank my readers. I am so grateful for each and every one of you. You'll never know how much it means to me that you take the time to read what I have written.

CHAPTER ONE

Sophie Daniels checked the clock as she straightened the clothes on the racks in her boutique. Today she was leaving work early to get ready for the wedding of two of her closest friends. Not only that, she had a date with a guy who met all the qualities of her potential Mr. Right.

She headed back to the counter where her mom was sitting with a crochet needle and a ball of yarn. "You're sure you don't mind closing?"

Her mom didn't skip a beat with her crocheting as she looked up and smiled at Sophie. "Of course not. Give Jack and Emma my best."

"I will." Sophie grabbed her purse from below the counter and leaned in to kiss her mother's cheek.

It was going to be a small wedding, including only Jack Hershey and Emma St. James's closest friends and family. Sophie was pleased to have made the guest list and to have narrowly missed the bridesmaids lineup. That meant she was free to wear a dress of her choosing from her own boutique. One with a hemline that swung well below the jagged scars on her left leg, a reminder of her climbing accident when she was eighteen.

"Good luck on your date." Her mom winked. "I hope this one has some sense."

Sophie laughed, easing some of the tension she felt coursing through her body. She hadn't had time to do her normal yoga routine this morning, which usually helped to ease the cramping in her leg muscle—another remnant of her injuries.

According to the town, Sophie was the girl who'd survived. She'd spent thirty-six hours on the side of a mountain, praying for rescue. And sometimes she felt like she hadn't fully escaped that cliff. Sometimes, even in a crowded room, she felt all alone.

Yeah, that would probably sound silly to some. Sophie had a lot of friends in town. She also had her family. But no one understood exactly what she'd been through. The girl who'd climbed up that mountain so many years ago wasn't the one who'd come down.

Sophie narrowed her gaze at her mom. "And by having sense, you mean that you hope my date falls madly in love with me?"

Her mother's gaze flicked from her crochet work to Sophie's eyes. "Any sane man would. What's not to love about my daughter?"

"You're my mother so you have to say that," Sophie said.

"But it's also the truth."

Sophie shook her head, laughing as she walked toward the boutique's door. "Bye, Mom. No half-off discounts while I'm gone," she said, only partly teasing. Her mom loved to mark down clothing for her friends. And everyone who came in was considered a friend by the time they left the store.

"Have fun tonight," her mom called as Sophie stepped onto the sidewalk of Main Street. Sophie waved again as she stood on the other side of the glass door. Then she turned and breathed in the springtime air. This was her favorite season. All things were new in the spring, and the thrill of possibilities always invigorated her this time of year. Instead of turning right toward her car in the parking area, she turned left and followed her craving for a hot tea from the Sweetwater Café. She'd be up late tonight, and a little caffeine would go a long way.

Tonight's date was a high school history teacher. That meant he had a job and liked kids. *Check, check.* She also knew that he had a house, which implied that he was responsible and didn't live with his parents. *Another check.* And he was an indoor kind of guy. That hadn't always been her type but given that it took thirty minutes of yoga every morning to tease out her muscle stiffness, a guy on the less active side—one she could actually keep up with—was preferable.

Sophie pulled open the café's door. Since Emma was the bride tonight, she wouldn't be working the counter today. Neither would her longtime employee Nina, who was one of the bridesmaids. Instead, a newcomer to town, Diana, greeted Sophie as she walked in.

"I'm afraid I haven't memorized everyone's drinks just yet," Diana said, talking about Emma's talent for knowing exactly what her customers wanted before they ordered. "What can I get you?"

Sophie ordered a hot tea with honey and waited patiently. Once Diana handed her the drink, Sophie paid and then turned to leave, when she noticed the couple at one of the tables against the wall. The man looked familiar but it took a moment for Sophie to process that he was her date tonight. It didn't make sense that a guy who'd be picking her up in an hour and a half would be sitting with his arm draped around another woman.

Sophie stood frozen, watching the happy couple and wondering what the appropriate response was. Confront them? Leave? Pour her hot beverage over his head? She was fairly sure the latter was a criminal offense and would land her in jail instead of at a wedding this evening.

She should probably feel angry but, instead, she felt relieved. She was tired of dating guys who, like her mother said, had no sense. Or were just plain rude. There was also the fact that she already knew every man in town. If The One were here, surely she would have realized it by now.

Deciding to do the mature thing, Sophie continued walking out of the café. When she got outside, she texted her would-be date and canceled their plans. Then she walked to where she'd parked her car this morning. She got in and sipped her tea as she drove down Main Street, taking a left on a connecting street and another right onto Dragonfly Lane, where she lived in her own home, sans her parents and purchased by way of her responsible job. She didn't work with kids but she liked them, and her best friend Trisha's son thought Sophie was the world's best babysitter.

If Sophie were a guy, she'd be her own Mr. Right. Maybe that was a sign that she was meant to be alone. Some people were perfectly happy living single after all. Perhaps she should get a pet to keep her company. A fish was low-maintenance.

Sophie carefully climbed her porch steps. She walked inside and headed to her bedroom. After taking an extended hot shower, she pulled the long, elegant dress she'd purchased for tonight from her closet. It was in a color called passion fruit, which was all the rage for spring. She slipped it over her body, loving the feel of silk against her skin. Then she turned to look at her reflection in the mirror. Her mood lifted just enough to make her release a pent-up breath.

Just like when she was eighteen and everything about her life had felt wrong, she stepped into a piece of clothing and her world righted just enough. That's when she'd fallen in love with clothes. She'd felt helpless, unattractive, and out of control after her climbing accident. She'd felt the pressing weight of everyone's expectations to lift her chin high, put on a smile, and get well.

She hadn't felt like smiling though. And back then, even though it had been during a spring much like this one, hope had been so far out of reach that she couldn't even conceive of the possibility that things would ever get better.

Clothes had become a kind of armor. They gave her confidence. They hid things from the outside world that she didn't want others to see.

Sophie swept her hair into an updo and slipped her feet into a pair of flats. Her days of wearing heels were long gone. Most days, she barely even had a limp. Ten minutes in a pair of high-heel shoes, however, would overstress the weak muscles in her left leg and ensure she couldn't even walk for the rest of the night.

Grabbing her keys off the counter, Sophie headed back out her door. She hurried to her car and started driving, distracted only a little by the question that had been plaguing her all day. Was Chase Lewis on the guest list? And truthfully, that was the reason she'd wanted a date to tonight's wedding in the first place.

Chase had returned to town three months ago but she'd done a fairly good job of avoiding her first love so far. And when they had run into each other, she'd managed to smile politely and excuse herself as quickly as possible. After over ten years, he still had the power to make her heart skip a beat. Too much had happened between them though. Some things couldn't be undone, like the boulder that had crushed her lower leg when she'd fallen off the face of a mountain. And some words could never be unsaid.

Sophie sighed, hoping she wouldn't have to dodge Chase tonight. Then she screamed as something darted in front of her car, and she slammed the brakes too late. Her bumper tapped against whatever it was with a jolting *thud*.

* * *

Chase had fully intended to leave the veterinary clinic early today so he could prepare for Jack and Emma's wedding. But it was one of those days where it literally seemed to be raining cats and dogs in his reception area. Then he'd needed to perform an emergency surgery on a patient of his, a retriever with a fancy for swallowing sweaty socks.

He'd known being the only vet in town would be hard when he'd accepted the job in late December. He couldn't work a normal schedule so plans were always getting fumbled. But if Chase hurried, he'd make it to the wedding on time, watch his longtime friends exchange their vows, and wish them the very best.

Chase stepped into a pair of leather shoes that he seldom wore and glanced at his reflection for a quick moment. At first, he didn't recognize himself. He was much more used to the scrubs and the dark five o'clock shadow that filled in after a long day at the clinic. Or a wet-dry tee and pair of athletic shorts, which was his typical climbing gear.

A suit, on the other hand…

He turned from the mirror and hurried toward the front of the house, slowing at the sight of a chew toy that still rested by his back door where Grizzly used to lay. Now Chase's beloved dog was gone.

Chase swallowed past the ache in his heart. Grizzly had been with him in college, his first job in South Carolina, and his return to his hometown a few months ago to take over the old veterinary clinic here. Grizzly had been a faithful companion through many tough times and could never be replaced. Chase had considered getting another dog but now he wondered if he ever would.

He stepped over the chew toy, grabbed his keys off the hook on the wall, and jogged out the door, his restless muscles reminding him that he hadn't had time to go for a run in two days. Maybe this weekend the clinic would slow down enough to give him a chance to satisfy his need for adrenaline.

As if on cue, his phone rang with an incoming call as he got into his truck. He checked the caller ID before holding his cell phone to his ear. "Hey, Will."

Will Marritt was a longtime friend and fellow outdoor fanatic.

"Hey, man, just wondering if you were free tonight. I was going to get some wings and a few drinks."

"I'm afraid I already have plans," Chase said. He pulled out of his driveway and onto the road.

"Hot date?"

"I'm going to Jack and Emma's wedding tonight." Chase wasn't surprised that Will wasn't invited. The guest list was intentionally kept small, and Will was older than Chase's high school friends. He and Chase had reconnected over their mutual love of the great outdoors since he'd been back home.

"Right, right," Will said. "I forgot. Man, I hate to eat wings alone but I like going to weddings alone even less."

Chase felt his lips pulling into a frown. He didn't enjoy going to weddings alone either but worse than that was going with someone he wasn't really into. "Actually, I'm taking Amelia Dover," he confessed.

"Oh yeah? You two dating?"

Chase hesitated. "This'll be our first date. Kind of." And he wished he were just going alone. Amelia was nice and they had a lot in common but there were no sparks. And she wasn't even good friends with Jack or Emma. She was only attending as Chase's date. "We'll get together another time," Chase said, veering the subject safely away from his dating life as he turned onto a neighboring street.

"We need to plan a climb. You free tomorrow?"

Chase wanted to say yes but his clinic schedule was

unpredictable. "As long as no pet emergencies come up. I'll let you know."

"Sounds good, bud."

They disconnected the call, and Chase slowed at the sight of a car pulled to the side of the road. He recognized the sporty yellow vehicle. Sophie Daniels had made it clear since he'd been back in town that she didn't really want to be friends. Who really stayed friends after a messy breakup anyway? At least after sharing the kind of young love they'd had. The kind of heartbreak that never truly healed, in his experience.

Unable to leave her stranded, he slowed and pulled behind her car. He got out, noticing that her hood wasn't up. He walked up to the driver's side window, preparing to knock until he realized that she wasn't sitting inside. Then he heard her quiet voice near the front of the hood. Her sniffles got his attention.

"It's okay. I'm so sorry. I just didn't see you," she said.

Chase quickened his steps and rounded the front of her car. "Sophie?"

She startled as she looked up at him, tears streaming down her flushed cheeks. Her reddish-brown hair was pulled back in a fancy clip at the base of her neck. "Chase! Oh my goodness. I'm so happy to see you."

He froze. "Are you okay?" Because the Sophie he knew these days seemed to avoid him at all costs.

"Yes, I'm fine but I hit this puppy." Tears made black rivers of mascara run down her cheeks. "He's still breathing. I didn't mean to hit him. He just appeared out of nowhere and I tried to stop but I still tapped him, and now he's just lying here." Her words ran together as she spoke quickly.

Chase trailed his gaze over the dog. He knew this puppy. It was a patient of his at the clinic.

"Please, help him," Sophie pleaded.

Chase headed over and knelt on one knee, dirtying the pants

leg of his suit. So much for polishing up nicely. "Hey, Comet," he said, gently rubbing the top of the pup's head.

"How do you know his name?" Sophie asked with surprise.

Chase slid his gaze to meet hers. Even in an emergency situation, his heart managed to squeeze at the sight of her. "He belongs to Mrs. Dozier." Mrs. Dozier was an elderly woman in town who lived alone and thought a pet would serve as a good companion.

Sophie covered her mouth with one hand. "Oh no, she'll be so upset. Is he going to die?"

Chase looked for any sign of injury on the dog. There was no visible blood but Comet's hind leg wasn't positioned right. "Best-case scenario, he could be in shock," Chase told her, hoping she wouldn't ask the next obvious question.

Sophie's light-green eyes widened as they filled with fear. She lowered her shaky hand from her mouth. "And the worst case?" she asked.

Chase hesitated because he knew Sophie wouldn't like the answer. "Let's not think about worst case just yet."

* * *

Sophie had never stepped foot into a veterinary clinic before. She'd never had a reason to until now.

The first thing she noticed was that the building had a distinct odor. Like wet fur and bleach. It wasn't necessarily bad but it wasn't a place where she'd want to work day in and day out either.

Sophie went up on her toes to see Chase and the limp black-and-white puppy better from where she was standing against the wall in the examining room.

"You don't have to stand way over there, you know." Chase glanced over his shoulder. "You can come closer."

"No, that's okay." She pressed her shoulder blades into the wall behind her. Her dress had an open back so her bare skin met the cold surface. A shiver ran through her, as much from the temperature as from the situation she found herself in. "I'm fine right here."

Chase was using a stethoscope to listen to the dog's chest and stomach as it lay on the table. Sophie guessed from her *Grey's Anatomy* television education that he was checking for the sound of something foreboding.

Please let the puppy be okay.

She watched Chase inspect Comet's leg next. The dog whined a little, and Sophie couldn't bear to watch another moment. This was all her fault. How had she not seen him run in front of her car? What was he doing out there all alone? Where was Mrs. Dozier?

Sophie turned and headed out of the examining room, needing air. Whatever she had to do to make things right with the little dog in the examining room, she'd do. She'd pay the vet bills and even go to Mrs. Dozier's home if necessary to care for him. It was the least she could do.

Sophie's stomach clenched but she kept walking, unfamiliar with the building's layout or where she was going. She just needed a moment and some room to move her restless muscles. She found a bathroom down the hall and stepped inside to wash her hands and wipe off the faded black trails of mascara from where she'd been crying. Then she stepped back into the hall and followed it a little farther down.

Meow.

The sound of a cat got her attention. Welcoming a distraction from her current state of panic, Sophie turned toward the sound and saw a room full of kennels, some empty and some with cats and dogs. Without thinking, she headed in that direction.

She stopped to say hello to several animals before standing

in front of a kennel with a handwritten sign that read MINNIE. "Hey, sweetheart. How are you doing tonight?"

The black cat pressed its nose against the cage trying to sniff her hand as she held it out. It meowed softly again. "I bet Dr. Lewis took very good care of you, and you're going to be just fine."

"I appreciate your faith in me. As a doctor, at least."

Sophie whirled to face Chase, who'd walked up behind her without her hearing him. He held Comet in his arms. "Oh. You're done with the examination already? How is he?"

"Well, he's not bleeding internally. But he does have a broken leg. I've stabilized it for right now, and I'll keep him here overnight." Chase bent down to gently lay Comet in one of the empty cages. It was lined with a large navy blue pillow that looked comfortable at least.

Sophie blew out a breath as she watched. Chase was definitely dressed for some kind of formal occasion. And he looked good. He was clean-shaven, and his honey-colored brown hair was combed neatly, curling slightly at the ends. She cleared her throat, focusing on the reason she was here. "Did you reach Mrs. Dozier?"

Chase nodded as he stood and faced her. "I left a message and told her that Comet was fine and that she could call my cell phone. When she does, I'll arrange for her to come see him tomorrow."

"On Sunday?" Sophie grimaced. "I'm guessing that's usually your day off."

Chase folded his arms in front of him. "One thing I didn't anticipate when I took over this clinic is that I'd rarely get a day off. Not without calling in one of the vets I know in Whispering Pines."

Whispering Pines was the next town over. The knowledge that Chase would be back here again in the morning because of her only compounded Sophie's guilt. "Thank you so much for helping. I know Mrs. Dozier would be heartbroken if something had happened to Comet."

"No need to thank me. I was glad to help. That's what I do."

Sophie realized that they were alone in this building, aside from all the animals watching them. The building was only half-lit and strangely quiet aside from the sound of claws tapping along the cage floors and scratching at fur. "I'll pay for the bill. I was the one who hit Comet after all."

Chase shook his head. "I don't need to be paid. I'll count this as my good deed for the month."

Sophie's hands fidgeted in front of her. "I want to make things right. What can I do to help?"

Chase shrugged. "Right now, there's nothing else to do. Comet is sedated, and he'll stay here tonight and rest."

Sophie felt helpless as she nervously turned to look at Comet. "He's a beautiful dog. A border collie, right?"

"That's correct. You know your breeds."

She turned to him. "You sound surprised."

"I've just never known you to be interested in animals."

She wanted to tell him he didn't really know her anymore at all. Instead, she looked around the room, anywhere but at him, and said, "A neighbor of mine used to have a border collie. He was such a gorgeous and smart dog."

"It's a good breed," Chase agreed. "Comet is a mix. He probably has a little retriever in him too."

Sophie listened as she took a step backward, needing to put some space between them. "Well, I better get going. I'm sure you have things to do with your evening."

Chase gestured between them. "Based on how we're dressed, I'm guessing we're both going to the same place."

"You're going to Jack and Emma's wedding too?" She was hoping there was some other fancy event in town tonight.

"Now you look surprised," he teased. Then his grin fell, and he slapped a hand to his forehead. "Oh no."

"What?" Without thinking, Sophie stepped toward him. "What's wrong?"

He pulled his cell phone from his pocket and looked at the screen. "I was supposed to pick up my date for Jack and Emma's wedding. I completely forgot."

The *d* word got Sophie's attention. Why wouldn't he bring a date though? She was supposed to be going with someone tonight too. "You had an animal emergency come up. I'm sure she'll understand."

"If she ever speaks to me again," Chase muttered. "I've missed three calls from her already." He blew out a breath. "I'll call her back after I lock up here."

"I'm sorry." But some part of Sophie wasn't sorry at all. She watched Chase fill a food and water bowl for Comet. "So, who is she?" she asked. "Your date."

Chase paused in what he was doing, glancing over his shoulder to meet her gaze. "You probably wouldn't know her."

Sophie folded her arms in front of her, tilting her head and narrowing her eyes. "If she's from Sweetwater Springs, I'm guessing I would. You're the one who's been gone for so many years. Not me."

He paused for a long beat. "Amelia Dover."

Sophie straightened a notch. "Oh." Amelia was younger than her by maybe five years. She was tall and curvy in all the places that a woman wanted to be. And she was undeniably gorgeous. She was also one of those genuinely nice people who you couldn't speak poorly of even if you tried.

"Well, she is someone who would definitely understand missing your date because of needing to rescue an animal."

Chase led the way down the hallway toward the front reception area. "You're probably right. I should have at least texted or called to let her know I wouldn't make it. I got distracted."

He turned to face Sophie in midstep, causing her to bump into him accidentally. His hands braced her arms, and her face reflexively tipped back to look at him. It'd been years but this position felt entirely too familiar. She didn't breathe for a moment. She just stared into his brown eyes, getting lost in the best kind of way.

"Sorry," he finally said, voice low. But his hands were still on her arms, and he didn't step back. Neither did she.

Her heart knocked hard against her ribs. "My fault. I wasn't watching where I was going." For the second time tonight.

"I turned on you too soon," he said.

"Because you had something to say. What was it?" At this close range, she could see the scar on his cheek from the time he'd fallen off his mountain bike on a ride with her. It'd been a nasty fall, and he'd gotten nine stitches that afternoon at the ER. She'd been there with him the whole time.

He held her gaze captive. She could barely blink as she waited, her heart thumping erratically. This was why she'd been avoiding Chase Lewis since he'd returned to town. She couldn't do this again. Wouldn't. They had nothing in common anymore. The only thing between them now was baggage.

"I can't seem to remember," he said.

She felt her lips pull into a slight smile. "Distracted again? I never pegged you as the inattentive type."

His hands fell away from her arms but he didn't budge otherwise. "Not when it comes to something I'm interested in."

Sophie pulled more air into her lungs as the room seemed to shrink, pulling her and Chase into their own tiny world. It was just the two of them—no one else. The way it used to be when they were inseparable and in love.

Then someone knocked on the glass entry door.

She and Chase both turned to look. It took a moment for Sophie to process the tall, curvaceous, gorgeous woman on the other side.

Amelia Dover.

Chase quickly stepped away. Sophie could imagine how this looked to an outsider looking in. And for a moment, she wondered if the way it looked was deceiving—or if it was all too real.

Chapter Two

Chase quickly walked to the door, not knowing what he'd say to Amelia when he opened it. He'd been mere inches from Sophie. There weren't a lot of good excuses for standing so close, and he wasn't one to lie. Except he didn't know what the truth was. Were he and Sophie about to kiss?

Either way, he shouldn't feel like he was cheating because he'd never even been on a date with Amelia. She was just supposed to accompany him to tonight's wedding. When he'd run into her at the park and had lamented about going alone, she'd offered to be his date. She was doing him a favor, and this was how he repaid her.

"Amelia," he said as he opened the vet clinic's door, "I need to explain."

Amelia's eyes were wide, like she was the one who'd been caught doing something wrong. She shook her head quickly, looking between him and Sophie. "No, you don't. I just... Well, when you didn't pick me up, I tried to call but you didn't answer. And it occurred to me that you might have had an emergency come up at the clinic so I thought I'd meet you here. That way we weren't late to the wedding." Chase noticed Amelia's satiny dress. She looked nice, and he felt like a big jerk.

"I did have an emergency. Sophie hit a dog this evening on the way to the wedding. I stopped to help her." He gestured back at Sophie, wondering again what would have happened if they'd had one more second alone together.

Amelia's hands flew over her mouth. "Oh no. Is the dog okay?" she asked, worry wrinkling her brow. Chase knew she was a huge animal lover. On paper, he and Amelia should have been a perfect match.

"Comet is going to be fine. He has a broken leg."

Amelia's eyes were suspiciously shiny, no doubt on the account of the dog and not him, but Chase felt guilty anyway.

Sophie stepped up beside him. "Amelia, I'm so sorry for holding Chase up. This is all my fault."

"Don't worry about it," Amelia said. "I completely understand."

"We've probably missed the wedding by now," Chase told her. "And I'm afraid after working on a dog, it probably wouldn't be advisable to dance with me."

Amelia offered a slight smile. She hesitated, which confirmed that she'd seen him standing too close to Sophie just now. She shook her head. "I'm not in the mood for dancing anyway. We can get together another time," she said nicely.

Chase appreciated that she wasn't making a huge deal out of this, even though he deserved her anger. "Thank you. Again, I'm sorry."

"Well, the dog needed you. And Sophie did too." Amelia took a retreating step. "I'll talk to you later. Nice to see you, Sophie."

Chase released a breath once Amelia was gone. Then he turned back to Sophie. "Was that as bad as it felt?"

Sophie grimaced. “You did stand her up. But it was for a good reason.”

“And she caught me with you,” he pointed out.

Sophie appeared startled by the comment. “We weren’t doing anything.” She narrowed her green eyes. “Were we?”

“Not exactly.” *Not yet.*

“So you’re fine. You can reschedule your date for another time. I’m sure she’ll agree.”

“Right. The thing is I wasn’t looking forward to our date tonight anyway.” Chase shrugged. “Amelia is nice but there aren’t any…”

“Sparks?” Sophie asked.

“Yeah.” And he felt a whole lot of sparks standing near Sophie.

“I can relate.” She folded her arms in front of her, as if guarding her heart. Did she still blame him after all this time?

Chase stepped away from the door. “Well, I won’t keep you any longer. I just need to lock up and then I’ll be on my way out too.”

“We missed the wedding but, if we hurry, we can still make it to the reception,” Sophie said.

Chase narrowed his eyes. “We?”

Her mouth fell open. “Not together, of course. That’s not what I meant. I just meant we’re both friends of the bride and groom, and there’s time to wish them well.”

“Right. I guess I could freshen up here. Do you need to do the same?”

Sophie shook her head. “I already washed my hands when you were examining Comet. I don’t plan on dancing with anyone anyway.”

“Doubtful you’ll succeed with those plans. All the single guys in the room would be crazy not to line up for a dance with you.” Him included, except he suspected she’d turn him down.

Sophie looked down at her feet. She was wearing a pair of

shiny flats in a pink color that complemented her dress. Back when they'd dated, she'd never been one to dress up. She'd been more of a tomboy—the prettiest one he'd ever seen. "I'll see you at the reception," she said.

Chase nodded. "Yeah."

"Thank you for everything, Chase. Really. I don't know what I would have done had you not driven up."

"I'm glad I could help." Chase released a breath as he watched her step out onto the sidewalk and head toward his side parking lot. He turned and headed down the hall to wash up in the bathroom. When he was finished, he locked up the clinic and drove to the wedding reception.

Better late than never, Chase stepped inside the large, open room full of music, friends, and family. Or actually, he was only supposed to have two family members here tonight. He didn't see Trisha or Petey but knowing his young nephew, who was a lot like his father at that age, Petey would make himself seen within a few minutes. If Chase had anything to say about it, Petey would be a far cry from what his father was like these days though.

Pete Senior was serving a lengthy sentence in a state prison two hours away. That was why Chase had moved back to Sweetwater Springs to begin with. He had grown up without a father or any real male influence but his young nephew didn't have to. Chase wanted to be close by to take Petey fishing, camping, and every other activity that boys enjoyed.

"Uncle Chase!"

Chase saw flashes of Petey as the boy weaved between the crowd and came barreling into his legs. Reflexively, Chase laughed at the boy's excitement. Then he looked up and saw Trisha watching them. She waved from the other side of the room, an easy smile sweeping across her face. Sophie was already sitting next to her at a round table with a floral centerpiece.

While Trisha had fallen for Chase's brother in high school, Chase had fallen for Sophie. The four of them had been inseparable for a time. Neither couple had found their happily ever after though. He guessed Trisha and Pete had for the last few years. But ultimately, they'd all been left with battered and bruised hearts—victims of bad choices and bad luck.

Petey tugged on Chase's arm, leading him to the table where his mom and Sophie were sitting.

"I was worried you weren't going to make it," Trisha said, standing from the table to give Chase a hug. Trisha was beautiful, smart, and one of the nicest people he knew. Chase had always felt like her real brother instead of only a brother-in-law. "Sounds like you and Sophie had quite the adventure tonight. She's been telling me all about it."

"I'd hardly call hitting and nursing a dog an adventure," Sophie said, sharing a look with him. Their idea of an adventure had once taken them to the highest peaks in the Carolinas. They'd chased one adventure after another together, getting as high from their thrill seeking as they had from their love.

"I'm happy to say that Mrs. Dozier's dog is resting comfortably," Chase reported, "and I got here just in time for the fun. I'm assuming Emma wasn't a runaway bride."

Trisha laughed as she sat back down at the table, placing her hands on the white lacy tablecloth. "No way. She and Jack are two people in love if I ever saw it."

"Glad to hear it." Chase shifted back and forth on his feet, trying to decide if he should stay or find another place to sit.

"We saved you a seat." Trisha gestured at an empty chair.

"Thanks." Chase started to head toward it but Petey was still holding on to his arm.

"I'm going to dance with my mom. You dance with Sophie," the boy ordered. It wasn't a question. Petey was a born leader just like his father.

Trisha stood and took Petey's hand, letting her son lead her onto the dance floor.

Chase looked at Sophie. She didn't budge from her seat. He didn't breathe. Then his instincts took over, and he did the only acceptable thing he could do in the moment. The only thing he wanted to do. He offered his hand, feeling vulnerable suddenly because she still had the power to crush his heart. "May I have this dance?"

* * *

Sophie stared at Chase's outstretched hand. How could she say no to the man who'd helped her save the dog she'd hit an hour ago? Without Chase's help, Comet might still be suffering on the side of the road.

"I promise I won't step on your feet this time," Chase said when she didn't immediately answer.

She laughed softly. He'd always been an awful dancer. High school dances left her feet swollen with dark-blue bruises but she'd never minded back then. "That's good because these are new shoes." She slipped her hand in his, ignoring the tingly sensation that zipped through her body as she stood.

"I guess that's the perk of owning your own clothing store," he said, leading her onto the dance floor and turning to face her.

Her mouth fell open. "Only a man would call my boutique a mere clothing store," she teased as he placed his hands on her waist. She resented the way her body reacted to him, with a racing heart and rush of blood. "Owning my own boutique has its drawbacks too. I can't take the goods home if I want to turn a profit."

"Ah. That is a dilemma."

The music was a familiar, slow tune that Sophie couldn't quite place. Not when she was too distracted by Chase's touch and the warmth of his breath on her cheek. She hadn't allowed him to hold her since before the accident. The feel of his arms around her was as familiar and unfamiliar as the music streaming through the speakers.

She made the mistake of looking up into his brown eyes. There was so much history between them. But he'd been gone long enough that she didn't know the man he'd become. Trisha had filled her in on some of the details, of course. He was still active, spending every free moment chasing another spike in adrenaline. He ran, biked, and climbed at every chance.

"Do you recognize the song?" Chase asked. "What are the odds?"

She drew her brows together in question as she listened a little closer. Then Chase began to hum along softly, the vibration tickling her skin.

Her heartbeat picked up speed.

"You don't recognize it?" he asked, looking slightly disappointed even though the corners of his lips were curling softly. "They're playing our song, Soph."

Her lips parted as the song registered in her memory. "Did you ask them to play this?" She regretted her defensive tone but she couldn't help it. Her guard was up whenever he was around. It was the only way to protect her heart from falling for him again. She'd believed they were made for each other once upon a time but she didn't think that was true anymore. People changed. She'd changed.

Chase chuckled. "I just got here, Sophie. How would I have had time to talk to the DJ?"

"Right." It was just a coincidence. Sophie took a breath, trying to recapture control of her thoughts and emotions. Then her left leg buckled. It was a quick loss of control that might've landed her on the floor if Chase weren't there holding her up.

"You okay?" he asked, concern wrinkling his brow.

She stood on two good legs. Sometimes she just lost control when she was tired. Or when she was hyperfocused on something other than standing. The damaged nerves and muscles had never fully healed after the traumatic break when the boulder fell on her leg. They would have if she'd been taken to the hospital immediately. But thirty-six hours on the mountain had allowed infection to set in. She was lucky to be alive. Lucky to still have this leg, according to the surgeon who'd operated on her after she was rescued.

"I guess you made me go weak in the knees for a moment," she joked, trying to ease the tension.

"Are you sure you're okay?" Chase asked a second time.

"I'm fine."

Chase seemed to accept this answer although he was holding on to her more tightly now. They were quiet for a moment but Sophie's thoughts were loud inside her brain. Memories of being held by Chase a long time ago surfaced. They'd had their own song, a million adventures, and a bright future that they were looking forward to.

The song ended, and Sophie stepped back. Their futures had gone in different directions, and she'd always believed it was for the best. No reason to second-guess that belief now.

"Thank you for thc dance," Chase said. "I hope your toes are okay."

Sophie nodded with a small smile. "They're fine," she said. Much better than her heart.

* * *

The next morning, Chase's stomach growled painfully as he stepped into his clinic. Until last month, he'd had a veterinary assistant who would come in on the weekends. Now, he and his office assistant, Penny, took turns handling all the nonemergency animal care. It was Penny's turn but Chase would've had to come in today regardless in order to check on Comet.

Chase walked down the hall, flipping on the lights as he entered the room of dogs and cats. Comet's eyes were large as Chase approached. Even after what he'd been through, his tail thumped happily on the pillowed floor of his cage.

"Hey, boy. How're you doing? Don't worry. Mrs. Dozier will be here to bring you home soon." Chase squatted and extended his index finger through the holes in the dog's kennel, laughing as the pup lapped a wet tongue across his skin. Then he checked on the other animals before walking back to his office.

He grabbed an energy bar from his desk drawer to temper his hunger, finishing it off in four bites. When he was done, he grabbed his phone. He was surprised that Mrs. Dozier hadn't contacted him yet. He dialed her number again, relieved when she answered this time.

"Good morning, Mrs. Dozier. Did you receive my message about Comet?"

"Oh yes. I did last night. I'm so relieved," she said.

Chase wondered why she hadn't called him back. "I'm at the clinic right now if you want to come by and visit Comet. I'll probably keep him one more day for observation."

"No, that's okay, Dr. Lewis," the older woman said. "I'm on my way to church. I'll just see Comet tomorrow. Is it okay to come by and talk to you in the morning?"

Chase glanced at his schedule on his laptop. "My eight thirty spot is open."

"Perfect," she said. "I'll see you and Comet then."

Chase said goodbye and sat at his desk for an awestruck moment. Most pet owners would have rushed down here at the first opportunity. But Mrs. Dozier was in her eighties. She had a routine, and he understood that.

Chase had a routine too. On the weekends, he traded his scrubs for athletic wear and did anything that worked his muscles to capacity. He brought up Will's contact in his phone and tapped Call. "Still interested in that climb?" he asked in lieu of hello when his friend answered.

"Always," Will said. "Meet you at your house in half an hour?"

"You're on." Chase disconnected the call and got up, walking through the clinic toward the front. Sophie was the one he used to call. She was the one who'd gotten him into climbing in the first place. She didn't climb anymore though. And even if she did, she wouldn't with him. Once again, he wondered if she still blamed him for her accident. He should have been there with her on the day of her fall. She'd asked but instead he'd opted to go off with a friend to ride horses.

Sophie had said she'd find another friend to climb with. Instead, she'd gone up that mountainside alone. After her rescue, which had seemed like a miracle because many had started to fear the worst, Chase had rushed to her side. But she'd wanted nothing to do with him.

Chase stepped out of his clinic and headed to his truck, remembering last night. For a moment, he'd thought that he and Sophie might kiss in his clinic's front room. Was that his imagination? Did she still want nothing to do with him? Or had something shifted between them?

Chapter Three

Early Monday morning, Sophie changed into her swimsuit and a cover-up to wear until she got to the indoor community pool. She was the only person here this early. Even the lifeguard wasn't on her stand just yet.

That was fine with Sophie. A couple of laps would ease her body and hopefully her mind too. Her sleep had been restless on Saturday and last night, too, thinking about the little dog she'd hit. That had stirred up memories of when she'd injured her own leg.

Hopefully the little dog's recovery would be easier than hers had been. It was all she could do not to check on Comet yesterday because that would've meant contacting Chase. And after that near kiss and too-close-for-comfort dance they'd shared on Saturday night, she'd wanted a little space from him.

Sophie pulled off the cover-up and left it draped over the bench along the wall. She slid off her shoes and then she pulled some goggles over her eyes before stepping to the edge of the deep end. She felt a small tremor in her left leg but she ignored it.

Instead, she inhaled deeply and dove into the crystal-blue

water. The sensation of water shocked her body momentarily, freeing her thoughts. Everything inside her focused on swimming. That was one reason she loved this exercise.

She moved her arms quickly, cutting through the water's surface until she reached the shallow end of the pool. Then she somersaulted underwater just like an Olympian and headed back toward the deep end. She somersaulted again. And again, going back and forth until her mind was focused on nothing other than the opposite end of the pool.

She was on autopilot, working to physical capacity the way she used to before her accident. She had never returned to climbing mountains, blaming her injuries. Her friend and former coach Denny Larson had tried many times to lure her back out there, saying amputees and even the town's wheelchair-bound mayor climbed. Sophie's injuries were minor in comparison. If they could scale a mountain, so could she.

Just the thought caused a swirl of anxiety and fear in her chest though. Her body tensed, which only increased the cramping in her left leg. Swimming and yoga were safe. They kept her on the ground. They didn't require a partner, and they didn't remind Sophie of Chase.

Focus, Sophie. Focus.

She swam faster and harder, lifting her head on every third stroke to take a breath. Sophie's head popped above the water's surface, and she gasped for air.

"Are you okay?" a voice asked from the edge of the pool. It was the lifeguard who'd shown up without Sophie realizing it. She was watching with concern wrinkling the skin above her brow.

Sophie stopped swimming and took a moment and another breath. "Yeah," she said, a little breathlessly, "it's just been a couple days since I've been for a swim. I'm off my game a little bit." She took several deep breaths.

"I wondered where you were last week," the lifeguard said with an easy smile. "It's good to see you."

Sophie nodded. "Thanks."

The lifeguard took her seat on her stand.

Instead of returning to laps, Sophie leaned against the wall of the pool, closed her eyes, and tipped her face back. Her body followed until it floated on the water's surface. She breathed in the chlorine smell that had become soothing to her over the years. She needed to soothe her nerves before the next item on her to-do list. She couldn't avoid the inevitable any longer. Today, as soon as she got to the boutique, she needed to make a call and check up on Comet. Which meant checking in with Chase.

* * *

At five minutes to eight, Chase unlocked the back door to his veterinary practice and walked inside. The muscles of his arms pulled tight as he straightened them. His legs were tired too. He loved the feeling of being pushed to his physical limits in a climb. His muscles usually ached the following day but it was a feel-good kind of pain that reminded him he was alive.

He carried the stack of mail that he'd pulled from the mailbox, thumbing through it as he walked to his office. His fingers paused on the familiar white envelope of a personal letter. A state prison's address was stamped at the top left-hand corner. He got one of these letters every Monday morning without fail. His brother, Pete, was persistent—he'd give him that.

Chase sat at his desk and quickly stashed the letter in the drawer with a dozen others. One letter for every Monday since he'd taken over the clinic. Their mom must have given Pete the address. Chase had thought that a one-sided conversation couldn't possibly go on for long but it had. What was Pete telling him in the letters? Was he talking about his days?

His weeks? His prison friends? Was he asking about Trisha and Petey?

Chase heaved a heavy sigh. He didn't care what his brother was saying. Pete had said everything with his actions. His brother wasn't a violent person but he'd hurt so many people, betraying his clients' trust and embezzling money from their accounts, leaving many of them in financial ruin. His brother had also left Trisha and Petey to fend for themselves. How could Pete let his son grow up without a father the way they had? It was unforgivable in Chase's mind.

Chase headed back down the hall toward the back area where he kept the animals overnight. He needed to check on Dory, the Lab pup that he'd operated on Saturday afternoon. He approached her cage, and her tail thumped happily against the floor.

"Having a case of sock regret?" Saturday's tube sock was the third that Dory had scarfed down in her short life. There was evidently something about a sweaty sock she couldn't resist.

Dory stood up as if nothing had happened and barked in response.

Chase chuckled, checked her vitals—pleased to see that they were good—and refreshed her water bowl. Next, Chase checked on Minnie, the black cat he'd spayed on Friday. She'd stayed longer than usual because her owner was out of town, and being a small-town vet, he obliged the extra days. Then he checked on Comet. The puppy seemed oblivious to his broken leg as he balanced on his cast, barking a soft hello at Chase.

"Don't worry. Your owner will be here this morning, buddy," Chase promised. "I bet she misses you as much as you miss her." Those words rang hollow in Chase's gut. Mrs. Dozier hadn't seemed overly eager to check on Comet when Chase had spoken to her yesterday.

Chase petted Comet a couple of minutes longer and then cared for the basic needs of his other patients. When he was done, he washed his hands one last time and headed back to the front door. He flipped the OPEN sign to face out in the window, his gaze catching on Mrs. Dozier as she rounded the corner.

Maybe he was wrong. Maybe she was eager to get her dog back.

Chase hurried to open the door for her, his muscles reminding him again of how hard he'd climbed yesterday with his buddy Will. "Good morning, Mrs. Dozier."

Mrs. Dozier stepped inside the clinic. "Good morning, Dr. Lewis."

"I just checked on Comet. He's doing great, and he's all set to go home."

Her kind face crumpled into a tiny frown. "I'm so glad to hear he's okay. He got away from me the other night, and I couldn't catch up with him. I tried; I really did."

Chase held up a hand. "Young dogs can be a lot of work. He'll calm down as he matures and he'll start to take commands better."

"I hope so." Mrs. Dozier was still frowning. There was something apologetic in her eyes. "For the next owner's sake."

Chase wasn't sure he understood. "What do you mean?"

"I can't keep Comet, Dr. Lewis." She held up a hand as if Chase was already arguing with her.

"What do you mean?"

"He's too much work. I bought a book to help me train him but I must not be doing it correctly. He barks at night, and I have to get up and take him outside at all hours. Then I can't get back to sleep. I toss and turn and..." Mrs. Dozier shook her head. "When I was younger, losing sleep wouldn't have been a big deal but if I don't sleep at night now, my days are just miserable. And Comet loves to go for walks."

Chase nodded. "Puppies have lots of energy to burn off. That's normal."

Mrs. Dozier's chin quivered. "I thought that would be good for me. To motivate me to get outside and soak up the sunshine. But it's a struggle to keep up. He pulls against the leash, and I pull back." She rubbed her forearm. "I'm getting pain from holding on to the leash so tightly."

Chase listened as she explained. "If this is about the vet bill, don't worry about it. It's covered." Sophie had offered to pay but Chase didn't need reimbursement. He just wanted Comet to be healthy and return home.

"It's not about the bill. It's about me." She folded her arms across her chest. "I love that dog but I'm afraid we're not a good match."

"You're giving Comet up."

"Believe me, I feel terrible about this. But I think it's what's best."

"I see." Typically, Chase didn't agree with owners giving up their pets. A pet was a commitment, like having a child. You couldn't just go back on that responsibility. But in this case, he understood. The growing dog could do a lot of harm to Mrs. Dozier if she wasn't careful. And Comet had already gotten hurt because of her inability to handle him.

"Will you please find him a good home?" she asked, her eyes pleading as she took a step backward.

"Of course." That meant that Comet would be under Chase's care for a while longer. At least until Chase could contact the local rescue that he dealt with.

"Thank you." Mrs. Dozier looked relieved. "He likes bacon treats. And if he sees a squirrel, you need to make sure you have a good hold on his leash," Mrs. Dozier warned. "He's a runner. He got out of my control another time, and my neighbor had to go after him for me."

Chase nodded as he listened. It was obvious that she cared about the dog.

"He won't come back if you call him. Maybe he can't hear or he just doesn't listen." She shrugged. "But he's a good dog." She held up a finger. "Oh, and he likes to watch *The Golden Girls*."

Chase couldn't help but smile at this. He'd heard a lot of things but that one was new.

"Will you make sure to tell his new owner for me?"

"I will," Chase promised.

Mrs. Dozier nodded. The color was back in her cheeks, and she was smiling faintly now. "Thank you, Dr. Lewis," she said before turning and walking out of the clinic.

Chase sighed and then turned toward his receptionist, Penny, who'd arrived while Mrs. Dozier was giving up her dog. Penny was in her midfifties and had been working at the clinic for years under the previous veterinarian. Chase guessed she'd seen it all when it came to pets and their owners too.

"Know anyone who might be looking for a dog?" he asked Penny.

She shook her head. "No. Do you?"

Chase hesitated, some part of him unwittingly contemplating volunteering himself. But he wasn't ready for another dog after Grizzly.

He shook his head as guilt formed a knot in his belly. "No."

"That's too bad," Penny said as she shuffled items on the counter and prepared for the day ahead.

Chase agreed. "I'll call the rescue at lunch." Until then, his schedule was full. There was no time to think about rehoming puppies with broken legs or nearly kissing long-lost loves who didn't want to be found again.

* * *

Sophie checked her phone for the millionth time as she sat on the floor of her boutique. She'd called Chase twice today and had left one voicemail for him to call her back. It was now late afternoon, and he had yet to call back. The suspense of how Comet was doing was driving her a bit crazy.

She groaned at her phone's blank screen. Why wasn't he returning her call?

She reached for one of the unopened boxes on the floor beside her and grabbed a pair of scissors to open it with. She'd gotten a big delivery of new clothing today, which had required unboxing and steaming before hanging each piece on a rack for display. She loved new shipments and new lines but it was also exhausting. At least today it had served to distract her from her mostly silent phone.

Sophie lifted the items out of the box as a giddy excitement reinvigorated her. The spring line for her boutique was going to fly off her racks. Her gaze moved over the newly hanging fabrics and rush of colors, stopping on the last of the items she'd ordered.

She stood and walked over, running her hand down the small section of gowns she always kept in stock. There wasn't a ton of demand for such fancy evening clothes. That's why it was genius for the women's shelter to have a black-tie affair instead of the annual spaghetti dinner this year. Sophie's best friend, Trisha, ran the shelter, and they'd come up with the idea together. It would give people a reason to get dressed up and hopefully bring in a lot more money to cover repairs and renovations for the shelter.

Speaking of Trisha, Sophie's cell phone rang, and her best friend's name flashed across the screen. She quickly connected the call. "I was just thinking of you. We need to get together soon. I didn't feel like we had much time to chat at Jack and Emma's wedding reception."

"Could that be because you were too focused on my ex-brother-in-law?" Trisha asked.

Sophie felt her cheeks burn. "We're old news," she said. "There is nothing between us." It was only a small lie. There was something there, a tiny spark, a buzz of awareness and remembrance of closer times. But Sophie had squashed it.

Trisha made a humming sound on the other end of the line. "If you say so. Catching up sounds good but that's not why I'm calling."

"Oh? What's up?" Sophie asked.

"Well, I have a client here at the shelter who will be going on a couple job interviews soon. The problem is she doesn't have anything to wear and can't afford to go shopping. Appearance is half of that first impression, as you always say. And I really want to set her up for success."

"Of course," Sophie said, still admiring the gowns from where she stood. "What do you need from me?"

"I was wondering if I could send her your way later this week? So you could work your fairy godmother magic."

Sophie kind of liked being compared to a fairy godmother. She'd never felt like the princess but she loved helping other women, especially those who were down on their luck. "Of course you can. What size is she?"

"She's an eight or ten," Trisha said. "She needs some shoes too. Size seven and a half."

Sophie grabbed a pen and notepad and wrote the details down. "Let me see what I can find. I'll give you a call back midweek?"

"Perfect. Thank you so much, Sophie."

"You know you can call me anytime."

"I do," Trisha said. "I never want to take advantage of our friendship though."

"This is not a favor between friends. This is my job, Trisha."

"No, your job is running a fancy boutique. That fairy godmother back room of yours is going above and beyond to help women in need. You give them more than clothes. You give them confidence, and that goes a long way. But you know that better than anyone."

Sophie was speechless for a moment. She did know that. That's why she'd started the back room to begin with.

"Anyway, I'm sure my client will also be grateful. She's working really hard to get back on her feet."

"We all need a little help every now and then," Sophie said, her eyes suddenly burning. She'd needed more than a little help in her life, and this town hadn't let her down. The people of Sweetwater Springs had rallied around her after her accident and during her recovery. And when she'd opened this boutique, half the town had showed up, buying her full stock on the first two days. She'd had to order more right away.

"I've also gotten a shipment of gowns," Sophie told Trisha before hanging up. "For people to wear to your black-tie affair next month."

"Oh, wonderful. I can't wait to take a peek," Trisha said excitedly.

"And to get your own dress," Sophie said. Trisha wasn't one to dress up in fancy clothing since her husband had been arrested. Trisha purposely dressed down as if to prove to everyone that she had not benefited from his crimes. "The whole point of your event is for people to be as fancy as possible, you included."

"Right," Trisha said, her tone notably more subdued. "I can't believe I was the one who came up with the idea."

"There was wine involved," Sophie reminded her. "And it was a great idea. That's why I pushed you to go for it."

"Remind me never to agree to anything under the influence of wine again," Trisha teased.

They talked a few more minutes and then hung up. After that, Sophie went to search her back room for clothes that might work for Trisha's client. The room in the back of her boutique looked worse than Sophie's closet at home. There were donated clothes from previous seasons and returns due to fabric flaws or damage.

Sophie shuffled through the things, finally finding a nice blouse and pair of pants that might work for the woman at the shelter. She had a size large blazer too but it might be too big. Sophie set the things aside. She still needed shoes but since Sophie wore the same size as the woman in need, she could find a pair from her own closet.

When she was done, she headed back to the front area and paused as she looked at the rack of gowns, excitement swirling in her chest once again.

"Wow, you look excited over something."

Sophie hadn't even heard the bell over her entry door jingle with an incoming customer. She looked up and smiled at a familiar face. Kaitlyn Russo-Hargrove owned the bed and breakfast on Mistletoe Lane. Sophie sometimes saw her around town but Kaitlyn didn't shop at the boutique.

"I am excited," Sophie shared. "I just put out new gowns for the black-tie affair that the women's shelter is putting on this year."

Kaitlyn had only been in Sweetwater Springs for a couple of years but she was already a pillar of the community. "I'm excited about the event but I must say I'll miss the annual spaghetti dinner."

"Really? You're not getting tired of it yet? You don't think they should do something new and exciting?"

Kaitlyn shrugged. "I don't know. There's a lot to be said for things that are familiar. Especially in Sweetwater Springs. The people here really love their traditions and charities, don't they?"

"You're one of us now. No talking like you're an outsider looking in."

Kaitlyn laughed as her gaze wandered around the store. "I guess that's what brought me in. Everyone I know shops at your boutique so I thought that I'd join your long list of customers."

"You moved here with all of your New York wardrobe. You haven't needed to do much shopping, I'd guess."

"That's true. But every time I rave over something that a friend of mine is wearing, they tell me they got it here."

"Well, you're in luck," Sophie said, "because I just got the new spring line on the racks today. You'll be one of the first to wear the pieces. You can be a walking advertisement for me."

Kaitlyn smiled. "Perfect."

Sophie returned to the counter as Kaitlyn shopped for the better part of an hour. When Kaitlyn was done, Sophie rang her items up and said goodbye. Her phone started to ring as soon as her boutique was empty. Sophie glanced at the caller ID and felt her heart flutter. She held the phone to her ear. "Hello?"

"Hey, Sophie. Sorry it took so long to return your call."

"No problem. I was calling earlier to check on Comet. Is he okay?"

"Yeah, he's doing great, actually."

Sophie blew out a breath, so relieved that her eyes teared up.

"You can come see for yourself if you want," Chase offered, his voice going low, making her wonder if he was suggesting more than just a friendly visit to see an injured dog.

Sophie hedged. Then she looked at the clock. It was still fifteen minutes until close but it was doubtful anyone else would be walking through her door this late in the day. "I'd love to."

"Great. I'll be here for the next half hour at least. Take your time."

They disconnected the call, and Sophie walked up front to turn the sign in the window to CLOSED. Then she headed out of her boutique, locking the door behind her. Her car wasn't in the parking lot, because she'd walked to work today, which wasn't unusual. Chase's clinic was one road past the route she normally took to get to her home on Dragonfly Lane. It was slightly out of her way but her leg wasn't acting up right now and a little extra exercise and fresh air would be good.

She needed to see for herself that the little black-and-white dog was okay. Even if it meant that she'd have to see Chase as well.

* * *

Chase felt the air become charged the moment that Sophie walked into his clinic. He turned and headed down the hall toward the front of the building to see if it was in fact Sophie and found her talking to Penny at the front desk.

Sophie looked at him as he approached, and he saw her quick intake of air.

"You came," he said.

She smiled. "I told you I was coming. You didn't believe me?"

He shrugged a shoulder. "I was just hoping nothing would hold you up, I guess."

She shook her head. "I walked today. I usually take Peony Road but Blossom Street also connects to Dragonfly Lane. It's just an extra block."

Sophie wasn't telling Chase anything he didn't already know. He wondered if the extra distance was a problem for her leg though. He knew Sophie still had issues with it, although he wasn't sure to what extent. Sometimes she had a subtle limp, but other times there was no visible evidence of her injuries. At least not with the long pants and skirts she wore. He'd visited her in the hospital right after her rescue but he'd never seen her scars.

Chase nodded as he stared at Sophie. His mind had suddenly gone blank, overrun with so many competing thoughts, all about her.

"You were going to let me see Comet," she prompted as the corners of her lips curled into a small smile.

"Right. Yes, I was."

Penny gave Chase a strange look as she watched the two of them.

Chase cleared his throat. "Comet is back here." He gestured to the back area where he'd taken the dog on Saturday.

"I'm surprised that he's not home with Mrs. Dozier already," Sophie commented as they walked.

Chase blew out a breath as they approached Comet's kennel. Immediately the little puppy stood to attention, balancing on the casted hind leg. He barked at Sophie, and she lowered to her knees to reach her hand through the cage and pet him.

"Here, I'll open it for you," Chase said. He released the latch, freeing Comet to come toward her. The little dog wasted no time getting the attention he was due.

"Is it okay that he's walking?" Sophie asked, looking up at Chase.

"I couldn't keep him from walking if I tried. That's why I casted his hind leg so well. It's stable. No need to worry."

Sophie nodded, running her hand down Comet's marbled coat and talking in a sweet voice that made Chase's heart squeeze.

"You two seem to like each other," he noted, as an idea seemed to take root in his mind. Sophie seemed to like Comet as much as the little dog liked her. "Mrs. Dozier isn't coming to take Comet home."

Sophie met his gaze again, a small divot forming between her brows as she looked at him in question. "What do you mean?"

"Well, Mrs. Dozier has decided that she can't handle Comet. She's giving him up."

Sophie's mouth dropped open. "No, she can't do that. Comet needs her."

Chase leaned against the kennel, folding his arms over his

chest. "Usually, I would agree but in this situation this is probably what's best for the both of them."

Sophie shook her head. "How could giving up someone you're supposed to love be best?"

Chase was tempted to call her out on the hypocrisy of that question. After her accident, Sophie had broken up with him, saying it was what was best for both of them. Chase was going to college, and she had a year of rehab ahead of her. When that hadn't worked to push him away, she'd revealed the truth. She blamed him for her injuries. He hadn't been there for her when she'd needed him most.

"Mrs. Dozier can't keep up with a puppy. That's why Comet got hit by a car in the first place," Chase explained. "So I'm rehoming him."

"You are?" Sophie asked.

He shrugged a shoulder. "Well, I'm trying. If you say no, I'll be calling the local rescue."

Sophie stood, her eyes narrowing. "If I say no?" she repeated.

"Comet obviously likes you."

"But I'm the reason Comet is even hurt," Sophie pointed out.

"No, it was an accident. Or a twist of fate," he said, remembering that Sophie didn't believe in coincidences. "Maybe you ran into Comet over the weekend for a reason. Maybe he's meant to be your dog."

Sophie looked unsure. She lowered her gaze to Comet, who was now whining at her feet, urging her to pay him more attention. A puppy's need for love was bottomless. "Why don't you take him home?" she asked, looking back up at him.

"I'm not ready. I just lost my dog, Grizzly, three months ago," he said quietly. And it still felt like yesterday in his heart. He saved everybody else's pets but he couldn't save his own.

"I'm sorry to hear that."

He nodded and reached out to touch her arm, gaining her

attention. “I think you and Comet are a good match. It’ll be an adventure, Sophie.”

Her gaze narrowed once more. “I don’t go on adventures anymore.” Now they were definitely talking about the past. Sophie looked down at the dog. “I’ve never even had a dog before. He needs someone who knows what they’re doing. Especially since he’s hurt.”

Sophie’s eyes were suspiciously shiny, and her hands were shaking. “I’m sorry, Chase, but I’m the last person who should be adopting him. I can’t take Comet home with me.”

Chapter Four

Chase had slept restlessly last night, and now he was reaching for his third cup of coffee before nine a.m. He'd gotten up early to go for a jog, showered, and had come in to care for the overnight animals, including Comet.

He'd really hoped that Sophie would have agreed to being Comet's new owner. He understood though. Taking on a pet was a lot of responsibility. A person didn't go into being a dog owner lightly. That's why he was waiting to get another dog himself. He'd loved Grizzly but owning a dog meant he had to change his plans sometimes or make arrangements so Grizzly was cared for when Chase couldn't take him on trips.

Chase had been on far fewer climbing trips since moving back to Sweetwater Springs. Agreeing to be the only vet in town wasn't a job one took on lightly either.

Chase plopped behind his desk and reached for his phone. Since Sophie had said no, Chase's next move was to call the local dog rescue. He'd known Mary Ellen forever. He pulled up her contact and connected the call.

"Hey, Chase," she said, "I haven't heard from you in a while."

"Well, I wish I could say this was a friendly call. One of my clients gave up her dog this week, and I'm trying to find him a good home."

"Oh no. I'm sorry to hear that. What kind of dog is it?" she asked.

"A young border collie mix, about six months old. He's got a broken hind leg," Chase said.

Mary Ellen made a noise on the other end of the line. "That's too bad. I'm afraid my rescue is full. And even if it weren't, I'm at capacity for homes willing to take on a dog with special needs."

"It'll only take a month or so to heal," Chase said, already getting the feeling that he was striking out yet again.

"That's a long time to ask someone to rearrange their life for a foster dog's needs, while caring for several other dogs in their home. I really wish I could help but I'm afraid I can't this time."

Chase's heart sank. He massaged his forehead as he listened to her continue to make valid excuses. "I understand," he finally said. "If something changes, please let me know."

"You bet," she said.

Chase disconnected the call and sat at his desk for a long moment. He had a few more calls he could make. He could keep Comet here. Maybe he could even take Comet home temporarily, if it came down to it. He had a belief that a person knew when they met the just-right pet for them. There was an immediate bond that happened. A kind of spark similar to what someone felt when they met the person that they were meant to spend their life with.

Chase hadn't had that connection with Comet. He'd only had that spark once with a pet. And once with a woman.

* * *

Late Tuesday afternoon, Sophie turned toward the sound of an incoming customer, a smile crossing her lips before she even saw who it was. Her smile grew even larger when she recognized Janet Lewis and Summer Rivera strolling in. They were two of her regular customers, and both were part of the Ladies' Day Out group that frequently got together in town for the sole purpose of good old-fashioned fun.

Sophie walked around the counter and headed in their direction. "So good to see you."

Janet was Chase's mom but there'd never been any awkwardness after the breakup. Janet held open her arms and gave her a big hug that warmed Sophie all the way to her core. She was a tall woman who greeted everyone she met with a large smile and a hug. In all the years that Sophie had known her, she never remembered hearing Janet speak an ill word about anyone.

Standing beside her, Summer Rivera was a sharp contrast. She was short and had at least one piece of gossip to throw out every time Sophie saw her, including today.

"Sophie, you will never believe what we just saw," Summer said as Janet pulled away from the hug.

Sophie turned her attention toward Summer, who was practically bursting at the seams to tell her the news. "Oh? What is that?"

Summer's tiny frame seemed to vibrate with excitement. "Well, Chief Baker was bringing flowers to Halona. I don't know where he got them, because, as you know, Halona owns the only florist shop in town. But the bigger question is why was he bringing his wife flowers? Either they're making up or they're celebrating something we don't know about yet." Summer's thin brows lifted high on her forehead, making golden McDonald's-shaped arches.

Janet shook her head with a laugh. "Or maybe he just loves his wife," she told her friend, "and he knows that she loves flowers. It's not our business to know why Alex was bringing Halona that bouquet." She turned to Sophie, gracefully transitioning to a new subject. "Our business is with you." She handed over a bag full of clothing. "I got your email. This is for the Fairy Godmother's Closet you've created in your back room."

Sophie hadn't officially named the room that but word of mouth had somehow made it official. "Oh, wow." Sophie took the bag and peeked inside. "This is so generous of you, Janet. Thank you."

"Of course. No thanks needed. It gave me an excuse to come shopping." Janet winked. "And to see my favorite boutique owner."

Sophie gestured toward the wall where she'd placed the new spring line of clothing. She always ordered a variety of sizes and made sure she had everything in tall just for Janet. "I know you two ladies are going to love the new line."

Janet clapped her hands. "I can already see that. I see some items that would look lovely on Trisha as well," she said of her former daughter-in-law.

Sophie shook her head. "Trisha doesn't shop at my boutique anymore, even when I offer the steepest of best-friend discounts."

"I know. That's my oldest son's doing," Janet said with a frown, talking about Pete. "At least one of my sons is doing the right thing. I didn't want Chase to drop his whole life and move home at first but it's nice to have him back. He really has stepped up to make sure Trisha and little Petey are okay. Trisha says he goes to her place at least once a week to do something with Petey."

"Hmm." Summer ran her hands over each new piece of clothing, scrutinizing them one by one as she listened to the conversation. "Chase and Pete were so young when they lost their own father. In a way, Pete was Chase's role model growing up. It can't be easy to have the person you admire most fall off their pedestal and go to prison. I'm sure Chase is very conflicted about his feelings right now."

Janet's smile fell away as she listened.

"I still can't believe how Pete pulled the wool over so many people's eyes," Summer went on. "Folks all over this part of the state trusted him with their money, and he just dipped into their accounts for himself."

Sophie searched her mind for a way to get Summer off the subject for Janet's sake. It had been six months since Pete had gone to prison but people's memories around here would likely keep the news ever present for the Lewis family. Janet was no doubt confronted with what her oldest son had done on a daily basis.

Summer shrugged. "At least one of your boys is doing the right thing by little Petey, Janet."

Janet offered a polite laugh to ease what might've ruffled some feathers. Janet was the picture of grace. She still loved Pete and went to visit him at the state prison at least once a month. Trisha went as well. Even though she and Pete were divorced—she'd started the paperwork during the lengthy trial—she wanted Petey to see his father. From what Trisha had told Sophie, Chase didn't go to the prison to visit his brother at all.

Sophie took a small step backward. "Well, I'll leave you ladies to check out the clothing. Thank you for the donations. Remember, you get fifty percent off one new item. I'll be at the counter to ring you up when you're ready."

"Thank you, sweetie," Janet said with a wink.

Sophie headed back to the cash register, thinking about what Summer had said and wondering if it was true. Sophie couldn't imagine feeling as if she had to atone for someone else's crimes.

But she did feel like she had to make up for all the burdens she'd placed on her family after her accident.

Her mom had to quit a job that she'd loved to take care of Sophie, and her dad had worked two jobs. They'd refused to touch the money they'd saved for Sophie's future. It was supposed to be a college fund but Sophie had ended up using it to open her boutique instead.

Sophie went through the donated pieces in the bag as her two customers shopped, pulling them out, inspecting them, and folding them back up. Twenty minutes later, Janet and Summer headed to the register with several new pieces of clothing to purchase.

"I'll be back in. I already have regrets over not buying some of the other things on the rack," Janet said sheepishly.

Sophie had no doubt Janet was being sincere. "My door is always open to you both."

Once they were gone, Sophie locked the boutique and headed home. In order to check on Comet, she took the long way again. As she approached Chase's veterinary clinic, she held her breath almost unwittingly.

The front door of the clinic opened as she approached, and Sophie stopped walking. Chase came down the steps, carrying Comet in his arms.

Sophie felt her heart squeeze at the sight of the little dog. His tail was wagging, and he looked otherwise healthy except for his leg. "What are you doing?" she asked as they drew closer.

"Walking Comet," he said.

Sophie reached out to touch Comet's head, running her fingers through the dog's silky fur. "Did you call the rescue?" she asked.

"I did. They're full, and they can't take on a dog with special needs right now." Chase kept walking so Sophie did as well, continuing toward her home on Dragonfly Lane.

Sophie felt a heavy disappointment. She had been certain that the rescue would have a capable person who would be able to care for Comet. "Special needs?"

"Well, he has a broken leg. It'll take about four weeks to heal so he'll be restricted to his crate a lot. He can't walk and run freely, which means he'll need extra TLC."

"I see." Guilt swirled in her belly, mixing with empathy because she'd been in a similar situation when she was eighteen, depending on everyone around her for help. Now Comet needed that same support, and there didn't seem to be anyone willing to give it to him.

"It's always hard to find a good foster home for injured or sick dogs," Chase said. "If Comet didn't have a broken leg, I think I could have found a place by now."

Sophie nodded as she listened. "That's a shame."

"So for the time being, I'll be caring for this little guy's needs at the clinic. And this is how he's getting his fresh air while he recovers," Chase explained.

"I wouldn't be able to carry a dog as I walk," Sophie said, continuing to justify her decision.

"No, but I could do that for you. You live right down the street from the clinic. You could even drop him off every morning so that Penny and I could take care of him while you're at the boutique."

Sophie glanced over. "You'd do that?"

"I care for animals. That's my job. And I care for you too," he said quietly.

Sophie felt her knees go weak. "Like I told you yesterday, I don't know how to care for a dog."

"Maybe, but this is the perfect time to learn because you'll have me."

She swallowed. She wasn't sure that was a selling point right now but she had to admit that she wanted to see Comet's recovery through until he was running and playing like any other frisky puppy. She owed him that much.

They turned onto Dragonfly Lane, walked a short way, and then turned into her driveway. Sophie stopped walking at her mailbox and turned to face Chase. "If I say no, where does Comet go?" She hoped he had a good answer to calm her concerns.

"Well, I suppose I'll keep him at my clinic until I make a few more calls."

"And if I say yes?" she asked. "Just to fostering. I'm nowhere near ready to adopt a puppy right now." She wasn't sure she was ready to bring one home for even a day.

Chase grinned as if he knew her answer was already yes. "Then I'll drop him off tomorrow afternoon for you."

Comet barked and looked straight at her, his large puppy eyes pleading as if he knew exactly what they were talking about. Maybe she didn't know the first thing about caring for dogs but how hard could taking care of one little puppy be?

"Okay." Sophie lifted her eyes to Chase's, which was a mistake. Butterflies stormed her stomach. She dropped her gaze back down to the dog. "I'll foster Comet while he recovers."

* * *

Chase didn't take Comet back to the clinic after leaving Sophie at her door. One night with him wouldn't hurt. Plus, he was on his way to Trisha's for dinner. Chase hadn't seen his nephew in a few days.

"Wanna go with me?" Chase asked Comet as he placed the dog gently in the passenger seat of his truck. Comet let his tongue hang out, looking at him lazily. "I'll take that as a yes."

Chase got in the driver's seat and drove toward his ex-sister-in-law's house. As soon as he pulled into the driveway and got out, Petey came flying down the porch steps and across the lawn.

Chase opened his arms, bracing himself for the tackle-hug. "Hey, bud. How are you?"

Petey started talking excitedly, tugging Chase's arm to lead him inside the house.

"Hold on. We can't go inside just yet. I brought a friend." Chase opened the passenger door of his truck and picked up Comet.

"Whoa! Is that dog for us?" Petey asked, his eyes rounding dramatically.

Chase suddenly wondered if Trisha was going to kill him. His nephew had been asking for a pet for a while now but Trisha was resisting the idea. She had enough on her plate without adding more responsibility. "I'm afraid not. Comet is going to stay with Sophie for a while. She's agreed to foster him. I'm just keeping him until she gets everything set up."

Petey looked crestfallen for just a moment. Then he was back to chattering excitedly as they walked toward the front door. Trisha met them as they entered, her gaze falling on Comet. She gave Chase a questioning look as her eyes narrowed.

"He's just with me for tonight. Tomorrow, he's going to live with his new foster. Sophie."

Trisha's mouth fell open. "Sophie is fostering a dog?"

"She is," Chase confirmed. "This little guy is what delayed us getting to the wedding on Saturday."

Trisha's eyes moved to the casted hind leg. "I see. Poor little guy."

No doubt she was making the connection between Sophie's past injuries and Comet's.

"Is it okay if Comet rests inside while I'm here?" Chase asked.

"Of course." Trisha smiled reassuringly. "Dinner is almost done. I'm making shrimp-and-pineapple fried rice. It's Petey's favorite," she said.

Chase's mouth watered. Trisha's cooking was one of the perks of spending so much time with his nephew.

"Petey has been waiting for you for the last hour," Trisha said. "He has something he wants to talk to you about." She lifted her brows, making Chase suspect that whatever Petey wanted to discuss was a big deal.

Chase looked down at his nephew. "Oh yeah? What did you want to talk about?"

"Next week is job day at my school," Petey said, his words stumbling over one another. "All my friends' parents are coming to speak to my class."

"Not all," Trisha corrected as she stood in front of the stove, stirring the ingredients in a cast iron pan.

"Well, a lot." Petey cast big, hopeful eyes at Chase. "And Mom can't go because she says her job isn't a good topic for first graders."

Chase could agree with that. Talking about the things that led one to live at a women's shelter probably wouldn't be advisable.

"And my dad's in prison," Petey said, his expression momentarily glum. "So you're the next best thing."

Chase stiffened and pointed a finger at his own chest. "Me?"

Petey nodded excitedly. "You can talk about fixing animals. My friends would think that was so cool. Please, Uncle Chase. Please, please, pleaaaaase!"

Chase had never been one to enjoy public speaking, and a class full of first graders terrified him even more than adults. But when he'd moved back to his hometown, he'd made a promise to himself to be exactly what his nephew needed him to be. Right now, it was an uncle with a cool job. "Well, I guess I could do that," he said.

"Yes!" Petey jumped up and down, looking about as thrilled as he did on his birthdays with large stacks of presents. "All those kids who've been picking on me will be so impressed by my uncle."

Chase shared a look with Trisha, who didn't seem surprised at all by Petey's remark. "What kids?"

Trisha wiped her hands on her apron. "Kids will be kids," she said as if that explained anything.

Chase guessed she didn't want to get into whatever troubles Petey was having in front of him. Before Chase left tonight though, he intended to find out exactly what was going on in his nephew's classroom.

Chapter Five

After closing her boutique the next afternoon, Sophie got into her car and headed to the local pet supply store. Chase was dropping Comet off tonight, and she could hardly wait to open her home to a new companion. At least temporarily.

She parked and walked into the large store. Sweetwater Springs was a small town but everyone had a pet, it seemed, so the demand was high for kibble, litter boxes, and chew toys.

Sophie was actually surprised that Chase was still the only veterinarian in town, considering all the animals that needed caring for. She supposed some people traveled to the clinic in Whispering Pines but most would be loyal to a homegrown, hometown local vet like Chase.

Just thinking of his name made her feel a fluttering sensation in her chest. When he'd first returned to town a few months ago, she'd bristled at the mention of his name. He'd left, and things were great the way they were. Why did he have to come back and make things awkward?

That almost kiss in his clinic over the weekend had really

stirred up old embers though. The fact that he was coming to her home tonight and that they'd find themselves alone again probably wasn't the best idea. Especially considering she didn't want to lead him on or tempt herself toward things better left in the past.

Sophie walked down the aisles, reading the signs that told her where to find what. She didn't exactly know which supplies she needed for a medium-size dog. Food would be a good start. She turned down the dog food aisle and blinked at the wide variety. There was every imaginable flavor in a dozen different brands. There was even dog food for sensitive stomachs. Did she need to get that for Comet? Chase had told her he was at least six months old. Did she get the puppy variety or the adult kind? Obviously not the food for senior dogs.

She chewed her lip, suddenly overwhelmed by all the choices. Finally, she decided on what she thought might work and tried to lift the twenty-pound bag into her arms. Her left leg threatened to buckle under the weight. She needed a cart, which had her walking back toward the front of the store to retrieve one.

After thirty minutes of debating various other items, she finally headed toward the register. She leaned heavily against her cart as she walked, realizing she'd probably overworked her muscles in the store. Her calf was tensing uncomfortably, threatening to clench into a full-on charley horse. The last thing she wanted was for Chase to come over tonight and suspect that she was anything less than fine.

Nerves arose in Sophie's stomach as she waited to pay. She started to second-guess her choices as her gaze scanned the items she'd picked out. Maybe she wasn't ready to take on a dog after all. What if she did more harm than good in giving Comet a temporary home?

"Did you find what you were looking for?" the cashier asked as Sophie stepped up. Sophie had seen the woman around town once or twice.

Sophie nodded. "I think so. The truth is I didn't really know what I was looking for when I walked in."

"Well, you must be new to being a pet owner," the woman said.

"Kind of. I'll be fostering a puppy."

Over the loud beep that sounded every time the cashier whipped one of the items across the scanner, she said, "A little advice: Animals are like kids. If they're misbehaving, it's because they aren't getting their needs met. It just means they need a little extra love and care. That's what we all need, don't you think?" She smiled brightly at Sophie.

"I guess so. Thanks for the advice."

"No extra charge," the cashier said on a laugh. "Is that all for you today?"

Sophie nodded as the cashier punched a few buttons at her register and read her the total.

Sophie pulled out her debit card and zipped it through the reader.

"There you go." The cashier handed Sophie her receipt. "Good luck, darling."

"Thanks." Sophie grabbed her bags and headed toward the door, feeling like she was going to need a little luck because she was nowhere near prepared for what was about to happen. She loaded her car, drove home, and quickly unpacked the items she'd purchased.

Chase would arrive with Comet any time now. That realization sent anxious tingles through her body. She wasn't sure what made her more nervous. Comet or his veterinarian.

The doorbell rang, and Sophie's heart skipped. She took a breath and opened the door, meeting Chase's gaze. *Definitely the veterinarian.*

* * *

Chase watched as Sophie and Comet got reacquainted. Comet snuggled into Sophie's hug as she knelt on the floor for a long moment. Then Sophie let out a soft squeal and lifted the dog off her body, revealing a small wet stain.

"I guess Comet got a little excited. Sorry about that," Chase said, trying not to laugh.

"He peed on me?" Sophie looked up in shock. Chase was sure whatever she was wearing cost a pretty penny. A woman who owned a boutique of designer clothing didn't have a cheap wardrobe.

Even so, there was a smile on her lips, and for a moment, he couldn't take his eyes off her. She'd never been superficial or materialistic. She had always appreciated beautiful things but they didn't run her life. His mom was the same way. Janet Lewis loved nice clothes but she didn't care if Petey ran up to her with filthy hands when he gave her a hug.

"Well," Sophie said, looking up at him and meeting his gaze, "I guess I need to give this little guy a bath. If that's okay." She looked concerned. "Can I bathe him with the cast on his back leg?"

Chase nodded. "We'll just wrap it with a plastic bag and a rubber band. Do you have those two things?"

"I do." She laughed again, which was a good sign. A lot of new and inexperienced pet owners might be having second thoughts right about now as they realized what they'd gotten themselves into. A dog was a nice thought but it was also a lot of work. There would be training, bathing, and losing a few precious items to a puppy's teething. "I told you this would be an adventure," he said.

Her smile fell just a notch. "You weren't kidding." She handed Comet back to him. "I'll just go change before we bathe him."

"We?" Chase asked.

"I assumed you were going to stay. You don't have to. I'm sure I can figure out the plastic bag over his cast."

Chase shook his head as she talked. "No, I'll stay," he said once she'd taken a breath. "I'm all yours tonight. I'll meet you in the bathroom."

She pointed down the hall. "It's the second door on the left. I'll change and then grab the plastic bag and rubber band to cover Comet's cast. It'll just take a minute."

Chase walked into her bathroom, noticing the tight quarters. Hers was a small house with equally small rooms. He glanced down at Comet. "Peeing on your new foster parent is not a good first impression," he said, even though Comet had already made his first impression on Sophie the other night.

He guessed Sophie's first impression when she'd hit Comet with her car hadn't been smooth either. "Don't worry though. She won't give up on you like your last owner."

Comet struggled to lick Chase's face but Chase held him firmly against his stomach.

Then Sophie walked into the bathroom, filling the rest of the open space. They were forced to stand close—not that he minded.

"I'm afraid I didn't buy any pet shampoo when I was at the store this afternoon. I guess that's one thing I didn't think of. I have some baby shampoo in my cabinet for the times that Petey stays over though."

"Petey stays over with you?" He didn't mean for the surprise in his voice but Trisha had never asked Chase to take his nephew overnight. He wouldn't mind doing so. That's why he'd returned home in the first place.

Sophie gave him an assessing look. "Petey comes over about once a month. That's why I've been dubbed Aunt Sophie."

Chase smiled. "I'm jealous of the sleepover factor. But I did get an invitation to talk to Petey's class about my job."

Sophie looked impressed. "Wow, that's nice of you."

Chase shrugged. "I'm just glad to help."

Sophie dipped into her bathroom cabinet and held up a bottle of kid-friendly shampoo. "Will this do the trick?"

"That'll work just fine." Chase reached for the bag and rubber band that she'd placed on the bathroom counter. He quickly covered Comet's cast and placed him on the floor as Sophie headed to the tub and began to prepare the bathwater. He tried his best not to notice the way her cropped top slid up her lower back when she leaned over the tub, revealing just a small area of skin. Once upon a time, she used to talk about getting a tattoo on that very spot. She'd wanted hearts or a butterfly. He guessed that had never happened.

"Does it matter what temperature the water is?" she asked, looking back and catching him watching her.

Chase cleared his throat and looked away quickly. "A warm temperature should be just fine. Not too cold, not too hot."

She gave a nod and returned to what she was doing. He watched as she ran the water, wiggling her fingers in its stream to test the temperature. Then she lifted Comet up and gently placed the struggling fur ball into the tub. Comet made a flurry of motion that resulted in Sophie being splashed across the front of her top once more, this time with bathwater. "He's really good at turning me into a mess. I'm going to need my own bath after all this."

Chase swallowed. *He* might end up needing a cold shower after all this.

He stood back, offering a few tips here and there as she massaged shampoo into Comet's fur. She seemed to be just fine on her own though. When she was done, he handed her a towel and watched as she lifted Comet out of the water.

Chase quickly stepped in because he knew the drill. As soon as Comet's paws hit the floor, he was going to shake his body free of all the excess water, and if Sophie wasn't careful, she'd be completely drenched.

Chase grabbed the towel and quickly whipped it over the

dog's back, catching all the water as Comet shook vigorously. "Sorry," Chase said, sweeping his gaze up at Sophie. In his haste, he hadn't realized he'd stepped so close. His arm was touching hers. Her face was next to his.

"We've got to stop doing this, huh?" she said in a soft voice.

"Doing what?" he asked. But he thought he knew exactly what she meant.

"Seems like we keep getting close enough to bump heads or..." Her voice trailed off.

Chase let the puppy go but he didn't take his eyes off Sophie for a long moment. Then he straightened and dropped his gaze to her lips. They really did have to stop doing this. Eventually, he was going to cave in to his desire.

Eventually being right now.

He dipped his head as his gaze returned to hers to make sure she was still looking at him with that twinkle in her eye. Then, because it was the right thing to do in his prekiss checklist, he asked, "Is this okay?"

Sophie seemed to swallow. Then she rolled her lips together, moistening them and giving them an irresistible shine. "Depends. Are you going to bump heads with me or kiss me?"

He could feel Comet's wet paws on his leg but he ignored it. "I was thinking the latter might be more pleasant," he said softly.

"I would agree," she whispered. Then she pressed her mouth to his. Chase's arms reflexively wrapped around her, holding her close.

Her lips were soft. Their kiss hypnotic. It wasn't their first kiss by any means but it'd been so long that he'd forgotten how perfect it was. Even though they were standing in a bathroom with a wet dog at their heels, this was the sexiest kiss he'd had since...well, since the last time he'd kissed Sophie Daniels.

"Wow." Sophie pulled away and looked at Chase with wide eyes. "That was..." She trailed off.

"Yeah. It was." He smiled. Then he looked down at Comet. "Sorry, buddy. We got a little distracted." He looked at Sophie again.

Where did they go from here? Was a kiss just a kiss? Or was it the beginning of a second chance?

"Well, Comet is bathed, and now I'll show him his food and water bowls. I've already set those up," Sophie said. "I think I've got things from here."

Chase felt disappointed for a brief moment. Was she trying to get rid of him?

He turned and headed out of the bathroom and down the hallway. She followed him into the entryway of the house. When he turned back, he smiled at her. "If you don't mind, I'd like to drop back in this week. To check on Comet."

He saw the hesitation in Sophie's eyes.

There was his answer. A kiss was just a kiss. It didn't mean this was the start of anything more. That didn't stop him from trying. "Sweetwater Springs Park has a great new dog park that I think Comet would love," Chase continued. "I think you'd love it too. How about I pick you two up on Saturday night and take you there?"

"But Comet isn't ready to walk, is he?" Sophie asked.

"I'll carry him. He'll love just watching the other dogs play."

She waited so long to answer that he was certain she was going to say no. "If you think he'd love it, then okay."

"I also think you'd love it," Chase said, scrutinizing her response and looking for some small sign that she'd felt something in their kiss.

She offered a slight smile. "The park sounds nice."

Chase felt a rush in his veins, similar to what he might feel when he scaled a ridge. "Great." He was tempted to call it a date but that might derail the whole thing. "I'll see you tomorrow at the clinic when you drop Comet off."

"Okay."

Chase reached for the doorknob. "Good night, Sophie." Then he turned and headed out of the house, walking toward his truck. Once he was inside, he blew out a breath. She hadn't said yes to a date but going to the dog park together was something. If not a second chance, it was an opportunity to spend more time with her. And for the time being, that was all he needed.

* * *

I made a huge mistake.

The next day, Sophie watched her phone screen and waited for Trisha to reply. When it didn't happen immediately, she unpacked the new box of gowns that had arrived in her boutique. Sophie had sold quite a few of the gowns she already had. People were beginning to shop for the upcoming black-tie affair, which meant Sophie had needed to order more.

Her phone dinged as she pulled out a straight black gown that was as simple as it was elegant. Sophie reached for her phone and read the text.

The dog?

Taking on Comet was definitely biting off more than she could chew but she didn't regret it by any means. She was looking forward to nursing Comet back to full health so that he had a better chance of finding his forever home.

No. Are you anywhere in the area today? I need your help.

Trisha's text came back quickly. Actually, I'm in town, running a few errands for the shelter. I'll come by your boutique in a bit.

Sophie breathed a sigh of relief. That would be great. Thank you.

Her best friend never failed to be there for her when she needed her. And that had always been the case. Sophie was as indebted to Trisha as she was to the entire town. A debt she'd never be able to fully repay.

The front door to her shop opened.

"I told you I'd be back in," Janet said.

Sophie stepped over and gave her a warm hug. "I didn't realize you meant so soon."

Janet laughed softly. "What can I say? Shopping makes me happy," she said. Then she beelined straight over to one of the racks. Sophie followed her. "I need a gown for the black-tie affair that Trisha is planning. It's only a month away, you know."

"I do know. It'll be here before you know it," Sophie agreed.

"Trisha is amazing to plan such a nice event with an even nicer cause. She's got such a good heart." Janet turned to look at Sophie. "Have you picked out one of these gowns for yourself yet?"

Sophie shook her head, her gaze falling on a light-purple gown that she'd been admiring. It was the right length to cover the unsightly scars on her leg, which made it the perfect dress for her. Assuming no one else bought it first. "No, these are for my customers."

"Don't tell me you're not attending. You volunteer over there with Trisha, and from what I hear, you helped come up with the idea. You have to go," Janet insisted.

Sophie shrugged. "Oh, I'll definitely be there to support the cause. But my customers get first pick of the boutique's gowns. I don't even have a date to impress."

Janet nudged Sophie with her elbow. "My son is still on the market."

Sophie looked away. She couldn't blame a mom for trying. It was bad enough Sophie had kissed Chase last night. And she'd agreed to go to the dog park with him this weekend. What was she thinking? They couldn't just pick up where they'd left off. She was a different person now but from what Trisha had told Sophie, Chase was still the same adrenaline chaser. He lived life on the edge at every chance he got, whereas Sophie didn't—not anymore.

"Which one of these dresses do you want to bring home and wear to the event?" Sophie asked, taking the focus off of herself. "I'll even give you a discount."

Janet's mouth dropped open. "Twice in one week? You're so sweet."

Sophie shrugged. "I just know your weakness."

Janet gave her a questioning look.

"You can't turn down a bargain," Sophie clarified.

Janet laughed. "Well, that's true enough. You do know me. Let me pick through these dresses and see what I want to try on. I'm not sure you have one in my size."

Sophie pointed toward the far right of the rack. "I always keep your size stocked. You're one of my best customers."

Janet beamed as she stepped over to start going through the gowns at the end.

"I'll be at the counter if you need me." Sophie headed back to her stool and sat, alternating between watching Janet and looking through the window at potential customers walking down Main Street. Her eyes lit up when she saw Trisha come into view. Then she looked at Janet again. She couldn't possibly discuss kissing Chase in front of his mother.

Trisha pushed through the door and headed straight toward Sophie. "Okay. What's this big mistake that you think you've made?"

Sophie felt like a deer in headlights. "I...I..." She looked at Janet, who was now watching them. Sophie gestured toward the rack of gowns. "Trisha, Janet is here."

Trisha looked over, noticing the other woman now. A smile swept over her face. Regardless of how her ex had treated her, Trisha obviously still loved her former in-laws. "Janet! Are you looking for a dress for the shelter's black-tie affair?"

Janet nodded. "Yes, and I'm going to buy you one as well. Come pick out any dress you want."

Trisha was already shaking her head. "I can purchase my own dress, Janet."

"I'm sure you can but I want to do this for you. Call it an early birthday present."

Trisha rolled her eyes as she laughed. "It's March. My birthday isn't until October."

"A half birthday, then," Janet said.

Trisha gave Sophie a look that said she was done arguing. She wouldn't win anyway. Janet was stubborn when she wanted to be. But Sophie knew from experience that Trisha was even more stubborn. "I'm afraid I don't have time to dress shop today." She looked at Sophie. "What did you want to talk to me about?"

Sophie shook her head and shrugged simultaneously. "Oh, it's no big deal."

The skin between Trisha's eyes knitted softly. "You called me over here for no big deal?"

"I just wanted to see my best friend. Is that so wrong?"

Trisha didn't look convinced. But she was smart and could probably put two and two together that Sophie didn't want to discuss her drama in front of Janet. "Okay. Well, Petey wants to come by and see Comet. He met him the other night when Chase brought him over. Can we stop in later this evening?"

Sophie nodded, suspecting the real truth was that Trisha wanted to give Sophie another chance to unload whatever was bothering her. "That would be perfect."

"Where is the little guy right now?" Trisha asked.

"I dropped Comet off at Chase's clinic on the way here this

morning," Sophie said. "He's caring for him in the daytime, and I'm caring for Comet at night. We're kind of like co–foster parents." Which sounded entirely too intimate. "We're a team."

Trisha's eyes widened a touch. So did Janet's.

"Actually, he's just being a good vet because I have no idea what I'm doing caring for a dog," Sophie said. "And he's being a good friend, I guess."

Janet beamed as she turned back to the rack of dresses. "It's so nice to see that you two are…friends again."

Chapter Six

At almost closing time, Chase heard Penny greeting a new patient who'd just walked in. The voice sounded vaguely familiar as he headed from his office toward the reception area.

"Amelia." He tempered the slight guilt he felt at seeing the woman he'd stood up last week. He was hoping that he'd be able to avoid her for a while until the awkwardness faded. "What brings you here?"

She frowned back at him. "My kitten. You're the only vet in town." Which implied that she would have rather not run into him either. She held up a midsize crate. "I found this little one this afternoon. She was under my porch but there weren't any other kittens and no sign of a mama cat. I wasn't sure what to do." Amelia shook her head as her eyes grew shiny. "It was like she was just left to fend for herself."

Chase didn't like the sound of that. He waved Amelia forward, leading her to the examination room. "Let me take a look."

"Thank you," Amelia said, following behind. "I know the

clinic is about to close but I started to worry about going through the night without her eating or drinking."

"I don't mind staying late." It was the least that Chase could do after Amelia got all dressed up for a date that never happened.

They stepped into the room and Amelia set the crate on the examining table. Chase unlocked the cage and gently pulled out the small tabby kitten that fit into the palm of his hand. The kitten mewed loudly for such a little creature.

"I'd say she's pretty hungry," Chase said on a laugh.

"But she won't eat. I put out a saucer of milk and tried to get her to." Amelia wrung her hands beside him. "Why won't she eat?"

"Well, she's still young. She needs to nurse. Any idea where the mother cat is?" Chase asked.

He saw Amelia shake her head from the corner of his eye. "I searched my street and asked all my neighbors. Nobody knows."

Chase listened as he checked the kitten's vitals. "She seems healthy overall," he finally said.

Amelia let out a breath. "Oh, that's good news."

"It is. To make sure she stays that way, you'll need to feed her yourself, every four hours." He glanced over. "I'll provide you with a small bottle and formula."

Amelia nodded. "Okay. I work from home so that won't be a problem."

"Good. She's about four weeks old. You can gradually space the feedings out as she grows bigger. At six to eight weeks, she'll begin to eat wet food, and that'll be all she needs."

Amelia looked up at him. Her eyes were warm. "I really appreciate your help." She offered a slight smile. "Maybe I can thank you properly by taking you to dinner for our rain check date."

Chase hesitated. He'd been mildly interested in a date with

Amelia before last weekend. But something had shifted in the air with Sophie. They'd kissed, and he was hoping that maybe one kiss would lead to another.

He must have waited too long to respond because Amelia collected her kitten and put it into the kennel. Then she took a step backward. "Just let me know if you want to take me up on dinner. But be warned—I won't be single forever. I'm quite the catch, Dr. Lewis."

He smiled, relieved by the way she'd avoided any weirdness. "I'd have to agree with that statement. Good luck with the new kitten. Don't hesitate to come by or call. That's what I'm here for."

Amelia glanced down at the crate. "I think this little kitten and I are a good match."

But she and Chase were not, and Chase was pretty sure they both knew it.

He saw her to the front of the clinic and watched her leave as Sophie came walking up the sidewalk. *She* had always been his perfect match, whether she thought so or not.

"Hi," she said with a wobbly smile. "What was Amelia doing here?"

Chase held the door open for Sophie. "Her kitten wasn't eating."

"Was it...awkward? I mean, you did stand her up the other day. My fault completely."

He shrugged as Sophie stepped inside the clinic. "Just a little but it ended fine. I'll get Comet and walk you home."

Sophie folded her arms over her chest. "You don't have to walk me home if you're busy. He's not that heavy. I can carry him."

Chase had noticed Sophie's slight limp as she'd walked up though. There was no way he was letting her carry a dog when she was already struggling—not that she'd ever admit to needing help. "A walk after working all day sounds nice. Wait right here, and I'll grab him for you."

Penny had left ten minutes ago to head to her weekly bunco group so it was just Chase and Sophie in the clinic now. He turned the sign to CLOSED and grabbed his keys from his office. Then he retrieved Comet from the overnight area and dodged a wet dog kiss across his cheek.

"We better let him have a moment outside before we start walking," Sophie suggested when Chase reappeared in the front of the clinic. "So that your shirt doesn't look like mine did last night."

Chase chuckled softly. "Good idea. See? You're already getting the hang of caring for a dog." He winked without thinking and saw her smile drop. The air between them was buzzing with an uncomfortable and completely addictive level of attraction.

They stepped outside, and Chase put Comet on the ground for a moment. Once Comet was done using the bathroom, he barked, and Chase picked the little dog back up. "Ready?" he asked Sophie.

"Yep."

They fell into stride beside each other, heading to the end of Blossom Street. The dusk air was cool as they made their way. The sounds of spring surrounded them.

"Good day?" he asked.

"It was," she said.

He could hear excitement in her voice as she talked about the gowns the boutique had gotten in for the black-tie affair at the women's shelter next month.

"Your mom came in for the second time this week," Sophie mentioned. "She picked out a gown for herself and practically ordered Trisha to do the same on her dime."

"Trisha stopped by too?" Chase glanced over.

"It seems your family enjoys my boutique." Sophie grinned.

"It seems my family likes you too." And he couldn't disagree with them.

Sophie's gaze hung on his for a long moment. "Anyway, you know Trisha is stubborn so she'll buy her own dress for the occasion." Sophie raised a finger as she looked forward again. "By the way, Trisha is bringing one of the women from the shelter to my boutique after hours tomorrow. I'm giving the woman one of my fairy godmother makeovers."

Chase nodded. "Trisha has told me about those. I think your charity is a great idea."

"Thanks. So I'll be late getting Comet tomorrow night. I can send my mom to get him, though, so it doesn't inconvenience you if you need to leave sooner."

Chase dodged another Comet kiss. "I'll wait for you," he said. It might have sounded unselfish to work late but his intentions on waiting were entirely selfish. He didn't want to miss a chance to see Sophie. The more time they spent together, the more he wanted to be with her.

He walked her to her door, the kiss from last night on the forefront of his mind. It felt like a new beginning to him but he couldn't figure out what Sophie was thinking or feeling.

"Well, thank you, Chase," she said, reaching for Comet and taking the puppy from his arms. She didn't dodge Comet's kisses as quickly. But she did seem to anticipate and dodge any potential kiss from Chase. Instead, she unlocked her front door and stepped over the threshold, turning back to him with an almost shy look. "Good night. I'll see you tomorrow."

"Night." He watched her close the door behind her. Then he turned to walk back down the street toward his truck in the clinic's parking lot. He needed the walk even more now to clear his head, which was entirely too full of thoughts about his first love.

* * *

Sophie took a deep breath and expelled it as she shut the door on Chase. Then she carried Comet over to his dog bed and gently set him down. She'd put up a baby gate to keep him contained when he was here.

"Doctor's orders," Sophie said, taking a moment to pet him. "You're supposed to rest. But I'll be back to play with you in just a second," she promised. Right now, she needed to stretch. Her leg was bothering her from standing all day. The long walk home hadn't helped either. However, it was nothing a little yoga couldn't help. After that, she would prepare herself dinner and a hot cup of tea.

Comet pressed his nose in the holes of the baby gate, watching her with large puppy dog eyes as she went through a yoga sequence and repeated it until her muscles relaxed and the ache in her left calf dialed down to being barely noticeable. Even so, she continued exercising because it also had a way of clearing her mind. At least, that was usually the case. But her mind was wired to Chase right now, and she couldn't seem to convince it that rekindling what they'd once had was a bad idea.

She didn't stop her yoga sequence until her cell phone started ringing from the kitchen counter. She walked over, pleased that her limp was gone, and picked up her phone.

"Hi," Trisha said. "I know you said we could come over tonight but Petey has a big project due for school that he somehow forgot to tell me about. Of course, Chase offered to help him with it since it's about animal life cycles."

Sophie could almost hear Trisha rolling her eyes. Trisha had said she understood why Chase wanted to be there for his nephew but she was also an independent woman.

"I could help Petey just as easily," Trisha said. "But the Lewis men are stubborn."

Sophie laughed. "Take advantage of the 'you time.' Go for a walk or read a book."

"Or I could just talk to my best friend on the phone," Trisha said. "You never told me about this big mistake of yours. What is it?"

"Right." Sophie stepped over to her kettle and started preparing hot water for her tea. "It doesn't matter anymore. I think I figured out what I need to do to fix it."

"Well, you called me over to your boutique earlier. The least you can do is tell me why."

Sophie watched the kettle, waiting for the water to heat up. "It's not a big deal." It only felt like one. "It's just, well... Chase and I kind of kissed last night."

"What?" Trisha practically squealed on the other end of the line. "Sophie, that's huge!"

"Shh," Sophie said, guessing that Chase was probably close by. "It was a mistake. He also kind of invited me and Comet out on Saturday night."

"You and Comet?" Trisha asked, confusion evident in her tone of voice.

"To go to the dog park."

"Like on a date?"

That was the big question. "I'm not sure. But it doesn't matter, because I'm going to cancel. There's no way I can go out with Chase. Our relationship is in the past, and I don't want to dredge it up."

"Why not?"

"Because I can't do all the things we used to do together," Sophie said. "I don't run or climb anymore."

"No, but I've heard Denny Larson offer to take you climbing. He said he could adapt things for you."

That was true. Maybe Sophie's injuries shouldn't prevent her from climbing again but her fear was paralyzing.

"What does that stuff have to do with dating Chase anyway?" Trisha asked.

The kettle's handle flipped up, signaling that the water was boiling. Sophie lifted it and poured hot water over a tea bag in her mug. "Chase is a reminder of the person I used to be and the things I used to do."

Sophie felt the muscles in her left leg begin to throb again. All her yoga efforts were nullified by the stress pulsing in her body. "He's a reminder of what I lost in my accident." And even if her heart was jumping at the idea of a second chance with him, the rest of her wasn't sure it was a good idea. In fact, she was certain that it wasn't.

* * *

The next evening at five o'clock sharp, Trisha walked into Sophie's Boutique with a woman that Sophie had never met.

Sophie gave Trisha a warm hug first. "Where's Petey tonight?"

"With Chase at the clinic. He offered because he's staying late, waiting for you." Trisha gave her a curious look, no doubt wondering if Sophie had canceled her date to the dog park yet. "Thank you so much for opening your store for us tonight," Trisha added, gesturing toward the other woman. The woman had dark-blond hair and tan skin that made Sophie suspect that she enjoyed being outside. Her smile was shy as she looked at Sophie. She and Sophie were about the same size, which meant most of the clothes that Sophie had set aside should work.

Trisha laid a hand on the woman's shoulder. "Sophie, this is Nadine."

Trisha didn't provide a last name, which Sophie understood. The women's shelter was a private place. Some of the women there were running from abusive circumstances. Others had found themselves homeless and just needed a place to get back on their feet. "Hi, Nadine. It's so nice to meet you."

Nadine smiled back at her. "Thank you for helping me. I want to look nice when I interview for jobs in town."

"So you're trying to stay in Sweetwater Springs?" Sophie asked.

"Oh yes. Sweetwater Springs is the ideal place for a fresh start," Nadine said, her shyness dissipating as she seemed to relax. "And that's what I need. I've served my time, and I'm ready to get back to living my life."

Sophie felt her mouth drop and her eyes widen a touch. "Served your time?"

"Five years in a women's prison." Nadine lowered her eyes before looking back up. "It won't be easy to find a job with my background."

Sophie couldn't argue with that. She didn't know what Nadine had served time for but the woman didn't look like she could hurt a fly. There was a kindness in her eyes and smile.

"It sounds superficial maybe but clothes really do help with first impressions," Sophie told the woman.

"That's why we're here," Trisha said. "We want Nadine to make the best first impression as possible during her interviews."

"Well, let's get started." Sophie led them back to the small back room of her boutique. "This is the Fairy Godmother's Closet," she said with a small laugh as she gestured toward makeshift racks of beautiful tops, pants, dresses, and coats. Sophie turned to Nadine. "What kind of job are you hoping to find? That'll make a difference in what we pick out for you."

"Any job, really. I'll do anything." Nadine's mouth dropped open, seemingly embarrassed by her answer. "I mean, not *anything*," she said. "But I'm not picky. After living where I've been, you can't afford to be choosy about your circumstances."

Sophie glanced over at Trisha to make sure this conversation was okay. Trisha was smiling, her shoulders low and relaxed, so Sophie continued chatting with Nadine.

"Well, if you had a certain kind of job that you would like to do, I might have inside information on where to look and who to ask."

Nadine's blue eyes widened a touch. "Really? That would be wonderful. But you should know I only finished high school. That's the only education I got."

Sophie shrugged. "Same with me."

"And you own your own boutique?" Nadine looked impressed.

"I was fortunate." At least in the fact that she could fund her dream. Not in the fact that it took a life-changing accident to alter her path. Sophie had been in rehab during what would have been her first semester of college. During her recovery, she'd become passionate about the power that clothing had to transform how a person felt, at least a little bit. She wanted to give that to other women. "I love clothes. What do you love?"

"I love . . ." Nadine paused thoughtfully. "I'm not sure what I love anymore. I just want to survive right now, I guess."

Sophie could understand that. "Okay, well let's look at the clothes I've laid out for you. I'm sure something in this pile will work for all situations." Nadine was smiling so big that it made Sophie's heart feel light and springy.

She set a pair of shoes at Nadine's feet. These flats had come from her very own closet at home. She'd barely ever worn them. "Here. Try these on."

Nadine kicked off a pair of worn sneakers and slid one foot into the left shoe. "Mm. These fit like a glove."

Sophie grinned. "That means they were made for you."

Nadine leaned over and gave her a spontaneous hug. She smelled like soap and hair spray, which reminded Sophie of her grandmother, who she needed to call, by the way. "Thank you so much." Nadine pulled back and slipped her right foot inside the other shoe.

"You're very welcome. If you think of a job that you might be interested in, please let me know so I can help with that too."

Nadine looked sheepish suddenly. "Well, there is something I would enjoy."

"Oh? What?" Sophie held her breath in anticipation of being able to help Nadine even further.

"I love animals. Like, really love animals," she said. "And I'm good with them too. Do you think there's a way I can find a job doing something with dogs or cats? Or any kind of animal, really."

Sophie sucked in a sharp breath. Her first thought was Chase but somehow she didn't think it was going to be easy to convince him to hire a woman he knew nothing about. Especially one with a criminal record. "I'm not sure." Sophie shared a look with Trisha, who seemed to be thinking the same thing. If Chase wouldn't even speak to his brother in prison, there was no way he would consider hiring Nadine. But maybe a local groomer that Sophie knew would. Or maybe Nadine could work at the stables. "I'll see what I can find out for you."

Nadine hugged her again. Soap and hair spray. "You really are a fairy godmother!"

An hour later, Trisha and Nadine walked toward the door with a large shopping bag full of gently used items.

"I don't know what the shelter would do without you." Trisha gave Sophie a meaningful look.

"This was amazing," Nadine added. "I needed the clothes but I feel like I have a new friend too. And I could probably use a few of those around here."

Once again, Sophie wondered what Nadine had done to find herself on the other side of the law. She seemed so sweet and unsuspecting. "Well, if you need anything else, anything at all, please let me know. I'm here to help." Like any good fairy godmother would.

Once the two women had left Sophie's Boutique, Sophie collected her bag and took a moment for herself. She knew what she had to do when she saw Chase tonight. She'd been going back and forth in her thoughts but as attracted as she was to him, she'd been down this road before. There was too much history between them. Too much baggage blocking their path forward. When she saw Chase tonight, she needed to cancel their Saturday-night plans.

* * *

Petey was talking a mile a minute as Chase watched the clinic window. It was getting dark, and Chase had fed his nephew an energy bar from his stockpile in his desk drawer but he didn't think that would suffice the boy for long.

Finally, Sophie's car pulled into his parking lot. Chase hadn't realized she'd driven today. Disappointment grew inside him. He'd been looking forward to walking her home all afternoon. He'd enjoyed the gorgeous sunsets and easy walks they'd shared the last couple of evenings. He'd also been happy to get to know Sophie again. He was relearning her quirks, some new, some old.

"Is that my mom?" Petey asked.

Chase looked down at his nephew. "No, it's Sophie, here to get Comet."

At the sound of his name, Comet's tail started wagging as he lay beside Petey. The little dog obviously adored Sophie. Smart pup.

"Your mom will be here any minute, I'm sure." As if on cue, another car pulled into his parking lot. "And there she is."

Petey stood up and grabbed his book bag. "You're still coming to my class next week, right? I told all my friends you were going to talk about animals. They're so excited."

Chase smiled and nodded. “I wouldn’t miss it, buddy.” He knew that Petey would probably have rather had his own dad come to his school. What kid wouldn’t? Anger festered in Chase’s chest. He pushed it down. There was no room for that right now. Sophie and Trisha were walking up the clinic steps.

Chase opened the door and he and Petey stepped out. “My two favorite women.”

Trisha grinned and looked at Petey. “Were you good for Uncle Chase?”

“Yep. I helped him feed all the animals who are having a sleepover here,” Petey confirmed.

Chase chuckled. “I’ll have to put him on the payroll one day.”

Trisha hugged her son to her waist. “Okay. Well, let’s get you home and fed.” She looked up at Chase. “Thank you.” Then she shared a look with Sophie. There was something about the look that got Chase’s attention. Was it apologetic? Regretful? Chase couldn’t put his finger on it. Maybe it had something to do with the woman they’d just helped at Sophie’s Boutique.

“Good night,” Chase told Trisha. “Night, buddy,” he told Petey, watching as they headed down the steps. Then he turned to Sophie. “Hey.”

Her smile was hesitant. “Hi.”

Chase got a weird vibe. His gut clenched nervously. “Everything okay?”

She nodded. “Yeah.” Then her smile fell, and she shook her head. “Actually, no.”

Chase swallowed. He was afraid that would be her answer. “What is it?”

She wasn’t meeting his gaze anymore. Instead, she was looking past him toward the clinic, where Comet was still resting inside. “Something has come up for tomorrow night. I can’t go to the dog park with you after all.”

Chase frowned. "Well, that's okay. We can just do Sunday night if you want."

Sophie shook her head. "I don't think that will be a good time either."

"I see," he said, understanding that she wasn't asking for a rain check.

"And actually, I just need to get Comet right now and head home," she said. "Thank you for keeping him today."

Chase wanted to ask more questions but he couldn't figure out what to say. So instead he stepped inside and picked up Comet. "I'll carry him to your car for you."

Sophie reached out and took the dog from his arms though, her skin caressing his. "I've got him," she said, meeting his eyes now. She offered a weak smile. "Thank you for being a good…friend." She emphasized the word *friend*.

There it was. Chase pulled his arms away. He got the message, loud and clear. No dates, no more kissing, and definitely no second chances.

Chapter Seven

Chase stepped over Grizzly's chew toy, still on his floor, untouched. He headed straight to his fridge for a cold soda and then walked out onto his back deck to sit on a chair. His usual MO after a long day at work was to do something active. Anything that pushed his muscles to their limits.

Tonight, though, he felt drained. He'd been looking forward to taking Sophie out on the pretense of showing her the dog park tomorrow night. He wondered again, like he'd done a dozen times lately, if she still blamed him for her accident. And if so, would she ever be able to forgive him?

Chase stared out at the dark sky. The sun was down now, and a sliver of the moon had revealed itself along with a spattering of stars.

He was just a young eighteen-year-old boy when he'd canceled his climbing plans with Sophie for what felt like a once-in-a-lifetime opportunity to ride horses all day in the woods. He'd wanted to go so badly that he'd been unable to refuse his friend's invitation, despite his commitment to Sophie. He'd never suspected that she'd go climbing alone.

Chase sipped his soda, enjoying the satisfying buzz on his tongue and at the back of his throat as he swallowed. He'd been riding horses that day, having the time of his life, as Sophie fought for hers. It'd been dark by the time anyone even realized she was missing.

He'd called and texted but she hadn't responded. He'd just assumed she was still peeved at him for canceling their plans. Then Sophie's mom had called him, wondering why he was keeping her daughter out so late. They'd all realized at once that Sophie was missing. A search party at night was futile, especially since none of them even knew where Sophie was. They'd called Trisha, who hadn't heard from her. They'd gone to all the local hot spots. They'd gone to the park—everywhere they could think of, except for the cliffs, which had to wait until daylight when it was safe for rescuers to search.

That night had been the longest of Chase's life. His only prayer was that Sophie returned home alive, which she'd done. But she hadn't returned to him. Instead, she'd pushed him away, angry and blaming him for her injuries. She'd refused to see him.

Part of Chase knew she was just hurting. Being an animal lover, he'd seen enough injured animals to make the comparison. She was frightened and confused. He'd suspected she'd just needed time. But as months went by, she never changed her mind. She recovered for the most part, and she was even friendly to him when he returned home from college and then from work on the holidays. But she never showed any sign that she was interested in rekindling what they'd had.

Until that kiss the other night. Chase had read too much into that kiss apparently because now she'd snuffed any sparks it had ignited.

He finished off his soda, wishing he had something stronger

in the fridge. He picked up his phone, and on an impulse, he texted his friend Will.

> I'm ready for those drinks you mentioned the other day. How about tomorrow night?

* * *

Sophie raised her arms up over her head, circling them in front of her to place her palms together at her chest for the sun salutation pose. She breathed in and out, stretching and completing several yoga poses until the blood was flowing easily through her body. When her muscles felt limber, she headed into her bedroom with Comet at her heels.

The playful dog nearly tripped her as he weaved between her feet. Even with a cast on his hind leg, he could move pretty well. She kept her balance as she dressed. Since it was the weekend, Comet wasn't going to the clinic today. Instead, she was keeping Comet with her at the boutique. She had a small baby gate to bring and a bag of treats and chew toys to keep the puppy busy.

Sophie stepped onto the porch and locked her front door behind her. Then she carried Comet down the steps and to her car. She loaded him into her passenger seat and drove to Main Street. The upside to keeping Comet with her today was that she didn't have to stop at the clinic. That would save her from having to smile politely and pretend like nothing had happened between her and Chase over the last week. Because it hadn't. One kiss did not equal a relationship. And one canceled date to a dog park did not make a breakup.

A short drive later, she parked and grabbed her bag and the kennel with Comet inside. She placed the baby gate under her arm and headed to open her boutique. Her leg was already aching from the morning's runaround. At least her mom would be coming by later to help run the shop.

Sophie unlocked her boutique door and stepped inside. She set the kennel down and quickly unfolded the baby gate behind her counter. "There you go," she said, placing Comet inside its confines. "You'll love it here, I promise." And maybe this should be the new arrangement. That way she didn't have to see Chase on a daily basis anymore. It would ease the awkwardness between them. Then they could return to what they were. Old friends who avoided each other when possible.

Sophie sighed. She needed a distraction from one particular handsome veterinarian. On an impulse, she pulled out her cell phone and texted Trisha.

> Can Janet watch Petey tonight?

The dots started bouncing.

Why? Trisha asked.

> Because I think we're overdue for a girls' night. What do you say?

> *I don't know. Last time was a bit of a disaster.*

The time Trisha was referring to was when they'd run into someone at the bar that Pete had conned money from. The guy was drunk, bitter, and adamant that Trisha buy all his drinks, saying it was the least she could do.

For every jerk like last time, there are a hundred people in town who love you, Sophie texted back. It'll be fun. Please?

It took a full minute before Trisha responded. I'll check with Janet to see if she can watch Petey for me. I'm sure she'll agree.

Yes! Sophie blew out a breath. There. Now she actually did have plans and a reason for not being able to go to the dog park with Chase tonight. Not that those plans made what she'd told Chase yesterday any less of a lie. But it did make her feel a little better. And tonight, hopefully, she'd feel a lot better after a few laughs and drinks with a friend.

* * *

Chase cranked the engine and started driving.

He was overdue for fun. He'd had far too little since taking on the veterinary clinic. Chase also needed a break from his Sophie-dominated thoughts. That's why he was heading to the Tipsy Tavern. Skip, another climbing buddy of his, owned the place. It'd been a while since he and Chase had gone up the cliffs together. That was overdue as well.

As Chase walked through the door of the noisy tavern and headed to the bar, his attention went to a loud cackle. For as petite as his ex-sister-in-law was, Trisha had a huge laugh, especially when she'd been drinking. Chase spotted her sitting at the end of the bar, talking to Skip.

"Hey, sis," he said as he approached where she was standing.

She looked surprised to see him. "What are you doing here?"

"Meeting up with Will," Chase told her as he looked around the room. "Have you seen him yet?"

Trisha shook her head and accepted the drink that Skip slid toward her. "No, but I've only been here long enough to be on my second drink."

Chase gave Skip a handshake. "Hey, buddy."

"Good to see you. We'll catch up after the crowd thins," Skip promised as he moved to the next customer.

Chase gestured to Trisha's glass. "Will you need a DD tonight?"

She angled her body to look at him. "Always the hero, hmm?"

Chase rolled his eyes. "Is it a crime to want to look out for you?" Chase flinched inwardly at the question.

"Because your brother can't look out for me anymore?" Judging by Trisha's tone of voice, she was already feeling tipsy. She wasn't one to bring up Pete readily.

"Are you here alone?" Chase asked, starting to worry about her. It wasn't like her to go drinking by herself. "Who has Petey?"

Trisha narrowed her eyes. "Petey is with your mom. And of course I'm not alone." She shook her head. "What fun would that be? Why don't you head over and join us?"

She didn't wait for him to respond. Instead, she stepped past him and headed toward one of the tables. Chase turned to follow her but stopped short when he saw who was sitting there. Sophie had bailed on him tonight because something had come up. Was this the something? Drinking with Trisha?

Chase didn't move until a hand grabbed his shoulder from behind. He knew it was Will before he turned to face him.

"There you are," Will said. "Already scoping out someone to dance with, I see."

Chase grimaced. "Trisha is my former sister-in-law. She might as well be my real sister."

"But Sophie is also over there," Will pointed out with a knowing look.

Chase didn't want to go sit with Trisha and Sophie. Especially since Sophie evidently didn't want to see him tonight. He gestured to the bar. "Let's just go get a couple drinks and talk to Skip."

Will clapped a hand on his back. "I won't argue with that plan."

Chase headed back to where he and Trisha had just stood. He was supposed to be having a carefree and relaxing night out with a friend. But instead he felt a restlessness inside him. He wanted to turn back, walk over to that table, and ask Sophie why she'd canceled their plans. Then he wanted to ask her to dance. He longed to press his lips to hers again and feel that rush that only she could give him.

"I don't mind being ditched if you want to walk over there and be with her instead," Will said.

"Sophie?" Chase took the drink that Skip handed him. Skip didn't have to ask because he knew what Chase wanted. Chase turned to Will and shook his head. "I'm not interested in Sophie."

"Liar."

Chase blew out a breath. "I'm not interested in dancing tonight. I'm here to catch up with you." Chase put on a smile that didn't feel sincere. Maybe after he'd finished this first drink it would be.

They chatted through their first and second drinks, and Skip headed over to chat with them for a while, although he was only drinking water on the job. Then they all stopped talking when Skip's gaze lifted to look out on the room. His usual smile fell into a hard line. "Looks like someone is bothering Trisha over there."

Chase whirled in his seat. There was a hulk of a man sitting at the table with his arm draped over Trisha's shoulders. She attempted to peel it off but the man's arm didn't budge. Without thinking, Chase got up and started walking in that direction. The restlessness was still swirling in his chest, collecting with other emotions in its tornado-like funnel. "Hey. Take your arm off her," Chase bit out as he stood at the table.

He recognized the guy. Jimmy Lorens. He owned a large Doberman-Lab mix that he'd brought into the clinic a couple of months back. Jimmy wasn't a big fan of Chase's brother, Pete—join the club. The Lorens family had lost money due to Pete's crimes, and Jimmy had been harassing Trisha about it.

"This is none of your business," Jimmy slurred.

Trisha squirmed to get out of his reach. She couldn't even stand up and walk away, because his fingers curled around her opposite shoulder.

"Let her go!" Sophie snapped at him.

Jimmy slid his gaze in her direction. "Are you getting jealous, sweetheart?"

That was the last straw. "Hands off, Jimmy," Chase ordered.

Jimmy glared at him. "What do you think you're going to do if I don't?"

Chase reached for Trisha's drink and lifted it over Jimmy's head. Then he poured the foamy beer all over the adult-size bully.

"Hey!" Jimmy shot up from his seat and stepped toward Chase. Physically, he was a bigger man. He was also angrier and a lot drunker. "I'm going to make you regret that."

Chase ducked as Jimmy swung a fist in his direction. How had five minutes turned into a bar fight?

Chase punched an arm out to defend himself and somehow landed his fist directly into Jimmy's nose.

Jimmy's hands went to his face as blood gushed from his right nostril. At the same moment, Chief of Police Alex Baker walked up. "Looks like you two will be sleeping it off in a jail cell tonight," he said. But not before Jimmy pulled back and took another swing at Chase. And this time, he didn't miss.

* * *

Thirty minutes later, Chase looked around his empty cell. It was dimly lit and clean for the most part. Not that he intended to stay here very long. He hadn't intended to find himself in a jail cell tonight either though. Or ever. It felt ironic, considering that his brother had been in a prison cell for the last six months. Chase couldn't imagine spending more than an hour here, much less years, which was Pete's sentence.

No wonder his brother wrote him a letter each week. Letters that Chase didn't read or reply to.

Chase dropped his face into his hands and then flinched. For a moment, he had forgotten about his black eye. He had a dull headache settling in at his temples too. It would probably be worse tomorrow morning when he hopefully awoke in his own bed.

Chase let that thought sink in. To wake up in his own bed, he would have to call someone to bail him out. Who would that person be? His mom already had one son locked up. He didn't want her to know that she had a second son locked up. He could call Trisha but she'd been at the tavern. She'd seen what had happened. If she were going to bail him out, she'd already be here. Maybe she blamed him. Chase would probably do best to give her space and not rub in the fact that he'd been hauled off in cuffs.

Chase flinched again because another thought came to mind. This was Sweetwater Springs. Everyone in town would know what had happened by tomorrow morning. His family. All his clients. His friends. The waitresses at the diner, the cashier at the local grocery store. And they would all compare him to his brother, Pete.

At one point in his life, being compared to Pete would have been a good thing. At this point, Chase wished he were an only child.

"Want some ice for that?" a woman's voice asked.

Chase looked up and squinted beneath the swelling of his eye at the police department's newest administrative assistant.

Marisa Kingsberry smiled back at him. There was no judgment or condemnation in her eyes, which he was thankful for. "Ice will help with the swelling."

"That would be great. Thanks." He watched her walk away and tried to figure out who he could call while she was gone.

He was certain that Will would come get him. Then again, Will had been in trouble with the law recently. Maybe he was avoiding Chief Baker and the police department. Skip would still be running the bar.

Chase dropped his head into his hands. There was only one person he could think of to call right now. And it was the last person he wanted to ask to come get him tonight.

Chapter Eight

Sophie stepped inside the local police station and looked around. Because she was tonight's designated driver, she'd had to swing by Janet's house to get Petey and then drop Trisha and her son off at home before coming here.

"I didn't want to haul Chase in but disorderly conduct can't be ignored," Alex said, standing behind the counter inside the station.

Sophie grimaced at the chief of police. "Jimmy started it."

Alex frowned. "I just wish Chase hadn't been the one to make the first assault. Pouring a drink on someone counts. He also took a swing at Jimmy."

Sophie raised a finger. "He didn't mean to swing. That was an accident."

"One that bloodied Jimmy's nose." Alex rested his hands on his hips. "I know both of these guys, and I'm pretty sure that Jimmy started the argument. But from a law enforcement standpoint..." Alex shrugged as he trailed off.

Sophie nodded. "I know. I'm here to bail Chase out. If that's allowed."

"It is. And there are no charges. I'm just holding them until they cool off." Alex stepped behind the front counter. "If it's any consolation, I probably would've poured a beer on any guy who talked trash about my family too."

"Jimmy wouldn't leave Trisha alone. Chase was just trying to help."

Alex chuckled. "No good deed goes unpunished, right?"

"Seems that way sometimes." Sophie followed Alex down a long corridor toward the jail cells. The place smelled of disinfectant and coffee, a weird combination in her view. Alex stopped in front of the cell where Chase was sitting on a bench.

"Lucky you. Someone loves you enough to come get you," Alex said.

Sophie felt her whole body go hot. She knew it was just a figure of speech but referencing love in the same sentence as her and Chase made her want to slink away and leave Chase behind bars. At least with him there, she'd stop running into him in town, and her heart would have a chance to build up a thicker wall.

Chase lifted his head to look at her, and she gasped when she saw the dark-blue bruise around his eye.

"Oh." Her hands flew over her mouth.

"You should see the other guy," Alex told her with a chuckle. "Jimmy's nose looks worse. He's got two black eyes. He kind of looks like a raccoon."

Chase stood and headed toward them. "I'm free to go?"

Alex unlocked the cell door and opened it for him. Then he turned to Sophie. "Are you driving him home? I know he's not drunk but sometimes a blow to the head can make a person woozy."

"I'll drive him. I have my car." Luckily, she hadn't had more than one drink tonight at the tavern.

Alex patted Chase's shoulder. "Things will be better in the morning. I promise." He removed his hand and offered it to Chase to shake.

Chase took it. "Sorry about tonight."

Alex shrugged. "I hope you understand that I was just doing my job."

"I do. We're still friends," Chase assured him.

"We'll have to plan a climb soon."

"Yeah."

Sophie looked at her feet for a moment. Then she and Chase followed Alex back up to the front and said their goodbyes. They stepped outside.

"I parked over here." She led Chase to her car in the parking lot and opened the passenger door for him.

"I should be opening the door for you," he said.

Sophie rolled her eyes. "If you want to think like a caveman, you should also be driving me home but, under the circumstances, I don't think that's a good idea." She waited until he sunk into her passenger seat. Then she got in on the driver's side, started the engine, and steered the car onto the main road. They were quiet for several long minutes as she navigated through the mostly empty streets. "I know you were just trying to help tonight."

Chase grunted beside her. "Jimmy wouldn't take his arm off Trisha. It wasn't right to stand by while he treated her that way."

Sophie wholeheartedly agreed. "Trisha always says that you act like an overprotective brother. I understand why she gets so frustrated by it."

"Frustrated?" Chase asked, sweeping his gaze to the side. "I'm being a nice guy, and she's upset?"

Sophie laughed. "Your niceness put you in jail tonight. Which meant I had to spend my girls' night bailing you out."

Chase was quiet beside her. "Your girls' night was our dog park night first. So I guess going to the bar was the thing that came up?"

Sophie's grasp tightened around the steering wheel. She glanced over. "That was a bit of a lie. I guess I realized that it would be better for us if we just forgot about that kiss the other night."

He was quiet again. Then he finally spoke. "I never forgot about the first kiss, and I'll have a pretty hard time forgetting about this last one."

Sophie didn't respond until she pulled into his driveway a few minutes later and cut the engine. "Chase, sometimes the past is best left in the past."

"I tend to agree with that sentiment," he said. "But if the past is truly in the past, there's nothing keeping us from being friends," he said. "I'm enjoying getting to know the woman you've become. I like spending time together, Sophie."

Her heart kicked. "I do too."

Chase reached for her hand. "I told you I'd help with Comet, and I intend to keep that commitment." He held her gaze. "If I promise not to kiss you again, will you agree to go to the dog park with me tomorrow night? I still think you and Comet would enjoy it. It's the least I can do to thank you for springing me out of jail."

Sophie hedged. That sounded an awful lot like a date to her.

"Since you ditched me tonight, which some might say led to me being put behind bars in the first place," he added.

Guilt swirled inside her belly. But there was something else too. Butterflies—lots of them. "Okay," she agreed, glancing down at Chase's hand on hers. The feel of his skin against hers made goose bumps flesh all over her body. This already felt like so much more than the start of a new friendship.

She looked back up at him, and he grinned. Then he pushed

open his passenger door. "Call me a caveman but you don't need to walk me to my door." He winked. More butterflies. "See you tomorrow, Sophie."

* * *

Chase held an ice pack to his eye as he lay back on his bed, looking up at the ceiling. He lifted the ice off his cheek to reposition it and grimaced. *Ouch.* This was really going to hurt tomorrow. So was the memory of what had happened tonight.

It wasn't necessarily his fault but it also wasn't his style to let someone get to him so easily. Why hadn't he put Jimmy in his place some other way?

An incoming text got his attention. He picked up his phone and blinked the screen into focus.

You okay? Trisha asked.

He appreciated his former sister-in-law's concern but he also hated the fact that he'd worried her. And that he'd ruined her rare girls' night out. He tapped his finger along the screen and texted a reply.

I'm okay. What about you? How did you get home?

He watched the dots bounce along the screen. His breathing matched the rhythmic motion. The dots seemed to go on and on, and he wondered what she was typing that was taking so long. Then her message finally came through.

Sophie dropped me off before going to the jail to get you.

It was only one sentence but it punched him in the gut. Trisha had been the one to go to the jail after Pete was arrested. She'd bailed Chase's brother out, believing in her husband's innocence with all her heart. Chase had believed the same. He'd been so sure that the charges were all a huge misunderstanding. They had to be.

Trisha texted again. I would have come with her but I really wanted to relieve your mom of babysitting duty.

Chase guessed that was an excuse. He imagined that the idea of going down to bail him out tonight had been too much for her. He tapped his finger along the screen. No problem. I'm sorry about tonight.

The dots took their time relaying the message again, letting Chase's mind run away with him. What if Trisha didn't forgive him? What if she no longer trusted him?

You don't have to apologize to me. Jimmy was being a jerk. You probably could've helped without starting a bar fight though. She followed that up with a winking face emoji. Don't think I'll let you live this down.

Chase laughed out loud. One, because it was funny. Two, because he was relieved that Trisha found the humor in the situation as well.

You'll have some explaining about that black eye at Petey's school on Monday though.

Chase frowned. The relaxation from being able to laugh at his situation was replaced by total-body muscle tension. He couldn't speak to Petey's class with a black eye. But he couldn't let his nephew down either.

* * *

On Sunday morning, Chase got up before the birds as always. Some people were lured out of bed by the thought of coffee. He was motivated by the athletic shoes in the corner of his closet and the promise of endorphins after hard exercise.

He dressed in a pair of jogging pants, pulled on a T-shirt, and sunk his feet into his shoes. Then he grabbed a bottled water and gulped down half before grabbing his keys from the kitchen counter. As he grabbed his phone, it began to ring in his hand.

The caller ID was the pet owner of one of his patients. His clinic wasn't open to seeing new patients on the weekend because no one thrived working 24-7. Except, somehow, that's exactly what Chase was on call for. He considered not answering. Or maybe he could call the owner back after his much-needed run.

Then Chase groaned. What if it was a life-or-death situation? Like Grizzly's had been.

Guilt mixed with raw emotion. Unable to ignore it, he answered the call. "This is Dr. Lewis."

"Oh, thank goodness. I was so worried you weren't going to answer. I need your help right away, Doc," a man's voice said.

Chase leaned against his counter, resigned to the fact that he wasn't going for that run just yet. It would have to wait. He listened to Grant Everson recount what was going on with his Great Dane. "Okay, I'll meet you at the clinic," Chase told him. "It'll probably take me ten minutes to get there."

"I hate to bother you on the weekend," Grant said.

"No bother at all." Chase's adrenaline rush could wait.

* * *

"You look awful," Sophie said as soon as she opened her door to Chase late Sunday afternoon. He was standing on her porch, dressed casually in a pair of jeans and a T-shirt.

His black eye squinted, giving him the appearance that he was winking at her. "It doesn't hurt as much as you would think."

Sophie shook her head. "I wasn't talking about the bruise. You look tired."

Chase massaged a hand over his face. "Yeah, I guess I am. I went into the clinic this morning to save a Great Dane. It was an urgent situation but I think the big guy will be okay. He's going to have to stay over a couple nights for monitoring."

"It must feel pretty good saving a life," she said.

Chase nodded as he slid the sunglasses from the top of his head over his eyes. "It usually energizes me but I didn't sleep well last night," he admitted. "I had too much on my mind to get much rest."

"I'm sure." Sophie smiled at him. "Maybe a walk in the park will take your mind off your troubles."

"We'll see. Let me get Comet for you," he offered.

Sophie moved aside so Chase could go in the house and retrieve the puppy.

"I'll take him out to my truck and get him settled," Chase said as he stepped back onto the porch.

She gestured inside her home. "Let me just get my bag, and I'll be right out."

Sophie quickly grabbed her purse and keys and then locked up her house behind her. She headed to the passenger side of the truck as Chase opened the door for her. He was still holding Comet. She stepped up on the floorboard and sat down. Then Chase placed Comet in her lap. He had to lean in to pass off the puppy but he probably didn't have to lean as far as he did. Sophie breathed in Chase's clean and minty scent. Too quickly, he straightened and closed the door.

Sophie took a steadying breath and bent to rub away the ache in her left leg. She'd overexerted herself this morning. She should have stretched more but Comet was a needy little pup, begging to play at every turn. She didn't mind. She actually enjoyed the little guy's company more than she'd expected to. And taking care of a dog wasn't as difficult as she'd thought. It was getting easier every day.

"So," she said as Chase started the engine and navigated toward Sweetwater Park, "how are you feeling after last night?"

Chase massaged a hand over his face again, flinching when he accidentally touched his swollen eye. "The truth is I don't know how I feel." He glanced over. "Didn't you go on a date with Jimmy once? I think Trisha mentioned something about that."

Sophie felt her cheeks burn. "Once," she agreed.

"I'm not sure what you ever saw in that guy to agree to a date with him."

"I didn't see or feel anything," she said. "That's why we didn't go out a second time."

Chase nodded. "I get it. I didn't feel anything with Amelia either. We made sense on paper but I didn't feel it here." He tapped his chest.

"Don't tell me you're a romantic."

He glanced over again before returning his eyes to the road. "You don't remember that about me?"

"I guess I do." Although she'd spent years trying to forget. Remembering any of the qualities that made her fall in love with Chase was a bad thing because they didn't make sense on paper anymore either. "Remember the time when you took me on a hike to Sunrise Point and read a poem you wrote for me? Now, *that* was romantic."

Chase smacked a hand over his face. "Ow. Don't embarrass me and make me slap myself."

Sophie shook her head as she laughed. "The poem was nothing to be embarrassed over. It was sweet." She went quiet for a moment, running her fingers through Comet's fur as she rode.

Chase lifted his hand and tapped his chest again, right over his heart. "There's only been one person who makes me feel something here," he said quietly. His gaze slid over briefly to meet hers.

Sophie swallowed hard. Then Comet yelped as her fingers

curled into his fur without thinking. "Oh, sorry, Comet. I guess I don't know my own strength."

Comet twisted his neck and panted in her direction.

Sophie didn't know what to say to Chase so she said nothing until he pulled into the parking lot and turned off his truck's engine.

Her mouth felt dry as Chase looked at her. She couldn't help remembering their kiss the night Comet had come to stay with her. She'd felt that kiss in the space that Chase had tapped on his own body. Her heart. But they'd agreed there'd be no more kissing between them. Or actually, Chase had agreed not to kiss her. She hadn't made any such promise.

"I'm not a romantic anymore, I guess," Sophie finally said. "I'm more of a realist."

"What fun is that?" Chase asked, his voice quiet, his gaze steady.

Not very much. But it was safer that way.

CHAPTER NINE

Sophie was starting to remind Chase of someone he used to know. As he watched her in the light of the setting sun and listened to her laugh and talk easily, she seemed like the Sophie he'd once been head over heels for.

"Comet will be walking out here on his own in just a couple weeks," he said. "He's healing up just fine."

Sophie nodded. They'd already circled the dog park, and Comet had barked at a dozen other dogs from the lazy comfort of Chase's arms.

Chase observed that Sophie was slowing down in her walk. He tried not to notice, and he definitely wasn't going to ruin this vibe between them by asking if she was all right. Her answer would be that she was, because that's what she always said. And he believed her for the most part. "Thanks for letting me hang out with you and Comet."

She glanced over with a small smile. "I should be the one thanking you. I couldn't foster him without your help."

"I'm sure you could have figured it out on your own."

She blew out a breath. “I certainly couldn’t have carried Comet around the park. To tell you the truth, I’m tired of walking. A mile is about my limit before my leg starts to give me grief.”

Chase was surprised at the admission. He gestured to a nearby bench. “Over there,” he said.

They walked over to the bench and sat down. Sophie was quiet for a moment as she looked out on the people in the park. It wasn’t crowded by any means but there were several couples and families taking strolls with their pets. “Sometimes I forget my own limitations but then my body reminds me,” Sophie finally said.

“We were up on our feet for a while,” Chase commented.

She faced him. “I doubt you’re tired.”

Chase opened his mouth to speak but he wasn’t quite sure what to say. He couldn’t disagree. He could run miles upon miles without stopping. He was conditioned to go for long distances.

Sophie laughed. “See? You want to say you are but you’re such a good man you can’t even lie.” She collected Comet in her arms, running her hands through his fur. “I’m glad you’re doing well. And I’m doing well too, just not at the same things.”

Chase expelled a breath. Since they were being open with one another, he asked, “Do you miss those other things?”

She gave him a strange look.

He was talking about the hikes and rock climbing they used to enjoy together.

“Yes,” she finally said, focusing her gaze forward. “Sometimes I wake up from a dream about being out there with the wind in my hair. The rush of freedom. Of invincibility. I miss it all. But what I miss most is doing them with you.” She visibly swallowed as she looked at him again.

“I never left,” Chase said, his throat suddenly dry. “I mean, yes, I went to college.”

“But you always came back.” Sophie lifted her hand to

smooth her hair out of her face. Comet seemed worn out for a brief second, which was a relief. Chase wanted to continue this honest conversation without interruption. "That's the problem. I didn't want you to come back," she said.

"Oh, I got that message loud and clear." And for the last several years, he'd respected her wishes. He'd stopped trying to call or visit. He stopped asking Trisha about Sophie too, only learning anything about his first love if Trisha offered it up in conversation on her own.

Sophie exhaled audibly beside him. "I never wanted you to give up your life for me, Chase. It was time for both of us to move on." She shook her head. "But there was also this selfish part of me that would fantasize about you crashing through my bedroom door and refusing to let me push you away."

Chase watched Sophie as she petted Comet. He'd had the same fantasy once or twice.

A vulnerability passed over her expression as she met his gaze. "In reality, there was no way I could have allowed you to put your life on hold for me."

"Allowed it to happen?" Chase couldn't explain it but he suddenly felt a wave of frustration. "Sophie, I was in love with you. I put my life on hold anyway. I waited for you to change your mind. I blamed myself for what happened to you. And if I remember correctly, you blamed me too."

Her lips parted, and her eyes widened. "I was hurt. I didn't mean anything I said."

"It sure felt like you did. You almost died. You had months of recovery to go through, and you told me, in no uncertain terms, that it was my fault. How was I supposed to take that?"

Sophie's eyes turned shiny. Given that she said nothing, Chase guessed he'd rendered her speechless. Now he felt like the selfish one but he'd held these feelings in for too long. He needed to get everything out on the table between them.

"I didn't blame you, Chase," she said. "I thought I was doing you a favor." She gestured at the seat of the bench. "I mean, we're sitting right now because my leg is tired. I slow us down even in a simple walk."

Chase wasn't sure why he felt so upset but he did. And he felt justified too. "I'm not the one who can't accept your limitations, Soph. You are. And yeah, those limitations might slow you down but they aren't what's stopping you."

She lifted her chin, looking like she was trying not to cry. "Oh? Then please tell me what is."

"Fear." Chase's gaze was unwavering. "I think you're afraid."

* * *

Sophie swallowed thickly. "Of course I'm afraid. I fell off the side of a mountain and got my leg crushed by a rock half my size. I was lost on a cliff and almost died." She swiped at a tear that slipped past her willpower. "And while, yes, I miss climbing, my life is full without it. I own my own boutique and walk to and from work sometimes. I volunteer at the women's shelter."

Comet barked as if sensing the tension and trying to get in on the conversation.

"Right," Sophie said, glancing at the dog. "And I'm fostering a dog for the first time."

Chase stared at her. She could almost see the wheels turning in his mind. "So you have an amazing life, and you haven't let your injuries slow you down?"

Sophie felt like this was a trick question. "That's right."

"But when you're with me, all you can do is dwell on the things you can't do anymore."

"I'm just highlighting those things so you understand why we don't make sense romantically. Those were the activities that bonded us."

"Maybe at first. But we also fell in love, and love doesn't take a record of how many things we have in common. If it did, I'd be dating Amelia. And I don't want to be with Amelia."

Sophie wanted to look away but she couldn't. Chase had been in love with her once. And she'd loved him back. Was that love still there? Had it survived all this time?

"At least that's not how it's supposed to work," Chase said. "Maybe it was that way for you though. You didn't run or climb anymore, so you didn't want me."

A lump formed in Sophie's throat. "You know that's not true."

"Do I?" He pulled back and narrowed his eyes. "I'm not the one who left, Sophie. I fought for us. I held on to our love and hope and every other emotion that you seemed to have lost on that mountain. You're the one who let blame and fear come between us. You decided that you were better off without me."

"No." She shook her head as tears burned in her eyes. "I decided that *you* were better off without *me*," she corrected.

"Well, that was my choice to make, not yours." He looked away now.

She heard him blow out a long breath. She wasn't sure she'd ever seen him this upset. Not with her at least.

"But that's history, right?" He looked at her again. "There's no need to dwell on what might have been. We've both moved on."

The lump in Sophie's throat grew bigger. She cleared her throat and gave him a definitive nod. "Right."

"It's getting late. We should probably head back to the parking lot," Chase said.

Sophie could feel the question he wanted to ask. Was she okay? The answer wasn't quite that simple. Physically, yes. But emotionally, she felt wrecked right now. "I'm fine," she said. Then to prove her point, she stood as she continued to hold Comet.

Chase stood as well, collecting Comet in his arms. "I'll follow your lead."

Sophie wondered if he was implying more than just the walk back to his truck. Had he really blamed himself all these years? Had she been wrong to push him away? Would she be just as wrong to do so now?

She walked with him back to his truck and stepped into the passenger seat. Questions raced through her mind as he got in on the other side and began the drive to her home.

"I think we wore him out," she finally said, speaking of Comet who immediately fell asleep, drool pooling on the thigh of her jeans.

"Lots of fresh air. That's my prescription for him." Chase's gaze lifted from the puppy in her lap to her before returning to the road. They were only a couple of minutes from turning onto Dragonfly Lane.

"Chase?" she found herself saying, even if she didn't know what she was going to ask just yet.

"Hmm?" He glanced over.

Her heartbeat sped up, and she summoned her courage to say what was in her heart and on her mind. It was so rare that those two agreed. "I'm sorry." She didn't list all the things she was apologizing for. There were too many, and she wasn't quite sure that she'd made the wrong choice anyway. Chase had been so stubborn the only way to get him to leave had been to blame him. At the time, it'd felt necessary.

"Me too."

"What are you sorry for?" she asked.

He looked straight ahead, following the road to her house. "For not climbing with you that day. For not realizing immediately that you were in trouble. For staying, for leaving, for not coming back. My reasons change depending on the day."

Sophie's heart broke for him. She hadn't realized she'd hurt him so deeply.

He pulled into her driveway and parked. Then he looked over at her, his gaze steady. She wished she knew what he was thinking. Was he thinking the same thing she was? That she wasn't ready to say good night just yet? That there was too much left unsaid?

"Come inside?" she finally asked.

* * *

Chase sucked in a breath. He would give Sophie the world if he could. He'd do anything for her but right now walking inside her house felt like an impossible feat that would either end with them fighting or kissing, neither of which his heart could handle right now. This weekend so far had been a roller coaster between being taken to jail and this heart-to-heart with Sophie.

He shook his head. "I think it's best we say good night right here."

He saw the disappointment in Sophie's eyes.

"I was only offering decaf coffee," she said quietly.

Chase reached for her hand. "That's the problem. I want more than coffee."

Her eyes widened, and he realized what she must be thinking. "I'm not talking about sex."

Just saying the word heated the space between them. They'd had sex before. They'd been each other's firsts. He would love to say she'd also been his last but she'd pushed and pushed until he'd moved on. "I'm just talking about spending more time together. As two people who enjoy each other's company."

"Funny, a month ago, we were barely friends."

"I'm glad that's changed. How about I come over next week? Maybe I can walk with you and Comet again one day."

Sophie tilted her head, making her hair spill over her shoulder. It was a subtle move that she'd always done when she was considering an option. As if looking at the world differently would give her the answers she needed. "I'd like that."

"Great." He started to open his truck door but Sophie stopped him. "I can see myself to the door." She didn't wait for his answer. Instead, she climbed out and pulled Comet into her arms. "I'll see you next week, Chase."

"I'll look forward to it." He waited until she had gone inside her house. He was relieved to see that she wasn't limping anymore. She was resilient and strong, and he admired the woman she'd become since their high school days. In his eyes, she was more beautiful than ever, on the outside and the inside. And if he wasn't careful, he'd lose his heart to her all over again, which was only a problem if she didn't feel the same way.

Chapter Ten

Chase felt like he was living inside that dream where you stood in front of a class without any clothes on. Instead, he was standing in front of his nephew's first-grade class with a large black eye.

Petey's teacher had gasped when Chase walked into the room thirty minutes ago. Chase couldn't very well tell her that he'd been in a bar fight over the weekend. He couldn't very well lie either, because this was a small town and people were going to hear about what had happened anyway. So he'd just smiled politely at Mrs. Winters and avoided the question. He'd avoided the other parent speakers' inquisitive looks as well. They'd spoken to the class first and now it was Chase's turn.

Chase dodged Petey's gaze as he stood in front of the class and talked about being an animal doctor. At this age, Chase had already known that was what he'd wanted to do when he grew up. He loved being outdoors. He loved sports. And he adored four-legged creatures.

Chase had considered canceling this little school talk today but Petey had been so excited about it. The last thing Chase ever wanted to do was let his nephew down.

Chase accidentally made eye contact with Petey, and he felt something akin to being kicked in the gut. Good intentions or not, he'd let Petey down anyway. The kid's usual big smile was drooping, and his bright eyes had gone dim. Chase had agreed to come talk to the class for Petey but Petey no longer seemed to want him here.

"Any questions?" Chase finally asked.

Several hands flew up excitedly. Maybe this had gone better than Chase had suspected. A thread of hope ran through him as he pointed at a large kid, seemingly too big to be a first grader. "Yes?"

"Are you a bad guy too?" the kid asked.

Chase frowned. "Too?"

"Everyone knows Petey's dad is in jail. Are you a bad guy like him? Is that why you have a black eye?"

Chase shook his head, noticing now that Petey had dropped his head to his desk. "No, I'm just a veterinarian. That's what I'm here to talk to your class about."

"How'd you get that black eye?" a little girl with braids asked without raising her hand.

Chase swallowed, his gaze darting around the room as whispers started between the students. "Well, it's, uh...it's a long story."

"My mom said you spent the weekend in jail. Just like Petey's dad," the girl with braids said.

At that comment, Petey pushed back from his desk, the legs of his chair scraping loudly on the floor. With one heartbroken look in Chase's direction, he ran out of the class.

Chase's own heart sunk like a rock in the river. He stood there for a stunned second, wondering if he should keep talking or go after Petey.

"I'll go check on him," Mrs. Winters said with an understanding smile, leaving Chase alone with the class for just a second. Then another teacher came to stand in the doorway. Evidently, a small-town veterinarian couldn't be trusted to watch a group of kids on his own. At least not one with a bruised face and a convicted felon for a brother.

"Does, uh, anyone have questions about animals?" Chase asked the class.

One brown-skinned child raised his hand. Chase braced himself for another question about his family. "What's your favorite animal?" the boy wanted to know.

Chase exhaled. That was more of the kind of questions he was expecting. "A dog," he said.

"Do you have a dog?" the boy asked next.

Chase found it hard to breathe again. Like Petey, he wanted to run out of the class at the reminder of Grizzly. "Um, I had a dog until a couple months ago. It, um, died."

The kids' faces all turned sad as they stared at him.

This wasn't going well but Chase had no idea how to turn it around. "His name was Grizzly because he looked like a small grizzly bear as a puppy. Then he grew up and looked like a big grizzly bear," Chase said.

"What happened to your dog?" a little boy with red hair asked.

Chase wasn't sure this was the best topic for the group. "He, uh, got very sick. There was nothing I could do for him." And that was the hardest part. Chase saved everyone else's pets but he'd been helpless to do that for his own.

"That happened to my grandma," the girl with braids said. "She died too."

Chase nodded. "I'm sorry to hear that."

Then the questions turned to how Chase had gotten Grizzly. What Grizzly liked to do. Chase found himself talking about his longtime furry companion, which he'd in no way come to talk about. The kids were fully attentive though so he continued.

Finally, Mrs. Winters walked into the classroom without Petey at her side.

Chase gave her a questioning look.

"He's in Mrs. Wilder's office," she explained. Chase knew that was the school counselor. *Great.* He'd driven his nephew to counseling when all he'd wanted was to stand in as a good role model.

"Class, thank Dr. Lewis for coming to talk to us today," Mrs. Winters said. That was Chase's cue that he was done. Chase thanked the class, wishing Petey could have heard the last part of his talk, which had gone considerably better.

"Dr. Lewis?" the little girl with braids asked.

Chase turned to look at her on the way out of the room. "Yes?"

"I'm sure Grizzly is in dog heaven watching over you. Like my grandma is for me."

Chase swallowed and gave a nod. "Thank you." Then he walked out of the class, feeling heavy with a dozen different emotions. His primary concern was for Petey but he was sure his nephew didn't want to see him right now. He continued walking past the counselor's office and outside the school. Then he reached for his cell phone and dialed Trisha.

"Hey," she said, answering almost immediately. "I can't wait to hear how it went at Petey's school."

Chase slid his sunglasses over his eyes. Maybe he should have kept these on inside the school building. "It was a disaster."

She hesitated on the other end of the line. "Oh? I'm sure it wasn't that bad."

"It was. In fact, I think you might want to come down to the school and pick Petey up."

* * *

Sophie looked up and smiled at the familiar face walking into her boutique. Nadine wasn't smiling though. Instead, her lips were grimly set, and her cheeks were flushed. She was wearing one of the new outfits that Sophie had given her for job interviews.

"What's wrong?" Sophie asked.

Nadine shook her head, her frizzy hair flying around her face. "I just went on an interview, and I bombed it. I know I did."

Sophie led Nadine to an armchair toward the back of the boutique. It was where husbands and boyfriends sat while their significant others dragged them out to shop.

Nadine plopped down. "I stuttered and stumbled and said stupid stuff." She put a hand to her forehead. "I just want to cry right now."

Sophie laid a hand on the woman's shoulder. "I'm so sorry, Nadine. Is there anything I can do?"

Nadine shook her head. "I just didn't know where else to go. I don't have a lot of friends in town yet, and I needed to talk to someone. Is it okay that I came here?" Nadine looked up at Sophie.

"Of course it is. I want to help you in any way that I can."

"It wasn't even a job I wanted," Nadine said, her eyes welling up with tears. "It was a desk job. I don't belong behind a desk."

"Well, then the bright side is that you can find a job more suited to you."

Nadine blew out a soft breath. "You said you'd check around for jobs working with animals. Did you find anything?"

Sophie leaned against the wall. "No." In fact, she hadn't checked at all. She'd considered asking Chase about the clinic but she'd ruled that out. But maybe she should reconsider. Nadine needed a job, and Sophie knew that Chase was overworked at the clinic. It might be a good fit. Except for the whole ex-convict thing. "I haven't checked yet but I will," Sophie promised. "I'll look into it this evening."

Nadine smiled for the first time since entering the boutique. "Thank you. For everything. To make matters worse, Trisha needs my room at the shelter for someone else. She's not kicking me out necessarily but I've overstayed my welcome. So I might be going back to the homeless shelter."

Sophie nodded as she listened.

"A job would help me afford rent. Then I could get my own place."

"Well, I'm here to help. It was never just about the clothes for me. I'm here for the long run," Sophie promised.

Nadine stood and angled her body toward Sophie's. "Talking to you has made me feel a little bit better."

"I'm glad." Sophie stepped forward and gave the woman a warm hug. "You look amazing in that outfit, by the way," she said as they pulled away.

Nadine offered a wide smile now. "And I felt amazing—until I started blabbering nervously." She laughed at herself, which, in Sophie's experience, was a good sign. "I guess nice clothes can only go so far in making a good impression. Thanks for listening."

"Anytime."

Once Nadine had gone, Sophie went back behind her counter, determined to do right by her new friend. She would see Chase tonight when she picked up Comet at the clinic, and she planned to ask him to consider interviewing Nadine. The worst thing that could happen is that he'd say no. He was a reasonable and rational guy though. Hopefully, he'd look past Nadine's criminal background and help her get back on her feet.

The boutique door opened, and two more crestfallen faces entered Sophie's Boutique. This time it was Trisha and Petey.

"Everything okay?" Sophie asked.

Trisha shook her head. "I'm afraid Petey had a bad day at school."

Sophie looked at the little boy. "Oh? I'm sorry to hear that." Sophie knew that some of the kids had taken to picking on him because of his dad. "What happened?"

Petey crossed his arms over his chest. "Uncle Chase talked to my class, and everyone is going to treat me even worse now," he said as tears brimmed in his eyes.

Trisha shared a look with Sophie. "Chase's black eye didn't go over so well with the kids," she explained.

Sophie's mouth fell open as her imagination filled in the blanks. *Oh no.*

"It was awful. I never want to go back to school again!" Petey declared. "And I never want to see Uncle Chase again either!"

* * *

Mondays had never been Chase's favorite day of the week but this one was the worst in the history of Mondays. Chase was so glad it was almost over.

He grabbed the mail that he'd been avoiding all day, pulling the usual letter from the prison from the stack and walking back to his office. He opened the bottom drawer and tossed it inside, unopened and unread as usual.

More resentment than normal brimmed at the surface because of what had happened at Petey's school earlier today. If Petey's dad weren't in prison, the kids wouldn't be making fun of him. And then they wouldn't have leaped to the conclusion that Chase was also a "bad guy."

Chase sat in his office chair for a second and massaged his hands over his face. What a disaster of a day. He'd checked in with Trisha earlier to make sure Petey was okay but that had done little to settle his mind. Apparently, his nephew wasn't ready to talk to him just yet. Some male role model he was turning out to be.

"Give Petey time," Trisha had told Chase over the phone. "He'll warm back up."

Chase leaned back in his chair and sighed. His nephew had enough to deal with without Chase adding to the heap.

"Hard day, huh?" His receptionist, Penny, stood in his office doorway. Chase hadn't even heard her walk up.

"You could say so," he muttered.

She folded her arms across her chest. "I'm sorry to hear that, Dr. Lewis. The good news is that Comet is fed, and he's been taken outside to use the bathroom. And," she said as her voice lifted just slightly, "he's ready to see his foster parent, who should be arriving anytime now." Penny gave Chase a knowing look.

Yeah, the thought of seeing Sophie did make Chase feel a little better, even if their last conversation had been tough. They'd laid out a lot of thoughts and feelings, some that Chase was still sorting through.

"I guess you'll probably be walking them home as usual," Penny said, "so I've gone ahead and locked everything up for you. When Sophie arrives, you can grab Comet and leave."

Chase nodded. "Thank you, Penny. That's helpful." Because he couldn't wait to get out of here and just go home and lick his wounds.

"Of course, Dr. Lewis. I'm heading out myself. I have dinner plans with my sister tonight."

"That's nice. Enjoy."

"We will." Penny turned and headed back down the hall. Chase heard her lock up and leave through the back door. Then he retrieved Comet and headed to the front of the clinic to wait for Sophie. His heart lifted in his throat as he saw her walk into view. Suddenly his Monday was looking up.

He headed down the steps and met her on the road. "Hi," he said, startling her. She must have been lost in thought.

She smiled easily when she saw him.

"Is it okay if I walk you?" he asked.

"I was hoping you would," she said, stepping up to him. She reached out and petted Comet's head, talking sweetly to the dog.

Chase had to admit that he was a little jealous, wishing she'd greeted him with the same amount of attention. He was also happy to see how much she and Comet were bonding. This arrangement was only temporary but maybe she'd change her mind. Perhaps, once the cast came off, she'd decide to keep Comet for good.

Sophie sighed as she lifted her gaze to Chase. "I've missed Comet. This is what I've been waiting for all day. I needed this."

This was exactly what Chase needed after the day he'd had too. A dose of Sophie was good medicine—the best kind.

* * *

Sophie fell into stride with Chase, as they walked toward Dragonfly Lane. Her left leg started to ache but she resisted letting herself limp, which would only draw attention and concern from Chase. And from what Trisha had reported, Chase was already having a rough Monday.

"So..." she said, glancing over, "do you want to talk about what happened at Petey's school this morning?"

Chase made a noise under his breath. "I guess Trisha told you, huh?"

Sophie pulled the cardigan sweater she was wearing tighter around her body, shielding herself from the slight wind. "She and Petey stopped by the boutique this afternoon."

Chase groaned. "I feel so bad about what happened. I was only trying to be there for Petey but I'm afraid I made things worse for him."

Without thinking, Sophie reached out and touched Chase's shoulder. She felt an immediate surge of attraction with just that simple contact.

"He'll come around. It can't be easy for him but he loves you."

Chase shifted Comet in his arms. "And I love him. I'd do

anything for that kid. Now I just need to figure out how to fix the damage I caused this morning."

Sophie removed her hand from his arm and petted Comet again as they walked up in silence, finally turning into her driveway a short time later. "Come inside for a drink?" He'd turned her down last night but she had a feeling that Chase didn't want to be alone at the moment.

"Hopefully, you have something stronger than coffee," he joked.

"I do, actually. I have a bottle of wine that just might hit the spot," she said, climbing up her porch steps. "If you want to stay a little while, I'll make dinner too."

"Wow." Chase looked over. "That sounds like an offer I can't refuse. What's the catch?"

She shrugged a shoulder as she twisted the key in her lock. She pushed her front door open and stepped inside. Chase followed behind her. "Well, I do have a favor I want to ask," she said, turning back to him.

Sophie watched as Chase put Comet down in the baby-gated area. Then he straightened and looked at her. He was suddenly standing closer than she expected. Her heart rate sped up.

"What kind of favor? I'm pretty much willing to say yes to whatever you ask of me right now."

"Really?" Sophie tilted her head. "Well, I was going to wait until after we'd had a glass of wine but maybe I should just go ahead and ask while you're inclined to agree."

Chase smiled, creating little dimples in his cheeks. She'd always loved that about him.

"There's a woman from the shelter that I've helped in my Fairy Godmother's Closet. She's been on one bad job interview so far and it really upset her. What she really wants to do is work with animals." Sophie nibbled at her lower lip. "I was thinking that you might need help at the clinic. She's super sweet and nice."

Chase narrowed his eyes. "You want me to give this woman a job?"

"No. Not exactly. I want you to give her a chance. Maybe interview her and see what you think?"

Chase hesitated.

Suddenly, Sophie needed him to say yes. She needed to tell him about Nadine's criminal history too, which pretty much guaranteed he'd say no. Maybe she'd wait for full disclosure until he at least considered the idea.

"Okay," Chase said. "A friend of yours is a friend of mine. And I actually could use help at the clinic these days."

"Really?"

"Tell her to stop by on Friday morning around eight thirty. My schedule is open at that time," he said.

Sophie grinned. "I could kiss you right now."

The space between them heated. His eyes seemed to take on a lazy look. "I wouldn't say no to a kiss."

Sophie stepped closer, tempted by the idea as well. "Maybe we'll have that glass of wine first."

Chapter Eleven

The woman sitting across from Chase in his office on Friday morning seemed kind. The corners of her eyes crinkled when she smiled, which seemed to be frequently. Probably because she was nervous.

Chase could sympathize with that. When he'd interviewed to work at this clinic last December, he'd sweated completely through his button-down shirt. And that was having known the previous vet all his life. Nadine had just met Chase.

"Sophie Daniels put in a good word for you," Chase told her.

Nadine nodded. "Oh, she's so sweet. She gave me these clothes to wear on any interviews I might go on. They're probably a little fancy for a vet clinic but I couldn't very well come here in jeans."

"Jeans would have been fine." Chase picked up his pen and pulled a pad of paper toward him. "Do you have experience with animals?" he asked.

"Oh yes. I grew up on a farm. I fed, watered, and groomed all the animals every morning and every night before bed. I don't mind getting dirty."

"Working on a farm is experience in and of itself," Chase said. "Do you have a vehicle, Nadine?"

This wasn't a question he'd usually ask during an interview but given that Nadine was staying at the women's shelter, it was a necessary one. If he was going to hire someone, they needed a way to get here.

"Actually, yes I do. Someone donated an old Chevy to me. It's a little grumbly, and it sounds like it might fall apart when I'm driving down the road but it's mine. And I'm happy to have it."

Chase gave her an assessing glance. "Well, if you're interested in the job, it's yours. I'd love some help around here."

Nadine nodded quickly. "Wow. Thank you. Yes, I'm interested. When can I start?"

Chase laughed as he stood from behind his desk. "Right now, if you want. But you probably don't want to ruin your nice clothes," he said, noticing her attire as she stood. The items in Sophie's Boutique were all quality clothing. Even the casual wear was made from expensive material.

Nadine frowned as she looked down at her women's dress suit. "No, I'd hate to do that. How about tomorrow? I can wear my jeans."

Chase smiled politely. He liked the woman but he probably wouldn't have hired her so easily if not for Sophie. She didn't come with the usual work references. He was sure she'd work out well here though. And the truth was he was swamped at the clinic and really could use an extra pair of hands to feed and water the animals, and groom them when needed. "We're not open for new patients on the weekend. If you're available, you can meet Penny here in the morning, though, and see how she tends to the overnighters," he told Nadine, walking her to the front of his clinic. Chase looked at Penny. "Is that okay with you?"

"Of course it is. I guess that means you're now part of the small crew here?" Penny asked Nadine.

Nadine was beaming. "I guess so. I'll be in the back with the animals mostly. Which is fine by me. I like animals more than people."

Penny's eyebrows lifted high on her forehead.

"I mean, I like people, and I already like you and Dr. Lewis." Nadine's cheeks darkened. "But ever since I was young, my heart belonged to the animals."

Chase patted her shoulder. "I totally get it. I think you're in the right place here."

Nadine nodded. "Me too. I'll be in tomorrow morning. Thank you again for giving me a shot." Nadine offered her hand for him to shake. Chase shook it before opening the clinic's front door for her.

"You're welcome." He watched her head down the steps.

After Nadine had gone, Chase closed the door and turned back to Penny at the counter. "Good morning."

"Morning. Looks like you've already been busy. She seemed nice," Penny said, her voice raising an octave on that last word.

Chase glanced out the window where Nadine disappeared around the corner. "We need help and so does she. So it's a win-win." He looked at his receptionist again.

"As long as I get to continue caring for Comet when he's here. I've grown fond of that little guy," Penny said. Then she held up a hand. "Not saying I want to adopt him though."

Chase smiled. He'd grown fond of Comet too, not that he was willing to give the pup his forever home either. "Nadine can look after the other animals. I'll let her know that you've got Comet."

Penny looked pleased as he walked back down the hall to retrieve the morning coffee he'd brought from home in a travel mug. While he was in his office, he tapped in a quick text to Trisha. Since Petey still wasn't talking to him, he'd dropped off a small gift before work this morning. It was a video game and a little bag of candy, better described as a bribe.

Did Petey get my surprise?

Yes, and you shouldn't have, Trisha texted back. An apology would have been enough.

Chase wanted to respond that you couldn't apologize to someone who wasn't speaking to you. His thoughts stumbled over each other, though, as his brother came to mind. But Pete's crimes and Chase's misgivings weren't the same thing.

He'll come around. No more gifts, Trisha texted.

Chase frowned at his phone's screen. Okay, he texted back. Then he gulped the rest of his coffee down and stood from his desk, preparing to start seeing patients.

For the rest of the day, he treated three cats, a hamster, a dachshund, and finally a pygmy goat. Then, at the end of the day, he retrieved his belongings from his office as he prepared to go home. His gaze moved to the letters from his brother in the bottom drawer.

He tried to be the guy who did the right thing. But sometimes it was hard to know what exactly that was. Hiring Nadine was right. Helping Trisha care for Petey in his brother's absence was right, despite a few epic fails. But Chase had no idea how to respond to these letters, if he responded at all.

He closed the drawer, locked up the clinic, and collected Comet. Since Sophie was working late again tonight, Chase had offered to drop Comet off later. Sophie hadn't texted him yet so he put Comet in his truck's passenger seat and drove back to his house to freshen up. He carried Comet over the threshold and then set him down on the hardwood floor.

As soon as Comet hit the floor, he lifted his nose in the air, getting the scent of a new place. Then the little dog ran over to

Grizzly's old chew toy, which had been lying in the same spot since Chase's beloved dog had passed.

Chase didn't move fast enough to stop it, and maybe he didn't need to. Grizzly didn't need that toy anymore, and Comet seemed to like it. Chase blew out a breath and nodded to himself as he watched, a bittersweet feeling coming over him. When he dropped Comet off at Sophie's later, he'd bring the chew toy with him. As the little girl in Petey's class had said, Grizzly was now in a better place. He probably had all the toys he wanted at his disposal.

Somehow that conversation with Petey's class had healed the hole Grizzly had left behind in Chase's heart. Maybe one day Chase would be ready to get another dog after all.

* * *

Sophie assessed the woman sitting on the bench in the Fairy Godmother's Closet. She had dark circles under her eyes. Her hair was dry and needed to be cut. She'd been through life struggles, and she wore them like her currently threadbare attire.

Trisha had driven the woman here, arriving just as Sophie was closing the boutique. Trisha nudged the woman sitting beside her. "Celeste has four job interviews next week."

"That's wonderful," Sophie said. If Celeste were to go to most interviews looking the way she did right now, however, it was doubtful she'd get very far in the process.

Celeste smiled shyly. "I've never held a job before," she admitted. "I got married at eighteen and became a mother straightaway."

"Well, motherhood is a job in and of itself," Sophie said. "Trisha here is the hardest working woman I know."

"Celeste has two children," Trisha offered. "They're staying at the shelter right now too."

Sophie listened as she walked toward the clothing donations she'd been collecting, looking for something that might work for Celeste. She had a good eye for size and color. "Well, those two kids of yours are going to be so proud of their mom when you get one of those jobs."

Celeste offered a weak smile. "I hope so. Everything I do is for them."

Trisha had already filled her in on Celeste's history. Her husband had left her and the kids. She'd waited for him to come home as the bills mounted. After her house went into foreclosure, she'd moved into the homeless shelter for a while. Then Trisha had taken her in at the women's shelter when a room became available.

Sophie held out a pair of black slacks and a no-iron blouse that was the perfect mix of dress casual. "What do you think of this? It's from last year's line here at the boutique."

Celeste ran her hand over the clothing. "I like that. The material feels so soft."

"Good." Sophie pointed to the dressing room down the hall. "You can try it on, and we'll wait in here. I have a few more things that might work. I'll bring them to you."

Celeste stood and took the hangers. Then she quietly walked toward the dressing room.

"She's a nice lady," Trisha said. "Thank you for helping her. This Fairy Godmother's Closet you have going is a godsend for these women."

"For the record, I'm just their fairy godmother's helper," Sophie said, nudging Trisha. "You're the fairy godmother in this scenario."

"Well, I couldn't do it without you. And Bea at Perfectly Pampered has agreed to fix Celeste's hair tomorrow. It's a regular Cinderella story. They all are. That's why I'm calling the black-tie event A Princess for a Night."

Sophie's lips parted. "I didn't realize the event was going to have a theme. I love that!"

"Yeah?" Trisha looked pleased. "I've also decided that I'm giving free entrance to the women who've stayed at the shelter over the last year."

"That's a great idea. Let me know if they need dresses. I can try to find something for them to wear for the occasion."

"I knew you'd say that." Trisha nudged her with her elbow. "You know, you'd be the perfect person to give a speech at the shelter's black-tie affair."

Sophie stiffened. "Me? Why me?"

"I think the question is, Why not you? You've helped the shelter so much, and you understand what getting a second chance means to these women. It would just be a short speech," Trisha said, making Sophie suspect that this wasn't a spur-of-the-moment suggestion. "And I'll be giving a little speech too."

Trisha was Sophie's best friend so Sophie had no problem saying no but some part of her wanted to say yes. She'd said no to herself too many times over the years. And the women's shelter was important to her. "Okay," she said, suddenly nervous even though she still had weeks before she actually had to get up in front of a large room of people. "I'll do it."

Trisha clapped her hands together at her chest. "Oh, I'm so glad. This is going to be a night to remember for everyone."

Sophie picked out a few more outfits while they chatted about the event. Then Celeste walked into the room wearing the black slacks and top. "Wow. That fits you perfectly."

Celeste gave a more confident smile than she had before. Clothes were only a small part of the journey. What was inside would take a lot more time to transform. Sophie knew that from her own experience. But she had no doubt that Celeste would be okay. This town took care of its own and adopted those who came in. Before long, Celeste would have a job and be on her feet, providing for her kids as a strong single mom with an entire town watching over them.

Sophie gave Celeste a few more things to try on. By the time Celeste and Trisha walked out of the boutique, it was getting dark. Sophie needed to hurry home because Chase was coming over this evening. He was bringing Comet but she had a sneaking suspicion he'd be staying awhile. At least she hoped so.

She hurried to lock up, walking past a rack of clothing. She'd been eying a shimmery top that had just come in this week. Now it seemed perfect for a low-key night with her favorite veterinarian.

She grabbed it as she headed out the door. The walk home wasn't long but she was tired by the time she reached her porch steps. She unlocked her door and stepped inside. She tapped out a quick text to Chase to let him know she was home. Then she took the new top down the hall and changed in her bedroom. After that, she took a moment and stretched. She didn't want anything throwing the night off balance.

Although she trusted that Chase would catch her if she fell. Falling on the ground wasn't nearly as scary as letting herself fall for Chase again though. And yet, that was inevitable if they continued spending so much time together.

* * *

Chase felt restless as he walked up the porch steps toward Sophie's door. It was a good kind of restless. The kind that made him want to run five miles or climb the side of a mountain.

He rang the doorbell as Comet barked in his arms, announcing their arrival. Then he heard Sophie's footsteps heading toward the front of the house.

She opened the door and smiled back at him. “Hi.”

“Hey.” Chase stepped inside her home as she closed the front door behind him. He also smelled the aroma of food cooking on the stove. He put Comet down on the floor and straightened to look at her. “Something smells good.”

“Well, I thought you might be hungry after working all day and then going above and beyond by dropping Comet off for me.”

That was good news to Chase’s ears. “Starving, actually. I also woke early and ran five miles before heading into the clinic this morning,” he said. He didn’t think anything of his words until he met her gaze. “Sorry.”

She waved a hand, dismissing his apology. “You don’t have to be sorry for working out, Chase. I still work out too, you know.”

Chase followed Sophie as she headed into the kitchen. He took the barstool at the counter. “No, I didn’t know.”

“I don’t run or climb anymore, of course,” she said with a shrug as she washed her hands at the kitchen sink. Chase watched as she reached for a pitcher of lemonade and filled two glasses. “But I often walk to and from the boutique. That’s exercise,” she said, narrowing her eyes at him like she thought he might argue otherwise.

Chase reached for the glass she offered him. “I agree.”

She smirked. “And if the weather is right, I swim at the community pool. That’s what I love doing most. I also practice yoga here in my living room. It’s a lifesaver for keeping my left leg relaxed.”

“Perhaps you can teach me a few tricks,” he suggested.

She raised a brow as she caught his eye. “You want to learn yoga?”

“Runners have to stay limber too, you know,” he explained, even though his motivation for wanting to learn wasn’t entirely innocent.

Sophie turned back to the stove. She stirred the contents of a large pot and set the ladle back down. “The food still needs another half hour. In the meantime, I was hoping you might show me and Comet a few tricks?”

He glanced over at the dog. “Oh?”

Sophie shrugged. “He’s doing so much better, and I was thinking that it might be fun. He doesn’t listen to me at all.”

“I have treats to help with that.” Chase patted his pocket, where he’d put a few before leaving his house earlier, suspecting that Comet might need a little motivation tonight. “We can work on sit, stay, and lie down.”

“Great. Then we can eat and see where the night takes us.”

Comet barked, evidently liking the sound of that. Chase liked it too.

They headed into the living room, and Chase sat on the floor with Comet while Sophie took the couch. He watched her move carefully, stiffly, and wanted to ask if she was okay. He guessed that some days were harder than others.

“Let’s teach Comet the art of a good sit first.” He went through the motions of teaching Comet to sit, offering the growing dog encouragement and treats. “Now you try.”

Sophie slid down on the floor beside him, sitting so close that he could smell the floral scent of her hair. She repeated the motions that he had just done while Comet struggled to chew on her bracelet. “Why isn’t he listening to me?” she finally asked, a bit of frustration playing in her voice.

“You have to be alpha. Use a more commanding voice. Tell him what you want him to do.”

“You make it sound so easy,” she said, looking at him.

“Things don’t always have to be hard.” They weren’t talking about Comet anymore. At least he wasn’t. His heart picked up pace, and his breathing grew shallow. “Every time I walked down Main Street, I had to resist stopping in your boutique.

Sometimes I saw you walking home and thought about parking my truck and walking with you."

"I probably would have told you I didn't need you to walk me home."

"You never needed me, Soph. I just wished you still wanted me."

Her lips parted. "Chase, it never felt that simple. Until now," she said quietly.

"What's changed?" he dared to ask.

"I'm not sure. It feels like everything has changed." She swiped a lock of hair behind her ear. "Or maybe I'm just tired of resisting you."

Chase drew in a breath. "It's a losing battle. At least from my perspective." He reached for her hand, hoping she wouldn't swipe it away. She didn't. Then he wrapped his fingers around hers. "So maybe tonight, we should just..."

"Surrender?" The corners of her mouth curled. Her gaze flitted to Comet and back up to his. "So I just need to ask for what I want?"

Were they talking about matters of her dog or her heart? "That's right," Chase said.

"Okay, then. To start with, I want you to kiss me." Like he'd suggested, her tone was bolder and more commanding.

Chase blinked. "Yeah, I think that's a good place to start."

* * *

There was something about kissing Chase that left Sophie feeling weak but not in a bad way. She melted into the kiss, and her muscles became loose and flimsy. She wanted to lean into his embrace and lose herself.

Why had she been fighting this for so long? The reasons felt blurry, lost in a fog somewhere in distance and time. Chase's hand wrapped around the back of her neck as his mouth explored hers. Sophie gave her hands permission to rest against his chest, feeling the mound of tight muscle there.

Chase did more than walk and swim. He ran and climbed. He hung off the sides of mountains and chased the sun the way they used to together.

Sophie pulled back and looked at him now, her breathing heavy. “Sometimes I still dream about being on Sunrise Point with you.”

He didn’t pull away. “Me too. That was one of the best memories of my life.” They’d climbed for hours, just the two of them, working as a team until they reached the highest point of the mountain. They’d sat there and talked about life. About their dreams and the future that they wanted together. Then they’d made tireless love.

“Chase,” she said, not knowing what she would say next. There were so many things left unsaid between them. “I’m not feeling sorry for myself but I can’t do all the things we used to.”

Chase reached out and stroked his hand through her hair. “We used to kiss a lot too, if I remember correctly. And from my vantage point, you kiss even better than I remember.”

Sophie felt a smile pull on her lips. “But we’re kissing in my living room instead of on a mountainside.”

Chase shook his head. “Do you trust me?”

“Of course I do.”

Comet chewed at the hem of her shirt but she didn’t care. She doubted the little dog was going to learn to sit, lie down, or stay tonight.

“Tomorrow is Saturday, and Penny is scheduled to tend to the animals in the morning. I’m going in during the afternoon. Spend the day with me. I want to take you somewhere.”

“Where?”

Chase grinned back at her. For a moment, he looked just like the boy she'd fallen in love with so long ago. "You said you trust me, right?"

She swallowed. "I do."

"Okay, then. It's settled. And just to make sure there's no confusion, this is a date."

Her breath caught even as she smiled.

"Do you want to change your mind?" he asked.

Fear gripped her but it wasn't nearly as strong as her desire. She shook her head. "No. Can we bring Comet?"

Chase grimaced. "It might be too risky for him. He'd be safer here—not to say you won't be completely safe."

She considered this. She certainly didn't want to put the dog's well-being at stake—again. "Okay, I trust you. A date sounds nice."

He leaned forward and kissed her once more. "Yeah, it does."

* * *

After dinner, Sophie walked Chase to the door and said good night.

"You better get your sleep. I'll be here around six thirty a.m."

"What?" Sophie's mouth dropped open. "Six thirty?"

Chase chuckled. "Oh, come on. Waking up early never used to bother you before."

"In case you haven't noticed, I'm not the same girl I once was."

Chase shook his head. "That's the point of tomorrow. I want to show you something new. Just for us. But it has to be early."

"Okay. I'll set my alarm clock." A giddy excitement grew inside Sophie. They'd always gone on miniadventures together when they were young. It was nothing for them to wake early, go hiking for miles, and have a picnic on some scenic ridge out in the woods.

Chase leaned in and kissed her. She'd lost count of how many kisses they'd shared tonight. Then he pointed at Comet. "Sit."

Comet sat awkwardly, tucking his casted leg under him.

"Stay," he said then, before taking a few retreating steps. Comet didn't budge. Neither did Sophie. She wasn't going to run from Chase this time. If he wanted a second chance, she'd give it to him.

She watched him descend her porch steps and then turned to close the door behind her, leaning against it. Comet barked at her. "You want to go out?" she asked, leading him to the back door. She let the puppy run free inside the confines of her fence and pulled out her cell phone as she waited for him to return.

There was a message from Trisha waiting for her.

Want to get together tomorrow? I have one house to clean but after that I'm free. Janet is taking Petey for the day.

Even though Trisha worked at the shelter during the week, she often cleaned houses on the weekends. Such was the life of many single moms. Trisha barely had time for herself. Sophie hated to disappoint her friend but she thought Trisha would be thrilled to know why she couldn't say yes. Sophie tapped her fingers along her screen as she texted back a response.

Actually, I have a date tomorrow, starting before sunrise.

The dots started bouncing on Sophie's screen. Comet walked past her back inside the house and settled on his dog bed as Sophie locked the back door. Her cell phone buzzed.

With my overbearing ex-brother-in-law?

Sophie couldn't contain her smile. It felt so good to stop resisting what her heart wanted. The one and only.

She could practically hear Trisha's squeal in her imagination.

Trisha had always thought that Sophie and Chase should get back together.

Trisha's text came quickly. I need details when the date is over.

Sophie grinned. You got it. Sorry I can't hang out with you tomorrow though.

Don't worry about me. I'll be fine, Trisha texted back.

Something about that statement left Sophie feeling unsettled. That was always Sophie's line. And it usually meant that she wasn't fine at all.

Chapter Twelve

The sky was still dark as Chase climbed Sophie's porch steps and rang her doorbell the next morning. After a moment, she opened the door and peered back at him sleepily. She had already gotten dressed, and her hair was pulled back in a ponytail. Even so, she covered her mouth as she yawned. "I haven't had my coffee yet."

Chase wasn't empty-handed this morning. He offered a travel mug full of hot coffee. "Just the way you like it. Unless that's changed over the years."

Sophie took the coffee and sipped it. Then sighed happily. "No, nothing has changed about the way I like my brew. Thank you. You're a lifesaver."

"Ready to go?" he asked, eager to get started on their morning date.

She nodded and reached for her purse, draping it across her body. Then she closed her front door behind her. "I'm not used to waking up and heading out this early anymore. I've learned the art of sleeping in on the weekends."

Chase chuckled. "Maybe you can teach me one of these days." Which would imply spending the night together. He hadn't intended anything by that remark but Sophie looked a little more awake now. Her cheeks blushed softly, and she took another sip of her coffee as he stepped ahead and opened the truck door for her.

"Thank you." She sat in his passenger seat and he closed the door. When he sat in the driver's seat, he reached for his own thermos of coffee.

"So where are we going?" she asked.

Chase clucked his tongue. "It's supposed to be a surprise. You really want to spoil it?"

She broke into another yawn beside him. "No, I am following you blindly today."

He tipped his head at her to-go cup. "You should drink more coffee. I want you fully awake for our morning adventure."

They talked easily as he drove to a clearing that allowed for just a few cars. There was a path that led into the woods for nature walkers. Chase parked and ran around his truck to open the passenger door. Sophie didn't step out immediately.

"Chase, I can't really go for long hikes anymore. And the uneven ground—" She shook her head, worry crinkling her forehead.

"We're not hiking. I come here all the time. It's just a short walk to the river."

"The river?" Sophie's eyes went wide.

Chase offered her his hand. "No backing out now. I promise this will be amazing. But we need to hurry so we don't miss it."

Sophie seemed to relax. "You're being very mysterious this morning." She stepped out of the truck and reached for her coffee. "I'm taking this with me."

"Good idea." He held her hand as they followed the path through the tall pines. It was still dark outside but daylight was starting to trickle in. Chase was used to walking fast but Sophie walked at a much slower pace. He didn't mind as long as they made it to the riverbank in time.

Sophie stopped walking for a moment.

Chase turned to look at her. "What's wrong?"

She gave him an apologetic smile. "I just need a minute. I didn't have time to stretch this morning. My leg is a little stiff."

"No problem," Chase said but he was anxious as the sky grew lighter. If they didn't keep going, they would miss the sunrise. He refocused his gaze and thoughts, realizing that Sophie was watching him.

"I'm sorry," she said, giving her leg one last rub and then straightening.

"Don't be. I'd pick you up and carry you if I didn't know for a fact that you'd hate it."

This made Sophie laugh. Then she reached for his hand. "I don't hate this. Okay, let's go."

"You sure?"

"Yep."

They continued walking again, following the path until they broke through the trees with the river in front of them.

Sophie gasped, her hand squeezing tightly around Chase's. The sun was just clearing the tops of the oak and beech trees beyond. He'd worried they'd be late but this was the most magical moment with the vibrant blend of colors illuminating the sky.

"It's breathtaking," Sophie marveled with her gaze pinned to the horizon.

Chase, however, couldn't take his eyes off her. *She* was what took his breath away.

"This is why you wanted to get here so early?" she asked.

"I thought maybe it'd been a while since you'd seen this."

"It has. I forgot how much I loved watching the sun rise."

"It's better than sleeping in?" Chase grinned as she turned to look at him.

"Especially when I share it with you." She stepped into his embrace and gave him a soft kiss.

"How's your leg?" he asked.

"It's not bothering me at all. I guess I'm a little distracted by the view. And by you."

Chase brushed his lips over hers again. They were soft and inviting, and he wanted to stay here for the rest of the day. "I couldn't wait a second longer to do that," he told her.

"I don't mind a bit. In fact, anytime you want to do that today, feel free."

"I have a feeling today's going to be right up there with that one we spent at Sunrise Point." He gestured toward the canoe that he'd placed on the banks of the river early this morning before picking her up. He didn't worry that anybody would take it in the short time that he left it there. Sweetwater Springs was generally a safe town.

"We're going out on a canoe?" Sophie asked, a look of surprise and excitement lighting up her green eyes.

"I can row it completely by myself if need be," Chase told her. "But I have an extra oar in case you want to help."

"That sounds amazing. It's been forever since I've been in a canoe," she told him.

"It's one of the things I enjoy doing on the weekends. I have fishing poles in there as well, and sometimes I'll bring home dinner. If I'm lucky."

"Wouldn't that be fun if we caught and cooked our own dinner tonight? Since we're spending the day together." She shrugged a shoulder.

"Anything we do today is going to be fun. As long as I'm with you."

She tilted her head and looked at him for a long moment.

Then she turned again to look at the sunrise. After the sun had risen halfway up the sky, she released a sigh. “If you don’t mind, I’d like to do a few stretches before we get in the canoe. It won’t take me long.”

Chase put his hands on his hips to keep from pulling her close again. “How about I do them with you? Stretching is good for everybody, right?”

She hesitated. “Okay,” she finally agreed. Then she led Chase through a few simple stretches.

He had only ever done a yoga class once so he didn’t know the names of some of the stretches. She bent completely at the waist and hung there until her arms touched the ground. Then she leaned forward, going even lower.

Her gaze swept sideways to look at him. She laughed because he was barely able to get his fingertips on the ground. “It takes time to limber up. But you’ll get there if you practice. Now we’re going to go into downward dog.” She walked her hands forward on the ground, away from her feet.

Chase followed along as best he could, losing his balance momentarily and making her laugh again. If that were his only accomplishment for the rest of the day, he’d be happy. Just to make her smile and laugh. Just to be here for her, as much as she’d let him.

“This is the sun salutation,” she informed him, sweeping her arms over her head and then bringing them to rest at her chest.

“Very appropriate, considering that we just watched it come up.”

“Indeed.” After several poses, she straightened and sighed. “There. I’m ready for anything now. But be warned, I’m drinking my coffee while you do all the rowing.”

* * *

"I can't believe you didn't remember what I like to eat for breakfast," Sophie commented, biting into a strawberry half an hour later. After crossing the river and getting out, Chase had laid down a blanket and unpacked a variety of fruit as they sat on the other side of the bank. The sun was high in the sky now, and the birds were in chorus all around them.

"Oh, I remember. S'mores Pop-Tarts." He grinned. "I was just going for something more romantic."

He reached out to touch her free hand, tracing a finger over the back the way he used to in class when they were younger. He used to write letters that created secret messages and distracted her from the teacher's lessons.

All her attention went to her hand as he wrote one letter after another.

"Beautiful?" she finally said with a growing smile. "Even with no makeup?"

Chase scooted closer, leaning his face toward hers. "I don't care about that stuff. You're beautiful because of who you are on the inside."

Sophie looked down at his hand still on hers. "Makeup and clothes help women feel pretty." She looked up and met his gaze. "I've always felt that way with you though. It's something about the way you look at me. It stopped after our breakup."

"You broke up with me. I was hurt and confused. I was an eighteen-year-old boy."

She nodded. "And I was an eighteen-year-old girl. I was too young and naive to understand that what we had was worth fighting for."

Chase's finger continued to trail along the back of her hand, making zigzags and curvy waves. "You were fighting for other things, like your health."

Sophie swallowed. It was true. But she'd made things so much harder on herself by pushing Chase away. He was the one person who could have made her feel whole even when her body was broken. "I said some awful things to you."

"You've already apologized for that." He looked away now, and his fingers stopped moving across her skin.

"When I was in the hospital, I told you that I never loved you. That I was only with you because we enjoyed the same things. I said you were convenient, and when you went away to college, I was planning to find someone new. I said I was going to break up with you anyway because I didn't want you to weigh me down."

Chase returned his gaze to hers. "If you're trying to refresh my memory, there's no need. I think I proved to you that my memory is good."

Sophie felt a wave of regret. "None of those things I said were true. I loved you too. I loved you too much to let you miss out on your future, which back then felt immediate. Back then, it felt like if you missed a day of anything, you missed everything. Time felt so different when we were younger. And every day after you left felt like a million at first."

Chase wrapped his fingers over hers now. "I wanted to be with you, no matter what. I still want to be with you, Sophie."

She sucked in a shuddery breath. "I know you wanted someone to go on adventures with."

Chase reached up and cradled a hand to the side of her face. "This morning has felt like the most amazing adventure I've ever had. Canoeing and watching the sunrise. Morning yoga on the riverbank and a breakfast picnic."

She smiled at him, feeling a sense of relief as she let go of the last of her reservations.

"And the day's adventures aren't over yet. We still need to go fishing, catch dinner, cook it, and eat it by candlelight."

"That sounds like quite the adventure. It also sounds very romantic," Sophie said with a lazy sigh as she leaned in closer.

He did the same until their lips were nearly touching. "Did I forget to mention the kissing? I'm looking forward to that part most of all."

"Warning," she said. "I might have coffee breath."

Chase chuckled softly and shook his head. "When are you going to stop trying to talk me out of what I want?" He tugged softly on her hand, pulling her even closer.

"Now," she said. "I'm stopping right this second."

"Good." His thumbs rubbed the back of her hand softly, sending shivers of pleasure through her body. "Because I'm about to kiss you. And it might take a while."

* * *

After a short walk along the river, they got back in the canoe and rowed to the other side. Then Chase loaded up their belongings and drove back to Dragonfly Lane. They'd already spent hours together but it was only midday.

Once they'd let Comet out and played with him for a few minutes, Chase turned to Sophie. "I need to check on the animals at the clinic. Want to come along?"

She hesitated for a moment. She'd had the best morning in a long time but her leg was aching. She'd already done a lot more than she normally would have. Part of her wanted to go anyway and pretend like she was okay. The other part wanted to make an excuse about why she needed to stay back. "Honestly, my leg is letting me know that I've reached my limits. I probably shouldn't do another lengthy walk right now."

Chase glanced down at her leg. "We can drive there," he said. "I can entertain you with my eighties rock music."

"Sounds torturous," she said. And it also sounded perfect. "I'm in."

* * *

There were only three animals staying overnight this weekend at the clinic. Chase checked on them all, spending a little extra time with Hercules, a tiny Chihuahua who'd had a bad case of parvo. He was on IV fluids and resting comfortably.

"Is he going to be okay?" Sophie asked as she rubbed a finger underneath the dog's chin.

"Oh yeah. Parvo can be deadly for dogs because of the dehydration. We caught this case early though. Hercules will be back to his feisty self by this time next week."

She nodded. "You're a good veterinarian. Thank you for your help with Comet."

"You've already thanked me, and it wasn't necessary."

Sophie seemed to have something on her mind as she continued to pet Hercules. "I'm worried about Trisha," she finally said, pulling her hand away and straightening.

Chase closed Hercules's kennel and took a seat on a nearby chair. He pulled one out for her as well, suspecting she needed to rest for a moment. The last thing he wanted to do was wear her out and make her wonder if she was holding him back in any way. He had a second chance in his sights, and he wasn't going to let it go. "She seems okay to me. It's Petey I'm worried about. He's just starting to experience the consequences of his father's actions."

Chase didn't want to let his good mood get ruined by his brother but anger festered just thinking about Pete. "It wasn't enough for Pete to rob his clients. He hurt his wife and son too."

"And you," Sophie said, laying her hand over his. "You two were best friends."

Chase nodded. "Past tense. We're not anything now."

"But maybe you should be."

Chase narrowed his eyes. "What's that supposed to mean?"

"Well, even Trisha and Petey go to visit your brother. Trisha says it's so that Petey understands where his dad is. It's helped her deal with the situation as well. She's been able to accept that the man she fell in love with isn't the same guy. It's helped her move on. Not that she's gone on any dates." Sophie sighed softly.

"She doesn't have time to date. She has Petey to think about," Chase said.

"Oh, I know. But a woman needs to think about herself too. And there's always time. She just needs to make time."

Chase guessed that was true but he felt protective of his former sister-in-law. He didn't want to see her get hurt again. "I'm not sure how seeing Pete would help me."

Sophie leaned back in the chair. "Every time his name comes up, you look like a million emotions rise to the surface. Maybe talking to him will give you some sort of peace." She shrugged. "You can't even bring yourself to open the letters he sends you."

Chase narrowed his eyes.

"Trisha told me," Sophie said. "You're carrying around a lot of festering emotion. You can't just keep that inside forever."

Chase appreciated what Sophie was trying to do. And maybe she was right. He'd been so focused on picking up the pieces after his brother left that his own heart was still fractured. "Why are you worried about Trisha?" he asked, deflecting the attention off himself and his emotions.

"I don't know. There's just something off about her lately." Sophie shook her head. "I can't put my finger on it." She looked at him as she seemed to chew on her thoughts. "She's not really one to tell you when something's wrong."

Chase couldn't help but laugh. "Yeah, I know someone else just like that."

Sophie punched him playfully. He caught her arm in midpunch and tugged her toward him, tempting her with another kiss.

"You had ideas for me," he said. "Got any good ideas about how we can help her?"

Sophie leaned into him, her body melting against his. "It's not easy being a single mom. Maybe we should offer to take Petey for a night. So she can have some time to take care of herself."

"I'm always up for more time with my nephew, although he's not exactly talking to me right now."

Sophie grimaced. "Maybe a night with him is just what the doctor ordered. Especially if his favorite 'aunt' Sophie is there," she teased.

Chase chuckled. "A night with Petey sounds like fun. It's not going to be easy for me to share you though."

"A bit greedy, are you?"

"Is that so wrong?" he asked, his voice dropping low.

She shook her head and laughed. "I feel the same way. But I really do want to do something for Trisha. I'll talk to her tomorrow and set up a time for us to take Petey."

"See? There's something else we can enjoy doing together. The list is getting longer by the minute. Before you know it, we'll be inseparable again, just like the old days."

Sophie didn't look so sure. "I don't want us to be just like the old days," she finally said.

An *uh-oh* bubbled up inside Chase's chest. He had enjoyed Sophie's company lately, and there was nothing he wanted more right now than a second chance with her. And he'd thought they were on the same page. "No?"

"No." She brushed her lips against his softly. "The old days were in our past. I just want to focus on what's ahead. Our future." Her eyes widened just a touch. "I mean, I didn't mean…"

He kissed her again. "I know exactly what you meant. And I want to focus on our future too."

Chapter Thirteen

This was the perfect end to a perfect day. Sophie melted into the crook of Chase's arm as they sat on her back porch together. They'd watched the sun rise this morning, and now they were watching it disappear behind the mountains. Even Comet was worn out and was resting at Chase's feet, snoring softly.

"So, tell me a little bit more about this backroom charity you've created," Chase said.

Sophie lifted her gaze lazily, too tired and happy to move another inch. "It's just something that kind of started over the past few months. It began with one person, and then the women's shelter sent me another. Before I knew it, I was getting referrals from the homeless shelter as well. I really enjoy helping these women find their second chances."

Chase ran his hand up and down the side of her arm, prodding her to continue talking. She never wanted to move again. Not if it meant that she would have to extract her body away from his. "I want to keep doing it. I enjoy it even more than I do working with my regular customers," she found herself saying. She hadn't even realized that detail until she said it out loud. But it was true. It was a chance for her to give back to the community that had done so much for her over the years. "I know it's just clothing but I believe it's making a real difference in these people's lives. That first impression in a job interview is real, and I'm dressing these women for success."

"I think that's amazing." Chase's voice was quiet in comparison to the springtime wildlife alive with chatter all around them. "Does it worry you at all that these people are coming from possibly dangerous situations? I mean, some of them are running from domestic violence, right? What if their significant other came to your store?"

Sophie thought about the question for a moment. It was a fair thing to ask but she'd never found herself in a situation that felt risky. She was never alone with the person, and she always locked up the front of the shop when she had someone in her back room. No one could get in without her letting them. "Trisha would never send anyone over to my boutique who would put me in danger."

"That's true," Chase agreed.

"Neither would Seymour at the homeless shelter. And since I only have women's clothes, they're only sending women. Not that women couldn't be dangerous but I can handle myself."

Chase's fingers continued to make delicious trails over her bare skin, lighting up her neural pathways. Being with Chase was its own sort of therapy.

"You've proven that to me in spades," he said. "Nadine seems nice. I think she is going to work out well at the clinic. I don't know what kind of situation she's coming out of but she seems harmless. And she really does seem to have a love for the animals."

Sophie was pleased to hear this. There was also a stirring of guilt interfering with her warm, fuzzy feelings though. Chase had assumed Nadine was a typical occupant at the women's shelter. He thought she was running from a domestic situation, which was the norm there. Sophie should've told him that Nadine had just gotten out of prison by now. Was it too late to tell him the truth? Did it even matter at this point if Nadine was happy and so was he?

"Chase?" Sophie said, lifting her head to look at him. "There's something I need to tell you about Nadine. About her past."

Chase's fingers stopped tracing patterns along her skin. "Oh?"

"She's lived through some things that would probably surprise you. And I think maybe we should talk about the circumstances that led her to the women's shelter."

Chase shook his head. "The truth is I don't want to know."

"What?" Sophie leaned up to get a better look at him.

"It's none of my business," he said. "I know that the women coming from the shelter have lived through rocky situations, including Nadine. I want to respect her privacy, and therefore, I don't want to know."

Sophie thought for a moment. Then she lowered her head back to his chest. "Fair enough." She'd tried. Granted, it'd been a weak attempt but it counted.

"So, you have a back room full of clothing," Chase said. "Is it kind of like a walk-in closet?"

Sophie laughed. "A messy one, I guess. It's more of a very large room than a closet space. I've been fantasizing about putting up commercial-quality racks and shelves for shoes. And turning it into a little boutique in its own right. I want these women to feel special when they go shopping in my back room. Even if the clothes are hand-me-downs. Part of that experience is affected by how the clothes are presented."

"If I remember correctly, you don't even know how to operate a drill," Chase commented.

"That's still true," she said. "But I can learn."

"Well, I'm sure you could. But you have a boyfriend who happens to be very handy with tools."

Sophie angled her body so that she could face him again. "Boyfriend?"

"Hopefully," he said quietly.

"I like that title on you." She tilted her head. "And you're offering to help me with my Fairy Godmother's Closet?"

"Only if you're willing to let me," he said with a growing smile.

She grinned back, a warm gooeyness spreading through her entire body. "Oh, I'll let you. I've decided that I'm done resisting you, Chase Lewis." She leaned in and gave him a soft kiss that made her yearn to keep on kissing him and never stop. "That was a thank-you kiss," she told him once she'd pulled away. "And there's more where that came from."

* * *

Watching the sunrise the next morning wasn't nearly as much fun without Sophie by his side. Still, reflecting on the memory of yesterday left Chase smiling as he sipped his cup of coffee while watching the sky from his front porch.

Some Sunday mornings, he would have already been out and have jogged several miles. This morning, however, he felt lazy in a good kind of way. And he was excited about all the prospects of the day ahead. First, he needed to go check on the animals at the clinic. After that, he fully intended to make good on his offer to Sophie. He was going to the hardware store and purchasing everything he needed to transform her boutique's back room into a place worthy of the cause she'd adopted.

Chase loved doing things for Sophie, and he loved that she was letting him. She tended to have a stubborn, independent streak. The fact that she'd so readily accepted his offer to help with the Fairy Godmother's Closet gave him hope that things would be different this time. She was done pushing him away when things got hard.

He finished off his coffee and then showered and dressed before heading to his clinic to check on his overnighters. Hercules stood at attention as he stepped into the kenneled area. Chase refreshed the food and water bowls for the animals and spent a little time petting each of them. Chase took Hercules outside to do his business and sniff around the bushes. Hercules was showing a lot more energy these days, which was a good sign that he was healing just fine.

After going back inside and administering necessary medications, Chase walked back to his office for a moment. He had a box of energy bars in his bottom drawer for occasions such as now when he'd left home without breakfast. He sat in his office chair, pulled out the bottom drawer, and reached past the pile of letters from his brother. Instead of grasping a bar, he grabbed the latest letter and stared at it for a long moment, thinking about what Sophie had said.

Maybe she was right. Maybe he was holding himself back by harboring resentment toward Pete. It was emotional baggage, and it was affecting him in more ways than he realized. Maybe the women who came to Sophie's back room weren't the only ones who deserved second chances.

He sucked in a deep breath and let it out slowly. Then he tore the top off the envelope before he could change his mind. He slid his index finger into the opening he'd created and pulled out a piece of college-ruled paper that was folded inside. What could his brother possibly say to make his crimes okay?

Dear Chase,

I'm sorry.

Love, Pete

Chase blinked past the sting in his eyes. Six words? That was all? He pulled out another letter and opened it.

Dear Chase,

I'm sorry.

Love, Pete.

Chase opened and read each letter in his drawer, one by one. They all said the same thing. There was no excuse. No begging or pleading or raging against the fact that Chase didn't come to visit. The message was simple, and yet it felt very complicated.

Chase stood and went to the bathroom to splash some cold water on his face. There was no more time to think about his brother, who hadn't thought of anyone but himself when he'd stolen people's money. It was easy to say you were sorry on a piece of paper. You could say it a million times but it wouldn't change what Pete had done to so many, including those in his own family.

Then again, maybe Sophie was right that Chase needed to get closure for himself. Maybe it was time to pay a visit to the prison and see his brother.

Chase's stomach growled loudly, reminding him of the reason he'd walked into the office to begin with. He headed back to his desk, sat down, and reached again for the box of energy bars. The box was empty.

He pulled the box out of the drawer and gazed inside just to make sure. He could have sworn he had a few more left. He didn't remember eating them, and no one else should have been in his desk. Penny rarely even came into his office. No one did. Or no one was supposed to.

His stomach clenched again. Maybe he was mistaken about having more. He put the envelopes back inside his desk for another day and headed out of his office to lock up the clinic. On an impulse, he went to check the back door. He rarely ever used it. He turned the knob, and it swung open. Unlocked. Was that just an accident? Or had someone left it open on purpose? There were only two people who could have done so. His receptionist, who he fully trusted, and Nadine, who he knew very little about.

Suspicion clenched his gut. It was probably unwarranted. His unresolved feelings for his brother really were leaking into his life, just like Sophie said. His resentment toward Pete was affecting his day-to-day in ways he didn't even realize. It was time to let that stuff go.

He locked the back door of the clinic and headed out the front as usual. Then he got into his truck and drove to the hardware store. He could hardly wait to get started on this project for Sophie. And he wasn't just going to hang some racks. He was going to completely transform the room. Being allowed to do something for her felt freeing in a way similar to being on the cliffs. Being with Sophie gave him that same adrenaline rush.

He parked at the hardware store and got out of the truck.

"Hey, Chase!"

Chase turned toward his name as Skip walked toward him.

Chase stepped over and shook his friend's hand. "What are you doing here?"

Skip walked alongside him toward the store's entrance. "I'm putting up a fence."

"Getting a dog?" Chase asked.

"Keeping out a dog, actually," Skip said. They entered the store, and Chase breathed in the scent of cement dust and tools of every kind. "What about you?" Skip asked.

"I'm hanging some racks and shelves for a friend."

Skip stopped walking and turned to face him. "Would this

friend be the one who bailed you out of jail after you threw down at my bar the other night?"

Chase lifted a hand to massage his face. "Sorry about that, man."

"I'm sure Jimmy deserved it."

Chase dropped his arm back down by his side and nodded. "Yeah, but I should be able to keep my cool better than I did." Another reason he needed to resolve things with Pete.

"Well, if you need a hand putting up those racks and shelves, I'd be more than happy to come by."

"Thanks. I might take you up on that," Chase said.

"Don't hesitate. It'd be nice to hang out awhile. We haven't been on the cliffs in a while. We're overdue," Skip said. "Nothing keeps your head on straight like clinging to the side of a mountain."

"That's true," Chase agreed. "We'll have to plan a day to do that."

Skip nodded. "Definitely."

Chase caught himself grinning. That sounded really good. Then he thought of Sophie. Would she feel bad if she knew that he wanted to go climbing? He brushed the thought away as silly. Being with her didn't mean he had to stop doing the things he loved. That was the flawed thought that had torn them apart in the first place. Well, her flawed thought. His was believing her when she'd blamed him for her accident. "Yeah, let's plan to do that," Chase agreed.

Skip offered his hand again. "Great. I'll call you this week and put the climb on our calendar. Right now, I'm going that way, and you're going that way." He pointed in the opposite direction. "So I'll see around, bro."

"Yeah. See you, buddy." Chase waved and headed toward the aisle with racks and shelving. He didn't have to give up the things he loved to be with the woman he loved. But maybe he didn't have to mention a climb to Sophie either.

* * *

After a round of yoga and dog training, Sophie drove to Trisha's house for breakfast. Trisha was making pancakes for Petey, and Sophie wanted to check on her friend. It'd been a couple of days since they'd gotten to talk without one of Trisha's residents from the shelter with her. And Sophie's gut was telling her that Trisha needed her right now.

Sophie started to put Comet in the backyard but then hesitated. "Do you feel like going for a ride?" she asked Comet, who barked excitedly. Even though he was still casted, he could walk on a leash now without her worrying that he'd reinjure himself. "It's settled, then," she told the pup. "Let's go."

Sophie loaded Comet in her car and drove to Trisha's. Petey was waiting at the front door when she arrived. As soon as he saw Comet, he started jumping up and down with childish excitement.

Maybe Sophie hadn't fully gotten a handle on the little dog yet because Comet launched his little body so hard that the leash fell out of her hand. Then Comet ran up the steps, leash dragging behind him, and propped his paws on the screen door where Petey was laughing and watching him on the other side.

Petey opened the door and scooped the little puppy into his arms. "You brought Comet!" he said excitedly. "That's better than pancakes!"

"Don't let your mom hear you say that," Sophie warned with a laugh.

"Too late." Trisha met them at the front door with an easy smile. As always, she was dressed in jeans and a T-shirt. The high-end clothing she'd worn when she'd been married to a high-profile financial tycoon was gone. "I'm glad you could tear yourself away for a morning to come see me."

Sophie rolled her eyes and followed her friend into the kitchen. "Have I been that MIA lately?"

Trisha nodded her head. "Yes, but I understand. You and Chase are destined for one another. It's just a matter of time before you're inseparable like you used to be."

"I still made time for you." Sophie sat on a barstool at the kitchen island, her leg already aching. She hadn't done enough yoga this morning. She'd been too distracted by thoughts of Chase.

"Yes, you did but I had my own person to be inseparable with back then," she said. There wasn't a trace of bitterness in her tone. She'd moved on from Pete.

Trisha brought a mixing bowl to the island to stir the batter as she talked. "Speaking of former flames, one of my housekeeping clients just realized that I was Pete's ex-wife yesterday. She followed me around the house as I cleaned, peppering me with questions. She was about as thorough as the FBI had been after they arrested Pete."

"What kinds of questions?" Sophie asked.

"Did I know? Did I suspect? Were there any signs?" Trisha shook her head like it didn't bother her. "I think the batter is ready. Do you want to do the honors at the stove, or should I?"

Sophie grimaced. "I want to earn my keep but I'm a little tired this morning."

Trisha always seemed to understand without Sophie spelling out exactly what was going on with her body. "No problem. I'll do it. Although I have a disclaimer. I can't make circle pancakes. They're always misshapen blobs. But they taste good."

"That's all that matters." Sophie watched as her friend made one pancake after another until there was a large stack on the counter beside her. Sophie could hear Petey's laughs in the living room as he played with Comet.

"Maybe you should get him a dog," Sophie suggested. "Comet will be ready to adopt soon."

Trisha shook her head. "As if I don't have enough on my plate."

"Speaking of which, Chase and I were discussing taking

Petey off your hands sometime this week and giving you a little time for yourself. What do you think?"

Trisha turned to face her now. "I think you're worried about me because my ex-husband is in prison."

Sophie offered a small grimace. "And because you're working so hard lately between your two jobs and planning the black-tie affair. Maybe go to Perfectly Pampered and get your hair done. Or treat yourself to a manicure."

"So people like yesterday's client can wonder if I'm just like Pete, and stealing their money?"

Sophie sighed. "You know most people don't think that. Everyone who knows you thinks you're a great person, Trisha. You would never steal from anyone."

Trisha offered a smile that didn't quite reach her eyes. "Let me think about your offer. Petey still isn't talking to Chase. Monday was pretty hard on him."

"All the more reason for them to spend time together."

"You're probably right." Trisha shook her head. "I'm not sure what I'd do without Petey or you though."

Sophie shrugged. "You could go out on the next Ladies' Day Out event."

"Then you'll miss it. I wouldn't want to go without you," Trisha said. "I do have a few errands I want to run on Wednesday evening without Petey tagging along," she mentioned. "And like you said, Petey and Chase need some time to work things out. You sure you don't mind?"

Sophie grinned. "I'm positive."

"Okay, then. I'll drop him off after school." Trisha brought the large stack of pancakes to the kitchen island and then reached into the fridge for syrup. "You really don't need to spend any time worrying about me though. You're getting a second chance with Chase. That's what you should be focusing on, and that's what I want to discuss this morning."

Despite her concern for Trisha, Sophie felt her cheeks warm. “All right.”

“Should we wait until after breakfast?” Trisha asked. “Because of Petey?”

“We can. Things between me and Chase are still PG though,” she said. That was always how she and Trisha discussed what happened in the bedroom. They rated their level of intimacy just like a movie.

“So you’re still just kissing?” Trisha asked, looking a little surprised.

“We’re taking things slow,” Sophie said. “Fast is overrated.”

“And you have all the time in the world,” Trisha agreed, sliding a stack of pancakes in front of her. “Because this time you’re not going to make the mistake of pushing him away. Which means this time you two are going to get the happily ever after you should have gotten a long time ago.”

Sophie swallowed. That’s what she was hoping for. And terrified of.

Petey ran up to the island and peered at his plate. “Whoa! Can Comet get a stack too?” he asked.

“No,” Trisha said. “Pancakes are for little boys.”

“And moms and aunts?” Petey asked.

Sophie laughed. She loved it when Petey adopted her as his aunt.

“Yes,” Trisha agreed.

They ate and laughed, and Sophie’s worry about her best friend dissipated a little bit. Trisha was tough. She’d get through whatever life threw in her direction. That’s who she was.

Sophie’s phone buzzed in her pocket as they cleaned up their plates. She pulled it out and grinned.

Trisha eyed her. “What’s my dear ex-brother-in-law saying? Is it appropriate for little ears?”

Sophie laughed. “He wants me to meet him at my boutique. He has a surprise for me.”

Chapter Fourteen

Chase was waiting by the back door of Sophie's Boutique when she walked his way with Comet at her feet. Her hair was pulled back in a ponytail, and she looked like she was ready to go on a morning run.

"Okay, I'm here for my surprise," she said with an easy smile.

"I thought you were here for me." He winked at her and then dipped to brush his lips against hers.

As he pulled away, Sophie playfully reached her hands into his pockets. "Where are you hiding it?"

Chase chuckled softly. "Your surprise is too big to fit inside my pocket."

She tipped her head back and looked at him. "And why did we need to meet at my boutique?"

"Because I didn't have a key to get in." Chase gestured at the boards, shelving racks, and other supplies he'd purchased from the hardware store. He hadn't known exactly how much he needed so he'd gotten enough to get started. He could always return to the store and purchase more later.

"What's that?" She took a few steps and then gasped before whirling back to face him. "Is that what I think it is?"

"I told you I wanted to help you transform your back room into something special. I meant it."

Her lips parted. "That was less than twenty-four hours ago. I didn't really think you'd make time for this so quickly."

"I'd do anything for you, Sophie. Haven't you figured that out yet?" He walked over and picked up the bags. "So, if you'll let me in, I'll go ahead and get started on this today."

Sophie unlocked the back door and then turned to grab one of the bags he hadn't gotten.

"Leave that there. I got it," he called behind him, remembering her limp. He didn't want to make it worse by asking her to carry heavy bags.

Stubborn that she was though, she followed behind him carrying a bag in one hand and holding Comet's leash in another.

Chase quickly grabbed the bag after freeing up his arms. "I don't want Comet to trip you."

"That's a good possibility." She shortened the leash the way Chase had taught her. "I might need a few more training sessions with you. Unless I've maxed out my favor card."

"Not possible," Chase said, enjoying the easiness of their conversation. He finished carrying all the supplies into the back room and visually assessed the space.

"What are you thinking?" she asked, a nervous edge to her voice.

"It's much bigger than I realized."

She nodded. "I know. This is where I usually keep new shipments. I was going to put a small kitchen back here since I practically live here some days. But the Sweetwater Café is right down the street. I usually run over there if I'm hungry."

"So a wall of shoes over there?" He pointed to the far wall. "And two walls with racks for hanging clothing?" He gestured at the walls running parallel to where they were standing.

"Yes. That's exactly what I was envisioning."

"Now the most important question. I purchased yellow but if you'd rather have a different color, I can go right back to the store."

"Yellow?" Sophie's mouth fell open. "You're going to paint the walls too?"

"You want these women to feel special, right? The employee in the paint section said yellow is fresh and inviting. It's a spring color," he said.

Sophie placed her hand on her chest. "Yellow is perfect."

Chase held out his arms. "That's all I need. Now you can return to your regularly scheduled Sunday."

"You don't want me to stay and help?" she asked, looking a little disappointed.

He really didn't want to cause undue stress on her body. He still didn't know exactly what her limitations were, and he was afraid to ask. "How can I surprise you if you're right here doing all the work?"

She seemed to accept that answer.

"Besides, I have reinforcements coming."

Sophie's eyes widened. "You do? Who?"

"I ran into Skip at the hardware store. He offered to swing by. Luke Marini has the day off from the fire department. He might come too."

The excited look in Sophie's eyes was addictive. "And I'm just supposed to leave and let you do all the work?"

"That's the plan."

He saw the moment when she relinquished her control and agreed. Her whole body relaxed as she smiled back at him. "Okay, then. I promised to take Comet over to my parents' house this weekend anyway. My mom has already grown quite fond of this little guy. She's calling him her grandpup, even though I've made sure she knows I'm only fostering him."

"Comet knows how to charm the ladies."

"And the kids," Sophie said. "Little Petey loves him."

Chase's gaze moved to Comet, who'd been exploring the room. "Oh no."

"What?" Sophie followed his gaze and then quickly moved to retrieve the puppy, who'd found a pair of nice shoes to chew on. "That's not charming."

She laughed as she stepped forward with Comet in her arms. She went up on her toes for a moment and kissed him. "Thank you for this, Chase. I can't wait to see the finished product."

"You're welcome. Enjoy your Sunday."

She held the leash and put Comet down in front of her. The little dog tugged forward, yanking her arm.

"How about I meet you here tomorrow before work for the unveiling?" Chase asked.

"I'll bring breakfast," she said.

"Sounds perfect. I'll look forward to it."

Chase worked for several hours, with the help of Skip, Luke, and Mitch Hargrove, who also had the day off from the local police department.

"I feel a little weird around so many pieces of women's clothing," Luke joked. "There's not one masculine thing in this place."

The guys laughed.

"I'm secure in my manhood," Skip countered.

"I'm the fire chief. That's a manly job, right?" Luke asked.

Mitch chuckled. "I hear Eve McConnell is aiming for your job one of these days," he teased.

Luke turned to Chase. "What about you? It's weird to be in a women's boutique, right?"

Chase shook his head. "I'm thrilled to be here, actually. How about this? We can counter all this feminine stuff with a day out in the woods. Skip and I were already talking about going on a climb. We're planning to invite Jack and Alex too. Are you in?"

Luke grinned. "Now you're talking."

"Great. How about two weekends from now?" Chase proposed. He was already scheming on something for next weekend. Maybe it was too soon to go on a weekend getaway with Sophie but she'd always loved his family's cabin. She and Chase used to go there with their friends once upon a time. It was peaceful, and while there was a lot of physical activity to be had, it was also conducive to rest and relaxation. And romance.

"Two weekends from now sounds good to me," Luke said.

Chase adjusted his tool belt. "But first, we finish this job for Sophie."

Luke and Skip looked at each other.

"What?" Chase asked.

"Nothing. It's just your turn," Skip said on a low laugh.

Chase shook his head, not following along. "Turn for what?"

"Turn for love," Luke said. "It's been contagious around here. Me and Brenna, Mitch and Kaitlyn, Alex and Halona. Now you and Sophie are an item again. Next thing we know, Skip here will be asking us to help him impress the woman he loves."

Skip put his hands up. "Leave me out of this, okay? We're harassing Chase right now."

Chase picked up a paintbrush and returned to coating the walls. He wasn't going to deny anything. "Harass me all you want. I don't mind as long as you're working." Because he had a woman to impress and he couldn't wait to see that excited look in her eyes again.

* * *

"He's a squirrelly little thing, isn't he?" Sophie's mom said as she sat on her living room floor playing with Comet.

Sophie sat on their couch, watching the seemingly tireless puppy launch himself at the small dog toy her parents had gotten him. This was a great way to spend the afternoon if she couldn't be with Chase. "Chase has given me a few pointers on training him. I'm not sure I've been the best foster pet owner so far."

"Well, I'm guessing it's because you've been a little distracted." Her mom looked up now.

Sophie's dad was snoring softly on the recliner in the corner of the room.

Sophie understood that her mom was talking about Chase. "Maybe a little."

Her mom stopped shaking the dog toy, and Comet proceeded to chew on her finger. "I remember the first time you and Chase fell in love. Suddenly my daughter was MIA for everything but him. You two were inseparable."

Sophie wanted to think back on those days with a smile but it was hard considering the way things had ended. She shifted and uncrossed her legs. Her left one still got stiff if she crossed them for too long. She needed to get up and move.

"I'm glad you're back together."

"Me too." Sophie stood and Comet dashed toward her, throwing her slightly off balance.

"Chase is good for you. The dog, on the other hand, is a fall risk. Don't let my new grandpup knock you down."

Sophie decided not to tell her mom for the millionth time that Comet wasn't hers to keep. She'd stopped telling herself that so often too. The idea that maybe she'd keep Comet was starting to set in. She couldn't imagine not having him with her in the mornings when she awoke. Or during the evenings when she got home from work.

"Next time, bring Chase over here for dinner," her mom suggested. "It's time to catch up with him."

Sophie glanced at her sleeping dad. "Will Dad promise not to interrogate him the way he did in high school?"

"No," her father barked from the other side of the room. Then he cracked open his eyes and looked at them. "I'm listening even when I'm sleeping."

Sophie's mom waved a hand at him. "He's harmless. Bring Chase next time."

Sophie nodded. "I will." Then she hugged her mom and stepped over to her father. "I'm going to give you a kiss even though you're sleeping."

He opened his eyes fully. "I always liked Chase," he said. "No one is worthy of my daughter but he comes close. Maybe try to keep him around this time."

Sophie leaned in and kissed her dad's cheek. "I'll see what I can do, Dad."

After leaving her parents' house, she drove back home and wondered if Chase was still working at her boutique. She was tempted to stop in and check but they'd already planned to meet tomorrow morning. She didn't want to ruin the surprise.

Instead, she turned onto Dragonfly Lane and slowed as she approached her driveway. Chase's truck was parked in front of her garage. He was leaning against it.

She parked and got out stiffly. "What are you doing here?"

"We finished, and I didn't want to go home without seeing you." He walked over to her and leaned in. Then they were kissing against her car.

"The neighbors might start talking," Sophie said. "They probably already are."

"Want me to leave?"

She shook her head. "No. I want you to come inside. And stay awhile."

"I like the sound of that."

Chase followed her in, holding Comet's leash. Sophie turned

to face him, deciding whether to offer him something to eat or drink. Or if she should just step into him and do what she really wanted. She wanted to pick up where they'd left off outside, and possibly keep going.

Was it too soon to make love? Chase was her first. And she wanted him to be her last.

While she was deciphering her feelings, she drew closer and tipped her head back to look into his eyes. There was no question what she wanted when she looked at him. Everything she ever wanted was right here within her reach. All she had to do was grab it.

Reaching for him, she went up on her toes and pressed her mouth to his. She was agreeing to a kiss but her hand took his and gave a gentle tug toward her bedroom.

Chase narrowed his eyes. "Are you sure this is what you want?"

"I'm sure," she said with a growing smile. Then she tugged again and led him to her bedroom, foregoing the lights so that, when the clothes came off, her scars would stay hidden.

* * *

Chase stirred in bed beside Sophie. His phone was buzzing on her bedside table.

Realization settled in around him about what had happened last night. They'd come to her bed together, and it had been one of the best nights of his life. Better than before. Better than ever.

He reached for his phone and noticed the emergency number from the clinic that paged him when someone was calling after hours. Not wanting to wake Sophie, he slipped out of bed and quickly stepped into the kitchen to listen to the voicemail. One of his patients, a large Saint Bernard that belonged to Julia Reynolds, was throwing up uncontrollably.

Chase sighed. He called Julia back and told her he was heading to the clinic right away. Then he quietly retrieved his discarded clothes from last night, dressed, and watched Sophie for just a moment as she slept. She looked so peaceful, and he wanted nothing more than to climb back into bed with her and sleep well past sunrise.

But duty called. He headed to the kitchen, texting Sophie a message on his phone. She'd get it when she woke up alone.

Regret settled over him. It couldn't be helped though. He was the only veterinarian in town. Perhaps it was time to fix that. If he and Sophie were going to get serious again, he wouldn't be able to go to the clinic for every emergency visit. He'd want to wake up with the woman he loved.

He chewed on that thought as he drove through the early morning darkness. Then he pulled into his lot. Julia's car wasn't here yet. That would give him time to turn on the lights and make the clinic more welcoming.

He headed around to the back of the clinic, remembering how the door had been unlocked before. Sure enough, it was unlocked again, which meant it was more than a onetime mistake. He pushed the door open and reached for the light switch beside him. "Hello?" he called.

The sounds of animals stirring met his greeting. Lula, a feisty orange tabby cat, meowed loudly back at him. He wished she could talk and tell him what was happening after hours.

Chase shut the door behind him, locking it this time. "Hello?" he called again as he walked toward the front entrance to flip the lights for his incoming emergency patient. There was no sign of anyone else but his gut told him that something was amiss. Before he could investigate any further, he saw Julia and her Saint Bernard coming toward the door. Chase opened it for them, already noticing that Harry was dry heaving as he was pulled along.

"Sorry to pull you out of bed," Julia said with an apologetic grimace. "I just didn't know what to do. Harry has been vomiting for hours."

"I don't mind," Chase said. Although he did regret leaving Sophie behind in bed. "My patients come first. Let's get Harry into an examining room and see what's going on."

By six o'clock that morning, Chase was once again alone in his clinic except for the animals that were staying overnight, which now included Harry. He'd sent Julia home to no doubt return to sleep while he waited to open the clinic for the day.

Chase went to his desk to grab an energy bar before realizing that he'd never purchased another box. His back door was being left unlocked, and his energy bars were missing. Was anything else missing?

He kept money at the front reception desk. He walked quickly there to check. He would have no idea how much should be there but some amount of cash should be on hand. He used the key to open the drawer and saw a good supply of dollar bills and change. Next, he checked the medicine cabinets in each of his examining rooms. There was a small supply of antibiotics and anesthetic that might be of interest to someone. The cabinets were all locked. He used his key and opened them to find everything in place.

Blowing out a breath, he headed back to the front of the clinic and took a visual assessment of the waiting room. Everything seemed okay. There wasn't much to take, though, except a few old magazines and books for patients to peruse while they waited. Maybe he was imagining things.

His phone buzzed in his pocket.

> You weren't here, and I thought last night was all a dream when I woke up.

A surge of heat shot through him. Not a dream, he texted in response. Are we still on for meeting at your boutique?

Definitely. I can't wait!

Chase grinned to himself as he leaned against the front counter and texted back. I know you offered but I've got time to spare. I'll bring the coffee and Danishes.

Perfect!

He headed out the back door, locking it behind him and double-checking this time. Perhaps the lock was faulty. That was really the only explanation he could think of. A veterinary clinic wasn't really a hot target for criminals. No, Chase knew from experience that criminals, like his brother, Pete, wanted more than energy bars. They would take everything if you let them. Which was why Chase didn't deal with criminals. Not even the ones in his own family.

Chapter Fifteen

Sophie had her eyes closed as she tipped her face to the rising sun outside her boutique. She'd already dropped Comet off at the veterinary clinic with Penny. Chase wasn't there because he was meeting her here first thing this morning.

Excitement bubbled up inside her. She couldn't wait to see what he'd done to her Fairy Godmother's Closet. She refused to go in until Chase got here though. She didn't even want to smell the fresh paint without him being right next to her. If she unlocked the door, she might not be able to control her impulse to run to the back room and check out the transformation.

"You waited," Chase said, walking up holding a drink carrier with two coffees and a bag of what she presumed were Danishes.

He reached out a hand to help her stand up from the bench she was seated on outside the shop. She looked between him and the food, her belly rumbling softly when she caught the sweet aroma. "Mm. I love you for this." Her heart jumped up into her throat when she realized what she'd said. "I mean…" She felt the blood drain from her face. It wasn't like she'd never told him she loved him before but not in a very long time.

"I know what you mean." He bent and kissed her mouth. "Ready to go inside?"

She nodded. It was just a back room but it meant so much to her. "I have a new client coming in today from the shelter. She'll be the first to experience the new room." She turned the key and pushed the front entrance open. Then she looked back at him.

"Well, go ahead," he said. "I'm right behind you."

She nodded and started walking quickly but then stopped as one of her muscles contracted tightly in her leg.

"You okay?" Chase asked.

She took a moment. "I'm...fine." She took a deep breath and then pulled away. "Okay, back to racing through the store." She walked more slowly this time until she was standing in the doorway of the back room.

Tears sprung to her eyes. The pale-yellow walls were fresh and cheery with the trim painted a new coat of white. There were racks lining the two long walls. The far back wall had a bench on one side and a floor-to-ceiling shelving system for shoes on the other. Sophie took a step inside, taking it all in. She didn't say anything for a long moment.

She looked up at the overhead lighting. Even that was different. The bulb was now encased in a small stained-glass covering with a dragonfly design. "Oh, wow. That's so beautiful."

"It reminded me of you on Dragonfly Lane."

"Dragonflies stand for change. It's symbolic," Sophie said, swiping a finger under her eye. She loved dragonflies for that reason.

"Do you like it?" he asked, a nervous edge to his voice. "I can change it if you don't. We can choose a new color of paint. The bench was donated from my mom. She was going to get rid of it, and when I told her what I was doing in here yesterday, she brought it by. We can reupholster it or give it away if you don't like it. It's up to you."

Sophie turned to face him and shook her head. "Don't you dare change a thing. This is absolutely perfect. Thank you." A tear slid down her cheek now.

This time he lifted a finger to swipe it away. "You're welcome."

"I love you for this," she said again.

Chase's eyes widened softly. "Don't worry. I know what you mean."

"No, I don't think you do. I meant it exactly how it sounded. I love you."

Chase's eyes narrowed. "That's a good thing because I love you back. I don't think I ever stopped."

She went up on her toes, not worrying if her muscles would rebel against the early morning stiffness. Chase would be there to catch her if she needed him to, and there was nothing weak about leaning on him for help.

When she returned to flat feet, she gestured toward one of the coffees. "After last night, I need that."

"Up late?" he asked innocently, as if he weren't the reason why.

"Mm-hmm. And I might be up late again tonight." She gave him a conspiratorial glance.

He kissed her forehead and then stepped away. "I'll look forward to it. I have a patient first thing so I need to head back to my clinic."

"Tell Nadine hello for me," Sophie said easily.

Chase's smile fell just a touch, which made Sophie wonder if something wasn't working out. "I will," he said before waving. "See you tonight when you pick up Comet."

Sophie nodded. He'd probably come inside for a little while too.

Chase seemed to hesitate before leaving. "I need to ask you something."

Sophie was willing to say yes to practically anything right now. "Okay."

He suddenly looked nervous. "I want to make the world disappear and for it to just be you and me for a weekend. Remember my family's cabin?"

"How could I forget?" she said, feeling herself blush. That's where so many firsts had happened for her and Chase. The first time he'd told her he loved her. The first time she'd fallen asleep in his arms.

"Let's go this weekend. I can call in a favor from one of the nearby vets to be on call. And Nadine can feed and water the overnight animals."

"A weekend getaway?" she asked. Last night was the first time Chase had stayed over. Were they taking things too fast? It didn't feel rushed though. Instead, the idea excited her.

"Yeah. Just the two of us. What do you say?" he asked.

"I say yes."

* * *

The next morning, Chase stopped at the Sweetwater Café prior to work. He'd had a craving for something sweet. If he'd woken with Sophie next to him, that craving could have easily been filled with her. He'd been careful not to overstay his welcome though.

Chase stepped up to the café's counter and glanced over at the display of treats. Then he surprised himself by asking for two Danishes instead of one.

"Oh?" Emma gave him a curious look across the counter. "Someone's buying another sweet treat for the woman in their life."

Chase laughed. "It's not for Sophie this time."

Emma looked disappointed. "I thought you two were back together. Everyone's been talking about it."

"I'm not surprised about that. But no need to worry. Sophie and I are doing amazing. We're actually going away together this weekend." Chase regretted saying so as soon as the words came out. He held up a hand. "That's just between you and me," he said, hoping Emma would understand.

"Of course." She pretended to zip her lips. "I listen to the hearsay but I don't spread it around. It's bad for business."

Chase chuckled. "The second Danish is for my new veterinary assistant. To show my appreciation for her." And because he felt a little guilty about his suspicions regarding her over the last couple of days. The only oddities at the clinic were missing energy bars, which he could've eaten himself without realizing, and his back door being left unlocked. That could've been an honest mistake by either Nadine or Penny. Or even him.

Emma grabbed some tongs and picked out the two prime Danishes in the display cabinet. "Aw. Well, she's lucky to have you as a boss."

"Thanks." Chase also ordered a coffee for himself, paid, and walked out of the café toward his clinic, passing Sophie's Boutique on the way to Blossom Street. For the past few months, this was the extent of him seeing Sophie every day. Some days she'd waved at him, and that was enough.

He didn't see her at the counter this morning as he continued walking. It was still early though, and the boutique wasn't open yet.

A few minutes later, he walked through the front door of the clinic and headed around back to see if the door was locked. Once again, he twisted the knob, and the door swung open. No key necessary.

"Good morning, Dr. Lewis," Nadine said, startling him and nearly making him drop his coffee.

"Nadine. You're here early."

She smiled back at him as if arriving an hour before her shift was nothing. "I woke up thinking about the animals. I could hardly wait to get here."

Chase's gut was firing its alarms again. Nadine was a nice woman though. There was no reason to think otherwise. "I remember those days. It means you're where you're supposed to be."

Nadine's smile dropped. "You said you remember those days as if you're not excited to get up and come here anymore."

Chase waved a hand, holding the bag of Danishes in his opposite hand. "It's not that. I think I just need a break from this place. I haven't been able to get away much since I took over ownership." But that was all about to change. He was leaving Sweetwater Springs this coming weekend.

Chase reached inside the paper bag and pulled out his Danish, noting how Nadine's eyes lit up. Then he handed the bag with the second Danish to her.

"What's this?" she asked, her mouth falling open in surprise.

"It's for you. If you're hungry." He shrugged. "I just thought I'd bring it in and save it for you. I had no idea you'd already be here and working."

Nadine looked touched. And kind of hungry. "I actually didn't have breakfast before I headed out this morning. So this is a wonderful surprise. Thank you."

"You're welcome." Chase started to step away but then turned. "How did you get in the clinic? You don't have a key, do you?"

Nadine looked a little taken aback. "Penny gave me a key."

"Oh." Chase hadn't been aware of that. He guessed that made sense for Nadine to have access to the animals. And if she was going to help out over the upcoming weekend, she'd need one anyway. "Well, it certainly worked out well this morning. I'm sure these guys were happy to see you." He gestured to the overnight patients.

"They were. And I was thrilled to see them too." Nadine held up the bag. "If you don't mind, I'm going to eat this right now."

Chase nodded. "I'm going back to my office and eating mine as well." Then he planned to contact Jason at the clinic in Whispering Pines to see if he was willing to cover any emergencies that came up this weekend.

After eating his Danish, he dialed Jason's number and waited for his friend and colleague to answer. It went straight to voicemail. Chase left a brief message and then considered what he'd do if Jason wasn't available. The clinic in Whispering Pines had three veterinarians. Surely one of them wouldn't mind coming in for emergencies only.

Chase had spoiled his clients a little, coming in for things that could wait until Monday. But the fill-in's criteria would be more restrictive. They'd make it work. All Chase was asking for was forty-eight hours with the woman he loved.

* * *

On Wednesday after work, Sophie picked Comet up from the clinic and drove home to prepare for Petey's visit tonight. Sophie was glad that Trisha had agreed to the visit. Sophie took Petey once a month and Janet helped out too but a single mom who worked two jobs could never get too much help.

Trisha was only running errands tonight but at least she was on her own for a couple of hours. Who knew? Maybe Trisha would meet a guy tonight, sparks would fly, and she'd find herself just as happy as Sophie was lately.

Sophie smiled to herself as she topped off Comet's water bowl and gave him some extra love. "You have a friend coming over this afternoon," she said. She was pretty sure that Comet had no idea what she was saying but he seemed pretty excited at the tone of her voice. He lapped up some water and then danced around her feet for a few moments. "Want to go outside?" she asked.

Comet immediately headed toward the back door. *Such a smart dog.*

She let him out and then turned toward the sound of her doorbell. Chase was coming over right after work, which would be anytime now. She hoped he got here first because she wouldn't mind sneaking in a few kisses before they had a tiny audience with them.

She opened the door and felt a soft zing in her chest. That zing was love. "Petey isn't here yet."

They shared a look that said Chase had been hoping that was the case. He stepped inside, closed the door behind him, and pulled her into his arms. One kiss is all they got in before the doorbell rang again.

Sophie looked up at Chase, who now looked like he was going into battle. She placed a hand on his arm. "He's a seven-year-old boy. He'll come around."

Chase nodded but he didn't look convinced. His relationship with Petey meant a lot to him. So it also meant a lot to Sophie. And before the night was over, she was determined to help her two favorite guys reconnect.

She opened the door and welcomed Trisha and Petey inside.

"I have my cell phone on me, of course," Trisha said. "I won't be far. If you need anything at all, just call. I can be back in five minutes."

Sophie pointed to the door again. "You have to stay gone for at least two hours. That's my condition. We'll be fine." She hugged Petey into her side. "Right, Petey?"

The boy glanced over at Chase with a glum expression. "I guess."

Sophie offered Trisha a reassuring smile. She knew Trisha wasn't worried about her babysitting ability. Petey was just having a hard time these days. Trisha was more likely concerned about his behavior tonight. "I'll call if we need you," Sophie relented. "I promise."

Trisha looked at Chase now, her expression clearly reading *Good luck.* Then she waved and headed back out the door.

"All right." Sophie turned to look between Petey and Chase. "You're stuck with us for two hours. We're going to have so much fun."

Petey didn't smile. Instead, he looked around. "Where's Comet?"

Sophie couldn't help but laugh. "He's in the backyard. I'm sure he'll be very happy to see you. Why don't you bring him in?" She watched Petey head toward the back door, and then she looked at Chase. "Maybe you should play with him and Comet. Petey adores that dog, and deep down, he adores you too."

Chase's gaze followed after Petey. "Think so?"

"I know so. I'll be here cooking for a little while. And also preparing dessert for later. Trust me—Petey is going to be smiling by the time Trisha picks him up tonight." She nudged Chase softly. "And you will too."

The back door opened, and Petey came running in with Comet.

"You two can play in the living room," Sophie told Petey. Then she turned to Chase and lowered her voice. "I'm guessing you have dog treats in your pockets."

"How is it you know me so well?" he asked.

She shrugged one shoulder. She did know him. For the most part, Chase was the same guy he'd always been, only amplified. He was smarter, stronger, funnier. She'd like to think that she had more of the qualities that had made him fall for her in the first place too but somehow she doubted it.

She took in a breath as a bit of fear and insecurity took root. Then she reminded herself that Chase was here because he wanted to be. And he'd invited her on a weekend getaway.

The connection was still there between them, perhaps stronger than ever.

Turning to the oven, she twisted the dial to 350 degrees. Then she got started preparing her Easy Cheesy Enchiladas. She wasn't a fancy cook by any means but she had a few simple recipes in her back pocket that guests always loved. Her recipe for three-cheese enchiladas was quick and would leave her plenty of time to spend with Chase and Petey.

She looked up, hearing Petey's laughter as Chase taught him how to make Comet sit, lie down, and roll over just like he'd done for Sophie. Petey was warming back up to Chase. No one could resist a puppy or Chase. Sophie certainly couldn't, at least.

And now she would be spending an entire weekend with the man, secluded and without interruptions in a cabin far away. They'd either come out on the other side more in love than ever, or they'd realize that too much had changed between them after all.

Chapter Sixteen

The drive to the family cabin was only an hour. It was a small getaway but it would be nice to block out the rest of the world and have Sophie all to himself. Chase wanted her to have a good time. It was supposed to be relaxing and a chance for them to bask in their second chance.

"I hope my boutique isn't too swamped this weekend."

"It's only forty-eight hours. I'm sure your mom can handle things," Chase said.

Sophie glanced across the seat. "You're not seriously going to try to tell me that you're not worried about your animals?"

Chase laughed. "My animals are in good hands with Jason." Chase reached across the seat for her hand. "It's just us. No one else."

She placed her other hand over his. "And that's what I'm most excited about. Forty-eight hours of uninterrupted Chase Lewis. And a hot tub. Let's not forget that."

His blood rushed at the thought of seeing Sophie in a bathing suit and pulling her close underneath mounds of foamy bubbles.

Maybe they should just spend the entire weekend in that one spot. He had other things on his agenda too though. He'd packed his climbing gear, and he was hoping to convince Sophie to take a chance with him. If the mayor of Sweetwater Springs, who was in a wheelchair, could climb, so could Sophie. Her arms and body were strong. It was just her left leg that was weak.

He paused at a stop sign and turned left, heading down a gravel road that suggested that they really were about to venture completely off the grid. He slowed at the end of the dead-end road, in front of a small log cabin with stained glass windows and a natural fence of tall pines, closing off the area and adding to its privacy.

"It's exactly the way I remember it," Sophie marveled, pushing her truck door open as soon as he'd parked. He couldn't admire the house because he was too busy watching her take it all in. Her smile made him feel something deep inside his heart. He didn't want it to disappear. He wanted to see that look on her face all weekend. Suddenly, that was his main mission for the next forty-eight hours.

He got out and lifted the bags from the trunk. "Ready to go inside?"

"Oh yeah," she said, practically skipping ahead like an excited child.

He laughed as he followed her up the porch steps and fumbled for the keys. He opened the door to a small, two-bedroom cabin with only the necessities inside. Well, except for the large Jacuzzi, which sat in the sunroom. That wasn't essential but it would be enjoyable. "This is called camping in style."

"Otherwise known as glamping." Sophie veered toward one of the bedrooms and stopped in front of a queen-size bed. She tossed a sexy look over her shoulder. "I know it's still daylight but I can't wait to turn in tonight." Something in her eyes told him she wasn't talking about sleeping.

His mind was no longer on the hot tub or the possibility of a climb. In fact, if he had it his way, they'd spend all afternoon in this bed. He'd noticed that Sophie didn't feel comfortable getting undressed without the cover of darkness. They were still getting reacquainted with each other though. Hopefully, this weekend would draw them closer.

* * *

"It's still early. Want to go for a walk?" Sophie asked after they'd settled in.

Chase tried to keep his poker face. "Are you sure you're up for a little physical activity?"

"Definitely. My leg isn't giving me any problems today."

Chase nodded, looking for the right way to broach what he felt might be a sensitive subject. "How about a, um, climb?"

Sophie's green eyes narrowed. "What?"

He cleared his throat, which had gone dry in a heartbeat. "I brought gear for two. Just in case."

"But I don't climb anymore," she said, her tone stiff.

Chase reached out for her hand, taking it in his. "Maybe you haven't climbed in a while but it's just like riding a bike. And I'll be right there with you. It's mostly mind over arms, remember? We can do a simple climb and stop as soon as you say the word."

Sophie looked absolutely horrified by the idea. "No," she said, shaking her head, eyes wide and skin suddenly pale. He thought he saw a tremor of fear run over her body. "Chase, I can't do that anymore."

Her eyes were suddenly shiny. This was not the reaction he'd intended. The last thing he'd ever want to do would be to make Sophie upset to the point of tears. He'd really just wanted to encourage her and show her that nothing should hold her back from what she wanted to do. She'd told him she still had dreams about being on the cliffs. He'd thought this would be a good idea.

"It's okay. It doesn't matter to me. I just thought it might make you happy. That's what this weekend is about—making you smile."

"Really? You're not disappointed?"

"No. Of course not." Chase reached out a hand to touch her cheek.

"Because you can go out without me if you want," she said.

Chase shook his head, dropping his hand to her arm. "I'm not leaving your side all weekend. You're stuck with me."

This made her smile. The blood had returned to her face, and she seemed to relax.

"How about we take that walk?" he asked, hoping the fresh air and exercise would completely remove what felt like the equivalent of putting his foot in his mouth. She wasn't ready to climb, and she might never be.

She cocked her head to one side as she looked at him. "The hot tub will feel so much better after a little physical activity. Then maybe we could enjoy a glass of wine too. Then..."

Chase swallowed as she trailed off and his imagination supplied the rest.

"You had me at hot tub and wine."

Sophie reached into her overnight bag and pulled out a pair of sneakers. "It's a beautiful day outside," she said. "I kind of wish Comet were here."

"Comet is fine. He's being spoiled by Petey right about now." Trisha had offered to take the dog for the weekend, hoping to give her son his dog fix without actually adopting one.

"I hate to add more work to Trisha's plate," Sophie said as she pulled on her shoes. Then they headed out of the cabin and into the sunshine along a trail just wide enough to walk hand in hand.

"I'm sure Trisha is happy to help. Comet is probably a good babysitter. I gave Petey a kid's book on training dogs. That'll keep him busy for hours while Trisha relaxes."

"That's true." Sophie glanced over as they walked. "I'm glad you and Petey are talking again. Everything's okay between you?"

Chase nodded. "Kids are so forgiving. I messed up big-time. At his age, being embarrassed in front of your entire class by your uncle probably feels like a disaster." Chase glanced over. "But the other night was good for us. Once I sat down with Petey and told him I wasn't perfect and that I was sorry, he forgave me." Chase shrugged. "It didn't hurt that I told him I was sticking up for his mom either. That actually kind of made me a hero in his eyes."

"You are a hero," Sophie said.

Chase slowed his pace and narrowed his eyes. "Me?"

"You dropped everything and moved back to Sweetwater Springs after Pete was arrested. That's heroic. You help Trisha with Petey, and you're there to give him a male role model. A lot of guys wouldn't care about that."

Chase wouldn't have it any other way. He knew how it felt to grow up without a dad.

"After I hit Comet on the street, you came to my rescue."

"Just being a good vet," he said.

She tugged his arm, making him look at her. "You're a good guy. And I know that your attempt to get me to go climbing with you was because you wanted to help me. And I appreciate it." She offered a small smile that made his heart squeeze. "You're definitely my hero."

"Thanks. I could say the same about you."

Sophie pretended to be insulted. "I would be a heroine, not a hero."

"I stand corrected. I really do admire what you're doing with your Fairy Godmother's Closet. Heroine material for sure."

She blushed softly. "A heroine wouldn't let her fears stand in the way of a little climb."

He tugged her hand this time. "Everyone's afraid of something. Even Superman has his kryptonite."

Sophie gave him a long look. "And you?"

Chase cleared his throat. "A lot of things. I was pretty scared that Petey would never speak to me again." Chase looked out at the cascade of trees ahead of him. "I guess I'm afraid of letting someone I love down again."

Sophie stopped walking and turned to him.

Chase really didn't want to get into a discussion about their past though. Instead, he wanted to focus on the moment they were in. "You're beautiful," he said, reaching out to sweep a lock of her hair out of her face.

She tilted her head like she always did as she looked at him. "I'm already a sure thing, Dr. Lewis. You don't have to sweet-talk me."

"Just telling the truth." He bent down and kissed her, unable to resist even a second longer. Then he pulled back and blew out a breath. Chase turned and ran his gaze over the rolling mountains. Then they continued walking. He was used to the valley but at this elevation, he had to take in deeper breaths.

Sophie stopped every few feet to admire the wildflowers. It was warm outside but she still wore long pants. "I wish Halona could see these flowers," she said.

"Maybe you can take a picture of the flowers with your phone and text them to her. See if she can name them," he suggested.

"That's a great idea." Sophie pulled her cell phone out of her pocket. She snapped a few pictures and then stepped off the path to get a few more. As she gazed at the skyline, Chase took a few pictures on his phone as well. His focus was on Sophie though. He took several of her hair blowing in the wind as she dipped to pick a bouquet. Just like the day they'd chased the sunrise and gone canoeing, they were on an adventure.

"I don't have reception out here," Sophie said a few minutes later. "I'll just send them to Halona when we get back to the cabin. Hopefully the reception is better there."

"Or you can quiz her when we return to Sweetwater Springs," Chase suggested.

Sophie cocked her head to one side, her hair spilling across her cheek. "You just want my undivided attention. That's what I think."

"Guilty."

She laughed easily and then stepped toward him, wrapping her arms around his neck. He kissed her again, savoring the softness and the sweetness.

* * *

By the time she and Chase returned to the cabin, Sophie had started itching. She bent, pulled up her pants leg slightly, and clawed at the skin around the edge of her sock. Just a few inches higher and her scars would be visible.

"What did you get into out there?" Chase asked. He stepped over to her and inspected her skin more closely. "That's not good."

She was afraid he was right.

"I'm not a human doctor by any means. My specialty is animals. But I think that's poison ivy."

Sophie knew he was right. She followed him inside and immediately went to wash off her leg. Not that she thought that would help. The damage was already done. She just hoped it didn't ruin her getaway weekend with Chase.

* * *

Two hours later, Sophie lay back on the couch with her head on Chase's lap. "I don't know when I've been this miserable. Maybe the chicken pox when I was seven," she said, knowing that first month after her accident was definitely worse. Chase smoothed her hair in a rhythmic motion, distracting her from clawing at her skin the way she wanted to.

"I'm sorry. I should've been watching out for you," he said.

She rolled her eyes. "I can watch out for myself. It was completely my fault. I know what poison ivy looks like. I just wasn't paying attention."

"Is the calamine lotion helping?" he asked.

He'd been so sweet to drive a half hour to the nearest drugstore to get her some after they'd returned to the cabin. He'd also brought multiple types of chocolate—a man after her own heart.

"I think so. It's hard to tell. Maybe it's just having you hold me and pet my hair that's working." She rolled her body to look up at him, her heart fluttering the way it did each time their eyes connected. "I'm sorry for being a drag."

She felt like she could cry. They were supposed to be reveling in their second chance, and here she was, coated in pink lotion to keep from tearing her skin off. So not sexy. They were binge-watching Netflix instead of soaking in the Jacuzzi, and she seriously doubted that either of them would be in the mood for stripping each other's clothes off later.

"I already told you my only hope for this weekend was to spend time with you and make you smile. It doesn't matter if we climb or if we stay here on the couch for the next forty-eight hours. Although I wish it weren't because you were covered in an itchy rash," Chase said.

Sophie felt even more like crying. "You're the sweetest man. How is it that no one has snatched you up already?"

He laughed softly, his hand still stroking her hair in such a way that she closed her eyes and sighed. "Because I was already taken a long time ago."

She opened her eyes and blinked up at him. And then she caved and scratched her ankle.

"More calamine?" he asked. "Or...I can find other ways to take your mind off that rash of yours." He bent forward, brushing his lips to hers in a soft kiss that left her laughing. "Something funny?"

"No. This is just an awkward position." She sat up and scooted toward him, drawing her face close to his. "That's better. Now let's try that again."

"My pleasure." He brushed his mouth over hers once more, this kiss going longer and deeper.

Eventually, Sophie completely forgot about the poison ivy. There were a lot of things that could be done while nursing a little rash. A lot of things that could distract in the best kind of way, and Chase did them all.

* * *

The next morning, Sophie stirred to the sound of birds' chattering outside the window. She stretched her body under the covers, her muscles pulling in a feel-good way. She also felt the nagging itch and reminder of her rash. Before she could reach down to scratch it, Chase appeared in the doorway.

"Good morning, beautiful." He stepped into the room, holding a mug of coffee. She could smell the hazelnut aroma from several feet away.

"I missed the sunrise, didn't I?" she asked, breaking into a yawn. Then she turned her lower lip out just slightly.

"Yes, but that's okay. I took a video of it with my phone," he said. "I'll show you over breakfast"—he gestured behind him—"which is cooking right now."

Sophie sat up. "Wow. You've been busy."

He handed her the mug.

"If I didn't already love you..." she said, trailing off and grinning widely over her cup of coffee.

"If you didn't already love me, I'd be pulling out all the stops this weekend."

"Seems to me that's already the case." She took a sip. "Mm. First coffee of the morning is the best. Where's your cup?"

"In the kitchen. I thought you could sip and wake up a little before you crawl out from under the covers. We're on vacation after all, so there's no rushing around today."

"So nice." Sophie took another sip of her coffee and closed her eyes. When she reopened them, she met Chase's lingering gaze. "So what are we doing today?"

"Another walk?" he asked. "As long as you promise to stay on the trail."

She laughed. "Trust me. I will. We can find some nice spots to take a selfie. Or do more kissing."

"Both sound perfect." He gestured at her leg. "How's the poison ivy?"

"Barely noticeable," she said.

Chase nodded. "Good." Then he turned back toward the kitchen. "I'm going to check on breakfast."

"I'll be out in a minute," she promised. When he was gone, she put her coffee mug down and grabbed her cell phone from the nightstand. She pulled up Trisha's contact and started tapping out a text.

> I'm drinking awful coffee but I woke up with Chase and he's making me breakfast.

Trisha texted a GIF of a baby dancing along with a message. YES! Bad coffee is a small price to pay. Sounds like an amazing weekend.

Well, the weekend hasn't been perfect. I managed to cover myself in poison ivy.

Cover was a bit of hyperbole but it got the reaction that Sophie was looking for.

Oh no! Trisha sent a dozen sad-face emojis. Don't you know what poison ivy looks like?

I was a bit distracted by one handsome veterinarian.

Trisha sent over laughing emojis now. You can share the deets over good coffee when you get back.

Deal.

Sophie put her cell phone down and grabbed some clothes out of her overnight bag. After dressing and pulling her hair into a ponytail, she walked down the hall and breathed in the aroma of eggs, bacon, and maple syrup.

When Chase saw her, he stepped over and wrapped his arms around her.

She reached behind him for a piece of crisp bacon that was lying on a greasy paper towel and plate. He swatted her hand playfully. "Hey, no bacon for you until you kiss me."

"Are you serious?"

"Always."

She shook her head as she giggled. Then she swiped a piece and bit into it anyway. "Mm. You make good bacon. Much better than your coffee."

Chase's mouth dropped. "Really? You're criticizing the brew?"

She shrugged and then took another bite of bacon.

"Let me get a taste of that," Chase teased, kissing her as she chewed and making her giggle again. "Bacon makes everything taste better—even you." He winked. Then he returned to the stove and flipped the bacon that was still in the pan. "So, speaking of this morning, what is it that you would like to do?" he asked.

Sophie tilted her head thoughtfully. "Actually, I was thinking that we might go for a climb this morning," she said nonchalantly. She didn't even know she was going to suggest it until the words came out of her mouth. She'd thought about the idea as she'd lain in Chase's arms falling asleep last night though. Then she'd dreamed of being on a cliff with him.

Chase glanced over his shoulder and narrowed his eyes. "Are you serious?"

She gave a nod. "Just don't let me fall, okay?" she said nervously.

Chase moved away from the stove and stepped toward her. "I'm the one falling right now." He kissed her. "We'll take the mountain slow, okay? One handhold at a time."

Slow. Right. She was definitely going to heed that suggestion. If she thought poison ivy put a damper on their weekend getaway, a full-fledged panic attack definitely would.

She nodded and sucked in a breath, followed by another. She was calm. There'd be no panicking, and her leg would be fine.

Chase looked concerned as she blinked him into focus. "You don't have to, you know."

"I know. But I need to."

* * *

Sophie was strapped in a harness. She took a breath and then another, her toes gripping the ground before she'd even left the surface. Every muscle in her body was tense—too tense.

"Relax," Chase coaxed. "I'm right here."

It was easy for him to say though.

"Just don't look down. Look at me," he reminded her. "I'll be right beside you."

She nodded and blew out a shaky breath. Then she shook out her hands. Her palms were sweaty. Her heart was racing too fast.

Sophie had done the research. People with much worse disabilities climbed all the time. There was no reason she shouldn't be able to do this with minor adaptations. No physical reason at least. Yes, it might be harder for her. It might hurt. It might cause her muscles to spasm. But she was capable.

Chase's hand found her lower back. "I'm here," he said.

Right. She wasn't alone. Not like last time. She'd been such a fool to go out on her own without telling anyone where she'd gone. Those thirty-six hours had been the longest of her life. Chase had no idea what she'd been through on that cliff. No one did. It was a personal experience that she'd lived through by herself.

She sucked in another breath, battling her emotions. Her breakfast threatened to resurface as she reached up and put her fingers on the smooth earth that towered before her.

"That's it," Chase said, cheering her on.

She knew he was just trying to help but somehow it made it worse. She knew this was what he wanted. She realized she was mostly doing this for him. Yes, she wanted to climb but she wasn't ready. Not yet. She didn't really want to be here right now.

She closed her eyes, willing her body to slow down and focus on her breaths like she did when she swam or practiced yoga.

"I know it's scary," Chase said. "But once you face that fear, it'll go away."

Sophie shook her head. Then she pulled her hands away from the cliff and turned to face him. "I'm sorry," she said. "I thought I could but I can't do this." Her whole body started to tremble.

Chase pulled her into his arms. “That’s okay.”

“No, it’s not. I wanted to do it. I wanted to do it for you.”

Chase pulled back and looked at her. “Well then, that’s the problem. You should only go back up there for yourself. No one else.”

Sophie shook her head. “First poison ivy and now this.”

Chase kissed her temple. “That’s not how I see it. First a walk through nature. Then a passionate night of lovemaking. Then the best coffee this side of the mountain.”

Sophie grimaced.

“And let’s not forget the amazing breakfast. Next…” He trailed off.

“Next?” she asked.

He reached for her hand. “Next, we return to the cabin and back to our bed. We stay there until we’re forced to get up and eat. Then we spend an hour or two in the Jacuzzi. After that, we’ll go back to bed and repeat it all.”

Sophie smiled up at him. “That sounds perfect.”

Chapter Seventeen

On Monday morning, Chase woke without his alarm and shoved his feet inside his sneakers. He ran five miles, all the while thinking of Sophie. Then he returned home to shower and head to work. Not long after he arrived, Nadine walked in through the clinic's back door.

"Thank you again for this job," she said.

"You don't have to keep thanking me, Nadine." She'd probably done so a dozen times already.

"Well, I want you to know I mean it. I'm just so grateful to Sophie for putting in a good word for me. First, she gave me clothes so I could feel good about going out on interviews. Then she sat down and talked to me. She didn't have to." Nadine glanced over at Chase as she scooped kibble from the large container, preparing to feed the one dog that had stayed this weekend. "Sophie has a really good heart. But I guess you already know that."

"Yeah." Chase had always known it. Even when she'd done her best to turn him away from her. She'd shown him the worst she had right after her accident, and he'd still seen through the act. "So what's next for you?" he asked his newest employee.

Nadine furrowed her brow. "What do you mean?"

"Well, you have a job. I'm assuming the women's shelter won't let you stay there forever."

Nadine shook her head. "No. And even if they did, I like to make my own way. I'm in the process of looking for a place to stay right now. Somewhere reasonable that I can afford." She held up a hand. "Not that I'm complaining about the pay here, Dr. Lewis. The pay is just fine. It's just hard for a single person to cover all their bills on their own."

"I completely understand. I'll keep an ear to the ground to see if I hear of a reasonably priced place."

Nadine smiled. "You're just like Sophie. You genuinely care about people. You are two of a kind."

"If you stay in Sweetwater Springs long enough, you'll see that most of the people around here are that way."

"Oh, I'm staying. I'm not from this area but I already feel at home."

That wasn't the first time Chase had ever heard that from a newcomer.

After chatting with Nadine a few minutes more, he checked on each of the animals in their overnight crates and headed to his office to check his schedule. He pulled open his bottom drawer for a snack and took a moment to pick up one of the letters from his brother. Surely, the prison had email. But maybe the inmates weren't allowed to communicate online. There was something sincerer about an apology in handwriting anyway.

Suddenly curious, he opened his laptop and tapped in the prison's name in his search bar. He took a virtual tour of a few of the areas. It wasn't in-depth but it showed an entertainment area, the inside of a cell, and an outdoor recreation area. Chase would never want to lose his freedom but it didn't look like such a bad place to be.

His mom had been going to the prison for months to visit her oldest son. She'd invited Chase along, of course, but he'd refused. He was too disappointed. Too angry. Too confused about how one of the people he looked up to the most could do such horrible things.

Like Sophie standing in front of a mountain, he wasn't sure he was ready. But maybe he was warming up to the idea.

Penny knocked on his office door. She smiled when Chase looked up. "Your next patient is here."

Chase pushed back from his desk and stood. He'd been looking forward to this particular appointment since he'd woken up.

"Should I go ahead and take Sophie and Comet back to one of the examining rooms?" Penny asked.

"No, thank you. I'll take them," Chase said, eager to see Sophie as always. He was also eager to finally take Comet's cast off. It was a big day for the little dog. Now he'd be able to run free just like a little dog should. He'd also be a better candidate to be adopted into his forever home.

Chase stepped into the waiting area. "You can come on back," he told Sophie. "Want me to take Comet?" he asked.

Comet wagged at the sound of his name. He was on a leash and standing at attention. Did he realize what was about to happen?

"I've got him," Sophie said. "Lead the way."

Chase started walking down the hall and then gestured inside one of the three examining rooms. She stepped in ahead of him and Comet started sniffing his surroundings anxiously.

"I've missed you," Chase said, helping Comet onto the table.

A slight blush rose in her cheeks as she met his gaze. It was like they were in high school all over again. "It's only been since yesterday," she reminded him.

"Too long."

Comet stood on the table and lapped his tongue quickly over Chase's cheek.

Sophie laughed. "You must be distracted, Dr. Lewis," she teased.

Chase wiped the puppy saliva away. "Just a little. But it's Comet's moment. You ready, big guy?" he asked, addressing Comet, who was half-puppy, half-full-grown-dog these days.

"Will this hurt?" Sophie asked Chase, a small divot forming between her furrowed brows. She truly loved Comet. They were the perfect match. Chase only hoped Sophie realized it before it was too late.

"It won't hurt. Not even a little." Chase reached inside his pocket and pulled out a dog treat for Comet. "There's another one of those for you once the cast is off, buddy," he told the dog. Then he reached for a small saw to cut away the cast from Comet's leg.

Comet panted loudly, a sign that he was as nervous as Sophie beside him. Sophie had been fidgeting for the last five minutes, her skin pale and her green eyes wide as she observed what was happening. This was progress from the first day Comet had come to the clinic. She hadn't even been able to stay in the room while Chase examined Comet. Today, she wasn't leaving Comet's side for anything.

Chase petted Comet's head. "Just a second longer and you'll be as good as new," he promised. He went ahead and fed Comet another treat as he manipulated Comet's leg, gently bending and straightening it at the joint to make sure it moved smoothly. He was pleased that it did.

Chase lifted his gaze to meet Sophie's. She still looked worried. "I wish I had a treat for you too. To help take the edge off."

She smiled weakly. "I just want him to be okay."

"It was a simple break. There's no reason to think Comet won't be as good as new. In fact, I think we should celebrate tonight by taking him to the dog park for a little walk on his own."

Chase pulled his hand away from Comet's leg and petted the fur along the dog's back, soothing the little guy and letting him know that the examination was all over. As if to prove that point, he offered a final treat. Comet snatched it from his palm.

"A walk in the park sounds nice." Sophie reached out and petted Comet as well. "What do you think?" she asked Comet in a softer voice. The pet voice, Chase called it.

Comet stood on all four legs, tail wagging like an exaggerated windshield wiper. His eyes were bright as he held the treat between his teeth, savoring this last one.

Chase lifted Comet off the table and put him on the floor. "Go ahead. Try it out," he told Comet, talking about the dog's legs.

Chase watched with bated breath as Comet hesitantly took a few steps. He took a few more and circled around Sophie as she laughed. Then Comet propped his front paws on Sophie's thighs, putting all his weight on both hind legs. There was no sign of pain in the dog's demeanor. "See? Good as new," Chase told Sophie, realizing now that she had tears in her eyes. Happy tears, which were the best kind.

She sniffled. "Well, I have to get to the boutique," she finally said after a moment. "I guess now that he's all healed up, he doesn't need to stay at the clinic during the day anymore. Should I keep him crated during the day or is it okay to let him free in the backyard?"

"He's okay to be out. If you don't mind, I'd still like to check on him today at lunch. Just to make sure he's doing all right."

"A house call?" Sophie tilted her head to the side. "We must be special."

"Very special," Chase told her, stepping closer. Then he did what he'd been waiting to do since she'd walked into this room. He kissed her.

Sophie looked at him as they pulled away from the kiss. "You did have a treat for me after all."

* * *

At midday, Sophie's mom stepped into the boutique.

"You sure you don't mind working?" Sophie asked.

Her mom headed behind the counter, sat down, and pulled out her crochet needle. "I don't mind. Go run your errands."

Writing a speech for the black-tie affair wasn't exactly an errand, per se. But it was definitely a pressing item on Sophie's to-do list. Sophie had tried to write it over the last week at the boutique's counter but there was always something to take her attention away from the task. She was hoping a change of scenery would be exactly what she needed. It was an honor to speak at the women's shelter event in a couple of weeks, and she wanted to do the moment justice.

"I'll close tonight. Don't even think about coming back. Just enjoy your day," her mom said as Sophie collected her purse from behind the counter.

"Thanks, Mom." Sophie kissed her mom's temple, careful not to distract her from crocheting. Then she stepped out of her boutique and tipped her face toward the sun, soaking in its warmth before heading down the sidewalk of Main Street toward Dawanda's Fudge Shop. She was hoping chocolate would fuel her creativity.

A short walk later, Dawanda looked up from behind the counter as Sophie stepped inside her shop. The petite woman with brightly colored hair and lipstick gave her a cheerful smile as always. "Well, look who walked into my shop!" she said excitedly. "I had a feeling you'd be here today."

Sophie paused midstep. "Did you happen to see that in your morning cup of cappuccino?"

Dawanda was known for her cappuccino readings where she read the fortunes of others in the frothy foam that lined their mugs. Sophie wasn't sure if it was coincidence but many of Dawanda's predictions had come true over the years.

Dawanda waved a dismissive hand. "No, nothing like that. I've just had you on my mind today for some reason. So I thought it must mean I was going to run into you."

"I didn't realize you were a psychic as well." Sophie approached the counter and started eying the fudge display. There was a wide variety of flavors ranging from chocolate to mint to caramel.

"I'm not psychic," Dawanda said. "I'm just old enough to know that nothing in life is coincidence. Everything is connected."

Sophie glanced up. "Well, I was hoping to occupy one of your tables to work on a speech that I'm giving for the black-tie affair at the women's shelter in a couple weeks."

"You're giving a speech?" Dawanda lifted a hand to her chest. "That's so exciting. What are you going to talk about?"

Sophie grimaced. That was the big question. "I'm not sure," she admitted. "I was hoping your fudge would inspire me."

"How about a taste of one of my new flavors?" Dawanda pointed in the display case at a light-colored fudge with a thread of orange running through it. "It's tangerine," she said. "It tastes just like spring in Sweetwater Springs."

Sophie straightened. She'd never considered that her hometown had a taste but okay. "That does sound nice. I'll take a square of that. And a coffee too, please." Before Dawanda could ask, Sophie held up an index finger. "No cappuccino readings for me today."

Dawanda's expression turned crestfallen, which made Sophie feel slightly guilty. "I don't need the foam to tell me what I can see with my own eyes anyway," Dawanda said, pulling out a square of parchment paper for the fudge.

Sophie tilted her head. "Okay, I'll bite. What are your eyes telling you?"

"I know a woman in love when I see her." Dawanda beamed. "You and Chase are going to work out this time. I just know it.

It was always meant to be with you two. It doesn't take foam or psychic abilities to see it."

Sophie felt herself beaming now too. "I hope so," she admitted.

"I know so." Dawanda collected a piece of the tangerine fudge from her case and put it on a paper plate. Then she made Sophie a cup of coffee and rang her up at the register. "If you change your mind about the reading, I'll give you one on the house."

Dawanda's readings were always on the house because she usually had to entice her customers to agree to have their fortunes read.

"Or if you want to practice your speech on me, I'm here for that too."

Sophie laughed as she collected her fudge and coffee. "Mind if I sit at one of your outside tables? The sunshine feels so good today." And Sophie had a sneaking suspicion that she'd get nothing done if she stayed in here with the chatty fudge shop owner.

"Go right ahead," Dawanda said.

Sophie thanked her and walked out. She sat down and bit into her fudge, practically moaning because it was so good. Then she pulled a notepad and pen from her oversize bag and stared at the blank page.

There was so much to say. Helping others was an honor. It was what people in Sweetwater Springs did. It's what they'd all done for Sophie when she was hurt. Sophie had made a point of giving back and paying forward the kindness that her hometown had shown her. Maybe Dawanda was right, and there were no coincidences. Maybe Sophie had needed to be helped when she was younger to set her on a path to help others.

She took another bite of her fudge, considering that thought. She'd never quite looked at her accident that way. She'd only looked at all the things it had taken from her and how she'd had to work to put herself back together. She refused to be a victim but she'd never considered what windows had been opened once a few doors had closed.

Her accident didn't define her but it had veered her life into the things that did. She'd found her passion for clothes and for helping women feel beautiful and confident. She'd found a passion for volunteering and second chances.

Sophie set her pen to paper, writing frantically as her thoughts and words flowed faster than her hand could keep up. Maybe it was Dawanda's fudge or the bright sunshine but Sophie suddenly knew exactly what she wanted to say to the people of Sweetwater Springs.

* * *

Chase heard Comet's barks from inside Sophie's house as he approached later that evening. He pressed the doorbell, and a moment later, Sophie opened the door, dressed in something bright and colorful just like the flowers he offered her. He'd stopped in at the Little Shop of Flowers on Main Street before coming here.

"These are for me?" Sophie took the bouquet and tipped her nose into the blooms. "They're beautiful. Thank you. What did I do to deserve these?"

Chase shrugged. "You don't have to do anything. If I could, I'd bring you flowers every time I came over."

She laughed. "I guess that would take the surprise factor out of receiving flowers."

She gestured inside her home. "I'll just set these inside, and we'll be ready to go to the dog park to celebrate Comet's full recovery."

"Perfect." Chase squatted to pet Comet on the porch as he waited. The dog danced around excitedly in front of him. It was as if he'd never been injured by a car. "I have something for you too," Chase told the dog, reaching into his pocket for an ever-present treat.

"You're spoiling us," Sophie said as she approached with Comet's leash in hand.

He straightened. "And I'm just getting started." He led Comet and Sophie toward his truck. He opened the passenger door for her and waited until she was seated to place Comet in her lap.

Once Chase was behind the steering wheel, he reversed out of the driveway and pointed the vehicle toward the dog park. They talked easily until he pulled into the parking lot and shut off the engine. "All right. Let's try out that leg," he told Comet, still in Sophie's lap. After getting Comet out of the truck, he and Sophie set out down a familiar path.

"Comet's new owner will have to train him to heel now that he's able to go for longer walks," Chase told her. He was fishing to see how she felt. She hadn't mentioned giving Comet up over the last week.

"Yes, she will," Sophie said. She glanced over. "Guess you'll need to come over to my place more often. To help."

Chase grinned. "Oh yeah? Why is that?"

She tilted her head as she met his gaze. "Because I've fallen head over heels for him. And now that I've found him, I'm never saying goodbye."

Chase swallowed, wondering if she felt the same way about him. "That's good to hear. I'll be happy to come over and help whenever you want," Chase said. "In fact, I'll insist on it." He leaned over and kissed Sophie. Then he heard a familiar voice calling his name. He looked up and saw Denny Larson walking toward them. Denny was a climbing instructor that had climbed with both Chase and Sophie once upon a time.

Denny offered his hand to Chase to shake and then to Sophie. "Hey, you two. Good to see you."

"You too," Chase said.

"Hi, Denny," Sophie added.

"Are you two"—Denny bounced a pointer finger between them—"dating?"

Chase looked over at Sophie. "We are."

"Well, that's great news. You two were a great couple back in the day."

Chase had hoped after the dating talk they'd say goodbye and continue on but Denny continued speaking before Chase could begin parting ways. He asked Chase the inevitable question. "So, have you been on any climbs recently?"

Chase shoved his hands in his pockets, looking for a way out of this conversation. "It's been about a month."

Denny flinched. "That's a long stretch. Any plans to go soon?"

Chase hesitated. He had plans for this coming weekend, actually, but he hadn't mentioned anything to Sophie just yet. He certainly didn't want the first she heard of this weekend's climb to be because of Denny. He should have told her but the subject felt awkward and uncomfortable. The longer he waited though, the more awkward it became. "Nothing solid," Chase said, which was only mildly true. The time he and his friends were setting out wasn't finalized but the rest of the plans were.

"Well, let me know when you go. It'd be great to do a climb together. Just like the old days." Denny turned to Sophie.

Chase could feel the tension. Denny wouldn't ask Sophie if she'd been on a climb lately. Being a large part of the climbing community, Denny already knew that she hadn't.

"Sophie, it's good to see you out. Looks like you got a new dog," Denny said instead.

She smiled politely but Chase could tell her spirits had fallen. "This is Comet," Sophie told Denny. "I just adopted him. Ten minutes ago, actually."

"Yeah? Congratulations. Maybe I need to get a dog," Denny said.

Chase gestured at where they were. "Why would you be at a dog park if you didn't have a dog?" Not that Chase hadn't done the same. He was a vet though, and he used to take Grizzly here all the time.

"It's a good place to meet women," Denny admitted. He held up his hands. "I'm not a stalker or a freak. I just don't like going to the bar. I like dogs," he said. "And women with dogs are more grounded."

Chase chuckled. "Well, whatever works." He shook Denny's hand again. "Good to see you."

"Yeah. Give me a call, and we'll discuss going up together."

"I will," Chase said but even that agreement made him feel guilty. He needed to find a good time to tell Sophie about his weekend plans with the guys. If they were going to be together, they needed to be able to tell each other everything.

Sophie was quiet as they said goodbye to Denny and continued walking in the opposite direction.

Chase could see that she was limping now. He wondered if stress affected her muscle tension somehow. "Do we need to sit down?"

She looked over, ignoring the question. "Climbing was my first love. I won't say it doesn't hurt when I think about it or hear about an amazing experience."

Chase swallowed. "Climbing was my second love," he said, reaching for her hand. "You were my first." And the last thing he ever wanted to do was hurt her. So maybe he shouldn't tell her about his weekend plans after all.

Chapter Eighteen

Chase couldn't fully enjoy his climb on Saturday morning because he hadn't told Sophie the full truth. For all Sophie knew, Chase was playing cards at someone's house.

"Focus!" Skip hollered over at him. "You can't fantasize about your girlfriend when you're climbing, buddy. I don't want to have to call search and rescue because you fell off the side of a mountain."

As if that was even a possibility. They all had ropes and pulleys. And they had each other's backs too. Unlike Sophie on her last climb.

All the memories, regrets, and fears surfaced in Chase's mind as his muscles worked to capacity. These climbs were usually good at clearing his head but today's climb was having the opposite effect.

Once they reached the top of Sunrise Point, they all collapsed onto their backs, pulled out energy bars, drank their water, and lay quietly for several long minutes.

"So," Alex finally said, his voice loud in the otherwise silent valley, "Halona is pregnant."

"What?" Skip sat up and twisted his body to look at his friend. He pulled his sunglasses off to narrow his eyes at Alex. "You two are going to have a baby?"

Alex could barely contain his smile. He was a happy man these days. "We are."

"That's great news," Chase said, sitting up as well. He held out a hand for Alex to shake. "Congratulations, man."

Alex was grinning bigger than Chase thought he'd ever seen the chief of police smile. "It's unexpected but we're both over the moon about it."

"Emma and I are trying," Jack confessed, sitting up now.

Chase turned to his newly married friend. "Not wasting any time, huh?"

Jack shrugged. "We want a houseful so we better get started."

Chase suddenly felt left behind. Skip apparently felt the same way.

"Well, I don't even have a girlfriend, so I'll just be your bachelor friend. And before you ask, no, I'm not available for babysitting duty."

Everyone howled with laughter.

"I wouldn't want my child being looked after in the back of a bar anyway," Alex quipped.

"Hey, that's how I grew up, and I turned out just fine." Skip took a bite out of his energy bar, feigning insult.

Eventually, all the attention turned to Chase.

"So Sophie, huh?" Jack finally said. "A repeat of the past?"

Chase shrugged. "I guess I've been waiting for her all this time."

"What's different this time?" Alex asked.

Chase shrugged. "We're older now, I guess. Before, we bonded over hiking and climbing and everything physical." He waved a hand when he saw Skip's expression, signaling that his brain was dipping into the gutter. "This time, a lot of that is off the table. We're discovering other things about each other that we enjoy." Chase looked at his friends. "Honestly, we don't have to do anything at all. I just want to be with her."

"Then why the hell are you up here with us lugs?" Skip teased. "If I had a girlfriend, I'd have totally bailed on you guys today."

The laughter started back up again. This was why Chase was here. He needed these guys.

Jack looked at Alex. "Can I toss Skip off the mountain without serving time?"

Alex seemed to consider the question. "I could go take a bathroom break in the woods and wouldn't see a thing. If you can get the other guys to back your story."

Jack nodded, tossing Chase a conspiratorial glance. "Good to know." Then he turned to Skip, who seemed entertained by the empty threat.

"All right, I have a real confession," Chase finally said.

Alex looked over. "You sure you want to incriminate yourself in front of me?" Chase knew he was only joking. Alex was honorable and law-abiding. He had no problem making a friend or even family member answer to justice. He'd proven that when he'd taken Chase to jail a couple of weeks ago.

Chase chugged the rest of his water bottle and then dropped his hands between his bent knees, letting the plastic bottle dangle there. "I didn't tell Sophie I was climbing this morning. I didn't want to hurt her feelings. This is something we used to do together, and after her accident, she can't really do that kind of stuff anymore. Or she might be able to but she's got a mental block on it."

"Understandable after what she went through," Skip said.

Chase nodded.

"You think she'd be mad at you for coming out with us?" Mitch asked.

"No. If I had mentioned this to her, she would have insisted that I go."

Alex shrugged. "So then why didn't you tell her?"

Chase really didn't know the answer to that question. "I felt guilty, I guess. I still love a good climb."

"And if you really loved her, you'd give up climbing to prove it?" Skip asked.

Chase shrugged a shoulder. "I guess so."

Skip looked at Jack. "Chase is the idiot of the group. Toss him off the mountain instead."

They all started laughing again. Finally, Chase joined in and laughed alongside them. When he'd put a voice to his fears, he guessed they did sound pretty silly.

"Well, you might not have told her, buddy, but she knows by now. Halona was planning to go shopping at Sophie's Boutique this morning. I somehow doubt the subject of our Men's Day Out won't come up," Alex said.

"Men's Day Out?" Chase asked.

Alex nodded. "If the women in Sweetwater Springs can have a Ladies' Day Out, why can't we have a Men's Day Out?"

"I've always thought we should," Mitch agreed. "It's only fair."

Chase was barely listening as the banter continued. He was too busy worrying that Alex was right and that Sophie already knew about his climbing trip. And she hadn't heard it from him.

* * *

"Mom, you don't have to come in every weekend. You deserve a break once in a while too." Sophie watched her mom unpack a new shipment of clothes to put on display.

"This isn't work for me," her mom insisted. Then her

expression grew serious. “Or are you trying to get rid of me? Am I being a nuisance?”

“Of course not. You’re a huge help.” Sophie sat on the stool behind the register. After playing and chasing Comet around the backyard last night, even an extended session of yoga hadn’t helped. “I just want you to know that I don’t necessarily need the help. I appreciate it but I’m fine.”

Her mom stopped pulling items out of the box. “I know you are. But I’m also your mom, and if there’s anything I can do to make your life easier, I want to do it for you. That’s my job, and there’s no retirement in motherhood. I wouldn’t take it if there were.”

Sophie felt her emotions come undone. She tried so hard to keep them at bay but sometimes they escaped. And lately, being with Chase had unleashed a lot of talk and unresolved feelings of the past. She’d thought she’d moved on but part of her was suddenly thrown back into things she hadn’t thought about in years. “Okay. Well, I’m glad you’re here. And I’m not sure I ever truly thanked you for being there after my accident.”

“You did. It was unnecessary then, and it’s unnecessary now. I didn’t think you were doing the right thing when you pushed Chase away all those years ago. I’ve always regretted letting you do that.”

“Letting me?”

Her mom continued. “I guess I didn’t say anything because I thought you needed to focus on getting well. I was concerned about you, and you two were so in love. I didn’t think Chase being there with you would help matters. Maybe I was selfish because I wanted to be the one to pull you through. I honestly don’t know but I’m sorry.” Her mom’s eyes were suddenly filling with tears.

Sophie shook her head. “Mom, I was eighteen. It was my decision. Me breaking up with Chase wasn’t your fault in any way." And she was surprised that her mom would have felt that it was.

"He should have been there for you, sweetheart. You needed him, and you weren't in the right mental space to know it. You've always been so fiercely independent. It was the first time you ever needed real help. You were terrified and confused, and I know I was there for you as much as I could be. But I also know that you needed more than me and your father."

Sophie got off the stool and stepped toward her mom. Then she wrapped her arms around her and hugged her so tightly that she worried for a moment that she was hurting her. "Well, I don't blame you for anything, and I don't want you to blame yourself. Chase and I are together now, and I think it's going to last this time."

Her mom pulled away and looked at her. "That's good news."

"We haven't talked about the future but it feels inevitable somehow."

"It was always inevitable with you two," her mom said. "That's how you know it's true love. Time doesn't make it go away. It just stays and waits patiently until you're ready."

The front door opened, and Halona walked in. She smiled at the two of them.

"Hi, Halona," Sophie said brightly, walking over to hug her friend. "What are you doing here? Not that I don't love to see you but I know that Saturdays are one of your biggest days at the flower shop."

"That's true but I needed to take a little break to go shopping. My clothes aren't fitting so well these days."

Sophie's gaze unwittingly traveled down the length of her friend. "Really? You look amazing to me. As always."

"Well, it's not because of my eating habits, although those have changed a bit. I just..." Her friend's cheeks flushed slightly. "Do you have any maternity items by chance?"

"What?" Sophie gasped and then turned to look at her mom to see if she'd heard. Judging by the look on her mom's face, she had. "Oh my goodness! Congratulations!" And now she knew why Alex had been seen bringing Halona flowers a few weeks ago. Summer had been so curious about the reason, and Sophie was thrilled that it wasn't because the couple was fighting.

"We're not telling everyone just yet. I mean, I'm sure Alex is telling all the guys on their guy trip today so I don't feel guilty at all about telling you." She laughed. "I was a little bummed that I couldn't tag along with them but I don't think climbing is the best activity for an expectant mother, do you?"

"Climbing?" Sophie's smile wilted.

Halona's smiled dropped, and her eyes narrowed. "You didn't know that's what they were doing today?"

"No. Chase didn't mention the specifics. He just said that he and the guys were hanging out." Sophie shrugged as if it were no big deal. And maybe it wasn't. Except he would've told her they were going on a climb if it weren't a big deal.

"Well, I'm sure they're having the time of their lives. Those guys love climbing, as you know." Halona turned and scanned the boutique.

Sophie looked down at her hands for a moment and took a deep breath. Why hadn't Chase told her what he was doing today? He was all about being up-front with people but he'd hid something from her.

"Did I say something wrong?" Halona asked.

"No, you didn't. And yes, I do have a few maternity items, although not nearly as many as I'd like. Now that I know you're expecting, I'll order some more." Sophie forced a smile.

"With all this love going around, you never know who'll end up pregnant next. I mean, I might know but my lips are sealed."

Sophie's eyes widened. "There's someone else?" The list of possibilities ran through her mind. Brenna was Halona's best friend, and she was dating Luke Marini at the fire station. Was Brenna also expecting?

"News will be out soon enough," Halona teased. "Now, point me in the direction of the maternity clothes before I say too much. I'm desperate for some things with breathing room."

Sophie suddenly needed breathing room as well. And lots of it.

After Halona left, Sophie retreated to the Fairy Godmother's Closet that Chase had renovated for her while her mom stayed up front to work the register. Sophie just needed a moment.

Chase must have felt like he needed to lie to protect her feelings about the climb today. Her feelings wouldn't have been hurt if he'd been honest though. She knew her limitations. The old Sophie would've taken this little lie by omission and let her fears run away with her. She would have worried that she was holding Chase back. That he couldn't do and be everything he wanted because of her.

However, the new Sophie took a few deep breaths and did a few yoga poses in the back room. Then she returned to the main boutique and carried on with her day. She ordered maternity clothes for Halona and the other secret pregnant friend, and despite her best efforts, she felt left out.

All her friends were getting married and having children. And she hoped that she and Chase were heading down a similar path. That's what she wanted. But if he couldn't even tell her about a simple climb, how stable was this relationship?

Thoughts like that made it hard to breathe.

Then she felt foolish. It was just a climb. He was just protecting her like he did everyone else in his life. And she'd been keeping something from him too. A secret that she somehow doubted he would see as simple or innocent. Sophie doubted he'd be understanding if he knew about Nadine's criminal background.

* * *

Chase let the shower's water beat against his skin, washing off the day at the cliffs. It would have been the perfect day except for his guilt over not telling Sophie where he was. And his worry that she had found out anyway.

He stepped out of the shower, reached for his cell phone, and called Sophie. He didn't want to wait a second longer to get his omission off his chest. He dialed but she didn't answer the phone. He was about to leave her a voicemail but a text came through.

> Sorry. I'm not feeling well tonight. Not up to talking.

Disappointment flooded through him. I can bring you something. What do you need?

He waited for her response as he sat on the edge of his bed. His guilt felt heavy on his shoulders. He needed to make things right with Sophie.

> I think I just need to be alone tonight. Sorry.

Chase frowned. It's okay. I get it. If you change your mind...

He hoped she would. He needed to see her.

> Thank you. I'm going to church and to my parents' house tomorrow. I'll talk to you later in the evening.

Chase felt unsettled by the texts for some reason. It was probably his conscience coming into play.

> No problem. I'll miss seeing you.

Chase waited for a reply that never came. With a sigh, he prepared to stay in for the night. He wasn't much of a TV watcher but he was too sore to exercise, and Grizzly, who'd once filled the empty space, was gone.

Chase turned on the television and started flipping channels, stopping when he saw his brother's face.

Chase blinked, wondering if this was a hallucination. Then he turned up the volume as he read the headlines on the bottom of the screen. Some other financial guru somewhere had stolen money from several clients' accounts just like Pete had. The news was comparing their crimes and dredging up famous past cases for extra dramatic flair.

Chase's stomach curled. He didn't feel so well either suddenly. Now, not only did he feel guilt over climbing and not telling Sophie, he also felt an edge of anger. He wanted to drive down to the prison where Pete was and yell at him. What if Trisha was seeing this news story right now? What if Petey was seeing it?

Chase massaged a hand over his face. He grabbed his phone and texted Trisha.

Please tell me you're not watching the news.

Her dots started bouncing.

I saw it.

Chase audibly sighed.

Petey? he asked.

He's asleep on my lap.

Chase collapsed into the back of the couch with relief. It was short-lived. Even though Petey was asleep, friends from his class were bound to see it. Then their parents would fill them in that the man in the picture was Petey's dad.

I'm sorry, Chase texted.

It's no more your fault than it is mine, Trisha responded. And my lesson has been learned.

What's that? Chase asked.

Never turn on the news before bed. She inserted a smiling emoji face.

Dinner Monday night? Trisha asked then. Petey misses you. You can bring Sophie, of course.

Chase wanted to spend some time alone with Sophie. He also knew his former sister-in-law needed her friends and family right now though. Sure. That sounds great.

Perfect! Don't forget to bring Comet. Good night, Chase.

'Night.

Chase aimed the remote at the television and turned it off. Too bad the remote didn't work to turn off the lingering thoughts and emotions that would rob him of sleep tonight.

CHAPTER NINETEEN

On Monday evening, Chase sat at his desk and finished up writing notes from the day's patients. He'd tried to see Sophie at lunchtime but she'd been busy. She'd agreed to meet him at Trisha's for dinner tonight though, and as soon as Chase had an opportunity, he planned to tell her about his weekend climb.

Chase looked up from his paperwork as he heard footsteps approaching his office.

The clinic had just closed ten minutes earlier. He was about to pack up his things to head out. He wanted to go for a jog and then shower before heading over to Trisha's.

"Hey, Nadine. Everything okay?" Chase asked as his newest hire lingered in his doorway.

"Oh yeah. Couldn't be better. I just wanted to see if you needed anything before I go home."

Chase thought for a moment. He assumed that she was still staying at the women's shelter. He didn't feel like it was okay to ask though. A boss-and-employee relationship was tricky. Some bosses were like family with their employees. Others kept a professional distance. "I don't think so. Thank you." He didn't want to overstep his relationship. "Do you need anything from me, Nadine?"

She looked taken aback for a moment. Then she shook her head. "You've already given me a job, which is the most I could ask for. And Sophie provided me with clothes, which I fully intend to return. I'm not going on any more interviews, so I don't need fancy clothes. Someone else can benefit from them."

"That's nice of you," Chase said, taking that as proof that Nadine was kind and honest. Any suspicion of her was unwarranted. "I'm sure Sophie will appreciate that."

Chase closed the bottom drawer of his desk, watching the empty energy bar box slide by. He hadn't thrown it away yet because he was still baffled. Had Nadine been in his desk? Would she steal from him? His drawer didn't lock so he couldn't keep the things inside protected. Not that there was anything of value. Just bars and letters from Pete.

Chase pushed back from his desk and stood. Then he reached for his keys. "I don't need anything else tonight. You can feel free to go home."

"Great." She turned to walk ahead of him.

"Mind making sure the back door is locked?" Chase asked, heading toward the front as usual.

"Not at all." She smiled politely at him and waved. "I'll leave that way."

Chase nodded, making a mental note to check the back door when he arrived in the morning. Even that thought made him feel like a jerk. "Thanks."

As he locked the front door behind him, he chastised himself for jumping to conclusions about Nadine. Hard times didn't make her a criminal in the same way that easy times didn't mean someone wouldn't turn into one. Chase and his brother had a great upbringing. There was no reason that Pete should have followed a path to prison. At least not one that seemed obvious to Chase.

Chase walked through the parking lot and got into his truck before pulling out his phone. The only way to lay his suspicions to rest once and for all was to figure out what was going on at his clinic. He pulled up Alex's number and tapped Dial.

"Hey, Chase," Alex answered. "How are you?"

Chase leaned back against the seat of his truck. "Good, for the most part. I was wondering if you could have someone do a couple extra patrols down Blossom Street this week?"

"Sure. Is something going on?" Alex asked.

"I'm not sure. The back door to my clinic has been unlocked a couple times lately and…I don't know. I just have a feeling that something is off." Chase decided not to mention the other odd details. He was sure that the police station had bigger fish to fry than a few missing energy bars.

"Well, there's a lot to be said for instinct," Alex said. "Always trust your gut. I'll have an officer drive that route a couple times tonight. No problem."

"I appreciate it. Give Halona my best."

"I will."

Chase disconnected the call and then cranked his truck's engine. He drove to the dog park and changed into his running shoes. Then he warmed up with a few stretches before beginning a steady jog.

He didn't see Denny or anyone he knew on the path today, which was good. He appreciated being alone with his thoughts on the trail. Sophie was uppermost on his brain. Also lingering in his thoughts were Nadine and his suspicions about her. His brother and the news story on Saturday night. And Trisha and Petey.

After he finished up his jog, he took a few minutes to stretch. Then he headed back to his truck just in time to see his cell phone ringing in the driver's seat. He grabbed it and glanced at the caller ID before answering.

He'd just spoken to Alex an hour ago. Why was he calling again so soon?

* * *

Sophie took her place at Trisha's table with an empty chair next to her.

"I don't think Chase has ever stood us up." Trisha reached for a piece of bread at the center of the table. She placed it on Petey's plate and then grabbed a piece for herself. "I mean, he's had to leave early for an emergency vet visit but he's never canceled altogether."

"Maybe something came up at the clinic," Sophie said. She couldn't think of anything else it could be. He'd texted both her and Trisha to let them know he wasn't coming tonight, not citing any real reason. "He left the other night for an emergency as well."

Trisha's eyes widened at that bit of information. Petey didn't seem to catch anything unusual about that statement.

Sophie grimaced and then cleared her throat. She mouthed *sorry* to Trisha across the table for all but saying that she and Chase were now spending nights together. They hadn't spent last night together though. She was still sorting through her feelings about him keeping his plans a secret.

"So things are moving right along with you two, huh?" Trisha asked.

Sophie reached for a piece of bread. "It seems so." But Sophie was still bothered by their secrets. What kind of relationship could last with a couple keeping things from one another? She was just as guilty as Chase. In the night, she'd resolved to come clean with him though.

"Well, it's about time you got your love life together," Trisha said. "I was getting tired of seeing you date guys who just broke your heart."

Sophie was tempted to say she was tired of seeing Trisha not dating at all but she didn't want to broach that conversation in front of Petey. The older he got, the more he listened and understood.

They kept the rest of the dinner conversation focused on Petey. Then when it was time to clean up, Trisha let him watch a show in the living room, which allowed her to have an adult conversation with Sophie.

"While I'm sad he didn't make it, I'm glad Chase isn't here for this topic." Trisha leaned against the kitchen counter and folded her arms over her chest.

"Oh? What's wrong?"

Trisha's lips settled into a deep frown. "One of my weekend housekeeping clients let me go today. A friend of a friend of hers was scammed by my ex-husband, and apparently, she feels disloyal for having me clean her house."

"That makes absolutely no sense." Sophie felt her temper flare in her friend's defense.

"It is what it is. A divorce doesn't mean your ex is completely out of your life. Looks like my ex will continue to haunt me." She looked down for a moment, and Sophie suspected her friend was collecting her emotions. "Anyway, I'm not going to play victim here. I was actually thinking about applying for a new job."

"What? Why? I thought you loved working at the women's shelter."

"I do. It's been my passion for a long time but sometimes you can just feel when it's time for something new. I think I'm ready to move on."

Sophie nodded. "Well, I hope it's a management position because you are a born leader. What and where is this job you're considering?"

Trisha waved her hand. "I don't want to jinx it so I'm not going to say just yet."

Sophie tilted her head and narrowed her eyes at her friend. "Since when are you superstitious?"

"Since I'm actually pretty excited about this job." Trisha nibbled at her lower lip, and Sophie could tell it was to keep a huge grin off her face. "And I was wondering if you would do me a favor."

"Of course. Just name it and I'll do it, whatever it is."

Trisha laughed softly but she had a sheepish expression about her. "I really want this job, and I think a makeover at your boutique might be helpful. I can't really afford your designer clothes in the front, not anymore, but I don't want to take advantage of our friendship either."

Sophie held up a hand. "Stop all your rationales and reasons that I shouldn't be your fairy godmother. My Fairy Godmother's Closet is at your disposal, and so am I. If anyone deserves a second chance at life and a fresh start, it's you." Sophie stepped toward her and gave her a tight hug. "I'm so excited I can hardly stand the suspense. You have this job in the bag. I have a sure feeling about this."

Trisha pulled back. The sheepishness was still there but so was the barely contained excitement. "I really hope so."

"So tomorrow, whenever you have time, I'll be at the boutique, waiting to wave my magic wand."

* * *

After Sophie got home later that night, she texted Chase. Everything okay?

She didn't get an immediate answer so she took a hot bath. Then she climbed onto the couch and turned on the TV. Just before she dozed off, her phone buzzed.

Everything is fine. Can you stop by my clinic on the way to the boutique tomorrow? We need to talk.

Sophie blinked the words into focus and read them again. Those last four words were never good in a relationship. She hadn't seen Chase on Saturday night or yesterday because she'd needed some space to calm down after learning he'd gone climbing without telling her. And then tonight he'd been MIA at Trisha's. Were they okay?

She texted back: Sure, I'll bring coffee and breakfast.

Sounds good. Sweet dreams.

Sophie stared at his words on her screen as she laid her head back on the arm of the couch. She set her phone down and watched something on TV, her eyelids drooping heavily. It was too early to go to sleep though, and her mind was wandering.

Maybe Chase was realizing that she was right all along. Maybe there was too much distance between them now, and they couldn't get back to the way they were.

* * *

Chase sat in the parking lot of the Sweetwater police station for a long moment. He'd already spoken to Alex on the phone. Nadine was inside, being held for breaking-and-entering charges.

Chase swallowed thickly. He hadn't told Sophie the truth just yet because he didn't have all the facts. And he didn't want her to lose sleep unnecessarily. They'd talk tomorrow morning, after a good night's sleep.

Maybe this was all one big misunderstanding. Maybe Nadine had gone back to the clinic because she'd left something inside. But when he'd called Penny tonight to ask, she'd told Chase that

Nadine didn't have a key—even if Nadine had told him that's how she'd gotten into the clinic the one morning he'd walked in on her.

Nadine had lied to him on top of who knew what else. Was she leaving windows and doors open so she could return when she didn't have permission to do so? Or had she taken one of the spare keys that Penny kept in the register drawer up front?

Chase's phone dinged with an incoming text from Sophie.

Good night.

He smiled at the screen. Then he shoved his phone into his pocket and got out of his truck, locking it up behind him.

His feet felt like they weighed twenty pounds each as he walked. The last time he'd stepped into the Sweetwater police station, he was on the other side of the law. This time, he was here because a crime had been committed against him. Kind of.

All Chase knew at this point was that one of the police officers at the station had patrolled the clinic after hours and they'd seen movement inside the building. When they'd checked things out, they'd found Nadine unrolling a sleeping bag. She'd tried to make excuses but the evidence pointed to the fact that she was setting up camp to stay the night. She'd had an overnight bag with her and a plastic grocery bag full of snack items, one of which was the same type of energy bar that Chase usually kept stocked in his desk drawer.

Alex walked into the station's reception area and shook Chase's hand. "Hey, buddy. Good to see you, although I wish it were under different circumstances."

After releasing Alex's grip, Chase folded his arms over his chest. "You guys work fast. Is Nadine under arrest?"

Alex shook his head. "Not yet. We just brought her in for questioning. An arrest depends on if you're pressing charges.

She says she's an employee of yours, so we need to know from you if it was okay that she was in the clinic. Did you give her permission?" Alex narrowed his eyes. "You and I spoke on the phone earlier this evening so I'm pretty sure I know the answer but I need your official statement. Making an arrest hinges on you."

Chase hesitated. He liked Nadine—he really did. She had proven to be a good employee, and he'd wanted to believe that his gut was wrong about her doing something illegal. "She works as a vet assistant for me," Chase confirmed. He shook his head. "But her shift was over when I left this evening. She didn't have my permission to return, and I never gave her a key. I surely never okayed her to camp out there after hours."

Alex frowned. "She told me as much when I brought her. She's honest, at least."

"Is it honest to return to my clinic when I'm not there? Without asking or telling me? That's a lie by omission," Chase said, feeling his frustration rise. He felt betrayed. He'd trusted Nadine, even though he'd also had suspicions. And Sophie had obviously trusted Nadine too. She wouldn't have recommended Nadine for the job if she hadn't.

Chase nodded definitively. He was firing Nadine but that didn't seem like enough in this circumstance. He'd given his new employee ample chance to ask for help if she needed it. If he didn't file a report, she'd go off to the next employer and betray them as well. One thing Chase knew about criminals was that they didn't stop after hurting one person. They continued.

"It's a hard decision. I understand." Alex put his hands on his waist. "Especially since this could send her back to prison."

Chase took a moment to let that statement sink in because it didn't make any sense to him. "What are you talking about?"

Alex narrowed his gaze. "You didn't know? Nadine already has a criminal history."

Chase shook his head, dumbfounded. "I didn't run a background check on her." He normally would have but he'd taken Sophie's referral at face value. And she'd probably taken Nadine at her word. Trisha probably had too. They hadn't known much about Nadine Charles, and not finding out more had proven to be a huge mistake. "I had no idea. Nadine didn't disclose her past to me."

Alex shrugged. "She just got released a month or so ago. She served five years for a nonviolent crime. I believe her record said larceny."

Pete's crimes had been considered nonviolent as well but he'd still hurt a lot of people. A crime was a crime in Chase's book. And not telling Chase about her past was another lie by omission. She had enough strikes against her right now that Chase felt justified by his anger. "You know what? Yes, I'd like to press charges against Nadine," he said with finality.

"You're sure?" Alex asked.

"Positive."

"All right. Let's go file the report." Alex led him back to his office down the hall.

An hour later, Chase walked out of the police station with not only heavy feet but a heavy heart too. He'd put his faith in the wrong person but, even worse, so had Sophie. She was going to be so disappointed tomorrow when she met him at the clinic. Chase almost didn't want to tell her what had happened tonight. But he'd kept too much from her lately, and she'd eventually find out anyway. It would be better if she heard the truth from him.

Chapter Twenty

Sophie woke early and did an extra-long yoga session before preparing for the busy day ahead. First on her to-do list was going to the Sweetwater Café to get coffee and breakfast for Chase and her. He'd said they needed to talk. That made her a little nervous but it was probably unwarranted.

After showering and dressing, she took a little time before heading out to play with Comet. Then she put him in the backyard. "How about I take you to the dog park again tonight?" she asked the frisky dog, hoping that Chase would want to come along with them. Whatever they needed to talk about, they'd do so over breakfast this morning. Then hopefully things would return to normal.

Instead of walking to work, she drove her car today, knowing the extra distance from the café to the clinic and back to the boutique might push her over her physical limits. The boutique had been a lot busier lately as the black-tie affair for the women's shelter drew closer. Sophie was spending more time on her feet, leading her customers to and from the dressing room to try on various styles of gowns for the big night.

A short drive later, she parked and headed down Main Street. When she entered the Sweetwater Café, Emma was back behind the counter with a newlywed glow about her. Was that all the glow was about? Sophie wondered again about the second pregnant friend that Halona had alluded to.

"I'd ask how your honeymoon went but I can tell it was amazing just by looking at you," Sophie said.

Emma started preparing Sophie's drink without even asking what she wanted. Emma always remembered. "It was better than amazing. I'm so in love with Jack."

Sophie laughed. "Well, I should hope so because you just said *I do* to forever."

Emma laughed. "And changed my name. I'm officially Emma Hershey now. And in honor of that, I have a new mocha-flavored drink called the Hershey Kiss." She pointed to a sign that announced the new beverage behind her.

"Oh, I love that!" Sophie said. "I'll have to get one of those sometime soon."

"When you do, it'll be on the house." Emma continued to prepare Sophie's usual order.

"Can I get two of those, actually?" Sophie asked, leaning against the front counter. "And two croissants?"

"So a second coffee and croissant for Chase, huh? I noticed you two dancing at my wedding reception. I had hoped it was a new beginning for you guys."

Sophie forced a smile. She hoped that she and Chase were still on track.

"I've heard the talk since we've been back from our honeymoon too. Even Chase has been in and told me how close you two were getting."

"Really?" Sophie straightened from the counter. "When was that?"

"The week before last," Emma said as she worked.

Nothing and everything had changed in two weeks though. "We've been spending a lot of time together," Sophie admitted, keeping her tone casual. "And we're having breakfast together this morning before work."

"Sounds like love to me," Emma said in a cheerful, possibly overly caffeinated voice. "Speaking of Chase, what happened last night?"

Sophie tried and failed to think of what Emma was referring to. "What do you mean?"

"Well, I heard the police got called over to his clinic after hours. Rumor has it one of Chase's new employees was arrested."

"Nadine?" Sophie asked with a growing sense of dread. "Why?"

Emma shrugged. "I thought you would know. Since you and Chase are dating now. He didn't tell you?" Emma asked as she returned to the counter with two beverages.

"No. We didn't see each other last night. Something came up." And now Sophie knew what it was. She guessed that was what he wanted to discuss this morning. Not the fact that he'd lied to her about climbing with his guy friends.

"Well, I hope everything's okay." Emma ran Sophie's debit card and handed it back to her as another customer stepped up behind Sophie. Emma needed to see to the rest of her customers, and Sophie needed to take this coffee and breakfast back to the veterinary clinic, where Chase would be waiting for her.

Her heartbeat raced as she left the café and walked to her car. She unlocked the door and plopped down behind the steering wheel. "Nadine, what did you do?" she muttered under her breath, hoping that it was all a big misunderstanding, the same as Chase's weekend outing.

She drove down Main Street, turning left on Blossom. She pulled into the parking lot and cut her engine, grabbing the cups and bag from the café. Her left leg ached despite her morning stretches as she climbed the steps and tapped on the clinic's glass door.

Chase stepped up to the entrance and smiled as he let her in. Then he kissed her before doing or saying anything. She melted into the heat of his lips, momentarily forgetting that their relationship was currently spinning off its axis. Or maybe that was all in her head. If they were about to break up, he wouldn't greet her with a smile and a kiss.

"Hey, beautiful," he said.

"Hey yourself."

He took the bag from her hand and gestured for her to follow him back to his office. "Penny won't be here for another half hour," he called behind him, glancing over his shoulder at her.

"And Nadine isn't coming," Sophie said.

Chase paused midstep and turned to look at her, his smile gone. "I guess you heard?"

Sophie nodded. "Just now at the café. Emma didn't know the details though."

He stepped toward her and wrapped his arms around her. "I'm so sorry, Sophie. I wanted to be the one to tell you. Nadine lied to us."

Sophie shook her head as she pulled back and looked up at him. "What do you mean?"

"She didn't tell us the complete truth." He turned and continued walking into his office, pulling out a chair for Sophie to sit down. Then he pulled up a small table to set their coffee and breakfast on.

"Chase, what's going on?" Sophie asked, fearing the worst.

He sat down in a neighboring chair, his gaze apologetic as if he was about to break some terrible news to her. "This might come as a surprise. I know it did for me last night." He took a breath. "Apparently, Nadine has a criminal history. She just got out of prison."

Sophie didn't say anything. She braced herself for more. Surely, as upset as he seemed, there must be more. Nadine's was a nonviolent crime. She was a good person, and she'd shown that to them all.

"You're not going to say anything?" Chase finally asked.

Sophie blinked, realizing that was the worst of what he had to tell. "I…I…"

"You already knew," Chase said, suddenly straightening. "Didn't you?" he asked quietly.

"I…well, I…" She trailed off, her gaze wandering to the licenses and certificates he had framed on his wall. He'd gotten those after her accident. She'd pushed him to leave, and he'd gone on to chase his lifelong dream of becoming a veterinarian. As far as she knew, he'd never had roadblocks or hurdles. Not like her. Or Nadine. "Yes, I knew," she finally said, meeting his gaze again.

The disappointment in Chase's eyes was obvious. It settled into the fine lines on his face, evidence that time had passed since they'd first been a couple. She hadn't been there to see those small lines form. They'd missed so much together.

He wore a grimly set frown as he stared at her.

"Chase, I'm sorry. But I knew if I told you Nadine had just gotten out of prison you wouldn't give her a chance. And she deserves a chance. Everyone does."

He let out a humorless laugh. "That was my decision to make. Not yours." He stood and walked to the window with his back facing her. He didn't talk for a long moment. "I trusted her…I trusted you."

Sophie swallowed past the sudden upset flooding through her. "Trust? Let's talk about how I trusted you."

Chase turned to face her, his expression clearly confused. "Okay?"

"You went climbing this weekend and didn't tell me. In fact, you went out of your way *not* to tell me what you were doing." She felt her cheeks flush. That omission had been festering inside her. She'd tried to pretend like it didn't bother her but if he was going to be upset about what she'd kept from him, she was going to return the favor.

"I was protecting you," Chase said. "I didn't want to hurt your feelings."

"How do you think I felt when I found out anyway and realized that you weren't going to tell me? You said you were okay with all the things I could no longer do but you're not. They make you uncomfortable and guilty."

"How did we go from your lie about Nadine to arguing about me trying to protect you?" Chase folded his arms over his chest.

"I don't need protecting, Chase." Sophie shot up from her chair as the muscles in her left leg tightened, throwing her off balance. She held up a hand as Chase stepped toward her. "What did Nadine do?" she asked.

Chase frowned. "Does it matter what she did? She broke the law. Several times, apparently."

Sophie asked again. "What did she do, Chase? Did she hurt someone?" Sophie couldn't stand the thought of being the reason that someone else may have gotten hurt. Tears started to burn behind her eyes as she waited, finding it hard to breathe. "Just tell me."

Chase blew out a breath. "Nadine has been coming back to the clinic and sleeping here at night."

Sophie blinked. She almost laughed at the absurdity of that crime. "That's all?"

Chase shook his head. "No. She's also been stealing from me."

* * *

Chase really thought he'd be comforting Sophie right now. Instead, she seemed to be as upset with him as he was at her.

He lifted his gaze to the sound of the clinic door opening and shutting. Penny was here, and it wasn't time for an argument. He didn't want to argue with Sophie anymore anyway. In the heat of the moment, things were said that couldn't be unsaid. And he didn't want to say or do anything that they'd later regret.

"Chase, I didn't know Nadine was staying here. I thought she was still at the women's shelter. But it wasn't a malicious crime. Nadine didn't hurt anyone," Sophie said. "All she was doing was trying to survive."

Chase massaged a hand over his face. "If she'd have asked, I'd have given her a place to stay and food, no problem."

"Sometimes pride gets in the way of us asking for what we need," Sophie said quietly. "I know that better than anyone."

Chase met her gaze. Sophie had never broken the law to get her needs met though. Once someone was willing to break one law, breaking another was easier. Then before they knew it, one quarter from a brother's piggy bank became twenty grand from a client's account.

Chase knew he was letting his personal history taint the situation but he couldn't help it. People who were willing to break the law weren't people he wanted to deal with, much less have work for him.

"I know Nadine is a good person," Sophie argued. "She has a kind heart, and I'm sure that she's sorry and—"

Chase held up a hand. "I fired her and pressed charges," he said, cutting Sophie off.

"What?" Sophie said, alarm rising in her features as she shifted more weight to her right leg, making him suspect that her left leg was bothering her. Not that she'd admit it. "You pressed charges over her staying at your clinic at night?"

Now Chase felt his own alarm. Whose side was Sophie

on anyway? "For breaking and entering. And for stealing from me."

"What did she take?"

Chase hesitated. "A few energy bars from my desk drawer."

Sophie released a humorless laugh. "That's it?" She stepped toward him. "If you want to blame someone, blame me."

"I blame you both," Chase said sharply, feeling heated. It took a lot to get him mad but he was on the edge this morning. Sophie knew how he felt about criminals. Nadine had served time. She was an ex-convict, and she'd broken the law. "I can't trust her," Chase said. "And honestly, I'm not sure I can trust you right now."

Sophie pulled back. "I see," she said quietly.

"Do you blame me for saying that? I mean, you tricked me into hiring a woman whose past you knew I'd be uncomfortable with."

"I tried to tell you the truth. You said you didn't want to know."

Chase shook his head. "You tried after the fact."

Sophie crossed her arms over her chest. "You kept things from me too."

"That's different, and you know it."

"A lie is a lie," Sophie countered. "You lied to me because you know that I resent you for being able to do what I can't anymore. You know that I still blame you for not being there with me that day on the mountain. For leaving me out there alone."

Chase's mouth fell open. "What?"

"I know it's not your fault. I know it but it doesn't change how I feel. I used to be fearless. That fearlessness almost got me killed, and now the thought of climbing again terrifies me. And it makes me angry. And resentful. Deep down you know that, and that's why you didn't tell me you were climbing on Saturday. Just like deep down I knew that you wouldn't give Nadine a chance because you haven't forgiven your brother. And you haven't forgiven your brother because you haven't been able to forgive yourself for what happened to me."

Chase wasn't sure what to say. He felt like someone had kicked him in the chest. But what she said felt like the only truth that had been shared between them lately. "You said you didn't blame me."

"I don't. I know it's not your fault," Sophie said as tears rolled down her cheeks. "But I think I'll feel wounded every time you go climbing. And you'll feel guilty. Two people in a relationship are supposed to bring out the best in one another but we'll be bringing out the worst."

"Then I won't go climbing," Chase said flatly. "I'll give that up. For you." And he wouldn't even think twice. He loved climbing, yeah, but he loved Sophie so much more.

"That's not the solution," she said softly.

Chase suddenly felt panic rising. They'd been here before. When Sophie felt hurt, she lashed out and pushed people away. She'd pushed him away. Was she doing that again? "What is the solution, then?" he asked.

"I think you know, Chase."

He shook his head. "That's your fear talking again."

"Aren't you listening? I'm not that fearless girl anymore. I'm terrified of climbing. I'm terrified of falling. It's not worth the risk."

Chase blinked, hearing what she really meant. Falling in love again was too dangerous, and he wasn't worth it. He shook his head, wondering what he could tell her to fix this situation but coming up empty-handed. "I don't know what to say right now."

"I do," she said quietly. "Goodbye, Chase."

* * *

Sophie had been staring off into space, thinking about her earlier fight with Chase. It was more than a fight. They'd broken up. It was like they were both carbonated bottles that had been shaken. The proverbial caps had come off, and she and Chase had exploded, saying things that couldn't be taken back. Not easily, at least, because it was all true. And now that everything was on the table, the truth couldn't just be ignored.

A tap on the front glass door of the boutique got Sophie's attention. She got up and headed quickly to open the door for Trisha. "Hey."

Trisha stepped inside, beaming. Whatever this job was that she was applying for, she seemed excited about it. The last thing Sophie wanted to do was kill her good mood by recapping her argument with Chase. Sophie wasn't even sure she could talk about it right now without dissolving into a puddle of messy tears. "You're sure this is okay?" Trisha asked.

"Of course I am." Sophie gestured for Trisha to follow her to the back of the boutique.

"I can't wait to see the renovations to your Fairy Godmother's Closet. Chase went on and on about it the other day when I spoke to him," Trisha said in an upbeat voice.

Sophie breathed past the deep ache in her chest. Trisha so rarely asked her for any favors, and she wanted this experience to be all about her friend. She stepped into the back room and turned to see Trisha's face as she entered.

Trisha's mouth dropped open. "Wow. I love the color," she said, looking around. "It looks like an official room in your boutique."

"That's exactly what I was envisioning." Sophie patted Trisha's shoulder. "And today, you are my VIP customer. So, I know you're being hush-hush on where this job interview is but can you at least tell me what it is you'd be doing if you got the job?"

Trisha flashed a full smile. "Well, I'd be managing a...place where people live," she said hesitantly. "So that's similar to my work at the women's shelter in the sense that women live there and I'm making sure their needs are met. Anyway, it's a good job with nice perks. I feel like it's made for me. And I'd only be working one job so I'd have more time to spend with Petey."

"Wow, sounds perfect." Sophie's mind ran through all the possible places in town where Trisha might be interviewing. Maybe the job was in Wild Blossom Bluffs, which was a larger neighboring town. Or Whispering Pines, another town that bordered the valley.

Sophie stepped over to the racks of clothing and started pulling items down for Trisha. "This would look great on you. And these pants are just your size." She grabbed five more things off the racks and carried them to the dressing room across the hallway. "Step in here and find the one that makes you feel the most confident."

"Thank you." Trisha disappeared into the dressing room.

While she waited, Sophie took the time to do more stretches. She breathed in and out, willing her muscles to relax. Her body felt so tense after her argument with Chase. Their fight had gained speed and momentum. Sophie had realized in the midst of it that there were obstacles between them too large to allow them to stay together. They'd come in with too much baggage from their pasts. It would never work.

So she'd pushed him away, just like she'd done when she was eighteen, but this time, she hadn't lied. Everything she'd said was true. She just hadn't realized it until that moment. She would resent Chase for doing what she couldn't anymore. And he would feel uncomfortable and guilty. He'd been right, too, when he'd said that it was fear stopping her. She was afraid. Terrified, actually. And that made her feel helpless and weak. Out of control.

Sophie straightened from her stretch as Trisha finally stepped out, wearing a pants suit that fit her perfectly.

"This one," she said, still beaming.

It was nice to see Trisha so happy. The last six months had been tough on her but she was strong. Trisha was taking her life back, her control back. It was inspiring to watch. Sophie wanted to do the same. Needed to.

Sophie did a once-over of her friend. "Now you need the right shoes." Sophie gestured for Trisha to follow her to a wall of slightly used shoes, all donated by loyal boutique customers. "Pick your pleasure."

Trisha's eyes lit up.

Sophie watched her. "I haven't seen you get excited over a shopping trip in a while. This is good for you."

Trisha looked down at her feet for a moment. Sophie could almost feel the emotion bubbling to the surface. "It feels good to be one of your VIPs today. I haven't felt this way in a long time."

"Well, maybe you should pamper yourself more often."

"Maybe. If I get this new job, I might have a reason to celebrate."

By the time Sophie led Trisha out of the back room and into the front of the boutique, she had a bag full of things. "Did you ever find out why Chase skipped dinner with us last night?" Trisha asked as she leaned against the front counter.

Sophie grimaced. If she got into that story, the rest of the story would follow. But they weren't in the back room anymore. Trisha had gotten the full fairy godmother experience. Tears burned in Sophie's eyes. There was no use trying to hide them. "I'm surprised you haven't heard by now."

Trisha shook her head. "Heard what? What's going on?"

"Apparently, Nadine had nowhere to stay so she started going back to the clinic to sleep."

Trisha straightened, her bright smile dropping like a stack of bricks. "What? I told her I needed the room at the shelter but she insisted she had somewhere to go. If I'd have known that wasn't true, I would've made some kind of arrangement for her."

"She didn't tell anyone," Sophie said. "She's just been returning to the clinic after hours and sleeping there. Which is harmless, really. But Chase started to suspect something going on at his clinic, and he asked Alex to patrol the area. Nadine was arrested last night." Sophie took a ragged breath. "And Chase fired her and pressed charges."

Trisha covered her mouth with one hand. "What?"

"He also found out that Nadine had a prior criminal history."

Trisha's eyes widened. She lowered her hand back to the counter. "What do you mean he found out? You didn't tell him before he hired Nadine?"

Sophie grimaced. "No. But only because I knew he wouldn't hire her if I did."

Trisha's mouth dropped open. "Sophie, I thought Chase knew. Otherwise, I would have told him myself. You know how Chase is."

Sophie plopped onto the stool behind her register. "Yeah, I do. Anyway, we got into a fight this morning about Nadine. Then I told him I knew he went climbing over the weekend with the guys, and that he lied to me about that."

Trisha frowned as she continued to listen.

"Then I told Chase that some part of me would always blame and resent him." Sophie wiped at a tear that slipped off her eyelashes.

"Wow. Is that true?" Trisha asked.

"I'm not sure. In my head, I know what happened to me isn't his fault. But I was the one who loved climbing. I taught him how to do it, and he's still out there. It hurts, and when he hides it from me, that hurts even more."

"Oh, Sophie. I'm so sorry. I had no idea."

Sophie shrugged. "We both said a lot of things. It just all came out in this huge, messy argument." She sniffled as she looked at her friend. "And I'm pretty sure we broke up."

Trisha gasped. "What? Who did the breaking up?"

Sophie took a shuddery breath. "Me. I shouldn't have let things move so fast. I should have taken things slower."

Trisha gave her a sympathetic smile. "No, you shouldn't have. You two are meant to be together."

"I'm not so sure anymore," Sophie said quietly.

Trisha reached for her hand. "Are you okay?"

"No. But I will be. Especially after I get the good news that you got this job you want so badly. Will you at least let me know what happens after your interview?"

Trisha gave a thumbs-up. "I promise." She nibbled her lower lip. "It's this Friday, actually, and it might take a little longer than expected. Do you think you could watch Petey for me after school?"

"Of course," Sophie said. Maybe Petey would distract her from her heartbreak. "Why don't you just let me take him for the night? You can pick him up here on Saturday morning."

Trisha pulled her hand away. "Okay, thank you. He'll be so excited."

"Me too." Sophie forced a smile. "Although I'm pretty sure it's my dog he really wants to play with."

Trisha laughed. "Try not to worry about Chase. Things will work out the way they're supposed to," she said. "They always do."

Sophie knew that was supposed to comfort her in some way but it didn't this time, because she wasn't sure she and Chase were supposed to work out anymore.

* * *

Today was not one for sleeping in. Chase had barely slept a wink for the past couple of nights from tossing and turning between his sheets. Sophie's voice haunted him, telling him again and again that he needed to let her go.

This morning, he'd finally given up, gotten out of bed, and was now drinking coffee well before dawn.

Chase lifted a hand and massaged his face wearily. He'd spent the night wrestling with a dozen questions over what had gone wrong with Sophie. He wasn't going to find the answers now so it was best he distracted himself. He stood and started collecting his things. Then he loaded his kayak into the back of his truck. If he hurried, he could be on the water to watch the sunrise and still be back in time to open the clinic.

Chase hopped in his truck. A short drive later, he parked in the clearing alongside the road, dragged his kayak to the riverbank, and launched it into the water. The sky was a dark canvas that slowly faded into light as the sun climbed over the trees and mountains behind him, just like it had three weeks ago when he'd brought Sophie here.

Chase sighed, adding to the mix of nature's noise. Every beat of his heart squeezed painfully. She'd lied to him; he'd lied to her. And now they felt even further apart than ever.

He swallowed and watched an eagle soar across the mountain skyline. A couple of egrets strolled onshore, observing him as much as he was them. Time seemed to disappear as he rowed.

Fifteen minutes later, he made it to the other side of the riverbank. Normally, he'd set off on a hike but he was drained of energy today so he just sat and enjoyed the sights and sounds of the outdoors.

His thoughts were clearer out here than they'd been alone in his bed all night. And his argument with Sophie seemed silly. At least the first part of it. He understood why she hadn't told him about Nadine's history. She'd been right that he wouldn't have hired her. His feelings about his brother would have overcast any chance for Nadine to work at his clinic.

A fish jumped out of the water, clearing the surface a good six inches before disappearing back into the murky river.

Chase didn't move. Instead, he continued to ponder, looking at things from a different point of view this morning. Nadine hadn't really done anything wrong by staying at his clinic. She hadn't hurt anyone. And he felt like a jackass for pressing charges instead of reaching out a hand to help her. Maybe Sophie was right, and it had everything to do with his brother. And with him.

He pulled out his cell phone, doubting it would have good reception, and dialed Alex Baker's number.

"Hey, buddy," Alex said after a couple of rings. "Everything okay?"

Chase was surprised the call connected. "Not really. I've had a change of heart. I want to drop the charges against Nadine."

"Oh yeah?" Alex asked. "Does this change of heart have anything to do with the woman who's stolen your heart?"

Chase swallowed. Sophie had stolen his heart a long time ago. They'd come to this second chance with a lot of baggage between them though. Maybe too much baggage. "Is it too late to drop the charges?"

"Not at all. I'm kind of glad you decided to go this way. I don't think Nadine had mal-intent."

"Me neither," Chase agreed.

"All right, then. I'll let Nadine know she's free to go."

"Thanks." Chase slid his sunglasses over his face as the sun came up in its full glory. "I have something else I need to do today but please tell her that I want her to stop in my clinic tomorrow morning if possible." Tomorrow was Saturday but Chase needed to go in and check on the overnight animals anyway.

"I'll do that," Alex said. "And I'll call Trisha and see if there are any beds open at the women's shelter for her temporarily."

Chase was pretty sure Trisha would make certain there was, even if she had to create one for Nadine in her office. "Thanks, buddy." They said their goodbyes, and Chase returned to his kayak and traveled back across the river. When he arrived home, he freshened up and headed to the clinic. Then he called Jason and asked if he could cover the schedule this afternoon.

"I know it's short notice."

"It's fine," Jason told him. "But if you keep calling me to Sweetwater Springs, I might decide to move there."

"Not gonna lie, I could use some help at the clinic. It's more than one vet can handle these days."

"Is that a job offer?" Jason asked.

"It's something for you to think about. So you can come today?" Chase asked again.

"Sure. I'll be there."

"Thanks." Chase disconnected the call and blew out a breath. He had something important he suddenly needed to do, and it couldn't wait another day.

Chapter Twenty-One

The spring line was front and center in the boutique, and along the wall were two full racks of evening gowns for customers who were shopping for the fund-raiser at the women's shelter. Sophie had thought that she and Chase would go together but they couldn't even speak right now.

An ache resonated in her chest. Eventually, she supposed they'd get back to being friends that waved at each other from a distance. They had to have some level of civility for Trisha's and Petey's sakes. There'd be holidays and birthdays where they'd show up and run into each other. There'd be more weddings like Emma and Jack's, where they'd sit at the same table and maybe even share a dance.

Sophie tapped her heart. No, if they were truly broken up, she couldn't allow herself to get that close to him.

A customer walked into the boutique and waved, pulling Sophie from her thoughts.

"Mrs. Goodman," she said, heading over to one of her

regulars. She put on a smile despite the ache in her chest. "How are you?"

Mrs. Goodman held up a large bag. "I'm doing well. I've heard about what you're doing here, and I brought some donations for the cause. I purchased these from the boutique last year. Now I would like to hand them off to someone who can use them. Which gives me an excuse to buy new things." Mrs. Goodman winked conspiratorially.

Sophie took the bag, surprised by how heavy it was. "That's so nice of you. Thank you."

"Well, it's wonderful of you to help the community. You're such a nice girl. Always have been." Mrs. Goodman looked over her thick bifocals, still conspiring about something. "I heard that you and Dr. Lewis are having troubles. I have a grandson about your age, you know. He's single and good-looking too, if you ask his grandmother."

Sophie felt her cheeks go hot. How did the folks in town hear things so quickly? "I'm afraid I'm not in the dating mood right now."

Mrs. Goodman nodded. "Well, when you're ready for another go at love, my grandson is quite the catch."

Sophie wasn't sure she'd ever be ready for another "go" at love. It seemed to be a merry-go-round of heartbreak that she could do without.

"I'll keep that in mind. Can I help you find something today?" Sophie asked, moving the conversation away from her dating life.

"I don't think I need help. I'll just take a look-see and then head up to your register when I'm ready."

"Perfect. And I'll take these donations to my Fairy Godmother's Closet." Sophie headed to the back of her store to drop off the bag. The beautiful yellow walls were supposed to brighten her spirits but they just made her think of Chase.

She lifted her gaze to the stained glass light fixture and its iridescent dragonflies. They were a symbol of new beginnings. It looked like Sophie wasn't going to get that for herself. She sat on the bench for a moment to collect her emotions. Tending her boutique on the verge of tears wasn't a good look.

When she had regained her composure, she headed back to the front of the boutique and found Mrs. Goodman standing at her register. "Already shopped out?"

"I know what I like when I see it. And I always find it here." Mrs. Goodman handed Sophie her credit card. "Here you go. Don't tell me the cost. I don't want to know." She winked again.

Sophie dutifully rang up the items and ran the card silently. Then she wished Mrs. Goodman a nice day and thanked her again for the bag of gently used clothing.

For the rest of the afternoon, customers streamed in and out, which Sophie was thankful for. It distracted her from moping. One last customer stopped in before Sophie had to leave and pick up Petey.

Sophie's lips parted. "Nadine. I'm surprised to see you here."

Nadine walked toward Sophie with a sheepish look. "You thought I'd be in jail? Chief Baker said I was free to go. The charges were dropped."

"What?" Sophie asked. "Chase dropped the charges?"

Nadine nodded. "I owe him a huge apology but he's not at the clinic today."

"He's not?" Sophie was trying her best to keep up with the conversation.

"That's what Chief Baker said. So I decided to come see you first. I owe you an apology too."

"Nadine, you don't owe me a thing. I knew about your history. You were honest the entire time."

"But I didn't tell anyone that I was sleeping at the clinic. I should have asked for help. What I did was wrong. I'm sorry I let you down."

Sophie stepped from around the counter and wrapped Nadine in a large hug. "It's okay. You could have told Trisha or me what was going on though. We would have made sure you were taken care of. You could have slept in my back room instead," Sophie said. "Or my guest room at my own home."

Nadine put a hand on her chest. "You're so kind. Thank you for saying so. But someone in town has already offered me a place. Trisha made a call, and a nice woman named Alice Hampton has a rental that's vacant. She said I could stay there for free until I'm able to pay. I told her it might be a while because I don't have a job but she didn't seem to care."

This warmed Sophie's heart. That was the Sweetwater Springs' way. Everyone took care of each other like family.

"Anyway, I wanted to tell you I'm sorry."

Sophie hugged her again. "When you're ready to interview for more jobs, come see me for another wardrobe makeover."

Nadine smiled. "My very own fairy godmother," she said.

They talked for a few minutes more. Then Nadine waved and headed out.

Sophie wanted to cry as Nadine left her boutique. She was so happy that Nadine was out of jail and had a place to go. Chase had dropped the charges. Did that mean he'd forgiven Nadine? That he'd forgiven Sophie?

That wasn't the only thing standing between them, of course. There were a lot more obstacles. One of them was Sophie's. It was one thing if she truly couldn't climb anymore and didn't want to. But she did want to, and she knew that she could. A leg injury wasn't holding her back. It was her own fear. And what she'd said to Chase in the heat of the moment was true. She would end up resenting him over time because he was still doing what they'd once loved doing together. That was no way to be in a relationship.

Sophie pulled up the contacts in her phone and found Denny's name. He was a friend and the best climbing instructor she knew. She also knew he worked with all kinds of people with disabilities, including Mayor Brian Everson, who was confined to a wheelchair. If Brian could climb with adaptations, so could Sophie.

Denny didn't answer so she left a message telling him that she wanted to get back on the cliffs. Ready or not, she was going to face her fears.

* * *

After Jason arrived to take over the clinic, Chase had gotten in his truck and started driving. He had no idea what he'd say when he saw Pete. All he knew was that he was crossing the distance to say *something*. And to give Pete a chance to explain.

Not that there was any explanation that would take away the pain he'd caused so many, including those in Chase's own family. This was a long time coming but it was time. He needed to work through his issues for his own sake. And if there was any hope for Sophie and him again.

There were so many layers of feelings that he'd been peeling back over the past few days. A breakup tended to do that. It made a person look long and hard at their own faults and weaknesses. And what they'd contributed to the relationship to steer it wrong.

Chase never thought he was perfect but he was a lot more imperfect than he'd realized. He wasn't sure what he'd say to Pete when he came face-to-face with him after all this time but he was certain that driving up to see his brother was the right first step to let go of all the junk weighing him down.

A few hours after setting out, Chase pulled into the parking lot for one of North Carolina's largest state prisons. It was surrounded by a barbed wire fence. Chase got the feeling that guns were pointed at his chest as he walked toward the front entrance. That most likely wasn't true and was probably just the product of watching one too many thriller movies.

He stepped inside the building and showed the man sitting at a reception counter his ID. Then he was led into a waiting room, where he sat in a plastic chair at a small rectangular table.

Time ticked by at a slow pace as he waited. Did Trisha sit in this same chair when she brought Petey to see his dad?

The thought of that lit anger inside Chase's chest. No little boy should ever have to see his dad like this. They wouldn't even be able to share a hug, and Petey loved to give hugs. Pete was missing his boy's life, and for what?

The door on the other side of the room opened and a vaguely familiar man was escorted in. Gone were the perfectly fitted Armani business suits that Pete used to wear so well. Gone were the gelled hair and smooth skin. The polished and pearly white smile. The man standing in front of Chase was an older, more tired version of Chase's brother.

Chase swallowed hard and wondered for a moment what Pete was thinking about the sight of him. It'd been less than a year since they'd seen each other but it felt like a decade.

Pete sat at the opposite end of the table where Chase was seated.

"Took you long enough," Pete said as a conversation starter.

Chase didn't respond immediately. He didn't owe his brother an excuse. Pete was lucky that he had even decided to come here today.

"You look good," Pete said. "Time has been kind to you, brother."

Chase nodded. "Thanks."

"Don't feel the need to reciprocate. I know I look like hell."

Chase didn't disagree. "I got your letters."

Pete looked down at his hands for a moment. "I didn't get yours."

Chase wasn't going to feel guilty or apologize. That wasn't why he was here. "Yeah, well, if you wouldn't have stolen from people, there would have been no need to write letters."

Pete stared at him, his head bobbing softly in agreement. "I'm sorry."

"Yeah, I got that message." Chase could hear the bitterness surfacing in his voice. He didn't want to be this guy. Why had he come here? What did he want to happen in this visit? "I, uh...I forgive you. No need to apologize anymore, Pete. Not to me."

Pete's eyes brightened. "Yeah?"

"Yeah. You made a mistake. Probably a lot of them. But you're human. I've done things I'm not proud of too. None that would land me in prison," he said, his tone lifting more into a teasing one. He wasn't about to admit to Pete that he'd been in jail in the last month, behind bars himself. "I'm the one who needs to apologize to you."

"For what?"

"For turning my back on you. I don't condone what you did but you're already paying the price. You didn't need to lose your brother too." Chase would have liked to think he was better than that. It was never too late to change your mind though. To try to do better. "I'm sorry."

Pete smiled. "If there wasn't a guard watching, I'd hug you."

"And I'd hug you back," Chase said.

Pete looked down again. "You don't realize how many things you take for granted until they're gone. Thanks for looking out for Trisha and Petey. And Mom too. For a kid who irritated me to death, you sure have stepped up to do the right thing."

Chase looked down this time. "It means a lot to hear you say so."

"These days, I'm the one looking up to you."

Chase swallowed past the sudden swell of emotion. "I've made my share of mistakes—believe me. Especially lately. Nobody's perfect."

"Well, the thing about mistakes is that none of them are unfixable," Pete said. "If they were, you wouldn't be here talking to me right now."

Chase nodded. His brother had always been good for advice. He was still the guy who'd advised Chase on friends, sports, and girls growing up. His brother had taught him so many things about being a man.

They continued talking for another hour, about everything and nothing. He'd missed talking to his older brother. It felt good to drop the resentment and remember the bond they'd once shared. The bond they still shared.

When Chase walked out of the prison, his steps felt lighter. He'd promised Pete that he'd return next month. And the month after that. This seemed to be the year of lost and founds. And now that he'd found what was lost, he was never letting go again.

That applied to his brother and to Sophie. Chase wasn't going to let her go so easily but he needed to work on himself a little more before asking for a third chance.

* * *

Petey hadn't stopped talking since Sophie picked him up from school. Sophie didn't necessarily mind but if this continued all night, the ache in her head would match the one in her leg.

"Can we go outside and play?" he asked. "Please. Comet doesn't want to stay inside."

Sophie laughed. "Comet, huh?"

Comet spun around in a circle and barked excitedly. One would never know he was hit by her car last month.

"Well, I suppose I do need to take Comet for a walk. He's a very active little guy like you."

Petey grinned, revealing a missing tooth on the top row.

"What do you say we go to the dog park nearby? Comet loves it there because he can see all the other dogs." And she loved going too, even if it reminded her of Chase. Everything in Sweetwater Springs reminded her of him.

"Yes, yes, yes! I love the park!" Petey cheered. "Let's go right now!"

Sophie laughed, ignoring the tiredness of her left leg that begged her to take the night off from walking. There was no night off when you were babysitting an active boy and dog who both needed lots of fresh air and room to burn off their energy.

Sophie grabbed her bag, looped it across her body, and reached for her keys. Then she snapped Comet's leash in place—she wasn't letting this dog out of her sight—and called for Petey to follow her to the car.

"Mom never takes me to the dog park," Petey said as they drove. "She says it'll make me want to get a dog of my own. And she's a single mom so she can't handle a dog."

Sophie flicked her gaze at Petey in the back seat. *Uh-oh.* Was she stirring up trouble for Trisha by making her son want a dog of his own? "Well, sometimes it's fun to see them but not necessarily take them home. Dogs are a lot of work." And Sophie might have jumped into this whole dog ownership thing without thinking first. She'd followed her heart though, and that could never steer her wrong.

A short drive later, she parked and helped Petey and Comet out. The evening was cool as the sun began to lower in the sky.

"Do you know where your mom went today?" Sophie asked Petey. Trisha had made it clear she didn't want to disclose the details just yet but Sophie's curiosity had been piqued.

"She went to a big lake," Petey said, looking up at Sophie. "She couldn't take me this time."

"A lake? Silver Lake?" Sophie asked. That was the only lake in Sweetwater Springs.

"No, an even bigger one. She's going to go again real soon. Maybe you and Comet can come with us next time."

Sophie looked down at the little boy. "I love a good lake spot. There are so many things to do." But none of them involved a new job for Trisha. "Do you remember the lake's name?"

Petey shrugged. "She wouldn't tell me. She said it's a big surprise." He grinned and flashed a smile revealing his missing tooth again.

Sophie draped her arm over his shoulders. Her best friend was smart not to tell Petey her secrets because Sophie surely would have pried them out of him right now. "Well, a lakeside surprise sounds exciting. Comet and I will definitely try to tag along if you and your mom head back that way."

Sophie's phone buzzed in her pocket. She pulled her arm from around Petey's shoulders and reached into her pocket to retrieve her phone and answer it. "Hey."

"Just wanted to let you know that I've closed the boutique," her mom told her.

"Thanks, Mom. How was the afternoon?" Sophie kept her gaze on Petey and Comet as they walked.

"Wonderful. We sold several gowns for customers going to the shelter's black-tie affair tomorrow night. You remember that pretty purple-colored one?"

Sophie swallowed thickly. That was the one she'd hoped to wear as she danced in Chase's arms. It was long and flowing, and it would definitely hide her scars. "It sold?"

"It sure did. Helen Mayberry snatched it up. It's going to be such a nice occasion," her mom continued.

"It is," Sophie agreed. Sophie stopped to sit on a park bench.

Petey dropped to his knees and started petting Comet, talking to him excitedly in a quiet voice. Something about Comet learning to shake and roll over.

Good luck with those tricks when he can barely heel on command.

"You're still going, aren't you, Mom?" Sophie asked. "You haven't bought a dress yet."

Her mom made a noise on the other end of the line. "Can't I just wear one of my Sunday dresses?"

Sophie rolled her eyes, scanning the darkening sky. "No. You need to pick out a fancy gown. That's the whole point of having a black-tie event. It's a reason to sparkle and shine."

"Fine, fine. I'll pick one out. I think you're just trying to make another sale though," her mom teased.

"No, I just want to see you and Dad all dressed up."

"Well, he'll probably go dressed in jeans, knowing your father."

Sophie rolled her eyes again, laughing because she knew her mom was probably right. "Can you at least get him to wear a sport coat?"

"I'll try. How's Petey doing?" her mom asked then, knowing that Sophie had taken the rest of the afternoon off to watch Trisha's son.

"He's a very energetic boy, and we haven't even visited Dawanda's Fudge Shop yet."

"Oh, he'll love a trip to the fudge shop. That's a kid's favorite treat."

"An adult's too," Sophie said. Especially an adult with a broken heart. She slumped against the bench. She hadn't realized how tired she was until she'd sat down. An incoming call beeped as she spoke to her mom. "Mom, I need to go. I'm getting another call."

"Maybe it's Chase," her mom said hopefully.

"It's not," Sophie said. "I'll see you tomorrow, Mom." Sophie disconnected with her mom and answered the other call.

"Sophie. This is Denny Larson. Just returning your call. I was glad to hear that you want to get back on the mountain."

Sophie watched as Petey and Comet played together. "I was hoping you'd go with me. I'm a little rusty, and, well, I'm not sure I can actually do it."

"I'm sure, and I'd love to take you. I actually have an opening tomorrow around noon. What do you say?"

Sophie swallowed. Trisha was coming to pick Petey up from the boutique first thing tomorrow. And Sophie's mom was already planning to work at the boutique in the afternoon.

"I know that black-tie event is tomorrow," Denny said, "but we can go out for a few hours and still be back in plenty of time to make it to the event. I promise. I have a date who'd be pretty miffed if I stood her up for the fanciest event of the year in Sweetwater Springs."

Sophie laughed. "No time like the present, right?"

CHAPTER TWENTY-TWO

On Saturday morning, Sophie unlocked the boutique with Petey and Comet in tow. Petey had woken Sophie early this morning, wanting to play and have breakfast. Sophie made him a large stack of pancakes with extra butter and syrup. She'd kept her stack small because nerves tingled through her body. It was an excited feeling mixed with a little bit of fear too. But she planned to conquer that fear today on the mountain.

Sophie set Petey and Comet up just outside the Fairy Godmother's Closet where she could see them from the front counter. Then she straightened things up before turning the sign in the window to OPEN. Almost immediately, the first customer of the day walked inside. She wanted a dress for tonight's black-tie affair. A second and third customer walked in wanting to shop for the same. Nothing like last-minute shopping.

Sophie happily rang them up, suspecting that most of today's customers would be here for the same reason.

Thirty minutes after opening the store, Sophie had already

sold four dresses. As one more satisfied customer walked out, Trisha walked in.

"Petey is playing with Comet in the back," Sophie told her. "He'll be happy to see you."

Trisha approached the counter. "Did he behave for you?"

"Always. We watched *Shrek* and *Shrek 2*, ate popcorn, and both of us passed out on the couch. It was awesome." Sophie smiled. "But I think he's ready to go home. Aunt Sophie and Comet don't compare to Mom."

Trisha beamed, and Sophie didn't think it was because she was happy to see her. There was something different about her this morning. "You got the job, didn't you?" Sophie asked, feeling excited for her friend.

Trisha's smile grew wider. "I did," she said, sweeping her gaze around the room.

Sophie bounced on her heels. Then she stepped toward her friend and gave her a congratulatory hug. "Management, right?" Sophie pulled back and looked at her friend. "I need all the details. Maybe we can get together tomorrow for lunch. Tonight will be a whirlwind with your big event."

Trisha nodded. "Yes, it will. Speaking of which, I still haven't gotten my dress yet."

"Seems to be the theme of the day. And I haven't gotten mine either. The one I had my eye on sold yesterday." She shrugged. "Not that I have a date either."

Trisha's smile drooped. "He'll be there. Maybe you two will share another dance and realize you can't live without each other."

Sophie looked down for a moment. Then she looked back up and gestured toward the dresses. "You choose yours first. There are a few left in your size."

Trisha walked over to the rack of dresses, taking her time to look at each one. Finally, she chose a gorgeous black dress for herself. She pulled a hanger with a pale-blue dress off the rack, walked it back over to Sophie, and held it up to her. "And I think you should wear this one."

Sophie took the hanger. "That's the one I was thinking about. You made my choice easy."

"Are you nervous about giving a speech tonight?" Trisha asked.

Sophie had almost forgotten about that. "Actually, I haven't even thought about it today. I'm too nervous about what I'm going to do before the event."

"Oh? What's that?"

Fresh nerves prickled inside Sophie's chest. She wasn't backing out this time. "I'm going climbing."

Trisha blinked but didn't say anything. "By yourself?" she finally asked.

Sophie shook her head. "No, I learned my lesson on that front a long time ago. I'm meeting Denny Larson."

Trisha seemed to relax. "You're sure you're ready?"

Sophie shook her head. "I'm not sure of much these days." The only thing she was sure of was that she wasn't going to let fear stand in her way anymore.

"Well, you can tell me all about the climb tomorrow," Trisha said. "And I'll tell you about my new job."

Sophie was afraid to ask, which was exactly why she needed to. "It's not in Sweetwater Springs, is it?"

Trisha sucked in a deep breath, her apologetic gaze giving Sophie her answer before she even said a word. "No, it's not."

Sophie felt her eyes begin to burn. "It's at a lake?"

Trisha nodded. "Somerset Lake."

Sophie felt her heart drop. Somerset Lake was two hours away. There'd be no more spur-of-the-moment visits. She swallowed and forced a smile, knowing this was what her friend needed—to move on. "I'm happy for you."

* * *

Even though it was Saturday, Chase had gotten up and headed to the veterinary clinic. He had a few overnight animals, and he'd told Nadine to meet him here this morning. Hopefully, she'd come.

He'd checked on the animals and then walked up front just as Nadine tapped on the glass. Chase smiled at her and let her in.

Her return smile was hesitant. "Thank you for dropping the charges, Dr. Lewis. I'm sorry about…everything. And I'll pay you for those bars in your desk," she said, looking genuinely apologetic.

Chase kind of felt embarrassed that she would even regret eating his food if she was hungry. "I'm the one who needs to apologize to you, Nadine. I didn't even see that you needed help. I should have asked you."

"You did ask," she reminded him. "I said I was fine."

Chase chuckled because that reminded him of another stubborn woman in his life. "Well, let's make a deal. From now on, while you're working here at the clinic, don't be afraid to tell me what you need."

Nadine looked at him like he was crazy. "You fired me. And had me arrested."

Chase grimaced. "So you don't want your job back? Because I really need some help around the clinic."

A glimmer of a smile touched Nadine's lips. "Yes, I would love my job back."

Chase nodded. "Then it's yours." He offered his hand for her to shake.

Nadine bypassed the hand and gave him a huge hug. "I couldn't be happier. Thank you."

Then, as a show of trust, he offered Nadine a key.

She stared at it a moment and then looked at him. "I have

a place to stay now so you don't have to worry that I'll be sleeping here."

"I'm not worried. But the animals might need attention tomorrow. And I'm hoping to be busy this evening," he said. Because before this day was over, he was going to find Sophie and lay his heart on the line.

Nadine took the key and put it on her keyring. Then she thanked him a dozen times more, waved goodbye, and walked out.

Chase locked up and walked out too. Next stop was looking for Sophie.

His cell phone rang, flashing Trisha's name on the screen. "Hey," he said.

He must have sounded disappointed because Trisha asked, "You were hoping I was Sophie?"

He didn't answer that. "Have you seen her?"

"Yes, actually, and you wouldn't believe what she's doing right now."

Chase clicked his key fob and got inside his truck. "Oh?"

"Unfortunately, it's not my story to tell. Maybe she'll tell you about it tonight."

"I was hoping to see her sooner than that."

Trisha made a noise. "She's not available. You'll have to wait until the big event to tell her you're hopelessly in love with her and beg for her to take you back."

Chase cleared his throat as he cranked his truck's engine. She wasn't far off from the truth of what he was planning. "Were you calling to give me grief?"

"No; actually, I need to talk to you. Is there a time we can get together?"

"How about right now? Since Sophie apparently isn't available."

"Come on over. Petey and I were going to have ice cream. We're celebrating."

"Oh?" he asked.

"We'll talk about it when you get here," she said.

A few minutes later, Chase pulled into Trisha's driveway and headed up to her door. Petey let him in excitedly and gave Chase a huge hug that melted away all his worries. At least for the moment. He never wanted to disappoint his nephew again. He knew that was probably unlikely but he intended to do his best.

He went inside, and they had ice cream with sprinkles and laughed while Petey recapped his week at school. Then Trisha set him up with a movie and headed back toward Chase.

"I don't know how to say this so I'm just going to lay it out." She folded her arms in front of her.

"Okay." He suddenly felt all kinds of anxious. Was she okay? Was Petey?

"I interviewed for a new job yesterday."

He nodded. "Yeah? I didn't realize you wanted to leave the women's shelter."

"I love working there but Petey and I need something... different."

What did Petey have to do with Trisha's job decisions? "Different how?" Chase asked.

Trisha visibly swallowed. She looked nervous as her hands fidgeted in front of her. "The job is at Somerset Lake."

Chase frowned. "That's two hours from here."

"Pretty much."

"Why would you leave Sweetwater Springs? This is your home." His anxiety dialed up a notch. "This is Petey's home."

"Because it's a good job. And because people have a long memory here."

Chase plopped onto a barstool. "Trisha, people who know you here know that you're an honest, hardworking person."

She shrugged. "Maybe, but it's hard, Chase. And I'm tired." Trisha took a breath. "I need a fresh start where no one knows me as Pete's ex-wife. And where no one knows that Petey's dad is in prison for stealing other people's money. Some of his friends' money." She looked down at her hands. Chase could see now that they were shaking.

"You took the job?" he asked, already suspecting that's what this was about. His heart sank like a heavy stone. He'd returned to Sweetwater Springs to be there for Trisha and Petey. But maybe that wasn't the whole truth. Deep down, he'd never stopped loving Sophie, and part of him had also returned for Sophie.

"I'm going to accept it. It's a management position." She looked at him again. "And a new beginning for me and Petey."

Chase's mind raced, looking for ways to fix this situation. To make things right so Trisha didn't have to feel like she needed to move so far away. But there was no need to fix this. It felt like a good decision for Trisha.

Chase stood and wrapped his arms around her. "Congratulations," he said.

Tears filled Trisha's eyes as she stepped back. "I said I wasn't going to cry. This is happy news. It's what I want."

"All I want is for you and Petey to be happy. No matter where that is."

"Thank you," she said softly. "Take care of Sophie for me?"

He hesitated. "If she'll let me."

"She will." Trisha looked up at him. "The first time you two broke up, you went in separate directions. You couldn't see your way back to each other. Now you're both headed toward each other. You dropped the charges against Nadine. And went to see Pete. You're letting go of the old stuff to make room for the new. And Sophie is..." Trisha trailed off.

"She's what?"

"She's out there working on herself today too, letting go of the old stuff that's been holding her back."

Chase's curiosity was piqued. So was his hope.

"I'm going to miss having you around for Petey. And for me," Trisha said with a sniffle.

"What are you talking about? You're moving but you're not getting rid of me so easily. You'll be back to visit because we're family."

Trisha didn't have any real relatives in Sweetwater Springs. But Chase and his mom had never stopped considering her family even after her divorce from Pete.

"I hope you'll have a guest room or a couch," Chase added, "because I'll be coming down as often as I can."

Trisha sucked in a breath, and he could tell she was trying not to get emotional.

He laid a hand on her shoulder. "I understand why you want a fresh start, and you deserve it."

She looked up at him again and nodded as her eyes turned glassy. "You deserve that too. I'm rooting for you and Sophie."

Chase pulled back from the hug. "Got any tips for me to win her back?"

Trisha grinned. "It's hard to resist a man in a tux."

Chase nodded. "I rented mine last week. It's not often a person gets to dress up around here. Not like this."

Trisha narrowed her eyes. "When Petey was upset with you, gifts and grand gestures didn't work. You won him over again by just being honest and being yourself."

Chase felt emotional now too. "Be myself? That's your tip?"

Trisha laughed softly. "That's what made Sophie fall in love with you the first time. It's pretty clear she never fell out of love with you, so your chances are good." Trisha held up a finger. "But she does have to give a speech at my event tonight. Can you wait to do whatever you're going to do or say until after her speech? Just in case it ends badly." Trisha grimaced.

Chase did too. "I thought you had faith in Sophie and me."

"I do. But when people are talking tomorrow, I want them

to be talking about how perfect this event was. I want to go out in style."

Chase chuckled. "I can do that for you."

She smiled as tears collected and streamed down her cheeks. Then she blew out a breath. "Okay. I've told Sophie and now you. Now I have to break the news to your mom."

"Good luck with that. She might move down to Somerset Lake with you just to be close to her grandson."

"Unless you and Sophie make up and get started on giving her a new one." Trisha swiped at her cheeks and winked at him.

Chase held up his hands. "Whoa. I have to win her back first. And I don't necessarily want to take things slow but I don't want to go that fast either." Except part of him did. Part of him was ready to make up for lost time with Sophie. He was inspired by Trisha's determination to pave a new way for her family.

He hugged Trisha before leaving her home. Then he drove back to his house, wishing he could go to Sophie. His arms ached to hold her. His body ached to be held by her. And he really needed to tell her how he felt. How he'd always felt and always would about her.

He loved her. The kind of love that left him breathless and unable to sleep when they weren't together. The kind that made him want to be a better man. That made him forgive his brother when he'd been refusing to do so and reach out a hand to someone who needed it, regardless of their past. The kind of love that made him want to look toward the future and consider things like marriage and children and growing old together. He wanted it all, and he wanted it with Sophie.

* * *

Fear gripped Sophie by the heart. She sucked in a deep breath through her nose, held it, and blew it out.

"You okay?" Denny asked.

Sophie's feet hadn't even left the ground yet, and her instructor looked concerned.

She shook her head honestly. "I'm freaking out but I'm also excited." She looked up at the towering mountainside in front of her. She'd mounted much steeper cliffs. This was more of a beginner's climb but it terrified her all the same. This was definitely not like riding a bike. "I can do this," she said out loud.

Denny patted her back. "Of course you can. I tell people it's all about the arms and the mind."

Sophie's arms were strong. She'd been doing yoga and swimming for years. Her mind was also strong.

"You ready?" Denny asked.

Sophie looked over. She took another cleansing breath, and then she nodded. "Ready."

They took the cliff slowly. At first, Sophie's entire body was shaking. She put one hand above the other, inching her way up. Her left leg began to tense but she leaned more on her arms. She focused on her breaths, just like she did in her yoga practice.

One arm reaching and then the next. Sophie vaguely heard Denny's words of encouragement in the background. She knew how to climb. She didn't need him to teach her. She just needed someone to be here. Some part of her wished that person were Chase.

Denny helped Sophie clear the edge of the cliff once she'd reached the top. Then she rolled onto her back with a large smile on her face. She closed her eyes as the sun beat down on her skin. She realized she had tears on her cheeks.

"You okay?" Denny asked, sitting up beside her.

She opened her eyes to look at him. "Better than okay. That. Was. Amazing."

Denny chuckled. "There's no better feeling."

Sophie had forgotten how it felt. She disagreed with Denny though. There was one better feeling. Being in love, being with Chase—that felt even better. And as soon as she got off this mountain, she was going to find him and tell him so.

CHAPTER TWENTY-THREE

Not even a hot shower could ease Chase's tense muscles. After leaving Trisha's house, he'd worked out. He'd jogged, and then he'd done several reps on the pull-up bar in his room. He'd exercised every muscle to the point of exhaustion because his emotions were frayed and this was how he dealt with them.

He stepped out of the tub and grabbed a towel to dry off, grimacing as he lifted his arms away from his body. Sophie had taught him yoga stretches that might help with his tight muscles. He'd only completed the poses on the riverbank with her. He wasn't sure he remembered the sequence but he was desperate to relieve his soreness in the same way he'd been desperate to relieve his stress. The only way he'd find relief, though, was to talk to Sophie. He didn't know where she went today but he knew where to find her tonight.

He walked into the living room and proceeded to do a few stretches. He bent at the waist, feeling the muscles along his back lengthen. It was painful but it also felt good so he let his body dangle there for a long minute as the blood rushed to his head. Then he walked his hands out in front of him and went into a downward dog pose, breathing in and out the way Sophie had taught him. She'd taught him so much this past month. Just being with her had influenced him to make changes in his life and the way he thought about things.

Dropping out of the downward dog, Chase moved his body into a plank. He focused on his breathing and thoughts of Sophie. And Petey. And Pete.

When he was done with the sequence, he felt compelled to sit down at the small personal desk in the corner of the room. He pulled out a pad of paper and reached for a pen. Then, for the first time in six months, he wrote his brother back.

He started by telling Pete about the weather. For some reason, that's what people did when they didn't know what to say. After that, the topic turned to their mom. Then the veterinary clinic. Chase didn't mention Trisha's decision to move. Chase was sure she'd tell him the next time she took Petey to visit. Lastly, Chase wrote about Sophie.

When he was done, he set his pen down and smiled to himself. For so long, all he could do was dwell on what his brother had done wrong. But like his brother said, no mistake was unfixable. Pete was serving his time, and he'd apologized to everyone he'd hurt. Now it was Chase's turn to make things right with the woman he loved—if he could.

Chase looked at the time on his phone. He needed to hurry and get dressed fast. He didn't want to be late to the black-tie affair. Chase stood and walked back to his bedroom where his tux was hanging off the closet door. He started to reach for it but stopped as his cell phone began to ring.

Chase pulled it out of his pocket and hesitated at the sight of the caller ID. It was an emergency vet call. He couldn't not answer. But he couldn't miss the women's shelter event either. Trisha had worked so hard on it. And Chase needed to be there for Sophie.

He didn't want to miss her speech, and he didn't want to let another second go by when they weren't talking to each other.

The phone continued to ring in Chase's hand. Finally, resigned, he connected the call.

"Dr. Lewis? I was worried you wouldn't answer. I need help with Chester," one of Chase's clients said.

Chase closed his eyes as he listened to the pet owner frantically relay the story of how his elderly dog wasn't going to the bathroom today. Chester wasn't eating or drinking either. It was a situation like what had happened with Grizzly just a few months ago. Chase would have done anything to save his dog at the time. "I'll be at the clinic in ten minutes," Chase promised. The dog had a good chance if he was seen right away. Chase would do everything he could to make him better.

"Thank you, Dr. Lewis. I owe you one."

Chase grabbed his tux from the hook on the door. He bent and grabbed his shoes from the floor too. He couldn't put the items on just yet. He'd have to dress at the clinic and hurry from there to the black-tie affair. Hopefully, he wouldn't be too late—for the dog or the event.

* * *

Sophie's body shivered. The dress she'd picked out from her boutique was long but it wasn't quite long enough. The slit that ran along the side gave a peek at the scars that ran up her left calf.

She angled her body in front of the mirror, her heart sinking at the sight of the raised pink labyrinth of scarred flesh. She'd kept it covered all these years. Even with Chase, she'd made sure he never saw it. They'd made love and shared the most intimate parts of their bodies but she hadn't shown him her scars.

She took a deep breath and recaptured the feeling she'd had earlier. She'd climbed up a mountain, and it'd felt like the very first time—only better. She was strong and vibrant, and these scars—well, they weren't a reminder of what she'd lost anymore. They were a reminder of what she refused to give up.

She took another breath and stepped out her left leg to give an even better view of her scars. She wasn't going to hide them tonight. She was going to be confident in every aspect of who she was. No more hiding behind long dresses and her fear of not being enough. Tonight, she was going to get up in front of her town, thank them for helping her when she was down, and applaud them for doing the same for the women that ended up at the shelter.

Everyone needed a hand up and a second chance at some point in their lives. Sophie was honored that she'd been the recipient once and that now she was able to be the giver.

Sophie smiled at her reflection in the mirror. Then she slipped her feet into a pair of flats. Although the days of high heels were gone, she was walking taller today than she had in a very long time. She felt proud and confident, which, in her book, was beautiful—scars and all.

Sophie looked at the time on her phone. She needed to hurry. She didn't want to be late, because suddenly tonight felt like the first night of the rest of her life.

* * *

Twenty minutes later, Sophie walked into the large event center where Emma and Jack had held their wedding reception just over a month ago.

"Wow! You look ah-mazing!" Trisha said, stepping up to Sophie.

"So do you!" Sophie ran her gaze down her friend's drop-dead-gorgeous body.

"I should look good," Trisha said. "I'm wearing a dress from the best boutique in town."

"All the guys here will be lining up to dance with you."

"And you, although I'm guessing Chase is the only one you're interested in."

At the mention of his name, Sophie's gaze unwittingly moved around the room to look for him.

"He's not here yet," Trisha said apologetically. "I called his cell phone because he was supposed to help me set up a few things but he's not answering."

Sophie felt her smile drop as she looked at her friend. "Where is he?"

Trisha shrugged. "I'm not sure. I saw him earlier. He was still coming when I spoke to him. He was actually anxious to talk to you but I told him that you were...preoccupied." Trisha held up a hand. "But don't worry. I didn't tell him with what." Trisha smiled. "How'd it go, by the way?"

"I made it. I leaned on my arms and my right leg, and I never looked down. It was more my fear keeping me from going back up. I faced it today, and it felt good."

Trisha opened her arms, and Sophie stepped into the hug.

As they pulled away, Sophie looked around the room again. What if Chase wasn't coming? What if he'd been looking for her to tell her so? What if he didn't want a third chance?

"Stop that." Trisha pointed a finger at Sophie's chest. "I can see you worrying about worst-case scenarios. He's coming. You two will talk things out, and you'll realize that you can't live without each other."

Sophie narrowed her eyes. "This night is yours. You're the one who planned this huge black-tie affair. You're the one who has brought the community together. Don't waste another second on my drama. What can I do for you?"

Trisha shook her head. "You are such a good friend. I'm going to miss you when I'm at Somerset Lake."

"No, you're not. Because I'll be FaceTiming you, texting you, calling. You'll see more of me after you move than you do right now." Sophie forced a smile.

"Promise?"

"Promise," Sophie confirmed. Then she turned to talk to Kaitlyn and Mitch as they made their way into the room, which was quickly filling up. Josie and Tuck entered behind them. They had Tuck's daughter, Maddie, with them but she quickly veered off to a group of other teens, including Jack Hershey's nephew, Sam.

Sophie's gaze stayed with Josie for a long moment. Josie looked different tonight. She had a glow about her. Sophie's gaze lowered to the small swell of Josie's usually flat stomach. The dress she was wearing was formfitting and revealing. Sophie smiled to herself. *Bingo.* There was the other secret pregnant friend. Although after tonight, Sophie doubted it'd be a secret to anyone.

Sophie continued to greet couples and their families, feeling suddenly alone in the crowded room. Her mom and dad would be here later, of course. But she would still be standing here on her own. She was so tired of being alone. She belonged with Chase. She'd always belonged with him. Where was he?

"Sophie?" a woman's voice called.

Sophie turned to see Nadine, who had come with her new landlady, Alice Hampton. "Hi," Sophie said. "You ladies look beautiful."

"You're so kind," Nadine said. She gestured down at her dress. "Alice had a dress for me to wear tonight. We're the same size. Isn't that a coincidence?"

Sophie recognized the dress from her boutique. It was from a line that she'd carried three years ago. "It looks great on you." Sophie gave them both a hug.

Then Nadine looked around. "Where's Chase?"

Sophie shook her head. "He's not here. I'm not sure."

"Oh, I hope he didn't get called into the clinic." Nadine frowned.

Sophie hadn't considered that. "I hope not too."

Alice touched her arm to gain Sophie's attention. "I hear you're giving a speech tonight."

"I am. Trisha is the host but she wanted me to talk about my Fairy Godmother's Closet."

"I've heard a lot about it," Alice said. "That's a wonderful thing you're doing. I have some dresses in my closet that I need to drop off for you."

"Thank you." Sophie greeted more friends as she made her way toward the front of the quickly filling event room. Her left leg tensed as she walked, making her pause for just a moment. Maybe she'd overexerted herself on the mountain earlier. She couldn't bring herself to regret it though. Instead, she found a chair and sat to rest. She bent and massaged her calf muscle until it relaxed. Usually she would only do this in private, not wanting to call attention to herself. But something inside her had unlocked on the mountain today. No more hiding. No more pretending. No more holding herself back from her heart's desires.

The lights dimmed, and Trisha walked onto the stage. She welcomed everyone and talked about where the idea for the black-tie affair had come from. She spoke about her time at the women's shelter and her passion for what she did. And how helping these women had helped her in her own life. Then she revealed that she was moving on but that the work here would continue.

It was a bittersweet moment for Sophie to watch, and it unleashed so many emotions. Sophie didn't want to get teary eyed prior to going onstage but the effort not to was futile.

After several minutes, Trisha reached out a hand toward Sophie and invited her to join her onstage. Sophie felt her entire body freeze. Then she stood on two stable legs and walked toward the steps. She lifted her right leg to take the first stair, and her left leg buckled under the weight. Sophie barely had time to gasp because suddenly a hand reached out to steady her. To the audience, it probably looked like Chase was just being a gentleman by offering his arm. But he had kept her from falling to the floor.

Trying not to fall in love, however, was another futile effort where he was concerned. He helped her all the way up to the stage and then he removed his arm.

"Thank you," Sophie said, catching his eye. There was so much she needed to say to him but this moment belonged to the audience and the women's shelter. To the town that had always backed Sophie.

"Break a leg," Chase said with a wink.

Sophie almost laughed. That was a misplaced joke, considering she'd almost fallen. And the fact that her dog had just recovered from a broken hind leg.

The shock of the humor worked to push Sophie's emotions down just enough. She continued walking toward Trisha, gave her friend a hug, and then stood behind the podium. Sophie stared out at all the familiar faces. She'd written a speech for tonight but suddenly it didn't feel like what she wanted to say.

"I'm not sure why Trisha chose me to speak tonight," Sophie began. "I don't really feel like I've done anything out of the ordinary. I just opened the tiny back room of my boutique the way Sweetwater Springs opened its hearts and homes to me when I was broken and needed help."

The tears were back in Sophie's eyes. "For those of you who don't know my story, I survived thirty-six hours on a mountain. I almost lost my leg. Sweetwater Springs rallied around me. Whatever I needed, this town stepped up to the plate and provided. I have always been grateful, and since my accident, I've been trying to pay that kindness and charity forward."

She took a moment to breathe. "Tonight, as I stand here, I want to thank you first for what you all did for me." Sophie pressed a hand to her heart, which was overflowing with love and gratitude. "And what you continue to do in this community. The women at the shelter needed a roof over their heads, so Trisha took them in as part of her job. They needed food, so all of you have donated faithfully over the years. They needed clothes and jobs and countless other things that you've all provided. That we've provided together. And one day, when these women are back on their feet, they'll join you in helping those who aren't as fortunate. That's why I love this town and everyone in it so much. We are a family here, even to the strangers that wander in."

Sophie looked out on the crowd, scanning the people in it. Brenna and Luke. Joy and Granger, along with Granger's girls. Halona and Alex. Paris and Lacy. Dawanda and her husband. Sophie took a shuddery breath, releasing the paper she'd written onto the podium. She wasn't going to use her speech. "So tonight is really to celebrate each of you for being so generous with your time, your money and resources, and your love. It makes a difference. It changes lives. I know because it changed mine. Thank you." Sophie found Chase's face in the crowd and her gaze stuck. "Now, find someone special and dance the night away."

Sophie heard the applause as she headed off the stage. Her focus was on Chase though. He stepped up to offer his hand as she descended the stairs.

"Can we talk?" she asked as soon as she was on the ground level.

He narrowed his eyes, looking slightly worried. The time he'd said those words, they'd broken up. However, this time, more than anything, she wanted to make up. “Sure. We can go outside where it’s quiet.”

She didn’t let go of his hand. “Lead the way.”

* * *

Chase removed his tux coat and placed it around Sophie’s bare shoulders as they stepped outside. The night was cool now that the sun had disappeared from the mountainous skyline. In its stead was a silvery moon with a dusting of stars.

“It’s a beautiful night,” Chase commented.

Sophie turned to him, suddenly looking nervous. “It is. How was the speech?”

“Heartfelt. The best kind,” Chase said. All he wanted to do was pull her into his arms but he wasn’t sure what she wanted. He knew what he hoped she wanted.

“It wasn’t at all what I planned to say,” Sophie said. “I wanted to talk more about the Fairy Godmother’s Closet and how the clothing donations have helped people like Nadine get job interviews. I wanted to mention all the wonderful donations that women have generously given. About how you and the others turned the room into something special.” Sophie shook her head. “There was so much I wanted to say but when I was up there, the only thing that mattered was saying thank you. Kind of like now.”

“You want to thank me?” Chase asked.

She laughed softly. “No. Yes. I want to say a million things all at once. I want to tell you that I’m sorry and I’m proud of you for going to see Pete. Trisha told me.”

Chase nodded. “It was overdue.”

“And I want to say that I think you’re brave and amazing. I also want to tell you that I went climbing today,” she said as a tear slipped down her cheek.

Chase's mouth fell open. "That's where you were today?"

"That was overdue too. Denny went with me to make sure I was okay." Sophie smiled widely. "And it was amazing. It felt just like I remembered. Even better. It was hard, and I was scared but I mounted that cliff, and then I stood and looked out on the valley." She reached for his hands. "I wish you could've been there with me."

"Me too," he said. "I'm happy for you, Soph."

She sucked in a breath. "But now that I'm standing here in front of you, there's only one thing I really want to tell you. Only one thing that matters."

Chase gave her hand a squeeze, willing her to continue. "Oh? What is that?"

"I want to tell you that I love you. I have always loved you, and I always will."

Chase lifted a hand and traced his finger alongside her cheek. "Funny, that's what I came here to tell you tonight."

"Great minds," Sophie said as more tears filled her eyes.

"I hope you didn't feel like you had to climb a mountain for me though," he said. Because he would've loved her no matter what.

Sophie's smile lifted her cheeks. "When I attempted to climb on our weekend getaway, I wasn't ready. It wasn't what I wanted. Today when I went up though, I did it for me. Because I'm tired of being resentful and afraid. I wanted to take back control over the things that scared me, and I did."

Chase was so proud of this woman standing in front of him.

Sophie tilted her head as she looked at him. "I hope you didn't feel like you had to make up with your brother for me."

"No, I did that for me too," Chase confirmed. "Because you were right. I needed to let go of my hard feelings... It seems you make me a better version of myself."

"I'd say we're both better together."

Chase finally pulled her close. They weren't on the dance floor but he didn't care. He could dance all night right here to the tune of her laughter and his heart. "So I guess we should just stay together, then. If that's okay with you."

Sophie pressed her body into his, tipping her head and looking up into his eyes. "It's more than okay with me. In fact, I wouldn't want it any other way."

Chase lowered his mouth to hers, needing to kiss her. When he pulled back again, he narrowed his eyes. "So, in your speech, you told everyone to find someone special and dance the night away."

"That I did," Sophie said. "Just don't step all over my toes. These are new shoes."

"I guess that's the perk of owning your own clothing store," he said, making Sophie smile. It was what he'd said a month ago when they'd danced at Emma and Jack's wedding reception. So much had happened since then.

"Only a man would call my boutique a mere clothing store," she shot back.

"Right. We've been through this, haven't we?" Chase looked down at her feet for a moment before returning his gaze to hers. They'd been through it all now, the good and the bad, and yet here they were. "I can't make any promises where our feet are concerned," he said.

Sophie tilted her head. "No? What promise can you make me?"

He pulled in a breath. "That I'll be here for you forever. If you'll have me."

Sophie tilted her head. "I have to warn you. My dog and I are a package deal. If you love me, you have to love my dog too."

Chase couldn't resist kissing her again. "You really are the perfect woman, aren't you?" he said as he pulled back.

"Hardly," she said on a laugh. "Just the perfect woman for you."

Chase absolutely agreed with her. “Shall we?” he asked, offering his hand.

Sophie nodded. “We shall.”

Then, taking her hand, he led her inside and onto the dance floor where all their friends and family were dancing the night away. But as he turned and pulled Sophie into his arms, it was just the two of them in their own little world—a world he wanted to live in for the rest of his life.

EPILOGUE

I love it here,” Sophie sighed as she lay back on a lawn chair, her hand in Chase’s as he lay on a chair beside her.

He looked over. Sophie could see her reflection in his sunglasses. She looked happy if she did say so. A lakeside vacation looked good on her. It looked good on Chase too. “I guess we’ll have to visit Trisha more often.”

“She’ll be sick of us,” Sophie said, tipping her face back to the sun.

They’d come to visit Trisha in Somerset Lake two days ago but Trisha was working during the day and Petey was tagging along. So the days belonged solely to Sophie and Chase.

A hawk squawked as it flew overhead, causing a flurry of movement below Sophie’s chair.

“I think Comet is afraid of the birds around here,” Chase commented.

Sophie laughed. “He’s not a lake dog, I guess.”

"He'll come around. But you're right. Somerset Lake is nice but we all belong in Sweetwater Springs."

"Except Trisha. She seems to fit here."

Chase squeezed her hand. "We'll visit often," he said again, reassuring Sophie. The last month had been good. Sophie and Chase were closer than ever now. They'd gone on a couple of climbs together. They'd swum in the community pool and spent lazy nights on Chase's back porch, watching Comet chase things that stirred in the bushes. They'd also spent long nights being lovers.

Third chance was a charm, and their relationship was going to stick this time.

Even still, Sophie had missed knowing her best friend was right around the corner. It was an adjustment but things changed. People moved on. And sometimes people returned to where they'd started, different and the same.

"So Jason is coming to work full-time at your clinic now?" Sophie asked.

Chase sighed deeply. "He accepted the job this morning. I guess covering for me these last couple days while we came to visit Trisha sealed the deal."

"That's great," Sophie said. "It'll free up more of your time for me."

Their lawn chairs were so close they touched. Chase rolled onto his side and reached out to her.

Sophie rolled toward him as well. She was wearing a bathing suit and a thin cover-up that only skimmed her thighs. The scars on her left leg were visible but she wore them proudly. She didn't care if people asked what had happened. She was the girl who'd survived against all odds, and she'd found the things she'd lost up there on that mountain ridge when she was eighteen. She'd found herself. Chase. And her passion for climbing again.

"I was thinking about things we could do today while we wait for Trisha and Petey to return home." Chase ran a hand along Sophie's curves.

"Oh?"

"If you're up for it," he added.

She was up for just about anything these days, as long as he was by her side.

"Windsailing. It would be an adventure."

"I do love an adventure with you, Chase Lewis."

"That's good because I've been dreaming up another adventure. One where we make this relationship official," he said.

Sophie's breath caught. She didn't think Chase was about to propose but he was definitely testing the waters on the subject. "Would we elope or would we have a huge wedding? Another excuse for the whole town to get fancy."

"I guess that would be up to you. A small wedding at the top of Sunrise Point might be fitting."

Sophie didn't care where or how or when they got married; all she cared about was spending the rest of her life with this man. "I guess we'll have to hold off on planning until you ask the question. You never know. My answer might be no."

Chase's smile fell.

Sophie laughed and punched him softly. Then she lifted off her chair and leaned over to brush her lips to his. "Or it might be one hundred percent yes."

"That's better," he sighed against her lips.

Comet whined below them, wanting to join in on the fun, but this moment was solely Sophie and Chase's.

"I could stay here and kiss you all day," Chase said.

"We could always go windsailing tomorrow. Or the next day."

"That's true. There's no rush," he said, landing soft kisses on her lips between words. "We have forever."

"Hmm," Sophie sighed. "I like the sound of that."

"Me too." Chase was still holding her hand. He let go for a

second and reached into his pocket. "I was hoping for something more romantic but this moment feels right."

Sophie lowered her gaze to Chase's hand, which was now holding a ring. She gasped softly. Then she reached up and moved Chase's sunglasses to rest on the top of his head. She wanted to see his eyes, to assess if this was real.

"You said the answer would be one hundred percent yes. Or might be. I didn't want to give you a chance to change your mind."

Sophie felt her eyes well up. "I'll never change my mind. Or my heart. It will always be yours."

"So your answer is yes?" Chase asked, suddenly looking vulnerable.

"You haven't asked a question yet," she teased.

"Sophie Daniels, will you be my climbing partner?"

Sophie furrowed her brow.

Chase was teasing her now. "And my swim partner. My canoeing partner. My dance partner."

"Only if you promise not to step on my toes for that last one." She stared into Chase's eyes, unable to look anywhere else.

"I promise a lot more than that. I'll always love you, and I'll always do my best to give you the life you dream about."

Sophie swallowed. Then she fanned the fingers of her left hand out, holding her ring finger steady and ready to wear his ring. "Yes," she said as tears slipped down her cheeks.

Chase slid the ring down her finger and then weaved his fingers in hers. "I can't wait to be your husband."

"And I can't wait to be your wife," she said. Then she tilted her head. "So maybe we shouldn't wait. Sunrise Point next weekend?"

Chase pulled back. "I was kind of joking about that. How on earth would we get Pastor Phillips up the side of a mountain?"

Sophie laughed because Pastor Phillips was in his seventies

now and she doubted he'd ever climbed even in his twenties. "Mayor Everson can officiate weddings. He goes climbing with Denny."

Chase nodded as he seemed to consider the idea. "Denny can be our witness…Don't you need something more romantic than that?"

Sophie laughed and kissed him again. "Aren't you listening? All I need for the rest of my life is you."

Comet finally found his way onto their laps, crashing the moment but also perfecting it as he gave them sloppy kisses.

"And you, Comet," Chase added. Then he pushed Comet away long enough to kiss Sophie one more time. "Sunrise Point next weekend, then. I love you."

Sophie's heart was full and overflowing as she returned those three words. "And I love you back," she said. Then she found her way into his lawn chair and snuggled into the crook of his arm, basking in the bright sunshine and their forever love.

SOPHIE'S EASY CHEESY ENCHILADAS

You don't have to be an expert at cooking for your food to look and taste like you are! These easy enchiladas will impress the youngest and oldest of guests. Great for Taco Tuesdays or any day of the week!

Ingredients:

- 1½ cups shredded Monterey Jack cheese (divided)
- 1½ cups shredded cheddar cheese (divided)
- 3 ounces softened cream cheese
- 1 cup picante sauce (divided)
- 1 medium red, green, or yellow bell pepper (diced)
- ½ cup sliced green onions
- 1 teaspoon cumin powder
- 2 cups precooked shredded chicken
- 8 flour tortillas (each 7–8 inches)
- Shredded lettuce
- Chopped tomato
- Optional: olives and sliced avocado

Directions:

1. Preheat oven to 350°F.
2. Combine 1 cup Monterey Jack cheese, 1 cup cheddar cheese, cream cheese, ¼ cup picante sauce, the diced pepper, onions, cumin powder, and precooked shredded chicken. Mix thoroughly.
3. Spoon ¼ cup cheese mixture down the center of each tortilla. Roll and place in a 13 x 9 inch baking dish. Make sure your rolls are seam-side down to prevent them from opening in the oven.
4. Spoon remaining picante sauce evenly over enchiladas. Cover with remaining cheeses—the cheesier the better!

5. Bake at 350°F for 20 minutes. While you wait, it's the perfect time for a little yoga or texting with your bestie.

6. Top with shredded lettuce and chopped tomato. You can add olives for more color and taste.

7. Serve with additional picante sauce and sliced avocado if desired.

PS Don't forget dessert! Lime chiffon pie would complement this meal like a pair of black ballet flats would any outfit!

Please turn the page to read

A WEDDING ON LAVENDER HILL

by Annie Rains!

Event planner Claire Donovan loves giving clients the weddings of their dreams. But that gets tricky when she has to work with the man who recently broke her heart—Bo Matthews. As the son of the groom and owner of the perfect venue in Sweetwater Springs, Bo will be impossible to avoid. But can Claire be this close to her sexy ex without falling for his charms all over again?

FOREVER

Chapter One

Claire Donovan had a bit of a reputation in Sweetwater Springs. She loved to shop.

As an event planner, she was always looking for a special item to make the *big day* just a touch more special. Last week she'd found a clown costume for a purse-size Chihuahua to wear to its owner's eightieth birthday bash. It was a huge hit with the crowd; not so much with the little dog, who yapped, ran in circles, and tore at the shiny fabric.

The only shopping Claire would be doing this morning, however, was glancing in storefront windows on her way to meet with her newest client, Pearson Matthews. Claire's reputation extended beyond shopping. In Sweetwater Springs, she was also known for being professional and punctual, and for putting on the best parties in town.

She passed Sophie's Boutique and admired the window display, wishing she had more time to pop inside and say hello to the store owner—and try on one of those dresses that she absolutely didn't need. Then she opened the neighboring door to the Sweetwater Café and stepped inside to a cool blast of air on her face. She was instantly accosted by the heavy scent of coffee brewing. *Best aroma in the world!*

"Good morning," Emma St. James said from behind the counter. She had the smile of someone who'd been sniffing coffee and sugary treats since five a.m.

"Morning." Claire glanced around the room, looking for Pearson. The only people seated in the coffee shop though were two twentysomething-year-old women and a man with his back toward her. Judging by his build, he was in his twenties or thirties and liked to work out. He wore a ball cap that shielded his face. Not that Claire needed to get a good look at him. If his face matched his body, then he was yummier than Emma's honeybuns in the display case. Claire would do better to have one of those instead.

Pulling her gaze away from him, she walked up to the counter.

"Your usual?" Emma asked.

"You know me so well."

Emma turned and started preparing a tall caffe latte with heavy cream and two raw sugars. "Your mom was here the other day," she said a moment later as she slid the cup of coffee toward Claire.

Claire's good mood immediately took a dive. She loved her mom, but she didn't exactly *like* her. "Oh?" she said, her tone heavy with disinterest. "That's nice."

Emma tilted her head. "She asked about you."

"Well, I hope you told her that I'm fine as long as she stays far away."

"She said she's going to AA now," Emma told her as she rang up Claire's items at the register.

Drinking had always been Claire's father's problem though. Nancy Donovan had so many other, more pressing issues to deal with, none of which Claire wanted to concern herself right now.

She paid Emma in cash, took her coffee and bagged honeybun, then turned and looked around the shop once more.

"Are you meeting someone here?" Emma asked.

"Pearson Matthews. I guess he's running late," Claire said, turning back.

Emma shrugged. "Not sure, but his son is over there." She pointed at the man in the ball cap, and Claire nearly dropped her coffee.

What is Bo Matthews doing here? She didn't have anything against his father, but the youngest Matthews son ranked as one of her least favorite people in Sweetwater Springs. Or he would have if he hadn't left town last April.

Bo glanced over and offered a small wave.

"Maybe he knows where his father is," Emma suggested.

A new customer walked in so Claire had no choice but to step away from the counter. She could either walk back out of the Sweetwater Café and text Pearson on the sidewalk or she could ask his son.

You hate him, she reminded herself as attraction stormed in her belly. She forced her feet to walk forward until she was standing at his table.

Hate him, double-hate him, triple-hate him.

But *wow*, she loved those blue-gray eyes of his, the color of a faded pair of blue jeans. The kind you wanted to shimmy inside of and never take off.

"What are you doing back in town?" she asked, pleased with the controlled level of irritation lining her voice.

He looked up. "I live in Sweetwater Springs, in case you've forgotten."

"You left." And good riddance.

"I had a job to do in Wild Blossom Bluffs. But now I'm home."

Like two sides of a football stadium during a touchdown, half of her cheered while the other side booed and hissed. She was not on Team Bo anymore and never would be again. "Where is your father?"

"I'm afraid he couldn't make it. He asked me to meet with you instead."

Claire's gaze flitted to the exit. Pearson Matthews was her biggest client right now. He was a businessman with money and influence, and she'd promised to do a good job for him and his fiancée, Rebecca Long. Claire also had her reputation to maintain. She took her responsibilities seriously and prided herself on going above and beyond the call of duty. Every time for every client.

And right now, her duty was to sit down and make nice with Bo Matthews.

* * *

Bo reached for his cup of black coffee and took a long sip as he listened to Claire do her best to be civil. If he had to guess, the conversation she really wanted to be having with him right now was anything but.

"The wedding is two months away," she said, avoiding eye contact with him. "We're on a time crunch, yes, but your father could've called and rescheduled the initial planning session." Her gaze flicked to meet his. "It's not really something you can do."

Bo reached for his cup of coffee and took another sip, taking his time in responding. He could tell by the twitch of her cheek that it irritated her. She couldn't wait to get out of that chair and create as much distance between them as possible. Regret festered up inside him. He couldn't blame her for being upset. He'd handled things with her all wrong last year. "There's a problem with the wedding."

Claire's stiff facial features twisted. "What? Pearson and Rebecca called the wedding off?"

"No, unfortunately," he said, although that would've made him happy. Bo had been certain his dad would eventually come to his senses about marrying a woman half his age. Then, a few months ago, the lovebirds had announced they were pregnant.

"If the wedding is still a go, then what's the problem?" Claire lifted her cup of coffee and took a sip.

Naturally that brought his focus to her heart-shaped lips. He'd kissed those lips once—okay, more than once—and he wouldn't mind doing it again. Clearing his throat, he looked down at the table. "Rebecca is in preterm labor. The doctor put her on hospital bed rest over the weekend. She's not leaving there until the baby is born. Not for long at least."

From his peripheral vision, he saw Claire lift her hand to cover that pretty pink mouth. "That's awful."

He nodded and looked back up. "She wants to be married before little Junior arrives, which could be a couple days to a couple of weeks from now, if we're lucky."

Women weren't supposed to be beautiful when they frowned, but Claire wore it well. "So the wedding is postponed?" she asked. "Is that why Pearson sent you here to talk to me?"

"Not exactly. Dad and Rebecca want to speed things up a bit. Rebecca can get approval to leave the hospital, but only for a couple hours."

"Speed things up how much?"

Bo grimaced. This was a lot to ask, but his dad was used to getting things done his way. Pearson Matthews demanded excellence, which was one of the reasons Bo guessed he'd hired Claire in the first place. "They want the wedding to happen this weekend."

"What?" Claire nearly shouted.

"No expense spared. Dad's words, not mine."

She shook her head and started rattling off rapid-fire thoughts. "I don't even know what they like or what they want. I haven't met with Rebecca for planning yet. She's the bride, it's her wedding. Today is Thursday. That only gives me—"

"—three days," he said, cutting her off. "They want to marry on Saturday evening."

Claire's face was flushed against her strawberry locks. Her green eyes were wide like a woman going into complete panic mode. He'd seen her in this mode when she'd woken up beside him in bed last spring, and that had been his fault as well.

She pulled a small notebook and pen out of her purse and started writing. "I guess I could meet with Rebecca in her hospital room to discuss colors and themes."

Bo cleared his throat, signaling for Claire to look up. "About that. Dad doesn't want Rebecca involved. No stress, per doctor's orders. Dad wants you and me to plan it."

Claire's mouth pinched shut.

Yeah, he wasn't exactly thrilled with the idea either. He had other things to do than plan a shotgun wedding that he didn't even want to happen. For one, he had architectural plans to finish by Friday for a potential client. Having just returned to town, it was important to reestablish his place as the preferred architect in Sweetwater Springs.

"You and me?" She folded her arms across her chest. "I don't think so."

He shrugged. "Dad said he'd double your fee for the trouble."

That pretty, heart-shaped mouth fell open. After a moment, she narrowed her eyes. "What's in it for you? Aren't you busy?"

"Very. But despite his poor sense in the love arena, Dad has always been there for me. He even bailed me out of jail once."

Her gaze flicked away for a moment. Claire had told him about her family history during their night together last spring. Not that he hadn't already heard the rumors. Her dad was a drunk, now serving time for a DWI. Claire's mom couldn't hold down a job and had a bad habit of sleeping with other women's husbands.

Most notably was her mom's affair with the previous mayor of Sweetwater Springs. That had ensured that the Donovan family's dirty laundry was aired for everyone to talk about.

Claire was cut from a different cloth though, and she did her best to make sure everyone saw that.

"Why am I not surprised that you would've spent the night in jail?" she asked with a shake of her head. The subtle movement made her red hair scrape along her bare shoulders.

"I guess because you have low expectations for me."

She pinned him with a look that spoke volumes. "How about *no* expectations?"

Maybe that was another reason Bo had agreed to help with this farce of a wedding. Claire might never forgive him, but maybe she'd stop being angry at him one day. For a reason he didn't want to explore too deeply, he hoped that was true.

* * *

Saying yes to this request would be insane.

Claire lifted her coffee to her mouth, wishing it had a splash of something stronger in it right now. "Okay, I'll do it." She'd never bailed on a job, and she wasn't about to start now.

Even if the wedding was in three days. And she had to plan it with Bo Matthews. And... "Oh no."

"What?" he asked.

"There aren't going to be any venues available. You can't book a place three days out. Everywhere in town will be taken. I wouldn't even be able to empty out a McDonald's for them to get married in with this short a notice."

Claire's hands were shaking. *The best and nothing less* was her personal motto. But she wasn't going to be able to deliver this time. There was no way. Her eyes stung with the realization.

"What about the Mayflower?" Bo asked.

That was a popular restaurant that she sometimes reserved for less formal events. "It'll be booked."

"The community center?"

Claire rolled her eyes. "Such a male thing to say. No woman dreams of getting married at the local community center." Claire dropped her head into her hands. *Think, think, think.*

She listened as Bo rattled off some more options, and shot them all down without even looking up.

"A wedding should be about the people, not the place," he said a moment later.

She looked up now. "I wouldn't have pegged you as a romantic."

He smiled, and it went straight through her chest like a poisonous barb. "It's true. If two people are in love, it shouldn't matter where they are. Saying vows under the stars should be enough."

She swooned against her will, immediately imagining herself in his arms under said stars. She'd danced with him at Liz and Mike's wedding reception last year. And he'd smelled of evergreens and mint. She remembered that when he'd held her in his arms, she'd thought he was the perfect size for her. Men who were too large put her head level at their chests. Too small put them face-to-face, which was just awkward.

But in Bo's arms, her head was at the perfect height to rest on his shoulder. Close enough to where she had to tip her face back to look into those faded denim eyes behind the Clark Kent glasses.

Bo reached for his coffee. "I couldn't care less where they get married. They'll be divorced within the year if my dad maintains his track record."

Right. Rebecca would be the third Mrs. Matthews.

"Maybe Rebecca is *the one*," Claire said, feeling a wee bit of empathy for the man sitting across from her.

"Nah. But I am going to have a new brother. *That* I'm excited about."

"You'll lose your spot as the spoiled youngest," she pointed out.

"Trust me, I was never spoiled." He tipped his coffee cup against his lips and took a sip. "I started working at the family business as a teenager after school. Dad made me save every penny to put myself through college."

Claire already knew the history of Peak Designs Architectural Firm and how it had grown from a one-man show to employing all three of Pearson's sons. Bo was the architect of the group. The middle son, Mark, was in construction management with the company. Cade did landscape design. The project he'd done that Claire liked best was Bo's own yard on Lavender Hill. The landscape, covered with purple wildflowers, was open and elevated over the water, with Bo's home—one of his own designs—seeming to touch the sky. She'd often looked out on that home while canoeing downriver and thought to herself that it was one of the most romantic places on earth.

"I've got it." She bolted upright. "Your place on Lavender Hill is the perfect place for a wedding!"

"My place?"

"I'm assuming your yard isn't taken for the weekend."

"It is. It's taken by me. No."

His expression was stiff, but she wasn't going to be deterred.

"Yes," she countered, leaning forward at the table. As she did, she caught a whiff of his evergreen scent, and her heart kicked at the memories it brought with it. Him and her, kissing and laughing. "It's your dad, your stepmom."

He groaned at the mention of Rebecca.

"And you owe me."

His eyes narrowed behind his glasses.

Yes, she knew she'd gone into his hotel room on her own volition last year. But he'd never called the following day, and she'd hoped he would. Instead, he'd taken a job in Wild Blossom Bluffs and promptly left town. She'd pined for his call even after the rumors had started popping up about them. Some people, more accurately, had compared her to her wanderlust mother. In reality, only a handful of people had talked, but even one comparison to Nancy Donovan stung. Claire wasn't like her mom and never would be.

Bo stared at her for a long moment behind those sexy glasses of his and then cursed under his breath. "Fine," he muttered. "You can have the wedding at my place."

Chapter Two

Bo was in over his head, and he'd barely waded into the water.

Helping Claire pick out colors or themes for his dad's wedding was harmless enough. Inviting her into his home on Lavender Hill, letting her rearrange things, and set up for a wedding was another.

And even though he was convincing himself of how awful this new turn of events was, there was some part of him that was excited to spend time with her. The night they'd shared last spring had been amazing. Being best man at the wedding of his childhood buddy and the woman who'd left Bo at the altar a year earlier had promised to be akin to having his appendix removed sans anesthesia. Instead, as the night was ending, Bo found himself kissing Claire, who'd tasted like some exotic, forbidden fruit. They'd both been too drunk to drive home and had gone up to the hotel room he'd booked. Best night of his life without question, even with hindsight and the events that followed tainting it.

In the morning when he'd woken, he'd watched Claire climb out of bed, looking sexy as anything he'd ever laid eyes on.

She'd had that sleepy, rumpled look he found so attractive. She'd smiled stiffly and had made some excuse about needing to go. Then he'd promised to call later, knowing good and well he wouldn't.

That was his main regret. What was he supposed to say though? *That was fun* or *Have a nice life*? Claire was the kind of woman who men fell in love with, and he wasn't a glutton for punishment. He'd gone that route once and had been publicly rejected by Liz. He didn't fancy doing it again.

He also hadn't looked forward to seeing Liz and Mike be newlyweds around town. So he'd taken a job opportunity outside of Sweetwater Springs to clear his head. Putting the lovely Claire out of his mind, however, hadn't proved as easy.

His cell phone buzzed in the center console of his car. He connected the call and put it on speakerphone. "Hello."

"Our new stepmom is in the hospital?" his older brother Cade asked.

"That's right. She's at Mount Pleasant Memorial on bed rest. And she's not our stepmom yet...not until Saturday," Bo corrected.

"So I hear. You're planning the wedding with the event planner? Isn't she the one you disappeared with after Liz and Mike's wedding?"

"Yes and yes," Bo said briskly. "I plan to give her free reign over all the details. Dad said money was no object, and I trust Claire's taste. I just hope she doesn't mess up my house in the process."

"Your house? That's where you're having it?"

"Outside." But guests had a way of finding themselves inside at events, either to use the bathroom or to lie down when they weren't feeling well. Bo wasn't naive enough to think that wouldn't happen. His cousins would likely want to put their small children to sleep in one of his guest rooms.

"Well, I'd say 'Let me know if I can help,' but..." Cade's voice trailed off.

"But you'd be lying."

"And I'm an honest guy," Cade said with a chuckle. "No, seriously. I'm designing some gardens behind the Sweetwater Bed and Breakfast right now. It's a big job, and Kaitlyn Russo wants it done before the Spring Festival and the influx of guests she has coming in for the event."

"It's okay. Claire will do most of the work. She's top-notch."

"You speaking from experience there, brother?" Cade teased.

Bo ground his back teeth. "I already told you what happened." And he took offense at people jumping to the worst conclusions about Claire just because of who her parents were. "Listen, I have to go," he said as he pulled into the driveway of his home. He'd taken years to design this house himself, working nights while creating the plan. He loved every curve and angle of the structure. He loved the rooms with their high ceilings. His bedroom even had a skylight that allowed him to stare up into the sky while lying in his bed at night. Set on a hill, the house overlooked the river and the mountains beyond. *This* was his idea of heaven. He'd missed it while he'd been licking his wounds in Wild Blossom Bluffs. But now that he was back, he didn't plan on leaving again.

He walked inside, went straight to the kitchen, and grabbed an apple. Taking it to his office, he started working on the proposal designs for Ken Martin. Landing this contract would be good for business.

An hour later, he let out a frustrated sigh. He couldn't concentrate. All he'd been able to think about was that night he'd shared with Claire last spring. And the next three days he'd get to spend with her.

* * *

Claire had briefly considered going to school to become a nurse. Then her grandmother had fallen sick during her senior year of high school, and Claire had spent quite a few months visiting her at Mount Pleasant Memorial. That experience had ended any nursing dreams. She didn't like hospitals. Didn't like the sounds, the smells, or the dull looks in the eyes of the people she passed.

Making her way down the second-floor hall, Claire avoided meeting anyone's gaze. She liked being an event planner because most of the time people were happy. They were excited and looking forward to the future.

Just like the patient she was here to see.

Stopping in front of the door to room 201, Claire adjusted the cheerful arrangement of daffodils she'd picked up at the Little Shop of Flowers on the way here and knocked.

"Come in," a woman's voice called.

Claire cracked the door and peered inside the dimly lit room. Rebecca was lying in bed wearing a diamond-print hospital gown. The TV was blasting a soap opera, and she had a magazine in her lap. "Hi. How are you feeling?" Claire asked, stepping inside.

"Like a beached whale," Rebecca said with a small smile. She was practically glowing with happiness.

"Well, you definitely don't look like one. Pregnancy looks great on you," Claire said. "I know you're not supposed to be doing work of any kind right now so I'm only here as a friend. I brought you flowers."

"Oh, they're so beautiful!...And that rule about no work of any kind is Pearson's," Rebecca added in a whisper, even though no one else was in the room. "He's so protective toward me. It's adorable, really."

Rebecca also had that look of love about her. Her brown eyes were lit up and dreamy. Bo might not think what his father and

Rebecca had was real, but Claire always got a good feeling for her clients. She could tell who was legit and who was getting married for all the wrong reasons. Maybe the baby was speeding things along, but Rebecca loved Pearson. It was as clear as her creamy white skin.

"I agree with Mr. Matthews. You should be taking it easy. We don't want that baby of yours coming any sooner than he needs to."

Rebecca sighed. "It's just, I've been dreaming about getting married since I was a little girl," she confided. "I wanted more time to plan this out and do it right."

"Relax. If you and Pearson are there, it will be perfect," Claire said, remembering how Bo had told her something similar this morning. "All you'll remember by the time it's over is the look in his eyes when he says I do. Assuming you can see through the blur of your own tears."

Rebecca's lips parted. "Wow. You're good."

"Thanks. And don't worry—your wedding day is going to be everything you ever dreamed."

"I hope so. The main thing I want now is to have it before the baby gets here."

"We'll make sure that happens," Claire promised. "Do you have any favorite colors?"

Rebecca drew her shoulders up to her ears excitedly. "I was thinking that soft purple and white would be pretty."

"That's a nice springtime combo." Claire pulled a little notebook out of her purse along with a pen and wrote down Rebecca's color preference. "I'll see if Halona at Little Shop of Flowers can do some arrangements in those colors. Maybe with a splash of yellows and pinks as well for the bouquets."

Rebecca's eyes sparkled under the bed's overhead light. "Perfect."

"What about food? Since it's such short notice, I was thinking we'd skip a full dinner and just have light hors d'oeuvres at the reception. And drinks too, of course, for everyone except you." Claire winked at the bride-to-be.

They sat and chatted for another ten minutes while Claire wrote down a few ideas. Then she stood up and shoved her little notebook back into her purse. "I promised I wouldn't stress you out so I better go. You need your rest. But I'm so glad we got a chance to talk. I'm clearing my schedule for the rest of the week to focus solely on your big day."

And not on Bo Matthews. Which would be easier said than done, since she would be spending the next several days at his house.

"Thank you so much," Rebecca said, bringing a hand to her swollen stomach.

"You're very welcome." With a final wave goodbye, Claire headed back down the hospital halls, keeping her gaze on the floor and not on passersby. She resisted a total body shudder as the smells and sounds accosted her. Once she was outside again, she sucked in a deep breath of fresh air. She walked to her car, got in, and then drove in the direction of Bo Matthews's home on Lavender Hill.

Butterflies fluttered up into her chest at the anticipation of seeing him again. But this was just business, nothing more, she reminded herself. And that was the way it needed to stay.

* * *

After a walk to clear his head, Bo settled back at his desk and worked steadily, making good progress on his proposal. Somehow, he put Claire out of his mind until the doorbell rang. Just when he'd gotten into the zone. With a groan, he headed to the door and opened it to find Claire staring back at him for the second time today.

She looked away shyly and then pulled the strap of her handbag higher on her shoulder as if she needed something to do with her hands. Did he make her nervous?

What would've happened had he called her the morning after they'd spent the night together? Would they be a couple right now? Would she be stepping into his arms to greet him instead of looking anxious and agitated? Would she be pressing her lips to his in a kiss that promised to turn into more later?

Bo cleared his throat and then gestured for her to come inside.

"I thought I'd go ahead and get started," she said. "I want to walk around the yard and get a good feel for the size and layout so I know where we can set up chairs and a gazebo."

"Okay." He was working hard to keep his eyes level with hers and not to admire the pretty floral dress she was wearing and the curves that filled it out so nicely. She had shiny sandals strapped to her feet that glinted in the light of the room.

"I stopped by to see Rebecca on the way here and brought her flowers." Claire held up her hand. "Don't worry. I didn't cause any stress. But she did give me her color preferences though."

"That's good," Bo said.

"I was thinking we should keep things simple. Even though your father said no expense spared, less is more depending on the venue. Your yard is the absolute perfect place for a wedding. The view is amazing, and as long as there's good music and food, it'll be as nice as some of the bigger events I plan in pricier spots."

Bo wasn't going to argue with her about saving money. Especially since his father was likely to have another wedding sometime in the next five years if history repeated itself.

"Feel free to walk around and do whatever you need to do," he said. As long as she kept her distance from him. He needed to work, and he had a feeling his brief streak of productivity was now broken for the rest of the afternoon. "There's a spare key on the kitchen counter for you to use over the weekend. You can come and go as you need." He gestured toward the back door. "That'll take you to the gardens. Let me know if you have any questions."

"Thanks." She turned and headed in the direction he pointed. His gaze unwillingly dropped as he watched her walk away. With a resigned sigh, he returned to his office to work.

This is going to be a very long three days.

An hour and a half later, he lifted his head to a soft knock on his open door. Then the door opened, and there was Claire, her cheeks rosy from her walk outside. The wind off the river was sometimes cool this time of year, and the humidity had left her hair with a slight wave to it. "Sorry to disturb you."

She'd been polite and civil toward him since their new arrangement. Whatever resentment she harbored toward him, she'd locked it away for the time being. The same way he was doing his best to keep his attraction toward her under wraps. "What do you think?" he asked. "Will Lavender Hill work?"

She nodded. "You have quite a few acres of land. We'll need to set up a few Porta Potties somewhere out of sight so that guests don't come in and out of your house all night. I think three will be enough, and I know a company that can arrange that on short notice. I'll also be having wooden fold-out chairs delivered. We rent them, and the company typically picks them back up on the day after the ceremony. The ground is nice and firm, and I checked the weather for Saturday. Sweetwater Springs isn't expecting rain again until later next week."

"Sounds like everything is falling into place."

"There's still more to do, of course. There are so many things to consider when you're planning an event for nearly a hundred people. But first I was thinking about having some food delivered. I'm starving, and I can't think when my stomach is growling. Are there any pizza places around here that deliver?"

He thought for a moment. "Jessie's Pizza delivers. It's my favorite." Just thinking about it made his mouth water. "The number is on my fridge."

She gave him a strange look as if she was debating whether to say something else. With a soft eye roll that he suspected was at herself rather than him, she folded her arms across her chest and met his gaze. "Are you hungry? I certainly can't eat a whole pie."

This was where he should practice self-control and say no. "I haven't eaten all day, actually. But if we're sharing, I'm buying. It's the least I can do considering the pinch my dad has put you in."

"Great. What do you like on your pizza?"

"I like it all," he said, not intending for the sexual tone in his voice.

Claire's skin flushed. "Okay, well, um…I'll let you work until it gets here," she called over her shoulder as she headed back out of his office.

Work. Yeah, right. With the anticipation of eating his favorite pizza with Claire, his brain had no intention of focusing on architectural plans right now. The only curves he was envisioning were those underneath that floral sundress she was wearing.

Chapter Three

While Claire waited for the pizza to arrive, she sat at Bo's kitchen counter and made a to-do list. Priority number one was lining up all the services for Saturday's wedding. Years of planning events meant she had close contacts for everything. Most would drop whatever they were doing and work extended hours to meet her needs. She'd already spoken to Halona about the floral arrangements, and that was a go. *Thank goodness.* She jotted down several people she planned to call after lunch, and then she found her mind wandering while she drew little hearts on the side of her paper and thought about Bo.

Whoa! She wasn't going down that path again. It'd been a long hike back the last time. Being seen coming out of Bo's hotel room had been mortifying enough. Even worse, she'd left that morning so smitten with him that she couldn't see straight. He was charming and funny, and undeniably gorgeous. She'd always thought so. He had this Clark Kent sexy nerd look about him that just *did it* for her.

Bo also had muscles plastered in all the right places. Not too bulky. No, his were long and lean. They'd run their hands all over each other's bodies last spring. That night had been hotter than anything she'd ever experienced, even though their clothes had stayed on—mostly. She was drunk, and he'd said he didn't want to take advantage of her. So they'd spent the night driving each other crazy with their roaming hands. They'd also spent it talking and laughing. Then, after Claire had left the next morning, it was out of sight, out of mind for Bo. But not for her.

The doorbell rang. As she walked down the hall, she turned at the sound of heavy footsteps behind her.

"I told you I'd pay." Bo caught up to her and reached to open the door ahead of her.

A young, lanky, twentysomething guy held a box in his hand. "Someone ordered an extra-large pizza and chicken wings?"

Bo glanced over his shoulder. "Wings, huh?"

Her cheeks burned. "I'm going to be here a while tonight so I thought it'd be a good idea to have plenty of fuel on hand." And pizza and wings were her biggest weaknesses, right after the clearance racks at Sophie's Boutique. And Bo, once upon a time.

Bo chuckled as he pulled out his wallet and paid the guy at the door. Taking the food, he closed the door with his foot and walked past her into the kitchen. "I'll get the plates. There's sweet tea and soda in the fridge. Help yourself."

She opened the fridge and peered inside. A man's fridge said a lot about him. If there was more alcohol than food, that might be a problem. Bo appeared to have only one bottle of brew, and a healthy selection of fresh fruit and vegetables were visible in the drawers. She reached for the pitcher of tea and brought it back to the counter, where Bo had put out two plates. The open box of pizza was at the center of the kitchen counter.

He placed a slice of pizza on each plate and carried them to the table. "I have two glasses over here," he said. "You can bring the pitcher over."

Apparently, they were eating together. She'd just assumed that he would take his food back to his office and work.

He glanced at her for a moment. "Everything okay?"

She softly bit the inside of her cheek. She'd already had breakfast with the man. Lunch too? Her stomach growled. "Yep. Just fine." She moved to the table and took a seat, where the delicious smell of Italian sauce and spices wafted under her nose. "Mmm. If that tastes as good as it smells, I'm going to be having seconds."

Bo laughed. It was a deep rumble that echoed through her. "It tastes even better than it smells," he promised. "Jessie's is the best."

Her eyes slid over as he brought the slice to his mouth and took a bite. A thin string of cheese connected his mouth to the pizza for a moment, reminding her of all the pizza commercials on TV. Bo could be the guy in those commercials. Watching him bite into a slice of pizza would have her craving it every time. Craving *him* every time.

She lifted a slice herself and took a bite, closing her eyes as her taste buds exploded with pleasure. "You're not kidding," she moaned. When she looked over, he was watching her.

She swallowed. "It's very good."

For the rest of the meal, she kept her eyes and moans to herself as she filled Bo in on Rebecca's thoughts for the wedding. "She's really excited. She has the bride-to-be and the mother-to-be glows combined."

Bo grunted.

"I've known Rebecca ever since she moved to town two years ago. I don't think she's the type to marry someone for anything other than love."

Bo finished off his third slice and reached for his glass of tea. "It's just hard to fathom that a twenty-eight-year-old woman would want to marry a fifty-year-old man."

Claire laughed. "Love is crazy that way. It doesn't let you choose who you fall for."

"True enough. Maybe if you did, it would turn out a whole lot better."

She knew the whole ugly story about his ex-fiancée, who'd fallen in love with his best friend. Even after their betrayal, Bo had stood in as best man for the wedding that had led to him and Claire spending the night together.

"Have you ever been in love?" he asked, surprising her. They'd talked about a lot that night last spring, but that topic hadn't come up.

She nearly choked on her bite of pizza.

"Sorry. You know my history. It's only fair."

She reached for her glass of tea and washed down her bite. "I've been in what I thought was love in college. It was really just infatuation though."

"How do you know the difference?"

"Well," she said, chewing on her thoughts, "infatuation fades. Love survives even after you know about all the other person's faults. Sometimes knowing the faults makes you like them more…This is not personal experience talking, of course. I'm talking as an event planner who has worked with countless couples in love. I've seen couples crumble under the pressure of big events, and I've seen others come out stronger."

He wore an unreadable expression on his face. "I guess I could say I've seen the same in my line of work. Making plans for the house you want to grow old in can be as stressful as it is exciting. Couples have torn into each other in the process, right in front of me. At those times, I'm almost glad that my ex walked away from me." He sat back in his chair. "That just meant I got to plan the home of my dreams all by myself. No drama involved."

Claire shook her head. "Well, you did a great job. This could very well be my dream house," she said. "I haven't seen the upstairs, but I'm sure it's just as perfect as the downstairs."

"I'll have to give you a tour at some point."

She shifted restlessly. Was his bedroom upstairs? She didn't think stepping inside alone with him would be wise. Probably asking him the question that sat right at the tip of her tongue wasn't wise either. She asked anyway. "Why didn't you call?"

Bo shifted his body and his gaze uncomfortably. She needed to know though. Yes, he'd left town, but he hadn't gone far and not for good. "I needed some space from everything. It had nothing to do with you. It wasn't personal."

But it was to her. She hadn't felt so connected to anyone in a long time. They'd had such a great time, and he'd promised to call. Only he never did. He must have been hurt watching his ex marry his best friend, and he'd used her as a crutch to get through the night. That was all.

"I see," she said briskly. Then she started cleaning up her lunch, even though she could stomach another slice of pizza or a chicken wing. What she couldn't stomach was continuing to sit with Bo right now.

"I had a good time that night," Bo said, as if backtracking from his response. "A *very* good time."

"So good that you never spoke to me again."

"We didn't sleep together, Claire. Why are you so mad at me?"

She slammed her paper plate and napkin in the trash and then whipped around to look at him. "Is that what defines whether a guy calls the next morning? Sex? You know, forget I asked the question. Forget everything. I have work to do and so do you."

* * *

It was well after eight p.m. when Claire arrived home. Her slice of pizza and sweet tea had worn off midafternoon, and she'd been running on adrenaline and fury since then.

It wasn't personal.

Those three little words had burrowed under her skin and had been festering for the last several hours. How dare he? She'd shared intimate details of her life with him that night. Hopes and dreams. She'd told him about her dysfunctional childhood that she never spoke of with anyone. It was *very* personal to her.

Stepping into her bedroom, she shed her clothes and traded them for something comfy. Then she turned off the lights, climbed into bed, and reached for the book on her nightstand. She kept rereading the same line because her brain was still trained on Bo. It'd only been one night, but that night could've filled several years' worth for some couples. She always left a wedding feeling romantic and hopeful for her own happily ever after. Like a fool, she'd felt there was a potential for that with Bo.

A few days later, she swung by his house on Lavender Hill. Instead of finding Bo, she'd run into his brother Cade, who'd informed her that Bo had taken a job out of town. He didn't know when Bo was coming back, but it wasn't anytime soon. With him, Bo had taken a little bit of her pride and a big piece of her foolish heart.

Well, not this time. In fact, she wasn't even going to waste any more energy being mad at him. Bo was right. This wasn't personal; it was work.

* * *

Bo startled at the sound of his front door opening and closing early the next morning. He jolted upright, realizing he'd fallen asleep at his desk, which wasn't uncommon. His muscles cried out as he moved. Even though he was only thirty years old, he was too old to be grabbing shut-eye in an upright office chair.

"Bo?" Claire's voice called out from the front entrance hall.

How had she even gotten in? Oh, right. He'd given her a key.

"Bo?"

He stood and met her in the hallway. Unlike him, she appeared to be well rested. Her hair was soft and shiny—perfect for running his fingers through. Today she was wearing pink cropped pants along with a short-sleeved top featuring a neckline that gave him ample view of her breastbone—the sexiest nonprivate part of a woman, if you asked him. Claire's was delicate with a splash of freckles over her fair skin. He'd spent time sprinkling kisses there once.

And if he didn't stop thinking about it, he was going to have a problem springing up real soon.

"I brought you a cappuccino and a cream cheese bagel." She lifted a cup holder tray and a bag from the Sweetwater Café. "And you look like you could use it." She laughed softly. She'd been royally ticked off the last time he'd seen her. What had changed since then?

"I fell asleep working on my latest design," he told her.

"And you have the facial creases to prove it." She smiled and breezed past him, leaving a delicious floral scent in her wake. He followed her into the kitchen and lifted the coffee from its tray.

"To what do I owe this act of mercy?" he asked suspiciously.

Claire lifted her own cup of coffee. "I'm calling a truce. What happened last spring is done and over. We won't think or talk about it ever again."

He sipped the bittersweet brew. The only problem with that suggestion was that he'd been thinking about that night for the past twelve months.

"I can put it behind me. It wasn't personal for you so I'm assuming you can as well." She notched up her chin, projecting confidence and strength even though something wavered in her eyes as she waited for him to reply.

"I can do the same," he lied.

"Great." She smiled stiffly. "Then I need your assistance this morning. If you're available."

"I got a lot done workwise last night so I guess I have some time. What do you need?"

"I brought some fairy lights to hang outside. You have some great gardens. Your brother Cade is so talented." She shifted her gaze, almost as if looking at him directly made her uncomfortable. "Since the ceremony will be at night," she continued, her voice becoming brisk, "I thought fairy lights in your garden beyond the arbor will add to the romantic feel. Do you have a ladder?"

"Of course."

"Great. I'm just going to take a walk around out there while you finish your cappuccino and bagel. I usually walk in the mornings down my street, but when I woke this morning, I just couldn't wait to go for a stroll behind your house. If that's okay?"

"Sure. I need to shower. I'll meet you out there with a ladder in about twenty minutes." Showers and coffee were his usual morning ritual. Perhaps he should start adding in a morning walk as well. Especially if it included a gorgeous redhead with dazzling green eyes.

He grabbed his cappuccino and went upstairs to prepare for the day ahead. It was Friday. Last night, he'd made a lot of progress on the Martin proposal. Tonight, he was meeting the couple over dinner to discuss his plans. He hated the social aspect of his job. Going to the Tipsy Tavern downtown with his buddies was fine, but having a nice dinner and wooing potential clients made his skin itch. It was a necessary evil though. He'd just have to suffer through it and hopefully come out of the night with a contract.

* * *

The gardens were a feast for Claire's eyes, but watching Bo string those fairy lights over the last hour was even yummier. His arms flexed and stretched while he hammered nails into the wooden posts that weaved in and around his garden. And the tool belt he'd looped around his waist was a visual aphrodisiac.

"You okay back there?" Bo asked, glancing over his shoulder.

She jolted as if she'd been caught with her hand in the proverbial cookie jar. Nope, she'd just been checking out the way he filled out the backside of those jeans. Her gaze flicked to his eyes, which were now twinkling with humor. *Yeah*, he knew exactly what she'd been doing. "Fine."

"Fine, huh? A woman who says she's fine never is. Am I hanging these things to your satisfaction?"

"You are. I might have to contract you for all my jobs."

"As much as I'd love to be at your beck and call, I'm afraid I already have a job that keeps me pretty busy." He climbed down the ladder and folded it, then carried it out of the garden and toward the arbor that had been delivered yesterday evening. He set the ladder back up and climbed to the top.

Claire handed him another string of fairy lights. "I'm meeting with the caterer in an hour and then swinging by the Little Shop of Flowers after that. Since your father asked you to help, I thought you might be interested in coming along."

Bo looped the lights around the arbor with an eye for spacing them out perfectly. "I'm not sure I'm the best person to ask for opinions on catering or flowers. Can't you get one of the women in that ladies group you go to?"

The group in question was a dozen or so Sweetwater Springs residents who regularly made a habit of having a Ladies' Day (or Night) Out. They went to movies, had dinner, volunteered for community functions, anything and everything. It was girl power at its finest.

"I spoke to Rebecca, but you know your dad's tastes. I always like to represent the groom as much as the bride. Going to a wedding or anniversary function that is one-sided is a pet peeve of mine."

She watched him shove his hammer into the loop on his tool belt. Part of her physical attraction to Bo was his intellectual look, complete with glasses and a ready ballpoint pen always in his pocket. He had those thoughtful eyes too, always seeming to be thinking about something.

But this handyman look was really appealing as well. She'd created an online dating profile on one of those popular websites a couple of months back with the ladies group, but she hadn't activated it. She was a bit chicken, and the spring and summer were her busy months for planning events. Maybe she'd make it active in the fall and expand her search for bookish professionals to include muscle-clad guys who did hard labor. Bo was a perfect blend of both, except he wasn't available. After the way his ex betrayed him with his best friend, he might never be again.

He climbed back down the ladder and faced her. "I've got a proposition for you. I'll go with you to meet the caterer and look at flowers if you have dinner with me tonight."

She blinked him into focus. "You mean a date?"

"No."

She swallowed and looked up at the work he'd done with the lights, pretending to assess the job. Why had her mind immediately jumped to the conclusion that he was asking her on a date? If he was going to do that, he would have last spring. "Why do you want me to have dinner with you?"

"I'm meeting a potential client and his wife. It's social as much as it is business, and I hate doing these things alone. So yes, I guess they'd see you as my date, but—"

"It isn't personal," she said with a nod. "Fair enough." She jutted out her hand.

As his hand slid against hers, her body betrayed her iron-clad decision not to want him. Those hands were magic, she recalled. The stuff that her fantasies would forever be made of.

She quickly yanked her hand away. "Deal."

* * *

Two hours later, Claire was standing beside Bo and sampling finger foods and hors d'oeuvres at Taste of Heaven Catering. Claire usually came to her friend Brenna Myer's business with the prospective brides and grooms. It was usually them sampling the cheese, crackers, and little finger sandwiches.

"This is divine," Claire said with a sigh. She turned to Bo. "What do you think?"

"It's good," he said with a nod.

Claire punched him softly. "It's better than good. Are you kidding me?"

He chuckled softly. "Okay, it's the best thing I've put into my mouth in a long time."

Those words sliced right through her like a knife on that soft cheese spread in front of them. *Get it together, Claire.*

Brenna was watching them the way she usually did with the clients that Claire brought in. Claire guessed that her friend, who was also a member of the Ladies' Day Out group, was scrutinizing every facial reaction and weighing whether her potential clients were satisfied.

Speaking of clients... "Do you think Pearson would like it?" Claire asked Bo.

"My dad is a carnivore. Put any meat in front of him, and he's a happy man."

"Especially with Rebecca at his side," Claire said, throwing in two cents for her currently bedridden client. If Rebecca made Pearson happy, then Bo should be happy too.

"Great. We'll definitely have a spread of various meats then," Brenna said, pulling a pen from behind her ear and writing something down on her clipboard.

"And the cheese," Claire said. "What pregnant woman doesn't love cheese?"

"I don't know any," Brenna said on a laugh. "You'll probably want something sweet as well."

"That's what I'm looking forward to sampling." Bo rubbed his hands together as a sexy smile curved his mouth.

"You have a sweet tooth, huh?" Claire asked.

"I do."

"Me too," she confessed. "Brenna's cheesecake squares are my favorite. I swear that's what she named this business after. They are the epitome of what heaven would taste like if it was food."

Brenna laugh-snorted.

Bo was also grinning. "Then we need to add them to the menu," he said, turning to Brenna.

"Oh no. This event is not about me and what I like," Claire protested. "It's about your dad and future stepmom."

The word *stepmom* drew a grunt from him. "We're the ones planning this wedding, and if cheesecake squares are your favorite, then cheesecake squares it will be."

Claire melted just a little bit at his insistence. "Let's add some chocolate maroons and white chocolate-dipped strawberries as well," Claire said, with a decisive nod in Brenna's direction. Those were also one of her favorites, but Rebecca had also mentioned how much she enjoyed those.

By the time they left Taste of Heaven, their bellies were full, and there was no need for lunch.

"That was actually a lot of fun." Bo walked on the traffic side of the sidewalk as they strolled down Main Street to their cars. They'd driven there separately so that she could go home and prepare for tonight.

"It was. Thanks for coming."

"Well, as you pointed out, it's my dad and his soon-to-be wife. Coming along with you is the least I can do. Plus, now I get you tonight." He raised his brows as he looked at her.

It wasn't a date. He'd said so himself. But her heart hadn't received that message, because it stopped for a brief second every time he looked at her.

He opened her driver's side door and then stared at her for a long, breathless second.

There went her heart skipping like a rock over Silver Lake. He leaned forward, and she forgot to breathe as his face lowered to hers and kissed the side of her cheek. Part of her had thought maybe he was targeting her mouth. Would she have turned away? Probably not.

"See you tonight." He straightened, holding her captive with his gaze.

Maybe she should've held on to her anger at him. At least that would have buffered this bone-deep attraction that she couldn't seem to kick.

"Yes. Tonight." She offered a wave, got into her car, and watched him head to his own vehicle. She could still feel the weight of his kiss on her cheek. His skin on hers. She touched the area softly and closed her eyes for a moment. When she opened her eyes again, she saw a familiar face crossing the parking lot.

Everything inside her contracted in an attempt to hide. Luckily, her mom didn't seem to notice her as she walked to her minivan and got in. Seeing Nancy Donovan was just a reminder of everything Claire wanted and didn't want.

She wanted respect, success, and a man who wanted her as much as she wanted him.

She didn't want to lose her heart or her pride to an unavailable man. No, Bo wasn't married, which was the kind of guy her mom preferred. But he was no less on the market. Being with him tonight would have to be more like window shopping. Claire could look, but there was no way she was taking him home.

Chapter Four

Bo wasn't sure if he was more nervous about meeting with the Martins tonight or about spending the evening with Claire.

He pulled up to her house, parked, and headed up the steps. As he rang the doorbell, he felt empty-handed somehow. Maybe he should've stopped and gotten flowers. That would've been stupid though. This wasn't a real date. But the tight, hard-to-breathe feeling in his chest begged to differ. It was a blend of anticipation and nerves with a healthy dose of desire for this woman.

The door opened, and Claire smiled back at him. She had on just a touch of makeup that brought out the green of her eyes. She'd swiped some blush across her cheeks as well, or maybe she really was flushed. With her strawberry tones and fair skin, she seemed to do that a lot.

There was something between them. There always had been. Their chemistry was off the charts, but it was more than that. Claire was funny and smart, and he admired the heck out of her. She would've had a right to view the world with bitterness and skepticism as much as anyone. Instead, she seemed to have unlimited optimism, and she romanticized everything. Bo could learn a lot from this woman, if he chose to spend more than three days with her.

"You're staring at me," Claire said. She looked at what she was wearing and back up at him with a frown. "Do I look okay? I wasn't sure what to wear for a business dinner, and there was no time to go shopping for something new. I can go back upstairs and change if you think this isn't good enough."

"It's perfect. You look beautiful." And heaven help him, it was all he could do not to move closer and taste those sweet lips of hers.

"Great," she said. "Let me just grab my purse. You can come on in."

Bo stepped inside her living room and looked around. It had been her granddad's place before he'd moved south to Florida and left it to her. Bo had never renovated a historic home before, but his mind was already swimming with ideas on how to modernize it just a touch by adding more windows for natural lighting.

As he waited for her to return, he walked over to the mantel and looked at the pictures encased in a variety of frames. There was a photo of Claire with her grandparents, who'd done a good bit of raising her while her parents shirked their duties. He thought he remembered that her grandmother had died several years back. There was one of Claire and her brother, Peter, whom Bo hadn't seen in quite some time. He wasn't even sure what Peter had been up to in the last decade since high school graduation.

Claire breezed back into the room. "Okay, got my purse, and I'm ready to go."

Bo turned to face her, and his breath caught. He wasn't dreading tonight's dinner like he had been this morning before inviting her along. On the contrary, now he was starting to look forward to it.

When they got to the restaurant, Ken and Evelyn Martin were already seated and waiting for them.

"Oh, you brought a date," Evelyn said, looking between them with a delighted smile. "This is such a nice surprise."

Bo wondered if he should clarify that Claire was just a friend. Evelyn didn't give him time to say anything, though, before launching into friendly chitchat.

"I'm Evelyn, and this is my husband, Ken," she said, reaching for Claire's hand.

Bo pulled out a chair for Claire and sat down while they all made their acquaintances. Then he made the mistake of looking around the restaurant. On the other side of the room, his vision snagged on Liz and Mike. They were expecting their first child if the rumors were true, which in Sweetwater Springs was fifty-fifty. A mix of emotions passed through him.

"I'm so glad you could meet us tonight," Ken said, pulling Bo back to his own dinner party.

Bo nodded. "Me too."

Liz had never been *the one* for him. He had come to terms with that during his time in Wild Blossom Bluffs. Perhaps he should walk over and thank them for that invitation to their wedding last year, because it'd led to an amazing night with the woman beside him. The *only* woman he had eyes for in the room tonight.

* * *

Claire had thought since this was a business dinner, that it would be tense or maybe a little stuffy. The Martins were probably twenty years older than her, but even so, Claire was having the best time. The older couple picked on each other in the most endearing way. And since Bo was paying, Claire helped herself to a steak with two sides of vegetables and a glass of wine. She didn't feel bad about it either. This was payback for last spring.

They might have called a truce this morning, but she hadn't forgotten.

"It must be so rewarding to plan so many life events for others," Evelyn said, stabbing at a piece of shrimp on her plate and looking up at Claire.

"Oh, it is. I couldn't imagine myself doing anything else."

"I was a schoolteacher for thirty-one years," Evelyn said proudly, "and I loved every moment. If you love what you do and who you're with, life is always a party."

Claire was midway through lifting her glass of wine to her lips, but she paused to process that statement. "I love that philosophy."

"Well, it's true. I fell in love with Ken thirty-three years ago, and we haven't stopped partying since."

Ken Martin reached for her hand.

After that, the conversation turned to Bo's architectural proposal. The Martins loved all his ideas, and they seemed to love him too. Why wouldn't they? She hadn't been lying when she'd told him earlier that he was talented. He was. He was the architect behind the designs for so many of Sweetwater Springs' big businesses and houses. He was amazing.

By the time they left the restaurant, Bo and the Martins seemed like old friends. And Claire was totally and completely smitten with her date. Exactly like she'd promised herself she wouldn't be. But being with him was so easy.

He walked her out to the parking lot and, like a good gentleman, opened the passenger door for her.

"Thank you," he said, once he was behind the wheel. He pulled out of the parking lot and started to drive her home.

"It was no problem. I had a good time, and I had to eat anyway, right? Thanks for buying me dinner. Usually, the night before a wedding, we'd be doing a dress rehearsal. But nothing is the norm about tomorrow's ceremony." She was chattering away for some reason.

"Looks like we make a good team."

There was a smolder in his blue eyes when he looked over. Was she imagining that?

"Yes, I guess so."

"Maybe you could call me for all your catering and flower needs, and I could ask you to be my date for all my client meetings."

She knew he was only teasing. "I daresay, you'd grow tired of sampling food and picking out flowers." She cleared her throat. "I saw Liz and Mike. You were fixated over there for a moment at dinner."

She saw the muscles along his jaw tighten. "They didn't stay long, thankfully."

"Is it hard to see them together?"

"A little," he admitted. "Not because I still love her. Just knowing that they did things behind my back. Trust isn't an easy thing to repair." He sucked in a deep breath. "All for the greater good, I guess. They have a baby on the way, from what I hear."

Claire had heard the same. She reached a hand across the car and touched his shoulder, wanting to offer comfort. The touch zinged through her body. She hadn't touched this man since last spring. She'd made a point not to. Now she felt his hard muscles at her fingertips, and her body answered.

She yanked her hand away and turned to look out the window. "Not every woman would do that to you, you know."

"I never thought Liz would do that to me. Or Mike. So no, I don't know." There was an edge to his voice, making her sorry she'd even brought it up. He was obviously bitter about relationships now. No doubt that spilled over into his view on his dad and Rebecca's nuptials tomorrow.

They rode in silence for a few minutes, and then Bo turned on the radio.

Claire looked at him with interest. "Jazz? I would've pegged you for classical."

To her relief, the hardness of his face softened.

"I've always thought classical was boring. I played the saxophone in high school band."

"I remember. Do you still play?"

"I have the sax, but all the neighborhood dogs start howling when I put my lips to the mouthpiece."

Claire laughed. "I play piano. I had six years of lessons."

"Really? I thought we spilled all our secrets the night we spent together." His gaze slid over. There was a definite smolder there, contained only by thick-rimmed glasses.

He pulled into her driveway and cut off the engine. "I'll walk you to your door."

"How about a nightcap? I have wine. Or beer if you'd rather." What was she doing? She'd resolved earlier this afternoon not to take him home with her.

"I'm not sure you can trust me not to kiss you if you invite me in," he admitted.

Gulp.

Without thinking, she ran her tongue along her bottom lip, wetting it. Which was just silly because she absolutely was not going to kiss this man. While her mind was starting to make a rational argument for saying good night, her body was warming up for first base, maybe second.

Bo leaned just slightly and tucked a strand of her hair behind her ear. Then his fingers slid across her skin as he took his time with the simple gesture. Her heart pattered excitedly. Then she leaned as well, almost against her will. One kiss wouldn't hurt anything, right? One tiny, little...

His mouth covered hers in an instant, pulling the plug on her mind. Her thoughts disappeared along with everything else, except Bo. It was just him and her and this scorching-hot kiss. His hand curled behind her neck, holding her captive. Not that she wanted to pull away. Nope. She was close to climbing across the seat and straddling him at this moment.

He tasted like white wine from the restaurant. Smelled like a walk through Evergreen Park. Kissed like a man who wanted her every bit as much as she wanted him.

She heard herself moan as their tongues tangled with one another. She remembered this. How good he kissed. It was like a starter match lighting a fire that burned in her belly. He broke away and started trailing soft kisses down her cheek and then her neck. There was a slight scruff of a five o'clock shadow on his jawline. It felt sinfully delicious.

She tilted her head to one side, giving him access. Eventually, his mouth traveled to her ear and nibbled softly. That fire in her belly raged to a full-on hungry blaze.

"That nightcap sounds good," he whispered, tickling the sensitive skin there. "And I don't want to think about Liz and Mike anymore tonight."

Claire's brain buzzed back to life. That was exactly why he'd invited her back to his hotel room last spring. She was a distraction, nothing more.

She opened her eyes and pulled away just enough to look at him. This was a mistake. There was no denying that she had it bad for this guy, but he wasn't emotionally available and she wasn't going to be used.

"Actually, I'm really tired." She averted her gaze because looking in his eyes, heavy lidded with lust, might sway her sudden resolve. "I'll see you in the morning. There are a few last-minute touches to do before the wedding. Thanks for dinner. Good night." She pushed her car door open, slammed it shut, and hurried up the porch steps as if running for her life.

But she was really running for her heart.

* * *

What happened tonight?

Bo sat out on his back deck and looked out to the garden. He'd turned on the fairy lights they'd strung earlier, giving the yard an ambient glow. Claire was right. It was a romantic touch.

He still couldn't decide if he was glad or disappointed that she'd slammed on the brakes to their make-out session. Going inside with her would have almost definitely led to her bed, and he didn't think Claire was the kind to have sex casually.

He'd been in a different place in his life last year. Liz and Mike's affair had plunged a knife through his heart, and he wasn't sure he'd ever be able to pull it out. It'd been hard to breathe for a long time after that. He'd dated casually, hooked up a few times, but he had no interest in anyone.

Until Claire. She'd sparked something deep inside him that was terrifying to him back then. The thought of allowing himself to have actual feelings for a woman felt like marching himself right up to Skye Point and preparing to jump off without a parachute. It was nuts.

But now…

He liked her. She evoked feelings he'd never experienced before. Not even with Liz, whom he'd planned to spend his life with.

Damn. He wasn't sure what exactly had happened tonight; all he knew was he needed to fix it. After tomorrow's wedding, there'd be no need to see Claire anymore. Not unless he climbed that proverbial mountain and forced himself to look off the ledge and jump. Getting into another relationship was a risk. Claire could hurt him even more than Liz had. But would she?

An hour later, he dragged himself to bed and flopped around restlessly until he drifted off. After what seemed like just a few minutes, he awoke with the chirping of springtime birds nesting by his window. A slant of sunlight hit his face, prompting him to sit up and shuffle down the hall. He made coffee, enough for two, and then showered.

Claire still hadn't arrived by the time he'd dressed and started preparing breakfast—also enough for two. A little worry elbowed its way to the forefront of his mind. Had he scared her off last night? He knew that she'd be here to finish the job no matter what. He trusted that she wouldn't let his dad and Rebecca down.

He trusted *her*.

That one thought stopped him momentarily in his tracks. His heart was more easily won than his trust, but it appeared that Claire had captured them both.

He continued walking to his office and opened his computer to scan his email. There was already a message waiting for him from Ken Martin:

> Loved having dinner with you and Claire last night. Evelyn and I both love your plans for the mother-in-law suite we want to add on. We were unanimous in our agreement that you are the right man for the job. We'd love to work with you. We'd also love to have you and Claire over for dinner at our place again sometime soon. She's a keeper. A wise man wouldn't let her slip away.
>
> Ken

Bo pumped a fist into the air. The deal was done. Success! He reread those last two lines.

It was good advice, and he planned on taking it.

Chapter Five

Claire was taking her time getting ready to go to Lavender Hill this morning. When she'd agreed to this business arrangement, she'd resolved not to let herself fall for Bo again. And who fell for a guy after only a few days anyway?

Apparently, she did. She wasn't in love with him, no. But she was long past lust.

Claire gave herself one last glance in the mirror. She hadn't put on the beautiful dress she'd purchased at Sophie's Boutique a few weeks back just yet. She still had work to do at Bo's house. Speaking of which, she guessed it was time to go.

She headed to her car, got in, and then, continuing to procrastinate, veered off toward the Sweetwater Café for a strong cup of coffee.

A few minutes later, Emma smiled up from the counter as a little jingle bell rang over Claire's head.

"Good morning, Claire," Emma said with all the warmth of one of her delicious hot cocoas. "You have a big event this evening."

"I do." Claire gave a nod. On the morning of a special event, she was usually buzzing with so much energy that she didn't even need to stop by the Sweetwater Café, even though she always did anyway. "Are you going to be there?" Claire asked.

"I wouldn't miss it. Rebecca is one of my favorite customers. I'm so happy for her."

"So you're not against the marriage because of the age gap?"

"No way. Not if she's happy, and I wholeheartedly believe she is." Emma was already preparing a cup of coffee for Claire per her usual specifications.

Claire fished her debit card out of her purse as she waited.

Turning back to her, Emma narrowed her eyes. "And you've been holed up for the last couple of days with Bo Matthews, I hear."

"Because the wedding is at his house," Claire clarified, handing her card over. "Not for any other reason."

Emma swiped the card and handed it back. "I wouldn't blame you if there was. He's hotter than that cup of brew you're holding. Don't tell him I said so though. He's not really my type."

Claire grabbed her cup of coffee and took a sip. Bo was *her* type. "No? What is your type?"

Emma shrugged. "I dunno. Chris Hemsworth, maybe."

"You do realize that he's a world-famous movie star, and that it's very unlikely he'll walk into your coffee shop, right?"

"Yeah, yeah. Just a technicality. It could happen," Emma said with a soft giggle.

Yeah, and Bo could realize he was falling for Claire too. Which would never happen.

Claire started to turn and leave, but Emma grabbed her forearm.

"I have to warn you," she said, biting down on her lower lip. "Your mom is here."

"What?" Claire looked over her shoulder, and sure enough,

there was Nancy Donovan. How had she missed seeing her when she'd walked in? And why hadn't Emma warned her sooner? Not that it would've helped. There was only one way out and it was past her mom.

Claire turned back to her friend. "Thanks for the heads-up. I'll see you tonight." She took her cup of coffee and turned to leave. As she headed toward the exit, her mom's gaze flicked up and stayed on her. Her mouth curved just slightly in a sheepish smile. Then she lifted her hand and waved.

Crap. If Claire kept walking, she'd be the bad guy here, and that wasn't fair. Claire was always the one trying to help her parents growing up. She was the one victimized by their lack of attention and their shaming of her family's name.

Forcing her feet forward, Claire walked over to her mom's table and slid into the booth across from her. "I can only stay a few minutes," she prefaced.

Her mom nodded. Soft lines formed at the corners of her eyes and mouth as her smile wobbled. "I'm just happy to get to talk to you. How are you?"

Claire swallowed, wondering if she should answer that question truthfully. And if so, what was the honest answer? Work was great, but her personal life was all screwed up because she'd once more allowed herself to have feelings for Bo. "Swell. And you?"

"Better these days." Her mom molded her hands around her own cup. "I'm working on things I wish I'd worked on a long time ago."

"Hindsight and everything," Claire said, hating how sarcastic she sounded. She blew out a breath as she looked around the shop and shook her head. Then she turned back to her mom. "Look, I'm sorry. I don't mean to be so rude."

"It's okay," her mother said. "I deserve it. I was hoping that we could work toward having some sort of relationship again though. Even if it's only five minutes every now and then over coffee."

Claire stared at the woman in front of her. Time hadn't been kind, mostly because of the way Nancy had chosen to live her life. "How's Dad?"

"Jail has helped him sober up. He's going to stay dry once he gets out next month," she told Claire with a hopeful lilt to her voice. "We're going to get a second chance to do right by each other. That's what we both want."

Claire sucked in a deep breath and let it go. It was hypocritical of her to expect Bo to believe his dad could change and settle down with Rebecca when she couldn't do the same with her own parents. It was easier said than done though. "I hope that happens, Mom."

They spoke for a few minutes more, and then Claire pushed back from the table and stood. "I really do have to go…But maybe we can do this again."

Her mom's brows lifted. "Really?"

"I'm usually here on Saturday mornings"—Claire shrugged a shoulder—"so maybe I'll see you next weekend."

"Yes. Maybe you will." Her mom reached for Claire's hand and gave it a quick squeeze, the closest to a hug that either of them were ready to give. "Thank you."

As Claire walked out of the coffee shop, she felt lighter. Maybe her mom would let her down again. But there was also the possibility that she wouldn't this time. Claire had always been an optimist. She never wanted to lose hope that things could change for the better.

There was no hope for Bo changing his mind about love and romance though. No matter how much her heart protested that maybe, just maybe, there was.

* * *

Claire had drained her cup of coffee by the time she pulled into Bo's driveway. She was surprised to find him outside setting up the chairs.

"Wow. You've been busy," she said, walking toward him. She kept her shoulders squared. Kissing him last night didn't change anything. She wasn't going to let it affect the task at hand.

Straightening, he looked at her. He was all hot and sweaty, with the same ball cap on that he'd been wearing at the coffee shop a few days before. "I promised to help, so I am. Ken Martin emailed this morning and offered me the contract, by the way."

Claire's smile was now sincere. "That's great, Bo. I thought he would. Last night went really well." Except for that last part.

Judging by the look in his eyes, he was thinking about that too.

"I'm, um, just going to call Halona and Brenna and make sure everything's on track. I'll use your kitchen for that, if you don't mind."

"I don't. There's coffee, eggs, and bacon in there too. I made plenty this morning."

It was official. Emma could have Chris Hemsworth, because he had nothing on Bo Matthews.

* * *

Claire was obviously ignoring him. Bo wasn't sure how to make things right, but he knew he wanted to. He wanted a lot more than that, and he was ready. Seeing Liz and Mike together last night at the restaurant had barely stung. In fact, he almost felt happy for the two of them. Yeah, they'd hurt him, but he knew they hadn't meant to.

Love didn't let you choose. He understood what Claire had meant by that now, because he was falling hard and fast for the sweet, smart, gorgeous event planner. *How the hell am I going to fix things with her?*

A delivery truck pulled into his driveway with SOUTHERN PORTA-JOHN written in large black letters on the side. Bo guided the guys toward the back of his house, where the porta-johns would be available to guests but not readily seen during the ceremony. After that, Halona Locklear showed up in a navy SUV with all the flower arrangements in the back. Claire came out of the back door to help her set things up.

It wasn't a good time to talk to her right now. Not when she had so many things to get done before tonight's wedding.

The next few hours were a blur of activity going on in and around his house. Brenna showed up with trays full of food. He helped her set up tables to display it all. A DJ showed up and set up a place to play music for the reception. The entire Ladies' Day Out group showed up after that and helped Claire with a host of other things that he never would've considered. They set out tablecloths and large baskets full of party mementos for the guests. Pearson's and Rebecca's names and the date were written on little paper hearts attached to each favor.

"Aren't these the cutest?" Lula Locklear asked as she walked up to peek inside one of the baskets. "The ladies and I were up all night making these." Lula was Halona's mom. She was often involved in the community, increasing awareness about her Cherokee Indian culture.

"They are," Bo agreed, unable to resist lifting his head and looking around to see where Claire was. He spotted her laughing with Kaitlyn Russo, the owner of the Sweetwater B&B. The sight of Claire happy and enjoying herself made his heart skip a beat. He longed to be the kind of guy who put that smile on her face.

"You are a man with the look of love," Lula said with a knowing nod. She followed his gaze to where Claire was standing. "She's such a nice girl. She needs someone who will treat her well." She gave him an assessing look as if trying to decipher if he was capable of being that kind of guy. *Was he?* "Maybe there'll be more weddings on Lavender Hill in the future," she said.

* * *

As the sun started to creep toward the mountains, the sky darkened, and guests started to arrive. Claire slipped on the beautiful satin dress she'd purchased from Sophie's Boutique and then headed outside to turn on the lights. The aroma of the food wafted in the air along with laughter and casual conversation.

Pearson and Rebecca would be on their way at any moment. Rebecca's obstetrician had okayed her to leave for two hours. That was enough time to greet guests, walk down the aisle, say their vows, and maybe even have a dance under the stars.

Claire sighed dreamily, imagining Rebecca getting the wedding of her dreams tonight.

Bo stepped up beside her, scrambling those happy thoughts and feelings. "I need to talk to you. There's a problem."

She whipped her head around to face him. "What kind of problem?"

"Rebecca is in labor. The wedding has been called off."

"What?" Claire's lungs contracted as if the wind had been knocked out of her. "But she wants to be married by the time the baby comes. She needs to get here."

Bo frowned. "I just spoke to Dad. Rebecca's water broke when she was putting on her wedding dress." He grimaced. "It's not going to happen tonight. They can do it after the baby is born. She can buy a new dress and have it anywhere or any way she wants."

Claire shook her head. "The only thing she really wanted was to exchange vows before she gave birth." Claire looked around at all the guests, seated in wooden fold-out chairs. The scenery was perfect. There were even hundreds of stars speckling the clear night's sky.

Her shoulders slumped as she blew out a resigned breath. This was out of her control, and she knew it. "I guess we'll tell the guests the news and send them all home." She hesitated before looking at Bo. Disappointment stung her eyes. She didn't want him to know that all she really felt like doing was sitting in one of those chairs and having a good cry on Rebecca's behalf.

"You stay here. I'll take care of the guests," he said.

"You don't have to. That's my job."

"You did your job already."

"Not really. The wedding is off. I've never let a client down before. Ever." And now she wanted to cry on her own behalf.

There was something gentle in his eyes when she looked up at him. "Stay here," he said again.

She watched him walk off toward the crowd, then she turned to face the garden. She wasn't sure exactly how long she stood there collecting herself before Bo came up behind her. When she turned, he was standing there with Pastor Phillips.

Claire started to apologize to the older man, but Bo patted the pastor's back and narrowed his gaze at her.

"Pastor Phillips is ready to go to the hospital."

Claire scrunched her brows. "What? Why?"

"Because there's a wedding to be had, and we don't have much time. If Rebecca wants to be married before my baby brother gets here, then that's what we'll make sure happens. Assuming we beat the clock."

Pastor Phillips chuckled. "My wife was in labor for twelve hours after her water broke with our first child. I think we'll be okay."

Bo reached for Claire's hand. "You've never let a client down, right? Why start now?"

"You don't even believe your father and Rebecca should be together. Why are you doing this?"

"Maybe I see things differently now. Because of you."

Chapter Six

Claire grabbed the wedding bouquet before climbing into Bo's car. It was an assortment of purple irises and white lilies—exactly what Rebecca had requested. In fact, aside from wanting to marry before her baby was born, the flower preferences were the only other thing Rebecca had asked for.

After a short drive, Bo parked in front of the labor and delivery wing, and they hurried inside. Claire clutched the arrangement tightly as she walked beside him toward the elevator. Pastor Phillips had driven separately. Hopefully he wasn't far behind.

"What's wrong?" Bo asked. "You were talking as fast as I could drive on the way here."

Claire shook her head. "A hospital isn't exactly my favorite place. I watched my grandmother die here." And ever since, Mount Pleasant Memorial had carried nothing but bad memories for her.

They stepped inside the elevator, and Bo reached for her hand. He didn't let go once the door opened on the second floor. The feel of his skin against hers distracted her from the repetitive beeping sounds and the smells of disinfectant as they walked.

"Let's make a few happy memories here today, shall we?" he asked, giving her a wink that short-circuited all the negativity in her mind.

"There's nothing more joyful than a wedding. I've always thought so."

His smile wobbled just a little as they walked.

"I'm sorry. I guess weddings hold as many bad memories for you as hospitals do for me."

"I used to think I never wanted to go to another wedding again. But there's nowhere I'd rather be tonight than at this one with you."

Her heart fluttered. "Same. Even if it is at a hospital."

They stopped behind Rebecca's door, and Claire knocked softly.

A moment later, it cracked open, and Pearson Matthews peeked out at her. Claire had seen him many times over the years. His presence was always confident and commanding. Now he looked like a man juggling half a dozen emotions: excitement, fear, anxiety, exhaustion, confusion, joy.

"How is Rebecca feeling?" Claire asked.

In response, they heard Rebecca groan in the background.

"The baby is coming fast," Pearson said. "What are you two doing here?"

"You couldn't come to the wedding so we brought the wedding to you," Bo answered. "Do you think Rebecca is up for it?"

Pearson smiled at his son, a dozen new emotions popping up on his face. "I think that will probably make her really happy... Thank you, son."

Claire's eyes stung just a little as she watched the brief father-son interaction. "Great. Can we come in?"

Pearson swung the door open wider. "Becky, look who's here?"

Rebecca looked between Claire and Bo and then to Pastor Phillips who stepped up behind them.

"Do you still want to get married before the baby arrives?" Claire asked.

"Yes." Rebecca shifted and tried to sit up in bed. She was wearing a hospital gown instead of a wedding gown. Her hair was a little disheveled, and the makeup she'd put on for tonight's ceremony needed a touch-up. Even so, she was as beautiful as any bride Claire had ever seen.

Rebecca flinched and squeezed her eyes shut, moving her hands to her lower belly. "But we better do this fast," she gritted out.

Pearson went to the head of Rebecca's bed as Pastor Phillips opened his Bible to read a short passage. Afterward, he looked up at the bride and groom and read off vows that they repeated.

Bo never let go of Claire's hand as they stood witness to the happy union. It was quick, but no less perfect. A tear slid off Claire's cheek as Rebecca said "I do." Then Pearson dipped to press his lips to Rebecca's—their first kiss as man and wife.

Claire would've wiped her eyes, but one hand still carried the bouquet and the other was held by Bo. He squeezed it softly as he glanced over. There was something warm in his gaze that melted any leftover resolve to resist this man.

Rebecca pulled away from her husband and turned to her guests, which had expanded to include two nurses. "My bouquet, please."

Claire finally broke contact with Bo and handed the arrangement over.

"Okay, ladies. Arms up," Rebecca said. "Bouquet tossing time!"

"Oh, no. I'm already married," one of the nurses said with a laugh.

Bo stepped off to the side, leaving Claire and the second nurse in the line of fire. Claire usually removed herself from this moment at weddings too. Fighting with a bunch of single ladies over a superstition had always seemed so silly, albeit fun to watch. As the bouquet went sailing across the room though, Claire lifted her hands reflexively and snatched it from the air, much to the second nurse's disappointment.

"You're next!" Rebecca said with a laugh. Then she flinched again as another contraction hit her.

"Okay, that's it," the married nurse said. "I think your baby wants to join this party."

Rebecca opened her eyes. "Okay." She looked at Claire. "Thank you. For everything. This was absolutely perfect."

"You're welcome. But I couldn't have done this without Bo."

Rebecca looked at him with tears in her eyes. "Thank you too."

"That's what family is for, right? Welcome to the Matthews clan."

Pearson stepped over and reached out his hand for Bo to shake. He shook Claire's hand as well.

"We're going to give you two some privacy now," Bo told him.

"Don't go too far," Rebecca called from across the room. "Your baby brother will be excited to meet you."

Bo seemed a little stunned by the invitation to stay. He looked at Claire.

"I'm in no hurry to go home," she said. Nor was she in a hurry to leave Bo's side right now.

* * *

"That was amazing!" Claire said, leaning back against the headrest of Bo's car as he drove her to his home three hours later. "And your baby brother is adorable. I can't believe I got to hold a newborn who's only been on this earth for an hour. That was such a rush. And the wedding was perfect, even though we were the only ones in attendance."

He glanced over, feeling a sense of pride and accomplishment at helping to put that contented look on her face. "You pulled it off."

"*We* pulled it off."

From his peripheral vision, he saw her turn and look at him.

"You said it yesterday, and it's true. We make a pretty good couple." Her relaxed posture stiffened. "Team. We make a good team," she corrected.

"I liked it better the first way." He'd been waiting to talk to her all day. The hospital hadn't seemed like the right place, but now he couldn't wait any longer. He pulled into his driveway, parked his car, and then looked across the seat at her.

Her contented, dreamy look was gone, replaced by a look of confusion. It was just last night that they'd kissed in this very car, but it felt like a lifetime ago.

"I like you, Claire Donovan. I liked you last spring, but I was a coward. I'll admit that."

"Sounds about right," she agreed.

"I'd just watched my best friend marry the woman I thought I wanted. But I was wrong. I was so wrong. You're the woman I want, Claire. And I want you like I've never wanted anything in my entire life." His heart was thundering in his ears as he made his confession.

Her eyes became shiny for the hundredth time that night.

"The last few days have breathed new life inside me. I don't want to think about waking up tomorrow and not knowing if I'll see you." He ran a hand through his hair to keep from reaching out and touching her. "Claire, I want another chance with you. If you say yes, I promise I won't mess things up this time."

She was so still that he wondered if she was okay.

"Say something," he finally said.

"I'm hungry." After a long moment, her lips curved ever so slightly.

He cleared his throat and turned to look out at his yard. "Well, there's probably still some food left over from the reception. The guests each took some, but it'd be a shame for the rest to go to waste. I even think I saw Janice Murphy spike the punch on her way out," he said.

Claire gave a small laugh and nodded when he looked at her. "There's also a place to dance under the stars."

"The evening is set for romance," he agreed.

"So let's enjoy it and see where the night takes us. On one condition." Her expression contorted to something stern with just a touch of playfulness lighting up her eyes. "If it ends up leading somewhere nice, you have to promise you'll call me tomorrow."

He chuckled. "I promise that it will lead somewhere nice, and when it does, you might never get rid of me."

She looked up into his eyes and smiled. "I might never want to."

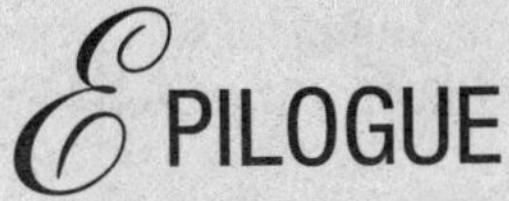

In the blink of an eye, everything could change. Or in Claire's case, one month's time. That was how long it'd been since she'd planned Rebecca and Pearson's wedding. It had all happened so fast, but everything had fallen into place perfectly.

Claire stepped out of the dressing room at Sophie's Boutique and did a twirl in front of the body-length mirror. The cotton dress was a deep rose color with tiny blue pin dots in the fabric. The hem brushed along her knees as she shifted in front of the mirror.

"That's the one," the shop owner said, stepping up beside her.

"I feel a little foolish. It's just our one-month anniversary, but Bo told me to wear something nice."

"One month together is definitely worth celebrating. Where is he taking you?" Sophie asked. "Any idea?"

Claire shook her head. "No." It didn't really matter though. It was the gesture that melted her heart like a marshmallow against an open flame. He was always doing little things for her to show her how much he cared. "Okay," she said, looking down. "This is the one. I'll take it off and let you ring it up for me."

"Do you have the right shoes?"

Claire laughed. She loved to shop as much as the next person, but she couldn't wait to get home and ready for whatever Bo had planned for them. "I do. But thanks."

An hour and a half later, Bo picked her up at her place and started driving.

"You're still not going to tell me where we're going?" she asked.

He was dressed in nice jeans with a polo top and a sport coat. She was almost disappointed to have to go out tonight because she would have rather been alone with him. They'd spent a lot of alone time together over the last month, and she wasn't sure she'd ever get enough.

"That would ruin the surprise."

She huffed playfully. "Fine. How's baby Noah?" she asked. He'd told her he was stopping by the hospital this afternoon. It had been all she could do not to invite herself along, but visitors were limited to family right now. She was just the girlfriend.

"A genius," Bo answered. "He takes after me."

This made Claire laugh out loud.

"And he'll be leaving the NICU tomorrow. The doctor says he's ready."

"That's wonderful news. I'm sure Pearson and Rebecca are so happy."

He nodded. "They are."

Claire blinked as she looked out the window, recognizing the route. Surely, she hadn't gotten all dressed up just to go back to his place.

He turned the car onto Lavender Road and drove all the way to the end. After pulling into his driveway and parking, he turned to her. She blinked and kept her gaze forward. The fairy lights were turned on—they'd never taken them down—and a table was set up at the peak of the hill behind his house.

Bo stepped out of the car and walked around to open her door for her. Then they approached what he'd put together. There was a small vase of fresh flowers at the table's center, sandwiched between two candles, not yet lit. Another table was set up to the right with what appeared to be catered food from Taste of Heaven.

"A candlelit dinner under the stars." She turned and stepped into him, wrapping her arms around his neck and staring into his eyes. "All this just to celebrate one month of being together?"

He leaned in and kissed her lips, soft and slow. Nothing in her life had ever felt so right as being with him.

"No. All this is to tell you that I love you, Claire Donovan. I love you so much."

She blinked him into focus. A man had never uttered those words to her before, but they were music to her ears. She wanted to hear them again and again. "I love you too, Bo Matthews."

She laughed as he pulled her in for another kiss under the starry night sky. Then they had dinner and shared a dance before retreating to his room, where he repeated those three little words again and again.

About the Author

Annie Rains is a *USA Today* bestselling contemporary romance author who writes small-town love stories set in fictional places in her home state of North Carolina. When Annie isn't writing, she's living out her own happily ever after with her husband and three children.

Learn more at:

AnnieRains.com
Twitter: @AnnieRainsBooks
Facebook.com/AnnieRainsBooks
Instagram: @AnnieRainsBooks

Fall in love with these charming contemporary romances!

A VERY MERRY MATCH
by Melinda Curtis

Mary Margaret Sneed usually spends her holiday baking and caroling with her students. But this year, she's swapped shortbread and sleigh bells to take a second job—one she can never admit to when the town mayor starts courting her. Only the town's meddling matchmakers have determined there's nothing a little mistletoe can't fix... and if the Widows Club has its way, Mary Margaret and the mayor may just get the best Christmas gift of all this year. Includes a bonus story by Hope Ramsay!

THE TWELVE DOGS OF CHRISTMAS
by Lizzie Shane

Ally Gilmore has only four weeks to find homes for a dozen dogs in her family's rescue shelter. But when she confronts the Scroogey councilman who pulled their funding, Ally finds he's far more reasonable—and handsome—than she ever expected... especially after he promises to help her. As they spend more time together, the Pine Hollow gossip mill is convinced that the Grinch might show Ally that Pine Hollow is her home for more than just the holidays.

Find more great reads on Instagram with @ReadForeverPub

CHRISTMAS ON REINDEER ROAD
by Debbie Mason

After his wife died, Gabriel Buchanan left his job as a New York City homicide detective to focus on raising his three sons. But back in Highland Falls, he doesn't have to go looking for trouble. It finds him—in the form of Mallory Maitland, a beautiful neighbor struggling to raise her misbehaving stepsons. When they must work together to give their boys the Christmas their hearts desire, they may find that the best gift they can give them is a family together.

SEASON OF JOY
by Annie Rains

For single father Granger Fields, Christmas is his busiest—and most profitable—time of the year. But when a fire devastates his tree farm, Granger convinces free spirit Joy Benson to care for his daughters while he focuses on saving his business. Soon Joy's festive ideas and merrymaking convince Granger he needs a business partner. As crowds return to the farm, life with Joy begins to feel like home. Can Granger convince Joy that this is where she belongs? Includes a bonus story by Melinda Curtis!

Connect with us at
Facebook.com/ReadForeverPub

HER AMISH WEDDING QUILT
by Winnie Griggs

When the man she thought she would wed chooses another woman, Greta Eicher pours her energy into crafting beautiful quilts at her shop and helping widower Noah Stoll care for his adorable young children. But when her feelings for Noah grow into something even deeper, will she be able to convince him to have enough faith to give love another chance?

THE AMISH MIDWIFE'S HOPE
by Barbara Cameron

Widow Rebecca Zook adores her work, but the young midwife secretly wonders if she'll ever find love again or have a family of her own. When she meets handsome newcomer Samuel Miller, her connection with the single father is immediate—Rebecca even bonds with his sweet little girl. It feels like a perfect match, and Rebecca is ready to embrace the future . . . if only Samuel can open his heart once more.

Discover bonus content and more on read-forever.com

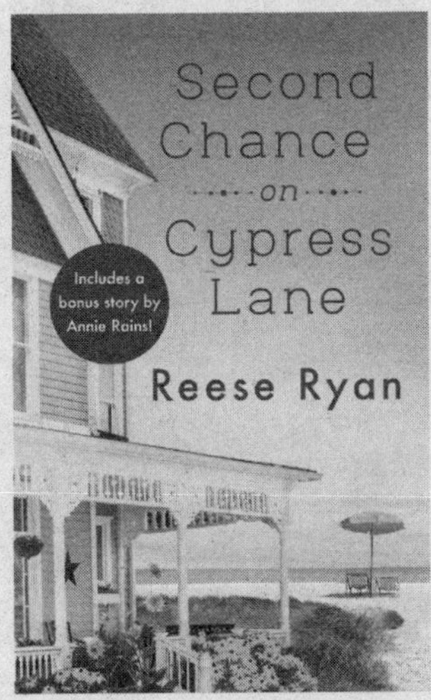

SECOND CHANCE ON CYPRESS LANE
by Reese Ryan

Rising-star reporter Dakota Jones is used to breaking the news, not making it. When a scandal costs her her job, there's only one place she can go to regroup. But her small South Carolina hometown comes with a major catch: Dexter Roberts. The first man to break Dakota's heart is suddenly back in her life. She won't give him another chance to hurt her, but she can't help wondering what might have been. Includes a bonus story by Annie Rains!

FOREVER WITH YOU
by Barb Curtis

Leyna Milan knows family legacies come with strings attached, but she's determined to prove that she can run her family's restaurant. Of course, Leyna never expected that honoring her grandfather's wishes meant opening a second location on her ex's winery—or having to ignore Jay's sexy grin and guard the heart he shattered years before. But as they work closely together, she begins to discover that maybe first love deserves a second chance…